THREE MURDERED MAGES

TWO BROKEN BONDS

HIYODORI

Contents

1

When had Wist and I last stood together before this iron gate?

Several years ago, yes. I dragged reluctant memories out of hiding. A ruined garden. A berserking mage. A bonded healer, skinny and cowed. I'd achieved my secret purpose during that visit, but it hadn't been pleasant.

"Nothing good will come of tangling with the Shiens," I pronounced.

"You've said that before." Wist looked at me as though wondering what I hoped to accomplish by stating the obvious.

My reply: "Repetitiveness is one of my virtues. Shows consistency."

The abyss behind my right eye—my prosthetic eye—throbbed as though laughing darkly. I can assure you that it was doing nothing of the sort. That blank space was not a being with a sense of humor, or any semblance of actual sentience. It was not a being at all, if you think about it. More of an absence than a presence. The most palpable part of the Void was its appetite.

The gate to the Shien estate had long bars matted with an excess of curling iron ivy. Naturally, this was only one of the clan's many estates. It was the oldest and grandest, however, and also happened to be the place where they'd raised Wisteria Shien.

Unlike last time, we hadn't dressed up. I wore fuzzy earmuffs and a big scarf and a jacket that would've kept me alive in the far northern wilderness. Overkill, perhaps.

It was late in the year, and unseasonably cold. The air smelled like flurries, though the area around the capital rarely saw snow.

Wist faced the gate without moving. She had on a very long twill trench coat; the fabric was a color like bleached honey. It would've dragged on the ground if worn by anyone else.

"Their security protocols have changed," she said.

The magic cuttings planted among the leaves of iron did look a lot fussier than in my memory.

Then again, I'd only been here twice before. Once a few years ago, and once as a cheeky student.

"Can you break in?" I asked.

Of course she could. She was the most powerful mage in the world.

"We're in no rush," said Wist.

"I'm cold."

She slid a hand beneath my scarf, seeking out the back of my neck. She wore a glove with tiny ticklish slits to let her fingertips breathe. Magic heated my spine like a fireplace.

I squinted balefully through the gate. The grounds were so vast that I couldn't glimpse a single building from here, nor any hint of the reason they'd summoned Wist.

Close-trimmed lawns had turned bright gold for the depths of winter. Austere formations of mature parasol pines, sixty to eighty feet high, lined private roads devoid of traffic.

I nudged Wist as she warmed me. "What're we in for this time? Scandalous bodies hidden in a vault of jewels? Madwomen locked in wine cellars?"

Wist declined to comment. It might've been funnier if it weren't so plausible. Her brothers and sisters used to make a game of trapping her: in abandoned wells, in walk-in refrigerators, in the family mausoleum.

At last a magically transmitted voice, brisk and clear, came through the bars before us. The voice instructed us to touch various shining leaves on the iron gate. I wondered idly if they were taking our fingerprints.

The gate slid open—seamlessly, soundlessly.

Wist moved half a step in front of me. Her hair had twisted itself into a sullen coal-black braid crown. The coils kept loosening and tightening and re-twisting all on their own.

I thought about saying something, but she must've known her hair was fidgeting. Anyway, by now we'd come face to face with the woman who'd appeared on the other side of the gate.

A healer with a dark bond thread around her neck.

She was younger than us by at least a full decade. Her clothing looked like a cross between a maid uniform and old-fashioned healer robes.

I'd never seen her before in my life. Neither, it seemed, had Wist.

"Apologies for the delay," she said in the same no-nonsense voice that had ordered us how and where to touch the gate. "There's been another visitor."

I stuck my head out from behind Wist. "The great Shien clan can't accommodate multiple guests in a timely manner? What a fall from grace."

Her pale eyes, guarded by large thin-rimmed glasses, remained fixed on Wist. So much for healer solidarity. Since the healer refused to look my way, I felt no compunction about studying her in detail. She had a small upturned nose that lent her a vague air of outrage, and platinum blond hair of the type that usually wouldn't last past childhood. She kept it pinned in two thick buns like cinnamon rolls stuck to the back of her head.

Remind you of anyone? I asked Wist. Just between us.

...Maybe, she replied.

I was still certain that I'd never met this healer-servant—who, whatever her faults, surely deserved better than being bonded for life to a Shien mage.

Nevertheless, something about her seemed peskily familiar. Those thin, compressed lips. Or maybe her overall aura of tight-buttoned blond superiority.

All of Wist's adoptive brothers and sisters were older than us. All were old enough to have raised adult offspring.

Then again, if any of her Shien siblings had spawned a healer child, would they really parade her around the main estate? Put your shame in a corner—that's the Shien way.

"Sure looks empty around here," I commented as the healer-servant escorted us to a portal set between stone pillars. I had yet to observe a single chipmunk or sparrow or overworked groundskeeper.

"Most of the staff have evacuated. So have most of the family."

"Now you've got the Kraken here to do clean-up," I said. "You'll be calling them all back soon enough."

The healer pressed her lips tighter.

I can tell when people dislike me. I often take perverse pleasure in encouraging it. (Gotta enjoy the small things in life.) This woman clearly needed no such encouragement.

Near the magical portal rested a bench with a seated bronze statue of some long-lost Shien ancestor. I reached out to bop them on the nose.

With a muttered word to our healer escort, Wist took me by the shoulders and propelled me through the portal as if I were a wayward shopping cart.

The portal plonked us down in a mudroom larger than my city apartment. It was stiflingly warm compared to outside. I hastily peeled off my scarf and earmuffs and various other winter accoutrements.

When I glanced at the waiting healer, though, that judgmental mouth of hers was still an unhealthy purplish hue. Maybe she always looked half-frozen.

We followed her to a receiving room with its floor painted an astonishing shade of glossy cerulean blue.

A dark-haired mage stood facing away from us, hands clasped behind his back, gazing at an abstract painting on canvas. It hung without a frame, large enough to dominate the entire wall.

As for the image painted there: I got a brief impression of an oversized starfish rendered in unearthly colors. Or a surreal, spiky pathogen seen through a microscope.

Then the healer announced our arrival. Well—Wist's arrival.

"Lady Wisteria Shien," she declared, as if calling a witness to testify.

The man in front of the painting turned. He wore a Mage Police dress uniform, neat black coat and all.

"Inspector Minashiro," said the healer.

She bowed in our general direction, as if to say her work here was done, then slipped away without a sound.

Minashiro? Not a Shien, then. The Minashiros were a mage clan of equal prestige. Minus the fact that they hadn't adopted the greatest mage of our time.

The good inspector regarded us with abject horror. Admittedly, this was the usual reaction I got from MPs.

"Anyone commit a crime?" I asked.

It did occur to me that I was without a doubt the only person in this room who'd already spent years in prison.

A flicker of understanding—half-alarmed, half-amused—filtered through my bond with Wist. She'd recognized something I'd missed.

I immediately focused the full power of my intellect and my magic perception on the inspector.

His magic—

Yes. I'd seen it before.

"*You*," he said, finally finding his voice. He could've meant either one of us.

"Wait." I held up both hands. "Almost got it. Right on the tip of my tongue. Minashiro, yeah? Your given name started with a T, didn't it? Something like—Tenner. Teddy. Temple. Tempest."

"Tempus," Wist said under her breath.

"That's the one. Minashiro Tempus."

I crossed the room, dirtying the pristine blue floor with every step, and threw myself down sideways in an armchair. Wist hovered nearby as if she were my roadie, rather than the eventual star of the show.

"Didn't know we were coming, did you?" I said to Minashiro Tempus. Our old high school adversary. He'd need to seek medical attention if his eyes bulged any harder.

2

I'D BEEN BRACED to confront someone from the core Shien family. One of Wist's many siblings, or her adoptive parents. Or her grandmother, the head of the clan—the only one who'd ever get called Lady Shien. No given name needed for clarification.

I hadn't expected Minashiro Tempus. I hadn't seen him in … not quite two decades, but close enough.

He wore his MP uniform far better than he'd worn his academy uniform, although that horrible skinny mustache wasn't doing him any favors.

I grinned at him like a back alley coyote. "So what is this, a high school reunion?"

"What," he said, "are you doing here?"

The years did not seem to have improved his sense of humor. There really was something a bit funny about us gathering here on the Shien estate. Like a pep rally for all my petty old enemies.

"Stopped bleaching your hair, did you?" I observed. "Good choice. But I'd advise getting rid of the mus—"

"No one asked your opinion," Tempus said through his teeth.

I wondered how we looked through his eyes, all these years later. He'd never quite caught up to Wist in terms of height. A taller heel on his boots might've made up the difference.

After flip-flopping between turning my hair fully white and fully black, I'd gone back to letting it grow mixed. Which was closest to its natural state, anyhow. Right now that meant I had two big white patches in a shape like floppy dog ears on either side of my face. Tempus doubtless thought I was the last person on the continent who ought to give out aesthetic advice.

Once upon a time, Tempus had felt like a dire threat. He'd been my worst enemy when I was a first-year student afraid of getting expelled.

Midway through our second year, after Wist and I dealt him defeat after defeat, his efforts began to strike me as being rather pathetic. Almost endearingly hapless. He was a remorseless bully, make no mistake. Unlike certain other mage students, however, he never actually killed anyone.

That's a low bar to clear, yes. As a thoroughly convicted felon myself, I wasn't about to harp on his teenage sins.

"Let's start over," I said magnanimously. "Nice to meet you. I'm Asa Lan—"

"Skip the false names."

"Asa Clematis, then. Call me Clem."

"Not over my dead—"

"What brings *you* here, Inspector?"

"I have an audience with Lady Shien." He looked pointedly at Wist. "Just like old times," he said coldly. "You still let your healer run her mouth."

"And you," Wist said with startling clarity, "still don't know when to shut up."

The bright threads of magic in her had gone unnaturally still. Tempus appeared to make a tremendous effort not to swallow, or glance away, or blot his temples with a handkerchief.

My turn to play the good cop. How ironic. Thank heaven that he hadn't been part of the crew sent to arrest me in my twenties. "I, for one, have nothing to hide," I said, shrugging. "We came to close the—"

"Where's your parole thread?" Tempus demanded.

I rolled my eyes as best I could. My prosthetic eye was somewhat more constrained in its movement. "Ask my parole officer. Manatree. You know her?"

He jotted something down on a pocket-sized scroll. Probably something insulting.

"You're here to close the vorpal hole?" he asked Wist.

She gave a single nod.

"You can't," he said. "You mustn't. Not yet."

What's he on about? I thought at Wist.

She had no idea, either.

"I hear it's quite a sizable hole," I said, in case poor Tempus had been misinformed. "It ate their entire rose garden. And it's expanding."

"Very slowly."

I straightened up in my armchair, swinging my feet down to meet the lavish blue floor. I spoke in tones of irreproachable kindness.

"You know, we only came because Wist has been under all kinds of political pressure to hurry up and do something about the giant hole eating the Shien estate. We put it off so long that absolutely no one could accuse her of showing favoritism toward her own family."

"Admirable," Tempus said without feeling. The painting at his back loomed like a portal to a land of nightmares.

"Actually closing it ought to be the work of a single afternoon. Then we can get on with our lives. Who are you, Inspector, to stop the Kraken from performing a good deed on private property owned by her own clan?"

He fiddled neurotically with his lapel. His mustache palpitated as if longing to leap off his face and gag me.

"You must know," he said suddenly, addressing Wist again. "Someone must have told you."

She met his plea with an expression of impeccable cluelessness.

It was uncannily quiet. No welcoming music. No distant voices or footsteps. The three of us may as well have been stranded in a mansion inhabited solely by ghosts.

Eventually Tempus lowered his hands from his much-abused lapel.

"Your sister," he said to Wist.

"Which one?" I asked.

He glared. "Shien Miyu. She's missing."

"Since when?"

"For over a week now."

Wist's expression didn't change one whit.

"Lady Miyu," he repeated, "is missing." He'd always thought Wist was a little slow on the uptake.

Three weeks ago, a vorpal hole had spawned in the middle of the Shien estate. I contemplated why the Mage Police might want Wist to wait even longer before sealing it.

"Think Miyu's dead?" I said baldly.

Tempus sucked in a breath, prepared to berate me for my lack of decorum. Then he caught Wist's eye again and stiffened, still inflated with corked-up reserves of indignation.

Before Tempus could decide what to say, I added, "Miyu has—"

"*Lady* Miyu."

"Lady Miyu has a bonded healer, doesn't she? You must have spoken with her bondmate. That answers everything."

"And yet," he said witheringly, "she's still missing."

If their bond were intact, it would serve as definitive proof that Miyu lived. If their bond were broken, then she was dead. Beyond a doubt. Only death could sever bondmates.

One day I wanted to be able to do it myself. To devise a way to break bonds (without killing anyone in the process). But I hadn't gotten there yet.

This was a secret project: the Osmanthian mageocracy would never support my aims. Although even if I did go around spouting off about my interest in severing mage-healer bonds, I'd be regarded more as a laughingstock than as an actual threat. It was a simple fact that nothing short of death could erase a bond, and everyone knew it.

Whether Shien Miyu had drowned in a river or gotten shot in the head, the end of her life would mean the end of her bond. Her bondmate would know the instant it happened. Conversely, an intact bond could signify that she was alive and in hiding, or in a coma, or suffering from memory loss, or otherwise rendered incapable of crawling home.

I'd met Miyu's current bondmate. Just once, the last time Wist and I came here. She'd been very different from the haughty blond healer who'd greeted us today at the gate, the one who'd reminded me of Miyu herself. Miyu's bondmate had been fatally skinny, with a voice incapable of rising above a whisper. I'd never learned her name.

On second thought, that skinny girl might no longer be Miyu's bondmate. Maybe Miyu had driven her into an early grave. Just like her predecessor. Maybe Miyu had moved on to yet another bondmate. Another healer to soak up her undiluted disappointment. Another healer to blame for healing her the wrong way, breathing the wrong way, looking at her the wrong way, apologizing the wrong way....

That new blond healer trussed up in stark long-sleeved robes, with a virulent look behind her large delicate glasses and a frigid purple tinge to her mouth—maybe she was Miyu's latest bondmate, after all.

"I can guess what Miyu's bondmate told you," I said to Tempus. (He no longer bothered with correcting my form of address.) "You described Miyu as missing. If their bond were broken, that wouldn't even be in question."

"The healer claims their bond is intact."

"You gonna be getting a professional in to confirm that?"

"You'll need Grandmother's permission to have Miyu's bondmate undergo a formal examination," Wist said.

"That's what I've come to request." There was something nastily fascinating about the anemic way his mustache moved as he spoke. "We also need clearance to send a forensics team to check the estate as a whole. Particularly the area around the fringe of the vorpal hole."

"Before Wist seals it up," I said.

"Before her magic contaminates the entire grounds, yes."

"Grandmother hasn't been very cooperative, has she?" I guessed.

His mouth pinched like a drawstring bag, mustache and all. "Lady Shien is—"

Wist said it for him. "She must be reluctant."

Any educated person would understand that a vorpal hole could spring up anywhere. In the countryside. In a pawn shop. On the grand estate of a preeminent mage clan. It had nothing to do with karma or bad omens, and everything to do with random chance.

And yet: when an acquaintance got stomach cancer, weren't there always people whispering about what they ate, where they lived, how they did or didn't exercise, their history with preventative medicine and magic? There would be a whiff of delicious scandal in the appearance of a vorpal hole on Shien property. In the sudden disappearance of

Shien Miyu, who only a few years ago had gone violently berserk and subsequently lost her position at the Ministry of Justice.

No one would be so crass as to blame any of these events on Grandmother Shien. At least not in so many words. No one could stop them from thinking it.

I held my hand out without looking. Wist took it with grace. I bounced to my feet.

"Well," I said to Tempus, "good luck convincing Grandma."

His nostrils flared. "Where are you going?"

"To take a gander at this vorpal hole." I waved dismissively. "Don't look so jittery. Wist won't spray magic all over the place. We'll wait to close it. You're very welcome, by the way."

On the way out, I turned back. Tempus braced himself as if I'd aimed a gun at him. Jumpy fellow.

It wasn't Tempus that kept catching my eye, though. It was that extravagant frameless painting on the wall behind him. That blazing shape akin to a sunken starfish limned in orange and gold.

Like the snub-nosed healer-maid with her hair done up in cinnamon-roll shapes, I was absolutely certain I'd never seen that painting before. Not in this life, nor in any other.

I knew the painting was new to me. I knew that. At the same time, it looked profoundly familiar.

3

Wist's relationship with her adoptive clan was so strained that nothing short of a giant vorpal hole could've convinced her to visit. I'd wondered if it were all a lie—a nonexistent vorpal hole; a gambit to trick her into coming over. I hadn't discarded that hypothesis until our conversation with Tempus.

I followed Wist out of the central manor. The gardens were still rife with blooming color. The relative mildness of winter near the capital—along with a few judiciously applied magic cuttings—made it possible.

The warmth we'd borrowed from our time indoors had yet to fade. I put my gloves in my pockets and draped my scarf over one arm. Wist's trench coat hung open, letting in intermittent gusts of wind. The sky was a shade of dull white that hurt to look at, somehow both dimmer than full sunlight and intolerably bright.

"We could just leave," I said. "Duck out and promise to return another day. Tempus doesn't want us here, anyway."

Wist contemplated the great sprawling manor. We stood in its shadow, too close to take in its whole shape at a glance.

"Remember what the estate is called?" she asked.

"It has a name?"

"Most estates like this do."

Way back in the day, her siblings and parents must've used its name in front of me. When pretending to welcome me. When sneering at how out of place I seemed.

I'd probably nodded and pretended I knew what they were talking about—if I'd even bothered to listen.

"No idea, sorry."

"Follyhope," said Wist.

I scrunched my nose. "Really? No accounting for taste. All right. Wanna ditch Follyhope?"

Her face remained as inscrutable as the building facade. "You're trying to give me an out."

"Can't accuse me of inconsistency. I was opposed to dropping by in the first place."

"*Nothing good will come of tangling with the Shiens*," she murmured.

"I also suggested putting it off till next year. It's just a few more weeks."

"If we waited till next year, then you'd be saying we should wait even longer."

"Yes. Make them stew. Avoid starting the new year on a bad note."

"This is time-sensitive."

"To the Shien clan," I said. "Not to us. Tempus says you can't close the hole right away, regardless."

She studied my prosthetic eye. "You didn't have to come."

"Well, I refuse to send you to Shien headquarters alone."

"You haven't been near a vorpal hole of this magnitude since…"

Since I'd internalized the Void.

Less than two months had passed since our return from a rather disastrous vacation. The whole trip had been a massive failure in some respects. Except for the fact that, by the end of it, we'd potentially saved the continent.

Not that anyone would ever know or understand. We couldn't brag about it. There would eventually be a terrible—and unknowable—price to pay, too. Not this winter, though. Not here at Follyhope.

I thought of this debt of ours in the same way I thought of death. Mortality might be inevitable, as was our impending karmic punishment. With luck, neither would have any bearing on our daily lives for a long time to come. Why dwell on it?

"I know the Void abhors vorpal holes," I said. "I can distinguish between its reaction and my own. Let the Void curl up and quake in fear. I'll be fine."

"Should we feed it first?"

The back of my lost eye emitted a thick pulse.

"Not necessary," I told her.

"You protest when I say I don't need healing."

"That's not the same," I argued. "Healing you doesn't take anything out of me. It's no more strenuous than getting up on a stool to braid your hair."

I didn't verbalize the other half of this thought. Feeding my Void would take a lot out of Wist.

We both imagined it. Wist made vulnerable beneath an unforgiving sky. The Void would slip out of me like a tongue of shadow. It would saw through the roots of her magic. It would slurp up her dense, ever-growing threads while I stuffed my scarf in her mouth to give her something to grind her teeth on, something to staunch her cries.

These images flared in our bond, unstoppable, echoing back and forth from mind to mind. We didn't discuss it further.

The Void I carried behind my right eye socket was nothing like a vorpal hole, although it'd be impossible to explain the distinction to a regular citizen.

Vorpal holes were an unpleasant rip in the jeans of reality. A gate to death, and to other worlds, but mostly to death.

The Void led nowhere except to the bottom of its own vacant belly. And it had a torturous hunger for magic. Especially Wist's magic. Now it nestled in me like an unremovable cyst.

The Void also had a dreadful aversion to vorpal holes. Perhaps it felt in them an echo of its own unsustainable voracity. Perhaps it reacted to them with the fury of a dog yapping hatefully at its own reflection.

It might seize my legs and make me run from the Shien vorpal hole until I collapsed in exhaustion. It might dive deep down inside me and hide like a wild creature going dormant for winter. No way to know for sure until the hole came into sight.

For the record, we weren't barging in here completely unprepared. After coming back to Osmanthus, we'd exposed the Void to a variety of vorpal holes. We'd diligently documented its range of reactions.

"So," I said as we walked. "What are the odds that your sister got drunk and fell in this vorpal hole all on her own?"

"Do we know that she fell in?"

"Tempus certainly isn't ready to rule it out. Must be a reason he's eager to get his forensics team poking around the border of the hole."

"That would mean her bondmate lied."

True. Only the Kraken could plunge into a vorpal hole and come back out of it alive.

I tried to picture Shien Miyu's healer, but I couldn't.

Was it the too-thin girl I'd met some years ago?

The new blond maidservant?

Someone else?

I backed off. "Sure, maybe it's got nothing to do with the hole. Miyu could've gotten kidnapped by terrorists. She could've absconded to another country. It all sounds about equally plausible."

"…I'm glad you weren't anywhere near her when she disappeared," Wist said, almost too quiet to hear.

To everyone except the two of us, Miyu's berserking episode had seemed like an awful coincidence. An accident that just so happened to take place during our previous visit to Follyhope. How very fortunate that Wist the Kraken had been right there to stop her.

How very unfortunate for Shien Miyu—a mage with every advantage, born into untold wealth, treated only by the best healers ever since she was a little girl—to have suddenly snapped without warning.

Only Wist knew about my interference. Only Wist knew I'd made Miyu lose it on purpose.

Now here we were, back at Follyhope, passing through an arcade between wings of the stupidly palatial manor. Soon we'd round a corner and see the scene of that very incident. The now-swallowed rose garden and graceful patio where Shien Miyu had gone berserk.

In the moment it manifested, the hole had devoured two groundskeepers. By now it would surely be roped off, or otherwise barricaded. Alarms would be set near the perimeter to alert residents in case its expansion accelerated.

We both stopped dead as soon as it came into view.

I was more used to encountering vorpal holes shaped like vertical scars in the air. This one hung horizontal: a crinkled lake of nothingness suspended a foot or two off the ground.

The perimeter was scattered with traffic cones. Monitoring devices perched on poles like birdhouses.

Remnants of rosebushes still grew in the uneaten space beneath, thick bare stems toothy with thorns. I could've gotten down on my hands and knees to wriggle among those thorns, crawling below the underbelly of the hole. If it rained, the hole would swallow every last drop before it reached me.

I looked fixedly at the scarf in my arms. It was all one color, a smooth bright parroty green. The vorpal hole repelled my sight. Returning its gaze seemed about as smart as holding a staring contest with a solar eclipse.

My mind kept snagging on thoughts of the dead gardeners. Had they fallen from toppled ladders? Or had the vorpal hole severed them at the knees when it appeared out of nowhere? Were their feet now rotting down there, trapped together with the roots of abandoned roses?

Pressure built in my head. There was a churning behind my eye like the Void had spiraled itself into a snail shell, small and tight and dense. Ripe for explosion.

Wist stepped between me and the vorpal hole that was still well out of reach. She turned her back to the hole; she faced me. As if I were the greater threat.

She touched my livid green scarf. She was saying something, both on the inside and on the outside, but I couldn't listen. Wind howled as if blasting through a narrow crack hidden at the back of my head. The seams of my skull screeched louder than a boiling kettle.

A lightning awareness rent my perception, a revelation like a hot brand on virgin skin. There were five mages on the estate. Wist right in front of me. Tempus and Grandmother Shien and two others back in the manor. Their branches shone like distant constellations.

The Void measured them and found them wanting—all of them except Wist. She was a titan compared to the other four.

"Wist." I had to pray that I was actually saying it. "Wist, you need to run."

I tried to shove her away. Both physically and through our bond. I couldn't get any purchase on her. I scrabbled as though running on ice in a dream.

Was this how it felt to be a mage who'd gone berserk?

"Don't just stand there," I said. Very clearly and calmly. "Please run."

Something hotter than blood streaked down my cheek. My prosthetic eye was melting away like ice cream.

Wist had stopped speaking. Her magic cringed in her torso, a horrified ball of yarn. The pain of it must've taken her breath away, all those branches cramped in one place. She still didn't step back.

She could've used magic to put me to sleep. (Not that it would've stopped the Void.) She could've hit me over the head and made me crumple to my feet. (That wouldn't have stopped the Void, either.) She could've ported one or both of us a thousand miles away. (That might've bought some time. Unless the Void decided to settle for snacking on other random mages.)

She placed herself between a looming vorpal hole and the Void, and she didn't activate a single skill in self-defense.

I don't know what I did next. I had only an impressionistic sense of physical and magical reality. I might've lunged at Wist, tearing the base of her throat with my teeth. I might've put my fingers on her neck.

She lay flung face-down on the stone-paved garden path. The vorpal hole hung in the air behind her like a drooping low-slung cloud, a cloud as thin as the edge of a knife.

My arms merged with her back. Maybe they weren't my arms at all. They were ropes of starved disintegrating flesh, a brood of disembodied throats that pulsed convulsively, always swallowing.

This was only one way to perceive it. Viewed another way, the Void came to life in my shadow. Blades without any substance grew from under my fingernails, shooting through her back, slicing her magic like a mandoline. I wanted to die. The Void ate Wist's magic. Wist wouldn't fight it. Wist wouldn't fight me.

Her branches grew and regrew, a paradise of self-perpetuating power, a neverending feast.

The last few drips of my molten false eye hit the back of her coat.

I didn't know how to open my mouth anymore. *Wist*, I said, from somewhere outside my Void-ridden body. *Wist, you need to scream.*

She couldn't. It was not a passive act, this consumption by the Void. It took everything she had to give and more.

She smelled of rigid terror. She'd done something to her fingers on the pavement. They looked pulpy, distended. Destroying her own hands was more bearable than doing nothing whatsoever while the Void shredded her magic.

She wouldn't let herself scream unless I made her do it.

I hijacked her magic even as the Void consumed it.

I hijacked a body with every magic branch flayed raw, almost insensible from the hurt of it—physical pain came a distant second.

I made her pry her mouth open against the stones beneath us. I made her voice split the air. It was a sound that belonged with blood and altars; it was the sound of a ritual slaughter.

4

I HEARD Tempus cursing. I glimpsed a dark-haired woman—not Wist—who spoke with a disturbing accent.

It felt as though the Void could've gorged itself forever. In truth, hardly any time passed between when I first saw the vorpal hole and when they discovered me attacking Wist, one eye melted clean out of my face. By then, the Void and I were already growing sluggish with satiation.

No idea how it looked to them. I don't want to know what they saw.

We'd fed the Void a couple times since returning from Manglesea. Small experiments. Just to prove I had the ability to make it stop eating.

The Void hadn't even needed those experimental feedings. I'd thought it was already full. But it wasn't an inborn organ like my stomach or my lungs. It was a parasite at best.

I'd carried it for less than three months. How could I have believed I knew anything?

We'd gone walking together near smaller vorpal holes, too. A newish cluster in the prairie by Wist's tower, for instance. As we approached, the Void made my feet drag. It made my breath come short.

Not once had it made me claw blindly at Wist.

I'd drawn the wrong conclusions from this.

I'd forgotten to be afraid.

Think of the Void as a muscular wild animal. A bear, or a great cat, or even a vorpal beast. Imagine that you'd raised it from birth as your pet. It might seem affectionate. It might seem predictable.

It might gore you on a seeming whim, on a day like any other. In the middle of getting its food or cleaning its pen or doing any other routine task you'd already done a thousand times before. A cruel and random assault—but would people blame the animal?

They would blame you. You should have known it was wild.

I couldn't abandon the Void in the countryside. I couldn't ship it off to a zoo. No matter how vicious it got, no matter how unpredictable, I would have to coexist with it for the rest of my life. Knowing all the while that it might lash out at any time. Not at me, but at Wist.

No. No.

It wasn't random. The Void hadn't erupted for no reason.

All this time, I'd stinted on feeding it. And the hole here at Follyhope was a hundred times larger and stranger than any of the holes near the tower.

Every attempt to give the Void satisfaction had felt like making Wist take a seat before me and punching her full in the face. I felt the clench of her gritted teeth in our bond. If I wouldn't break a bottle on her head and drag the jagged edges down her back, why would I let the Void gnash her magic from root to tip?

For a mage, the Void's predation would be far worse and far deeper than a simple slash with a knife, a simple beating with fists.

Something ate at me when the Void ate at Wist. I didn't breathe a word about it. Only one of us had the right to complain.

Instead, I held the Void back as much as I possibly could. I could at least attempt to master its appetite. The Void would learn to make do with less.

That was your mistake, Asa Clematis. You lacked the grit to quench the Void's thirst. You denied it even when Wist would've willingly sacrificed more magic. Even when—unlike today—she would've had a chance to brace herself before the Void sank its teeth in her.

You told yourself you could train away the Void's vampiric wildness. In a matter of months, no less. The height of arrogance. You fancied yourself in control of the uncontrollable. You let its desire build unfulfilled, week after week, giving it only miserly hummingbird sips.

Then you threatened it with an enormous vorpal hole on one side and Wist on the other. Existential fear versus infinite satiation: a bottomless well of nectar, enough magic to fill the greatest emptiness in all the world. Why would the Void flee in terror when it could feast away its dread?

Some time later, I revived from a dreamless swoon.

I lay on a daybed. The Void slept without a sound at the back of my eye socket, glutted by its meal.

Wist wasn't here in the room with me. The line of our bond stretched further away. Not all the way off the estate.

I knew before squinting my eye open that a different mage sat nearby. A nine-branch mage.

Inspector Minashiro Tempus.

I blinked at the faraway ceiling, which was covered from corner to corner in a mural of angels. White light fixtures hung in twisted ribbony shapes like seaweed. I was in handcuffs, my right eye empty and uncovered. The Void remained sedate.

At the clink of my handcuffs shifting, Tempus twitched in his seat.

"What the hell were you doing?" he said.

"Where's Wist?"

"What'd you *do* to her?"

I rattled my wrists like maracas. "I've been cuffed many times. But I've never gotten along well with MPs."

He preemptively went red before I got out more than a couple of syllables. He spluttered, choking. He inhaled.

"I'll explain if you bring Wist here," I said. The only door I could see was closed. Presumably locked.

All that furious tension gusted out of him. "You're out of your mind," he said dully. "We all saw you attack her. I dragged you off her. Her hands—your face—her magic—"

"Who's *we*?"

Tempus stared.

"You said *we all saw you*. Who else was there?"

"Oh, for—that doesn't matter!"

"I'd like to know who else thinks I'm a dangerous lunatic."

"Asa, anyone who knows your background already thinks you're a dangerous lunatic. Rightfully so! You just—"

"You haven't asked about my eye."

Tempus graduated from staring to outright gaping. I opened my right eyelid at him.

"I know you wear a prosthetic," he said, stilted.

"Well, I've lost it. Look—I'm just going to keep stalling till you let Wist in. You're wasting your time."

His previously spotless uniform now bore bruise-like smudges of dirt and chalky dust. Must've acquired them when he came rushing out of the manor to wrestle me off Wist.

He squared himself.

"If you saw someone commit assault and battery out in broad daylight, and the first thing they did afterward was ask to see their victim face to face, would you go along with it? Would you say—of course, go ahead, my pleasure? Would a reasonable, sane person permit that?"

He was absolutely correct. I couldn't argue that I hadn't been hurting her. But I wouldn't get anywhere if I didn't argue at all.

"Tell me, then," I said. "You're ready to name my crimes. Describe exactly what I did to her."

His face twisted.

"You were horrified. Did you retch? Did someone have to come bury your vomit with a fresh layer of mulch?"

His mouth moved—his mustache gave it away—but failed to let out any sound.

"You must've asked Wist what I did to her."

"She wouldn't answer," he growled.

I understood his position. I'd attacked Wist in front of witnesses. I was the aggressor. She was the victim.

He might not comprehend how a mere weaponless healer could have done anything to wound the Kraken. He might not comprehend what precisely had taken place as the Void wolfed down raw hunks of her living magic. But he would've cringed to his core in sympathy. He would've known, without being able to articulate why, that it was an atrocity.

Better stop trying to convince him to bring us together. I had other options, anyway.

I reached for my bond with my mind as if tugging on a rope in a dark cave. Wist materialized between us with the preternatural smoothness of a high diver entering faraway water. Then she buckled. She caught herself on the foot of the daybed. Tempus's startle response devolved rapidly into contempt—directed at me, not at Wist.

She heard my handcuffs and turned. She ran her eyes over the short chain between my wrists. Magic clicked in the air with a sound akin to fingers snapped at a servant, imperious. Both cuffs came open like dropped jaws.

Wist tossed the cuffs to Tempus. He caught them one-handed and wordlessly slotted them into a holster on his belt.

She sat—not quite next to me, but close enough. On my left, where it was easier to see her. She hadn't touched me once, not even when removing the handcuffs, but a constant gentle pressure weighed on our bond all the while. A sensation of dry reassurance. Like holding hands where no one could see us, nudging feet together under a table.

"You got what you wanted," Tempus said to me, disdainful.

I hadn't even questioned whether Wist would come when I called her. I'd immediately forced her back into close proximity with me, and thus with the Void—however satiated it might be now.

I'd assumed too much, and I'd waited too long to give the Void a real meal. Whatever Tempus thought of me, I felt inclined to agree.

"Your hands," I said. To Wist, not to Tempus. Her fingers were no longer purple and leaking.

"Give your thanks to Lady Shien's physician," said Tempus.

Grandmother's personal doctor would, of course, be a mage.

As the Void fed on her magic, Wist could've flung me off and fled at any moment. I'd sensed through our bond that she hadn't been paralyzed by shock alone.

She was still physically stronger than me. She could've used her magic even while the Void ate it. Debilitating terror hadn't nailed her to the pavement, either. She'd made a deliberate choice to stay beneath me until the Void had its fill. I couldn't wrap my mind around the calculus behind that. Could you lie there without thrashing while feral pigs picked the flesh off your legs? This was no different.

Could you then—without shuddering, without hyperventilating—sit right here next to the human body that carried the amorphous entity so intent on ingesting you?

If not for our unchanged bond, if not for how I could feel her there without even trying, I wouldn't have been able to face her. I would've fled to the far ends of the continent to stop hurting her.

I would've twisted the Void into a tool for hunting other mages. Depraved and evil ones, hopefully. Perhaps sometimes they would just be unlucky. Sometimes the Void would need to feed, and I'd run out of time to find anyone appropriately villainous.

Because of our bond, I knew she wanted me here more than she dreaded the Void. I knew it as an absolute truth, a factual physical sensation like air filling my lungs, something that existed in me without any need for a believable explanation.

I looked Tempus in the eye and told him that Wist the Kraken had certain unique healing needs. That what had looked to him like torture was actually a type of vital treatment.

He didn't buy it.

"That's the truth," Wist said. "It was necessary. It was inevitable."

She sounded as wooden as ever. Hopefully Tempus hadn't forgotten that she never spoke with a wealth of emotion.

I chimed in. "Spread the word to whoever saw us. Demand their discretion. The Kraken's secrets are a matter of national security."

Tempus looked like he'd swallowed a spoonful of pepper flakes.

"Anyway, don't let this distract from your job," I said. "It's got nothing to do with Shien Miyu's disappearance."

"The last time you met her, she went berserk."

"I'm telling you, don't get distracted." I leaned back on my hands. "You warred with us in school. Didn't go very well for you, did it? You're a grown-ass man now. Don't make the same mistake."

He didn't acknowledge a word of this. He didn't bristle, either. Maybe our school days felt just as ancient to him as they did to me.

"Don't go anywhere," he warned. "Or I swear…"

"What?"

"Just. Don't."

He strode out of the room. The angels on the ceiling radiated an air of relief.

Wist immediately flopped down on the daybed. I asked without words if I could touch her magic. Her threads were worse than a thicket of brambles, chafed and knotted, bent and aching from the rapidity of their forced regrowth.

She scooted up so I could reach her lower back. She lacked the energy to say anything more.

This would've been more bearable if the Void had some form of utility. So far, it was nothing but a liability. It made wounding Wist inevitable. Not just inevitable, but a guaranteed price that would need to be paid over and over to keep it safe, to keep it tame.

I'd entertained all sorts of thoughts about putting the Void to good use. I'd been frustrated by Wist's reluctance to cooperate.

She'd been right to discourage further experimentation with the Void. After today, how could I fantasize about controlling it?

5

WHAT FOLLOWED were several dozen minutes of mute healing. Wist breathed as though hypnotized.

My hands moved in a stupor. Sometimes they didn't move at all. Healing was not a process fundamentally bound to physical actions and reactions. Through our bond, I could stir her branches without lifting a finger.

"The letter," Wist said as I finished. She sounded like she'd slept for fifteen hours straight.

"The—oh."

I'd brought a letter in my jacket. Between meeting Tempus, learning about Miyu, and unleashing the Void, I'd forgotten all about it.

"Think it has to do with Miyu?" I asked.

She shook her head slowly against the side of my leg, then pushed herself up. Numerous dark wisps had escaped her crown of braids. It still held itself in place with nary a pin.

My jacket lay on a coffee table without any legs: smooth white stone shaped like half an egg. As I rummaged through my pockets, I remarked on how the mansion's interior design had evolved over time. Many furnishings now appeared more contemporary—or at least more adventurous—if no less luxurious.

"Miyu," Wist said. "She stayed sequestered at Follyhope after getting out on parole. Did a lot of redecorating."

"You've been keeping closer tabs on the Shiens than you let on. Ah—here we go." I pulled out the letter.

It was written on Shien letterhead. Their family crest featured a stylized monoceros. Wist hadn't been able to answer when I asked her to explain the difference between a monoceros and a unicorn.

The letter had been delivered to my city apartment. It was addressed not to the name I used for business correspondence, but rather to my real full name of Asa Clematis. After we got back from Manglesea, I'd found it waiting together with a note about my water bill.

Dearest Magebreaker,

I write this to you on the eve of the equinox. Did you see spider lilies blooming in Manglesea? They must have been breathtaking. Do you prefer the red ones, or the white ones?

That reminds me: you hail from a family with a great passion for gardening. Here at the manor, all the garden staff are getting ready to hold our annual chrysanthemum showcase in October and November. Please do come visit. It would be a shame if you missed it.

Perhaps I digress. There are other reasons it might behoove you to pay us Shiens a visit. A promise of new meetings and old reunions. Above all, a chance to put your recent studies into practice.

The best way to become comfortable with a new skill is simply to keep using it over and over, don't you think?

Allow me to risk making a tiny prediction. One way or another, you will end up at the manor. Your time there might be miserable, or it might be surprisingly productive. Why not make the best of it?

We look forward to having you.

Fondly,
An Admirer

P.S. Please do give my love to Wisteria.

I'd joked with Wist that this was my first fan letter. Plenty such messages made their way to Wist the Kraken, one way or another. Mori usually took it on himself to sort them for her.

On the whole, Wist was more comfortable with death threats than with being admired or thanked by total strangers. She had unlimited confidence in her ability to save her own life. Innocent gratitude and shining praise cut much deeper. Maybe she liked me because I'd never given her much of either.

My anonymous letter, unfortunately, felt more like a threat. The writer knew my address. They knew that said address belonged to the criminal called the Magebreaker. They knew about my parents' horticultural hobbies. And, worst of all, they knew about my studies.

These past couple years, I'd covertly brushed up on my skills in two totally divergent fields.

First—not long after our previous visit to Follyhope—I'd begun researching bonds. I wanted to do something unprecedented: to invent a non-murderous way to break them. I read books on bond authentication. I took classes as if I planned on getting certified. To break bonds, I'd need a better idea of how they worked. I'd need to understand them at least as well as an entry-level notary.

The more I researched, the more I realized how devastatingly little anyone knew about bonds. Period. Granted, no one could afford to run bonding experiments in the first place. Mage-healer bonding was for life. It'd be unethical to throw people together solely for the sake of science.

I found various observational studies—some spanning decades—but these were primarily interested in analyzing how bonding boosted mages' magic.

I used to assume that my extremely sharp magic perception would let me identify bondmates at a glance. Maybe not with perfect accuracy, but better than your average chump. It was humbling to discover just how wrong I'd been.

Like magic forensics, bond identification was a skill that could only be developed through intensive hands-on training. An amateur might make a lucky guess. They might also get fooled by fake bonds; they might overlook a true bond due to lack of experience.

I'd mined Wist's connections for a chance to shadow professional bond notaries. They were surprisingly diverse—mages, low-level healers, even quite a few subliminals. Some theorized that healers had natural advantages when it came to bond authentication, but everyone went through the same training.

My other field of study was a touchier subject. Not long after obtaining my very first passport (thanks to Wist pulling strings), I'd invited my parole officer to Wist's tower and informed her that I wanted to get back into learning Jacian. She laughed at my sheer audacity.

"Of course," she said, cradling the cup of spica I'd obsequiously poured for her. "Of course you would. What makes you think you'll ever get a chance to use it? No—don't answer that. I don't want to know."

I asked if she'd like a shot of whiskey in her spica. (She vehemently declined.) I explained patiently that I was telling her upfront because

I knew just how bad it would look if I ever got caught practicing from a Jacian phrasebook behind her back.

I was a convicted traitor. You could say I owed it all to my past association with troublesome Jacians. Since getting sentenced, I hadn't seen or spoken to a single Jacian outside prison. Very few ever made it over to our shores to begin with.

I did understand why the seemingly innocent act of working on my language skills could reflect poorly on me, and on Wist by extension. Not to mention my harried parole officer.

Said parole officer knew me too well to try to stop me. "Be discreet," she said balefully.

"I am the very soul of—"

"Don't."

I'd never taken formal classes. Jacian classes wouldn't be offered anywhere in Osmanthus, anyway, except perhaps to intelligence officers.

Back before my arrest, I'd pored over old textbooks (most of which were technically banned, censored, etc.) and illegal imports. But I'd improved mainly by figuring out where real-life Jacians hung out in Osmanthus City. I'd amused them with my willingness to sound like an idiot.

As the Magebreaker, I occasionally got tasked with hobbling imprisoned Jacian mages. Guards would beat me over the head if I started jabbering in a language they didn't understand, though. All in all, my Jacian abilities had deteriorated to almost nothing over time.

Why pick it up again? There'd been rumors that the International Vorpal Defense Council might send Wist on a mission to Jace. Such rumors were rather questionable, considering that Jace wasn't even a member of VorDef. Years later, nothing had come of it.

As for me, I was the least likely person in Osmanthus to be permitted anywhere near a hostile country.

And yet—if Wist ever crossed the sea to Jace, I was determined to go with her, and to make myself useful.

Jacian technology remained a mystery to much of the continent. Jacian healing techniques were even more of a black box. There might be a chance, however slim, that they'd independently developed the same techniques I'd once thought were mine alone. Hobbling. Reverse healing. Hijacking. I couldn't risk shipping Wist off to Jace on her own.

I'd abandoned my various attempts at self-education during our trip to Manglesea, of course. It was supposed to have been a vacation.

According to Wist, the monoceros crest on the unsigned letter didn't look like a forgery. But she couldn't say for sure.

It might not have come from a Shien family member at all. It could just as easily have been sent by a rogue employee, or a third party (like the ever-scheming Extinguishers?) with their own nefarious reasons for wanting to trick us.

We'd decided to ignore the letter. It lacked both clarity and urgency. And, as I'd grown fond of telling Wist: nothing good would come of tangling with the Shiens.

Then came the news that a giant vorpal hole had torn open right in the middle of the Shien estate. We revisited the letter. The writing style told us nothing. Anyone could sound a little stuffy if they tried.

Well, almost anyone. Ficus—one of Wist's older brothers—had never struck me as being tremendously literate. Maybe he had hidden depths.

I'd also been tempted to rule out Miyu, Grandmother Shien, and Wist's adoptive parents, all of whom seemed too proud and too ill-humored to write to me with even the thinnest veneer of courtesy. Not even for the sake of some dastardly plot.

Wist's oldest brother, Nerium, seemed like the most obvious candidate. I could picture him composing this missive ... which might've been exactly what the mysterious writer wanted us to think.

I remembered too little of Wist's other siblings to judge whether they could've authored the letter instead. The handwriting provided no clues, either. It was an organic script, elegantly generic. It bore all the markers of text transcribed with a touch of magic.

I waved the letter at Wist. "My deductive abilities tell me that it probably wasn't Tempus."

"What wasn't me?" Tempus asked sourly.

I tucked the letter away just as he came through the door.

"I've had a genius idea," I said.

Wist, who had begun lolling sideways again, sat up abruptly on the daybed. Tempus looked appalled, and made zero effort to hide it.

"I'll save you time," I continued, dauntless. "I'll help you investigate."

6

"WHAT?"

Tempus said it out loud.

Wist said it in my head.

Trust me, I told her.

"Hear me out," I told him.

I bent to lace up my clunky work boots, which had been awaiting me below the daybed. The floor here was prissy old hardwood. My soles might leave black marks on the glistening basketweave boards.

"I've studied bond authentication," I said. "I've already got the most basic certification."

"A learner's permit?" said Tempus.

"Wist can vouch for me. My papers are back at her tower. If you really want to see them—"

He cut me off. "What are you getting at?"

Wist had already guessed. Our bond felt as taut as a sore throat.

"You're negotiating with Grandmother Shien to bring more outsiders to the estate," I said. "Bond notaries and your forensics crew and what have you. You'll have to make appointments, draw up a schedule, argue over confidentiality and the necessity of it all. But what you really want to know is whether Shien Miyu is dead. A broken bond is as good as finding a body."

"You don't have any authority to formally certify—"

"No," I agreed. "I can't give you anything legal to stand on. My license is still provisional. I can look at Miyu's bondmate and tell you the facts, though. Even if you've got to get a real bond notary to sign off on it later—today I can tell you whether or not the bond is still there. Whether or not Shien Miyu is dead. Everything hinges on that one point, no?"

Tempus couldn't decide whether he ought to look at my good eye or my missing eye. "You used to be all about healer liberation. Why offer to expose Lady Miyu's healer as a liar?"

"Their bond might still be intact," I pointed out. "I might prove that her healer's been telling the truth all along. Besides, the faster you get this sorted, the faster Wist can close that vorpal hole."

He scoffed. "You aren't even attempting to act distressed." He seemed to mean both of us.

"Distressed over what?"

"Her sister is missing. Potentially dead." His eyes were on Wist again. "I swear, if your movements weren't so well accounted for...."

I laughed. "Some Board members would love to see the Kraken accused of murder, wouldn't they? But that'd be tough to pull off, Inspector. Your family's always been too chummy with the Shiens. You of all people ought to understand why Wist wouldn't shed false tears over Shien Miyu. Don't you dare keep telling me to call Miyu a lady, either. I'll gag you with your own mustache."

He pivoted toward Wist. "Can we talk without your lapdog yapping?" he said coolly. "Just for a minute?"

They stepped out of the room. I found myself mildly impressed. The Tempus I'd known would've long since lost his temper and attempted to put us under arrest for things we'd never done.

He'd hit me where it hurt, too. If Miyu's bondmate had indeed lied to cover up Miyu's death, then revealing that lie would by no means be a shining act of healer solidarity. I could fib about the results of my bond examination—I could pretend I'd made a novice error—but that would only delay the inevitable.

The thing is, I wanted to know the truth.

Wist had all but cut ties with the Shien clan, and they'd despised me since long before I got thrown in prison. The death of one of her siblings would make no material difference in our lives.

And yet a strange feeling coiled in me, a foreign sensation like the bloodless swirling presence of the Void. A conviction that I had set this in motion. I had knocked over the first domino in a long row, as carelessly vindictive as a cat swiping a porcelain trinket off a shelf.

A couple of years ago, I had judged Shien Miyu, and I had found her wanting. I'd exacted my own unspoken form of justice by twisting her magic till it drove her berserk.

She lost a lot of things: her reputation, her job at the Ministry of Justice, her ability to show her face in high society without shaming Grandmother Shien. But she hadn't lost her bondmate. I hadn't known of any way to separate them without becoming a self-appointed executioner.

That one berserking incident couldn't possibly have anything to do with Miyu's current disappearance (or death). Even so, I felt irrationally convinced that there must be some kind of destined connection—however thin, however tenuous. That slender sense of causality ran from the present to the past like an unbreakable bond, a string as bloody red as my hidden scarlet parole thread.

I'd promised myself that if I ever did figure out how to break bonds, I'd come back and offer my services to Miyu's bondmate. She'd be the first healer I'd give a chance to escape.

At the moment, I was still stuck fiddling with unprovable theorems. The problem with bondbreaking was that I couldn't experiment on myself. What if a broken bond could never be reforged?

I couldn't test it out on random strangers, either. I couldn't openly canvass for volunteers. Even if I found a healer desperate to get out at any cost—what if I ended up maiming their bond without actually breaking it?

I sat back on the daybed. To Tempus—and any other witnesses—it must've looked as though I'd assaulted Wist at random. If anyone suspected that venturing near the vorpal hole had set me off, the most sensible response would be to send me far away from the estate.

I didn't think the Void would react the same way twice in short succession. But I'd misread it before. Better keep my distance from that hole. When Wist got clearance to close it, she'd have to visit the old rose garden alone.

I found a spare eyepatch in a long-forgotten jacket pocket. I finished picking all the lint off and had donned it by the time Wist and Tempus returned.

Wist gave me a measuring look. Under normal circumstances, this was the closest she would get to outright frowning.

She held a palm out as if cupping water. *I can fetch a spare eye from the tower.*

Save your magic, I told her.

The eyepatch was good for throwing people off. For eliciting curiosity, and sometimes pity.

At any rate, we had no good backup for the prosthetic eye I'd destroyed today. My spares were only equipped with basic defensive magic. Nothing nearly as sophisticated or precious as the one I'd lost.

Wist could recreate it for me, taking new cuttings from all her relevant branch skills, but doing so would demand way more time and concentration than she could afford at the moment. Especially after how the Void had savaged her magic.

Tempus announced in clipped tones that he would make arrangements for me to examine Miyu's bondmate as soon as possible. First, Wist would help him run this proposal by Grandmother Shien.

He caught Wist sidling toward me, reaching to take my arm.

"No," he said in a voice like a stomped foot. "No way. Bringing her in would be a great way to guarantee that Lady Shien turns us down."

"I know when to keep my mouth shut," I said.

"Asa, you've got this uncanny ability to rub mages the wrong way even when you don't breathe a damn word."

I gave him the most pious look I could muster. "Speak for yourself, Inspector."

7

WIST REMAINED reluctant to leave my side again.

"Your healer can survive half an hour on her own," Tempus said acerbically.

I knew the reason for Wist's hesitation. The eye that had dissolved from my face in wet strings and globs like foamed-up toothpaste—that lost eye had been implanted with a cutting I could trigger to summon her from anywhere in the world, at any time. Even if she were unconscious. Even if she couldn't hear my inner voice.

Tempus installed me back in the same blue-floored receiving room as before, and warned me not to wander. He claimed to have passed my story on, telling other witnesses that what I'd done to Wist was in truth an unfathomably intricate healing ritual, one tailored exclusively to the esoteric needs of the Kraken.

Who had seen us? The blond healer? Grandmother's in-house physician? Grandmother herself, staring from a window?

Tempus pried Wist away from me, urging her not to keep Grandmother waiting; he gave no further answers. I took advantage of my solitude to look more closely at the starfish painting mounted on the far wall.

It wasn't actually a starfish, despite its tropical colors and five long tentacles. It could've been a rubbery dead hand with spindly water-warped fingers, or a maimed five-legged spider.

Five. I'd sensed five mages around the estate when the starving Void came spewing out of me and latched onto Wist.

I could account for four of them off the top of my head. Wist. Tempus. Grandmother Shien. Her doctor. Who was the fifth?

This was an estate large enough to house an army, with multiple standalone mansions flanking the central manor building. Yet once a vorpal hole consumed a sizable swathe of the gardens, Grandmother Shien had evacuated most live-in staffers, and presumably most live-in relatives.

The hole's progress might have been immeasurably slow, but it was metastasizing nevertheless, growing outward bit by bit like human fingernails.

Which other Shien mage would've been permitted to stay?

I'd felt the burning magic of those five mages with painful lucidity, but only through the lens of the Void's indiscriminate hunger. I hadn't been able to count their branches, or to discern if the layout of their magic matched anyone I'd met in the past.

Which meant that—hypothetically—the mysterious fifth mage could very well be Shien Miyu. Not dead, not on the lam: imprisoned here by her own family. Buried alive in a cellar for—I dunno, a mortal offense against her grandmother.

"What do you think?" said a woman's voice.

She stood in the middle of the room as if she'd been there all along. Glossy off-black hair with purplish undertones. Winged eyeliner. A plethora of pearl jewelry against cool brown skin. There was something more leonine than feminine in her stance, in how radically relaxed she seemed in her own body.

She was a—

Was she a mage?

She had a magic core. For a second, I'd thought she had branches. Short branches, fatally deformed branches, but branches nonetheless.

I concentrated harder. The illusion scattered.

This woman was a subliminal mage, branchless, nothing but a smooth magic core buried in her like a ripe golden mango. No real power.

But she could also have been the fifth mage staying at Follyhope. Rather—the one I'd mistaken for a fifth real mage. At first glance, her core argued very convincingly that it ought to have branches.

"Did I surprise you?" she asked, unperturbed by my gawping.

At last my brain caught up with my ears. I heard the peculiarity of her pronunciation. Her accent.

Her Jacian accent.

Clem?

Wist's voice reached me like a distant echo between mountains.

I'm—not hurt, I managed. *I'll be fine.*

The blond healer wearing maid robes glided into the room behind the stranger. "Do try to control yourself," she said repressively. "That's a very offensive reaction."

It took me an extra second to realize that the healer was talking to me.

"She's just taken aback," the Jacian stranger said easily. "Don't pick on her, Danny."

"Don't call me that."

The Jacian looked me in the eye, unfazed by my eyepatch, and switched smoothly to her own language.

"I'm Lear," she said, with nonchalant clarity. "Lovely to meet you. Remember any Jacian phrases? I've heard from compatriots that you used to be quite the chatterbox."

To my dismay, I understood every syllable. I was still tongue-tied. How might the government react to news of me fraternizing with a Jacian?

But I'd done nothing incriminating. Really and truly. I hadn't uttered a word yet.

It might still be a trap.

The blond healer turned up her stubby little nose. She, at least, was definitely Osmanthian. "Rude," she sniffed. "Don't speak in languages that half your audience can't understand."

The Jacian—Lear—reverted to Continental. "Wasn't talking to you, Danny."

"Danver."

"Danver, then." Lear sounded amused. "Feeling left out?"

"Look," I croaked. (Also in Continental.) "I'm not—I can't—"

"What an extraordinary show of xenophobia," said the healer called Danver.

"Most city folk keep it well under wraps," agreed Lear.

"Looks like she's having an allergy attack."

"You're one to talk, Danny. You just lectured me about using my own mother tongue."

"That's different."

My outlook shifted like a tilting picture frame.

Whoever this foreigner was, getting caught (almost) alone with me might be just as bad for her as it was for me. I'd left prison as a result of my association with Wist. All the same, I was one of the most infamous Osmanthian criminals of our time. I'd gotten in trouble specifically by conspiring with Jacians.

There's a Jacian here, I told Wist. *I'll tread carefully.*

She answered with a light press through our bond like a squeeze from an unseen hand.

Lear strolled up to the other end of the rectangular painting, keeping a kindly distance from me. Danver the healer hung back with her arms crossed.

"I'm not a spy or an assassin," Lear said. "I promise."

"Neither am I," I replied. "At least not at the moment."

She chuckled politely, which was pretty much all that comment deserved.

"I'm just a harmless layperson." She raised her eyes to the painting. "And an artist."

"Your work?" I ventured.

She pointed out her signature in the corner: a stylized mush of old Jacian characters.

"I'm here legally," she said, matter-of-fact. "Got a generous international grant. Cultural exchange and all that. I'm the Shien clan's artist-in-residence."

"...Congratulations."

"Thanks." She swept a bow. "I often get called an abstract painter, but I've never considered myself anything but a realist."

I eyed her giant stringy starfish.

"Pure and faithful realism." An obscure satisfaction entered her voice.

"Where are you from?" I asked.

She raised an eyebrow. "In Jace? You know much about Jacian geography?"

"I barely know anything about continental geography."

"Heh. My family's in the tiny islands sprinkled far to the south. The ones everyone tends to forget about." She gestured gracefully at her jewelry. "They dive for pearls and abalone. The grannies would harvest a lot of other seafood, too. Dunno what it's called in Continental. You'd be amazed at how long I can hold my breath."

"You've come a long way," I said banally.

Lear pretended to shudder. "I only regret it in winter. Lord, it's cold here."

"Not nearly as cold as it gets up north."

She grimaced. "You people and your seasons. Four seasons are way too many."

"There are parts of Jace with just as many seasons, no?"

"Doesn't bother me if I don't have to live there."

"If you're done flirting," Danver said, "the MP and the Kraken are on their way back."

She had excellent ears. Or perhaps her magic perception had alerted her. Cuttings had been applied to her querulous glasses, cleverly blending with the wiry golden rims. But why would a healer—even a Shien family healer—be given such a valuable perception-enhancing artifact?

Who was her bondmate, anyway? Grandmother? That might explain this healer's continued presence on the nigh-empty estate. It might also explain her attitude.

Wist and Tempus returned to the receiving room a few seconds later.

Tempus nodded curtly at Lear.

Wist, in contrast, stopped and stared as though confronted by a piece of trick art, a life-size optical illusion. Then she shook herself (rather doggishly) and came over to me without comment.

A branchless core was nothing unusual. Every subliminal mage had one, and they far outnumbered mages with actual power. But Lear's seemed somehow as though it ought to be growing branches. One or two, at minimum.

I'd never met a subliminal who threw me off like this. At least it wasn't just me who found her confusing.

Lear, for her part, looked very briefly and sharply at Wist's inner forest of magic.

Most people would gawk when they first found themselves in the same room as the Kraken. There was a perturbing element of professionalism in how penetratingly Lear regarded her, and how swiftly she shifted her focus elsewhere.

Tempus paid no heed. "You've got permission to perform a cursory examination," he said to me. "I'll have your head if you screw this up."

"Aye aye, sir."

He named a building and asked Wist if she knew the way. Lear suggested using one of the enchanted mirrors down the hall as a shortcut.

"Wait."

Danver's voice had jumped a full octave higher.

She cleared her throat. "You're going to—"

"To see Shien Miyu's healer," Tempus said, impatient. Even as he spoke, I could see him growing perplexed about why he'd bothered answering to the equivalent of a household servant.

"You already interrogated her. Multiple times. She needs rest. You can't—"

"Lady Shien authorized it. Nothing to be concerned about."

Wist and I followed Tempus out of the blue-floored room. I turned at the sound of Danver hurrying on our heels with quick little steps. Lear watched her go for a moment, then shrugged and began to amble after.

8

T‍HE HALL FED US into a terminal of towering mirrors laid out in angles like facets of a gem.

Each sheet of glass bore a unique set of intricate etchings. If anyone had told me how to interpret these marks in the past, I'd long since forgotten.

We stepped through a half-hidden mirror tucked off to one side, concealed by all those other flashy competing reflections. It was much shorter than the rest; Wist ducked to fit.

Our chosen portal transferred us to the front yard of a large boarding house some distance from the manor. A dormitory for live-in help.

Dead hairy vines crawled over discolored stone walls. Turkey vultures teetered on thermals high in the sky. Holly and other evergreens formed a tall screen at our backs. Heaven forbid that any Shiens sully their vision with an accidental glance at servants' quarters.

Tempus looked at Danver the healer with ill-concealed consternation.

"Why are you—"

"I live here, too," she said.

She swept up to the front door and motioned officiously for us to come in.

The dormitory had airy ceilings, ambitious vaulted bones. Homespun window treatments and sun-faded furniture kept it humble. Green onions sprouted vigorous roots in glass canning jars clustered on a water-stained sill.

Tempus took out an expensive-looking pocket watch. "We have to wait for Doctor Hazeldine."

"Who?" I said.

"Lady Shien's doctor. She requested his presence as a witness."

Next he eyed Danver and said: "Make yourself useful. Go fetch your friend."

Was it just me, or did she look like she wanted to clock Tempus in the jaw?

Lear leaned over and introduced herself to Wist as if they'd just met at a party. "The Shiens have been very welcoming," she said warmly. "Despite me being a foreigner. They've given me an entire atelier of my own to work in—more space than I've ever had in my life."

"Did Grandmother invite you to stay?" Wist asked.

Her tone didn't vary in the slightest. If they didn't know her, even someone attempting to give her the benefit of the doubt would hear a challenging edge in the flatness of that voice. The absence of emotion shouldn't have sounded like anything—but it came out sounding like rude disinterest, arrogance, unvarnished hostility.

On the other hand, the Kraken was widely reputed to be a little eccentric. And a Jacian who'd come to Osmanthus would be even better-educated about the Kraken than most native Osmanthians. Know your enemy, and all that.

"One of your brothers brought me here," Lear said genially. "Shien Ficus. Friendly fellow. Took a real shine to me and my art."

She cupped her hand near her mouth and false-whispered, "I'd love to think that he got totally bowled over by my massive talent."

"He wasn't?"

"Doubt it. Bet he liked the novelty of a continent-crossing Jacian making a living off painting. No matter! I'm grateful all the same."

"A lovely sentiment," Tempus sniped, "but we aren't in your art studio."

"Really? You don't say."

"You've insinuated yourself into this situation as if you belong here. You had no reason to follow us."

"Come, now. Listen to my accent. I don't belong anywhere in Osmanthus."

Lear clapped him on the shoulder. He failed to react.

She continued, undeterred. "Whatever you're about to do, it's not some classified matter of national security. Right? If it is, kick me out. If it's not—you remember what Ficus said, don't you? There's no telling when inspiration might strike. Inconvenient, but that's how it is."

"You only paint—"

"Artistic inspiration can come from anywhere," she declared. "A stomach cramp. A dead mouse. A certain ray of light. It might not have anything to do with the final product. Anyway, Ficus gave me free rein to run all over Follyhope, and Lady Shien has been kind enough not to throw me out on my ass. Ah, pardon my language. I know I'm lucky."

This struck me as being the sort of blather I myself might've coughed up if I were pretending to be a visual artist. But what do I know? There are all kinds of people out there. She could've been serious.

We'd come to Follyhope around mid-morning. By now it was past lunchtime. The moment Lear stopped ribbing Tempus, my stomach growled like a guard dog. Lear made a sympathetic face. Tempus's mustache wriggled in a frisson of disgust. Really, how dare I have working organs. So uncouth of me.

Wist tapped me through our bond. I knew without looking that she was holding out a crunchy candy bar. I'd heard her tear the wrapper.

I love and adore you, I thought goopily. *Knew you'd come through for me.*

Wist started withdrawing the candy bar. Too late—I snatched it up like a mongoose. I made cursory excuses to Lear and Tempus as I chewed. I had no intention of sharing. Not that they would've wanted my leftovers, anyway.

Wist was a different matter. I tossed the last chunk high over my shoulder—no advance notice—and listened with satisfaction as she caught it in her mouth. We'd have been able to forge a decent career for ourselves in a third-rate circus.

I was licking my fingertips when Danver came back downstairs, a taller woman behind her.

Miyu's healer.

Was this the same healer I'd met when Miyu went berserk?

Yes. Yes, of course. Still startlingly thin and young, with the haunted look of a greyhound.

She wore the same long robe-based uniform as Danver, although hers came with gloves. She was so pallid that she made light-skinned Danver look downright tan.

"We're still waiting on the doctor," Tempus said gruffly.

"I'm Asa. Asa Clematis," I said to Miyu's healer. "You know Wist over here? She's the Kraken."

The healer folded her gloved hands together. "Ginko," she replied.

It had the sound of a given name. *Danver* was likely a given name, too. *Lear* I couldn't be too sure about. Jacian names came flipped by default—given name first, family name last—as if they were all adoptees like Wist.

Ginko spoke only when spoken to; she didn't seem to wonder why we'd called on her. She nodded when I asked if she recognized us.

"I remember you. Both of you."

Her voice was very soft and high and breathy. Under different circumstances, I might've assumed she was putting on an act.

Lear—infinitely comfortable in her pearl jewelry and patchy rolled-cuff jeans—wandered the fringes of the entrance hall and kitchen with an air of avid curiosity.

Tempus's grip tightened on his pocket watch. He'd better put that thing away before he cracked it.

I sidled into the nook next to a broken grandfather clock and observed Danver and Ginko as they went around wiping surfaces that didn't look dirty.

The main reason I didn't think Ginko's whispery little voice was an affectation: Danver didn't seem like someone who would put up with coquettish fakery for more than two seconds. They moved in perfect harmony in their matching healer robes, bleakly colored from head to toe like a pair of industrious crows.

Ginko, too, had a bond thread around her neck. A symbol of her ties to Shien Miyu. I still didn't know who Danver's bond thread was meant to represent.

They stood on tiptoe to reach for hollow glass baubles that hung from curtain rods and dangling plants. Dust-collecting globes, gleaming with embedded magic.

If similar dust traps had been set up around the rest of the manor, they were cunningly hidden. I'd never seen any in Wist's tower, either. Her walls had a way of inhaling excess grit when no one was looking. Although they'd never done a very good job of catching cat hair.

Danver and Ginko emptied their glittering globes into a bin. Out tumbled dust globs the size and color of well-fed rats.

Nearby, Lear scrutinized pressed flowers hung in a sequence of small irregular frames. Sometimes she glanced over at Danver and Ginko as if searching for the dangerous hidden crack in a flawed drinking glass, one that would need to be disposed of even if it hadn't fallen apart yet. She looked at them as if they were already lost.

Maybe they were. They were both bonded to mages, and one of those mages was Shien Miyu. They wouldn't have been given much real choice regarding who to bond, or when.

Wist and Tempus and I were all the same age, in our mid-thirties. Despite her worldly air, Lear could've been anywhere between thirty and forty. Danver and Ginko could've passed for university students.

People say you should experience life by yourself before shacking up with a lover. People say you should live with someone and learn what they're really like before starting a family.

But there's no way to do a trial run of having a bondmate. You're either bonded or you're not. There's no way to undo it except for murder, suicide, or a terrible accident.

And once you're bonded, you'll never have another chance to live truly on your own, to learn independence, to hear your own uncontaminated thoughts, to feel your own undiluted feelings.

You could be by yourself in an otherwise empty room in an abandoned house in a bombed-out city—and even if your bondmate was on the other side of the continent, you still wouldn't be alone in any way that mattered.

I don't mean to imply that there was anything unusual about Danver and Ginko being in their early twenties. Healers considered skilled enough to pursue as bondmates would often get bonded right out of school. If not earlier.

Back when I'd had delusions of dabbling in politics, I'd pushed to raise the legal age of bonding consent. Every attempt at reform fell through in the end. Now all that struggle and disappointment felt like something that had happened to a pitifully idealistic stranger in a different world, a different life.

The door swung open. Tempus jumped, although he should've been primed to expect it.

Cold air seeped in together with a swarthy middle-aged mage in a tailored sports coat. He wore a neat monocle and a lush black beard trimmed with off-putting precision. Tempus must've been jealous.

"It's brisk out there!" the man cried, as if this would be news to us. His eyes landed on Wist. "How are your hands?"

"Usable," she said. "Thank you."

He didn't introduce himself. If he were the estate doctor, then everyone—except for me, just another random healer—already knew him. He would no more go out of his way to address me than he would begin earnestly gossiping with the nearest houseplants.

On the plus side, this lack of reaction probably meant that he hadn't seen the Void devouring Wist firsthand. Who had, then? Tempus for sure. Lear, too—I'd heard snatches of her accent as I lapsed out of consciousness. She hadn't betrayed any particular revulsion toward me, but a Jacian like her would need guts of steel to make it through life in Osmanthus.

To my surprise, Tempus hemmed and hawed and then gestured my way. "She's with the Kraken," he said to the doctor. "Asa..."

"Clematis." I followed this up with, "How do you do," in the poshest tone I'd ever used in my life.

"Oh!" The doctor looked me over through his monocle. "Hazeldine Shien." Given name first: an adoptee into the clan, like Wist. "Delighted to make your acquaintance."

He pivoted back towards Wist and Tempus. They were clearly the only people who mattered. Danver and Ginko were mere staff, and healers to boot. Lear (who still seemed content to half-listen as she explored the kitchen) was a foreigner and a subliminal.

The doctor asked Tempus why we'd gathered here.

"Lady Shien didn't tell you?" Tempus said with a frown.

"Had my hands tied with some delicate tasks after seeing to the Kraken"—a quick bow at her—"and I'm afraid there was just no time to go over any details. Terribly sorry to have kept you waiting."

Tempus pointed at me again. "This woman, Asa—"

Wist regarded him expressionlessly. I watched him war with his absolute abhorrence at the notion of calling me a lady.

"This, uh, this healer has training in bond authentication," he finished.

Magic rang out at the periphery of my awareness. A streak like a falling star.

"Nice catch," Lear called as the air held its breath.

Someone had dropped one of the gleaming glass dust traps. As it fell, Wist's magic pounced like a bird snatching insects in flight.

She had her back to Danver and Ginko. Physically, she hadn't moved an inch. Behind her, in a total blind spot, her magic suspended the fallen globe an inch above the linoleum floor.

Ginko stooped to retrieve the globe with gloved fingers. It had already been emptied of dust. As soon as she took it, Wist's cushioning magic winked out like a firefly.

Wist's fist hovered near her mouth, though she showed no other outward signs of strain. A shared queasiness spilled through our bond, ricocheting from her body to mine. It hadn't been pleasant for her to use reflexive magic so soon after being ravaged by the Void. It would've felt like straining while you still had stitches in, pulling at the contours of never-healed wounds.

Empty-handed, Danver looked down at the mouth of the open trash can.

It had been Danver who dropped the dust trap. Not Ginko.

Doctor Hazeldine began to say something to lighten the mood.

"Her? Asa Clematis?" Danver's voice splintered, squeaking. The doctor blinked—probably unaccustomed to being interrupted by healers.

"I saw what you did to the Kraken," Danver said to me.

"A necessary procedure," I half-lied.

"The Kraken has singular needs," Tempus added. Not very convincingly.

Danver whirled on him. "There's something wrong with them. Both of them."

"Danny, my girl," said the doctor, "you can't just insult the Kraken like—"

She remained laser-focused on Tempus. "You can't do this. You need Lady Miyu's consent. You can't subject her healer to—"

"The head of the clan gave permission," Tempus snapped. "We've been over this."

Ginko plucked ineffectually at Danver's long fluttering sleeves.

Lear moseyed over and put a friendly hand on Tempus's shoulder. He shrugged her off like a horse twitching away a fly.

"Now, now," she said. "Danny's just feeling a little overprotective. Who could blame her?"

"I can," Tempus snarled, "if she obstructs—"

"Now, now, now, now."

It really did begin to sound as though Lear were soothing a temperamental horse. She eased herself between Tempus and the two healers. All traces of amusement left her voice. "Lord forbid, if Lady Miyu turns out to be dead—they'll wonder why you reacted so strongly, Danny."

"I'll—"

"Don't say you'll kill me. Please. Don't say anything violent. Wouldn't be advisable, given the circumstances."

Ginko whispered something to Danver, who clammed up and stared mulishly at her feet. Doctor Hazeldine let out an audible breath of relief.

Wist sat down in a squeaky chair and closed her eyes as the magic in her clenched like cramping muscle fibers. Tempus had his eyes closed, too. He must've been fantasizing about arresting each and every one of us.

9

For all the kerfuffle beforehand, the actual bond exam took less time than we'd spent waiting around for Doctor Hazeldine.

Danver demanded to be allowed to attend the examination. Lear took her arm and maneuvered her outside before she could say anything to get herself disciplined.

Wist quietly pulled her legs in to avoid tripping them as they passed her.

I told Tempus to let Wist keep dozing. (She was only pretending to sleep in her chair. But she did deserve a breather.)

The remaining four of us—me, Ginko, Tempus, and the doctor—went upstairs. I'd wanted to conduct the exam in a place where Ginko would be comfortable, and which might provide a modicum of privacy.

Her third-floor room had a compact bed, diamond-pane windows, and not much else. Garden rocks stood lined up on a chest of drawers, meticulously ordered from largest to smallest.

It was noticeably warmer than on the lower floors. I asked Ginko to take off her gloves.

She hesitated. "She hates when I touch her."

She was talking about Miyu. And she didn't just mean physical touch.

"Have you called to her?" I asked. "Have you asked why she disappeared? Where she went?"

Tempus answered before Ginko could say a word. "Obviously. That's the first thing we did when Shien Miyu was reported missing. We reached out through her bondmate."

"She never responds," Ginko said quietly.

There weren't any chairs or other such niceties for guests. With Ginko's permission, I sat next to her on the low-slung bed. She began working her gloves off one finger at a time.

Tempus and Doctor Hazeldine hung back by the opposite wall, just inside the narrow door.

Tempus seemed skeptical about the fact that I hadn't requisitioned any special tools. Doctor Hazeldine offered me a magnifying glass, one coated in a sheen of iridescent magic. I declined.

I explained to Ginko that I would need to touch her. I took her bare hands. They were cold and parched—the type of skin that would absorb copious amounts of cream in seconds, and then immediately go dry again.

Hazeldine rambled at Tempus while I tried to focus. "I've got a daughter at Guralta Academy. Very proud of her! You went there, too, didn't you? You and the Kraken."

And me, I thought, but I said nothing.

"Graduated from Guralta myself, actually." The doctor was the sort of conversationalist who didn't require much reaction. "Got out of there before they went co-ed—not a healer in sight. Not as students, I mean. That dates me, doesn't it? A lot has changed since my time."

I could imagine that Tempus had little desire to chitchat. If he could, he'd tell the doctor to shut his trap and devote himself to his role as Grandmother's appointed observer. But he wouldn't risk offending a fellow alumnus.

Hazeldine just kept going. "Never bonded, myself—just wasn't in the cards—not sure how my wife would've felt about that, haha! Totally valid choice to have both a spouse and a bondmate, of course, perfectly, professional, nothing wrong with that. But it's not for everyone!"

"Uh-huh," Tempus said, sounding trapped.

"Of course, it would've been easier to work my way up at major medical institutions if I'd gotten the boost of being bonded. Luckily, that was never my main ambition. I'm a family man, you see. To have a family, and to provide for them—what greater joy could there be? My favorite part of the job is helping other Shiens grow their own little families.

"Yes, originally I trained as a fertility specialist. Funny bit of trivia, isn't it? No matter where life takes me, I've always made a point of keeping up with..."

With some effort, I stopped hearing him. I proceeded to drag the examination out for as long as possible. Even then, I couldn't quite make it to fifteen minutes.

As a general rule, healers were easier to inspect for bonding than mages. They didn't have any magic branches writhing around to confuse the question.

It was also easier to confirm the definitive lack of a bond than to endorse its presence, or to sign off on the fact that two specific individuals were bonded to one another.

Bond authentication was frankly more of an art than a science. Most seasoned professionals eschewed the use of tools. Analog equipment wasn't much help, and magical equipment could spit out extremely misleading results. Magic never did a very good job of analyzing itself.

Notaries in training were instead taught to refract their magic perception through other senses.

Most people with any degree of magic perception already experienced this without thinking about it. Many would describe magic in visual terms, even though they didn't actually perceive it with their eyes. A light, a glow, a flare, a spark.

I sometimes thought I heard magic—buzzing, humming, ringing someplace other than my ears. Or else I might smell it, or taste it like static on my skin.

Mage-healer bonds could be uniquely slippery, difficult to trace accurately with magic perception alone. Intentionally cultivated synesthesia—recruiting other senses to your cause—allowed trained notaries to assert that yes, these people were bonded, or no, that person was lying.

Ginko was lying.

Ten seconds after taking her hands, I knew there was no point in continuing.

She didn't try to snatch her hands away. She didn't deny anything, or start protesting. She sat there obediently, at my mercy.

I went through the motions of examining her (not that it looked as if I were doing much of anything from the outside). If I could, I would've prattled on about this and that in the way of a hairdresser soothing a client with meaningless conversation. I failed: I couldn't speak coherently while Doctor Hazeldine droned on behind me.

I'd heard all about how Shien Miyu had treated her previous bond-mate. Ginko's predecessor, now deceased. I remembered those stories not because they were strikingly unusual, but because they weren't. A cruel and domineering mage: how dreadfully hackneyed. How archetypal. How *common*.

Shall we concoct theories to explain Miyu's behavior?

She had less magic than her siblings. Any amateur could diagnose her with a debilitating inferiority complex, one exacerbated by her adopted sister Wisteria—who'd turned out to carry more magic branches than anyone else in the world.

Or perhaps it had little to do with the cutthroat competition between all those brothers and sisters. They'd banded together quickly enough, hadn't they? They'd found a common enemy in Wist.

I wasn't inclined to cut Miyu much slack for the distance and coldness and crushing expectations of her parents, either. My Wist had been raised by the exact same people.

Let's say it was something innate, then. In Miyu's view of the world, other people might in theory possess feelings and desires and a capacity for being wounded. Ultimately none of that meant anything to her when measured against her own hunger, her own suppressed fears, her own howling needs.

Nothing would have been more threatening to a woman like her than to be magically bound to another human being. To viscerally feel, for the first time, in a way that no amount of words or heartfelt persuasion could ever make her admit—to feel that this other person had pains and hopes every bit as real and urgent as hers. Nothing could've been more revolting.

To preserve her own sanctity, she'd have to stomp her bondmate down into the smallest possible corner of her awareness. Still, she'd pick at her bondmate as though digging compulsively at a pus-filled scab. Waking or sleeping, that awful alien scab—the intolerable presence of another—would stick to her like lesions on her brain.

I'd snooped around for more intel on Miyu after the berserking incident. It wasn't only her bondmate that she'd struggled to get along with. She saw conspiracies everywhere, at work and at home. Everyone was—here we go, the biggest cliche of them all—out to get her.

She had a keen sense of the ridiculous. She would never have let those precise words pass her lips. But she sincerely believed it.

She cared desperately for appearances, and yet she couldn't or wouldn't stop herself from picking needless fights. A kind inquiry about her health or her weekend would be interpreted as a backhanded attempt to criticize her looks, her comportment, how she spent or wasted her time. A timid request for help from an underling would be taken as a jab at the inadequacy of the training she'd provided, or snide commentary on how she must not have anything better to do at the moment.

It must have been miserable to live as Shien Miyu.

It must have been much more miserable to live as her bondmate. To be raked constantly by the fingers of her impotent rage, to exist as the dump where she inevitably poured every last drop of her poisoned runoff. To be told—during good times—how selfish you were, how immoral, how stupid, how forgetful, how slutty, how worthless. How undeserving of life, love, or a second's worth of peace.

It would not just be her voice invading your head. It would be her resentment, her very loathing, her need to hurt something that was not her. Before she shaped any of it into words.

Hear that raging narration day in and day out, feel those intrusive emotions as your own, and before long it would all become yours, rooting in your soil, growing from within you as if it had been your own voice berating you all along.

She would stake out victory by virtue of her absolute certitude. She would become your sole moral authority. She would rewrite history and personality in the way of a colonizing power. And she would do it not through the predetermined machinations of a master manipulator, but completely unplanned, the forceful instinctive counterattack of a cornered child, the rabid tenacity of an animal fighting bloodily to cling to life.

She would win the battle before it even started. She would win because you were made vulnerable by your own tendency to listen and try to understand— your reasonableness, your commendable empathy, your willingness to admit when you were wrong. Yield a single millimeter out of compassion, and she would automatically crush you. There was no room for compromise in the inexhaustible storm of her inner world.

I slowly released Ginko's hands.

She put her gloves back on. The diamond-pane window glass had begun collecting condensation, overpowered by the disparity between the breath-laced warmth around us and the winter air outside.

The doctor had at last fallen silent. Tempus's eyes bored into my back.

To put it lightly: I felt like a snitch.

But if it wasn't me who revealed the truth, then it would be someone else, and not much later. It would be someone far less sympathetic to a healer who'd lied to hide the severance of her bond, and therefore the death of her bondmate.

"The bond is gone," I said to the bedroom. "Shien Miyu is dead."

10

Doctor Hazeldine took in a hissing breath, like something in him had been punctured. He put a hand over his mouth in the way of a man trying to cover a wound.

Tempus wore a bleak look but evinced no real surprise. This outcome was one of only two possibilities. He would've been braced for it from the moment he first took the case.

Ginko didn't fumble with her gloves. Her gaze fixed itself to the curved glass trap dangling by the window; it held a smattering of dust. She sat next to me as if she weighed nothing, barely denting the bed.

She might've been waiting numbly for someone to tell her what to do. She might've been incapable of panic, even on her own behalf, without first receiving detailed instructions.

To me she appeared stuck in the behavioral rut where Miyu had buried her alive. That same Miyu had now abandoned her after battering her psyche for years on end.

Or: Ginko might have known that her cover-up would be revealed sooner or later. She'd lied anyway. She hadn't displayed so much as a flicker of either agony or relief when I pronounced her bondmate dead.

"Miyu ordered you not to tell anyone, didn't she?" I said.

Ginko looked at me with dark hopeless eyes that reminded me, briefly and eerily, of Wist. She nodded.

Tempus tried to speak. I beat him to it. "Must be quite a blow," I said to Doctor Hazeldine. "You should report to Lady Shien. So she hears it first from family."

Tempus could tell what I was doing, but he went along with it, encouraging the doctor to break the news to Miyu's grandmother. At the last second he remembered to tack on: "I'm deeply sorry for your loss."

"Yeah," I said, unhelpfully. "Condolences."

Doctor Hazeldine had begun breathing as audibly as a congested bulldog. He took out a very fine handkerchief, one likely not intended for any practical function other than adding a spot of color to his breast pocket. He patted his face all over. As if wiping sweat rather than tears.

Tempus glowered at me after the doctor hustled out of the cramped bedroom. "Don't get any clever ideas."

"I would never."

"You're not a lawyer. You're not an MP. You're despised by everyone in the whole clan."

"Except for Wist."

"Except for Wisteria Shien. Your involvement won't help prevent a miscarriage of justice. Your involvement will make justice scream, throw up its hands, and run in the opposite direction. Do we understand each other?"

I faked a yawn, then gave Tempus a humorless grin. This was starting to feel vaguely nostalgic.

He motioned me nearer to the hallway and spoke in a whisper. "We can't believe anything she tells us. She lied about her bond."

I caught Ginko's eye. "What did Miyu want you to keep to yourself?"

"That night—"

"Which night?" Tempus asked sharply.

Ginko named a date about two weeks ago. "Lady Miyu went out late at night. She warned me not to probe. Not to follow her. Not to speak of it."

"I doubt she intended for that to extend to concealing her death," he said, thick with sarcasm. "How faithful of you. How very literal."

Such mute, dumb obedience would not be judged kindly in retrospect. Despite the fact that it would be expected of a bonded healer in every other conceivable context. Despite the fact that it had been installed in her with the merciless force of a smith hammering metal.

A knock sounded at the bedroom door. "Come in!" I called.

Wist came through, as I'd known she would, stooping to fit.

Trapped between us, Tempus gave in. "I'll question you later," he said to Ginko. "Without ... without further intrusions." He started to indicate me and Wist. He stopped once he realized he was being rude to the Kraken.

He told Ginko to stand. She obeyed, hands folded in front of her.

"I'm marking you as a person of interest," he said formally. "All rights derive from the state."

He pressed his thumb to her forehead. When he lowered his hand, a blot of magic lingered on her skin like a translucent sticker.

"My previous warning still stands," he added. "Don't go anywhere off the estate."

Ginko bowed to him as he walked out the door. She held her bow as Wist and I followed, and even when I turned to peep in on her from the hallway. She was very well trained.

Tempus left the boarding house. So did we.

"Can't you tell that I'm trying to get rid of you?" he demanded.

"Can't get rid of us yet." I touched the side of my head as if receiving a message through vibrations in my skull. "The Kraken has something important to tell you," I fibbed.

Tempus stopped in the cold garden and sardonically put a hand to one ear.

What should I say? Wist asked.

Don't worry about it. Leave him hanging.

"The wind's too loud," said Tempus. "Can't hear a word of the Kraken's staggering wisdom. My loss. If you'll excuse me—"

He set off across the grounds. Big strides. I broke into a jog. (Wist had no difficulty keeping up.)

The estate was sprinkled with surreal art installations, some magical and some analog. Miyu's doing? Perhaps she'd sourced these during her frenzy of redecorating. A titanic humanoid figure—as large as the manor itself—lay prone among gentle hills behind a far-off wing of the building. It could've represented a dead body. Or an indolent nudist.

I poked Wist. "Wonder how your grandma feels about looking out her window and seeing a naked ass the size of—"

"I need to report to HQ," Tempus said. "I need to call on Lady Shien. I need to gather my thoughts."

"Then why're you stalking around the gardens?"

"To shake you off my tail, you—"

"You can't seriously think that Ginko killed Shien Miyu and buried her out back behind the manor."

"Biased as you are," he said, "you have to understand that it's a possibility."

"A slim one." I peered harder at him. "Since when did you ever care about truth, justice, and beauty?"

Oh—but Tempus *had* always cared about beauty. I remembered how he used to look at Shien Ficus.

Without taking the lead in any noticeable way, Wist steered us far from the vorpal hole that had eaten the rose garden. It was a thin irregularity in distant air, an obscured yet blinding presence like sunlit water glittering madly through the gaps in a wall of trees.

We skirted around the broken preserved foundations of historical houses. Verbose signboards explained their significance. Wist and I used to take refuge here during my first visit to the estate.

I reminisced loudly about each archaeological landmark. To no avail—Tempus seemed to have absolved himself of any obligation to respond to my jibes.

The Minashiro Tempus that I'd known at Guralta Academy would've had a lot in common with Shien Miyu.

Now, for all the sourness of his tone, his behavior towards me and Wist was astonishingly civil. His bitterness only went skin-deep. Miyu's acidic hatred—of Wist, of me, of her rivals at work, of her successive bondmates, and maybe herself—had penetrated down to her core.

I couldn't begin to tell you why Tempus had turned out different. He used to be famously friendly with Wist's Shien brothers. In a truly just legal system, his current investigation would've been considered a conflict of interest.

On that note: no one, least of all Tempus, had audibly informed Wist of Miyu's death. He'd rightly assumed that I'd already let her know through our bond.

Nor did he attempt to offer condolences. For better or for worse, the three of us went way back. He knew a thing or two about Wist's relationship with her adoptive clan.

I reluctantly relinquished my crackpot theory about Miyu being held prisoner deep in the manor. I didn't care much about how or why she'd died. I cared more about why Ginko had lied: to buy time? To protect someone dear to her? (Or, if she were the killer, to protect herself.)

About two years ago, I'd made Miyu go berserk. For that one slip-up—a mistake I'd forced on her—she'd been stripped of her elite position and all her social prestige, doomed to a life of eternal stigma.

In my view, it wasn't nearly enough. Her punishment would feel feather-light when weighed against her relentless abuse of her previous bondmate. Society would crack down on her for a single episode of berserking, but not for driving a young man to suicide.

I'd done what I could to exact a modicum of revenge. Except then I'd left the estate. I'd left Ginko behind, still bound to Miyu for life.

It would be an easy matter for the Shien clan to close ranks. To rope in Tempus, an old family friend. To devise a story about Miyu's death (whether they called it accidental or otherwise) in which her healer Ginko was the only person on the continent who bore any semblance of fault.

She had, in fact, lied to investigators. She could defend herself only by claiming that the dead woman had made her do it.

Ginko might have killed Shien Miyu. Even if she hadn't, she might still get blamed for Miyu's death. I couldn't leave her to the mercy of the Shien clan. Not for a second time.

Frankly, I'd have been driven to murder ages ago if I'd gotten bonded to any Shien sibling other than Wist. She'd made me the most privileged and protected healer in Osmanthus.

Growing older (and spending years in prison) had also made me increasingly selfish and self-contained. I didn't like to think too hard about what I owed my fellow Osmanthian healers.

Consider the facts, and the only moral conclusion would be that I owed them everything. I owed them a revolution.

But I hadn't bargained my way out of a prison cell and back into Wist's arms only to waste the rest of our lives waging bloody war. Or to install her as an absolute tyrant, controlling the minds of the entire populace to avert violence. (We'd given that something of a trial run in Manglesea.)

By taking in the Void, I'd arguably saved the continent. That would have to be enough. I wouldn't transform Wist into a conquering warrior like the first Kraken.

I wouldn't completely abandon my responsibility to other healers, either. I would stand by Ginko, despite the fact that she might turn out to be a killer. Despite the fact that I'd only just learned her name.

Wist and Tempus and I walked alongside a comically long rectangular pool crowded with lilies, no two blooms the same color. Steam and mist-fine magic residue rose off the artificially heated water.

Tempus was an MP. He therefore belonged to a division of Public Security, which in turn was governed by the Ministry of Justice. Which was where Shien Miyu had been employed before her downfall.

I asked him if they'd ever worked together.

"Not directly," he said.

"Did you like her?"

"Does that matter?"

"Just curious about whether you've become a better judge of character over the years."

He looked away. "Of course you would love speaking ill of the dead. In front of her own sister, no less."

"I haven't uttered a word of disparagement," I said haughtily. "If you'd like to know what I really think—"

"I really wouldn't."

We reached a life-size train crossing surrounded by trees pruned to look like amputees. Another art installation. A yellow-striped gate arm came down to block our path. Stand in just the right spot, and the illusory tracks would go on forever on both sides, cutting through gardens and stone buildings and private tracts of preserved wilderness.

A signal bell rang out. No train cars came or went. Instead a magical weight of killing heft—an invisible presence—whooshed past us, whipping at the strands of hair that had escaped from Wist's braids.

The bell stopped, the crossing gate rose, and we walked past. A few steps away, and the tracks vanished. The gate infrastructure stood isolated, guarding future pedestrians from nothing whatsoever.

"Okay," I said, "but what does it *mean*?"

Tempus sneered. "You never did have much of an eye for art."

"So you don't know either. Good."

I glanced up. Colossal mobiles floated over the estate like a skeletal imitation of the exotic aerials we'd seen in Manglesea.

"The Jacian," I said. "Lear. Her presence here would make more sense if she pumped out that kind of art. Stuff with magic."

"You think Jace would let a functioning mage come alone to the continent? That'd be practically begging them to defect."

"You trying to convert her?"

"Not my job."

"Maybe the Shiens have been working on her," I murmured. "There's gotta be people in the family affiliated with intelligence agencies. She might be preparing to defect. She might already be a double agent. Or a triple agent. Or a—"

"Not your concern," Tempus said. Which was true.

After letting him go, Wist and I stayed out in the brittle cold. We stayed until she had no choice but to head in for token face time with her grandmother.

We agreed to linger at Follyhope until Wist received clearance to close the vorpal hole. I figured it wouldn't be much of a wait. With Miyu confirmed dead, Tempus could call in a magical forensics team much faster.

We'd hang around longer, if needed. Long enough to intervene—with the full gravity of Wist's personal influence as the Kraken—if Tempus and his backers tried to pin it all on Ginko. (Minus actual evidence, and without proper consideration for mitigating factors.)

My newfound resolve soon had occasion to falter. After hearing about Miyu, Wist's two oldest brothers both decided to come over that evening for dinner.

11

Around a grandiose table sat Shien Nerium, Shien Ficus, Doctor Hazeldine, Tempus, Lear the Jacian, Ginko, Danver, Wist, and everyone's favorite Magebreaker: Asa Clematis.

Lear would have been invited to dinner as a token courtesy. She was an artist-in-residence, a guest from abroad, and one of the few non-family members left at Follyhope. But would they really expect her to accept the invitation at a time like this? By evening, everyone knew that Miyu was dead.

As for Tempus—would an MP inspector normally enjoy fine dining with an entire family of potential suspects? There might have been foul play involved in Miyu's death. He had yet to prove otherwise.

The Minashiros and the Shiens had always been close. Now the Shien clan would have extra motivation to keep him closer. It was only natural that they'd asked him to stay for dinner, although I wasn't so sure about the propriety of him actually taking them up on it.

What I couldn't explain was why they'd included the other two healers: Ginko and Danver. I'd never seen fellow healers eating at the same table as Shien mages. The only reason I'd ever been allowed to join them was because of Wist.

No sign of Grandmother. Maybe she was sick with grief. Or maybe she'd excused herself because she found it beneath her to attend a dinner in her own home on equal footing with healers.

Ficus and Nerium came in last, after stopping by their grandmother's office or lair or wherever she habitually lurked. Doctor Hazeldine was so excited to see them that he leapt out of his seat. How sprightly.

Nerium (the oldest of Wist's six siblings) gave the doctor a genial greeting. Ficus (the second oldest) commandeered the empty chair across from Wist. He said little, but the air in the room felt as though he'd slapped the tabletop hard enough to make the silverware jump.

Ginko and Danver, seated to my left, were unnaturally motionless. Both still wore modified healer robes, although they'd switched to lavender aprons for mourning. No one else wore mourning colors yet.

"Wisteria," Shien Nerium said. "Asa Clematis. It's been so long."

Through magic-infested glasses, he looked straight at my eyepatch. As if addressing the Void—as if he knew it was there. But of course that was impossible.

Before we filed in, I'd asked Wist if I ought to make an effort to avoid antagonizing anyone.

"Speak your mind," she said evenly. "I can pick the pieces up afterward."

So I returned Nerium's gaze and let my intrusive thoughts win. "You've gotten old, sir."

Someone squeaked. Possibly Danver. Nerium laughed it off as he hung his cane from the edge of the table beside him. "I daresay the same amount of time has passed for both of us."

"You sure about that?"

"Let it be known that I'm still under fifty. I can only hope to age as well as Hazeldine over here."

With a sigh, he lowered himself into the chair at the head of the table. I realized with a frisson of unease that the last time I'd seen him up close—during my first visit to Follyhope—he would've been just about thirty. Younger than I was now.

That first visit to Follyhope hadn't been my first encounter with Nerium or Ficus. I'd met both of them when they were still in their twenties.

The texture of their skin was now markedly different, but in some ways, neither had changed much. Even at twenty-six, Nerium had shown signs of premature aging. His hairline had already been beating a hasty retreat. Today he had no hairline to speak of, just some sad tufts of ambiguously colored dandelion fluff.

Ficus was the exact opposite. He had been beautiful back then, and he was still beautiful now, albeit rougher around the edges. If Nerium were in his late forties, then Ficus would be forty-four or so (a couple years older than Miyu). From across the table, he could pass for a man in his thirties, careless stubble and disheveled gold-tinged hair and all.

It was the sort of beauty that had a lot to do with bottomless amounts of money. The kind of money that could make stress dissolve like sugar, that could buy you infinite nights of dreamless guilt-free sleep and monopolize the services of the best aestheticians in the country.

At first glance, of course, one would come away with the impression that he'd been made this way, that he'd never checked himself in a mirror or given even a second's thought to the power of his appearance.

That power was already exerting its effects on at least one of us. Deliberately or not, he'd put himself next to Tempus, who was beginning to look a touch short of breath.

Some things never change.

Lear, positioned down by the far end of the table, waved a cheerful greeting at Ficus and Nerium. Rather to my shock, Ficus waved back at her.

Afterward, she looked at me with undisguised curiosity.

What?

I glanced furtively at Tempus, frozen anxiously in his seat. Then at Nerium, who wore a benevolent smile. Then Ficus. Doctor Hazeldine, now in his element, had struck up a new conversation with the brothers. One in which he talked twice as much as Nerium and ten times as much as Ficus.

There were five mages at the table. Plus Lear: a subliminal mage without any branches.

Wist, needless to say, was a Kraken-class mage. Hazeldine was only Class 2—but like Wist, he also happened to be an originator, with the ability to invent new custom magic skills all on his own. (A fact that I'd gleaned from his vociferous chatter.)

Tempus was Class 9, which meant he had more branches than anyone here except Wist. Nerium was Class 6. Ficus was Class 5.

Class 5. Five branches. Five elongated limbs. Five flexible fingers. A radiant starfish.

Pure and faithful realism.

Lear hadn't been pulling my leg. She wasn't an abstract artist. She was punishingly devoted to depicting reality, insofar as the reality of magic could ever be translated to the limitations of a two-dimensional visual medium.

Her gargantuan starfish painting was a sincere rendition of Shien Ficus's magic core and five grasping branches.

Lear caught my eye. She smiled irrepressibly.

I wasn't in a good enough mood to smirk back at her. On my right, Wist had begun jiggling her leg under the table.

This wasn't the chamber I remembered eating in as a teenager. No doubt the manor had dining rooms aplenty. Perhaps tomorrow we'd get called to gather somewhere altogether different.

Preserved oxblood lilies hung upside-down in bundles from the ceiling. They were shaped rather like the red spider lilies of Manglesea—although these had been treated to last far beyond any fall equinox.

Aquarium-style wall tanks ran around the entire perimeter, filled not with water but instead with a flabbergasting assembly of limbless wooden dolls. The dolls had flat, minimalistic painted faces and were overall about the size and shape of a rattle for a baby. Wist owned a similar set of mana stamps.

"A northern tradition," said Shien Nerium, following my gaze.

Lear gestured with a glazed ceramic cup of liquor, one not much larger than a thimble. "It's a remarkable display of folk art. Saw a lot of them when I traveled up north. They're rarer down here."

"Your grandmother didn't have any opinion on these design choices?" I asked Nerium.

"She let Miyu pull all sorts of old collections out of storage. It kept her occupied."

It felt as though he'd mentioned Miyu on purpose.

"Such a shame." Doctor Hazeldine sounded choked. "Such a shame."

After a few painfully awkward minutes, they began discussing Nerium's business. Something to do with magic imaging, diagnostic equipment, special refractors, loupes and telescopes and microscopes and various other optical instruments....

"Thought you worked in real estate," I remarked, although in truth I hadn't thought much about Nerium and his money at all.

"Real estate is more of a hobby," he said cheerfully.

I nibbled a slice of some anonymous fish. Meanwhile, I kept an eye on Shien Ficus. Lear had leaned way back in her chair to banter with him, bypassing the doctor and Tempus. Ficus flipped a knife around in his fingers as he listened. They shouldn't have set the table with all these excess utensils. The sharpest knives seemed completely unnecessary.

"I really must apologize for the fact that we couldn't all be here today," Nerium said, to no one in particular.

He named Wist's other three adoptive siblings, those older than her but younger than him, Ficus, and Miyu. He alluded vaguely to how they'd been called far away by work and family obligations.

"You should go be with your grandmother," I suggested. Lady Shien was still conspicuously absent. "She needs comforting more than we do."

"Don't be callous," he said reproachfully. "Miyu's healer has suffered the greatest loss of all."

I just barely managed not to shoot a look over at said healer.

"Grandmother never neglects her duties," Nerium continued. "Even as we dine, she's been discussing matters with our parents."

Speaking of conspicuously absent—their parents hadn't come up very much, had they?

Given my druthers, I'd rather deal with Wist's parents than with Grandmother Shien. They were ordinary snobs. Less spiteful than Miyu, less frightening than Ficus, less artful than Nerium, and much weaker than Grandmother.

I dipped into a creamy white porridge made of pine nuts. My mind kept whittling away at the question of why Danver and Ginko had been given a seat at the table. Certainly not because of their scintillating contributions to the conversation. Both were—wisely—trying to blend with the furniture.

Danver had at first reminded me superficially of Miyu. Now that I saw her in the same room as Shien Nerium, a more unsettling resemblance began to take shape. An impression like a face in a fog-blurred mirror. They both wore round magical glasses, almost similar enough to be a matched set. They had the same large forehead; his was still peculiarly smooth. They had the same mouth, with a pronounced dip cutting into a small upper lip. Their ears had the same slant.

The doctor had bragged about his daughter, a mage at Guralta Academy. What was Danver's family name? What would become of a Shien born as a healer?

Nerium wasn't too young to be her father. If—a big leap—if Danver were Nerium's daughter, she'd already been born when Wist and I first met as schoolgirls. When I first ran across Wist's brothers.

A strange thought. Nerium had never hinted at having a child. But why would he?

Paternity aside, who did Danver's bond thread symbolize? If not Grandmother, then her bondmate could very well be Ficus or Nerium. It wouldn't matter whether or not Danver had Shien blood, too.

I'd been shocked to learn that during my studies. I'd always thought bonding between relatives (and even childhood friends) would be flat-out impossible. This was an extremely common misconception among those without specialized knowledge.

On the contrary, bonding a close family member was neither impossible nor illegal. And it wouldn't be incestuous, strictly speaking. Not in the same way as marriage or romance.

It was just extremely rare. Not socially encouraged, but not an outright taboo. The sort of eccentricity that would be easier to get away with if you were already secure in your power and replete with generational wealth. Akin to a vice like hoarding tendencies, or mild kleptomania, or a tedious obsession with yachts.

Based on behavior and observations alone, I couldn't tell if Danver were bonded to either brother. They studiously ignored her, and she returned the favor.

So of the two healers at this table other than myself, one was potentially a Shien by blood—or at least bonded to some Shien relative, on or off the main estate. The other had no bondmate anymore, and was therefore up for grabs.

Had the brothers come to mourn Miyu, or to call first dibs on her possessions?

I lost my appetite, both for food and for probing. Wist hadn't eaten a single bite.

As if he'd read my mind, Ficus pointed his knife at Ginko. "I'll take her."

Danver clenched her chopsticks in a way that made my eye ache.

"Let's wait till after the funeral, shall we?" Nerium told Ficus.

"Hard to have a funeral without a body."

"Don't lose hope. I'm sure Tempus will leave no stone unturned in his search."

"Yeah," I said. "I'm sure he'll do exactly as you wish."

Tempus shifted uncomfortably.

"The Minashiros are like family," Nerium agreed. "But Tempus has also become quite an avatar of justice over the years. Of course, he was always one to commit himself thoroughly to a cause."

"That's not a compliment," Ficus said, in case anyone had been wondering.

Nerium had two different glasses of water and three different glasses of alcohol. No clue how he chose which one to sip from at any given moment.

"You're astounding, Wisteria," he commented, apropos of nothing. "You get taller every time I see you."

"I'm sitting down," said Wist.

"A brother can tell." He touched a finger to the temple of his glasses. "You aren't wearing the complimentary pair I sent you."

"Ficus isn't wearing glasses, either," I said.

"I've long since given up on him. He's much too vain." Nerium smiled indulgently. Ficus, looking bored, ran a hand through his shining hair.

From there, Nerium pivoted to idle talk about our time in Manglesea. Lear set down her utensils and peppered us with questions.

It made me wonder if she dreamt of life there. Of fleeing to a country without magic, ruled neither by mages (like Osmanthus) nor healers (like Jace—although putting it that way might be a dreadful oversimplification).

I answered to the best of my ability. We'd only stayed in Manglesea once, and under highly unusual circumstances.

On my left, Danver and Ginko took microscopic bites of delicate jade-green vegetables. Whatever they were eating, it brought to mind a salad made from decorative succulents. They chewed like hostages held at gunpoint.

Wist rested against the back of her chair with her eyes closed. It didn't go high enough to lend any support to her neck.

She was neither sleeping nor lost in thought. Our bond had drawn as taut as a bowstring.

Ficus had been sitting across from her.

Ficus was gone.

12

WHILE I HEROICALLY held up my end of the conversation, Shien Ficus had vanished.

He's—

I forced myself to shut the hell up. Wist already knew.

My ears rang. A woody scent permeated the room. Something like high-end designer sawdust. A whiff of magic? A hallucination? It was there and gone as soon as I smelled it.

Head lowered, Wist twisted at the blue bond thread around her wrist. Lear kept speaking as if to smooth over the heightening tension.

Nerium's cane was gone, too. It had been hooked on the table; now it wasn't. Nerium's hands remained empty.

Ficus hadn't ported away. We'd have noticed the burst of magic when he left. He was still here—and he'd erased himself from every single one of our senses. Including magic perception. Neither Wist nor I could detect him.

He wouldn't have gone invisible just to stroll out of the room and find dessert. He wouldn't sneak around behind Wist to strike at her directly, either. Not even if he were deluded enough to think he could wound her in any meaningful way.

He'd known her since she was six years old. He could intuit much more effective ways to hurt her.

Nerium touched the edge of the table. He'd noticed his cane missing. The opaque magic glazing his glasses made it impossible to discern the exact direction of his gaze. But his head moved a fraction. Those shielded eyes pointed past Wist, then past me.

Nerium sees him, I hissed to Wist. *He—*

A crash. A cry. A thump like dough hurled down on a counter.

By the time I heard these, I'd already been ported. I was on my feet: weak-kneed, soles tingling, Wist's arm clamping me to her side.

Our chairs stood empty. She'd jumped us back behind Nerium, as if she had half a mind to take him hostage.

Danver was on her feet, too. She clutched a plate of picked-over bones.

Ginko's chair had toppled. Right next to Ficus, now visible, his face as serene as the face of a monk.

Ginko had crumpled to the floor. Ficus prodded her with the end of his stolen cane. She was too thin to have much softness to protect her.

She started to crawl away under the table. The cane came down harder, pinning her in place. She shivered and went still.

Something crunched—a sound from out in the room, or from deep in my ears?

Lear looked thoughtfully at the disproportionately tall and flower-covered ceiling. Doctor Hazeldine raised his napkin to his face like a smothering blindfold.

Tempus was half out of his chair. An empty gesture that would no doubt have greatly cheered Ginko if she were in any sort of state to notice it. Danver quivered; she must've meant to hurl her loaded plate at Ficus. Her body betrayed her, locking in place.

Nerium gave a small, weary shake of his head.

My brain ground to a halt. Wist's arm tightened around me. Enough for it to hurt. It hurt a lot, actually. I didn't say anything. She'd gone too numb to notice through our bond.

The oxblood lilies on the ceiling began to wilt and fall in clumps like volcanic ash, contaminating the leftovers still on the table. Magically treated warming plates smoked with a stench like burning toast.

Danver yelped and released the plate in her hands. It bounced on the zebra-carpet floor without breaking. Peafowl bones scattered.

Only a couple seconds had passed since the initial burst of noise. Since Ficus had struck Ginko out of her chair.

Gray-brown flowers kept falling.

"No one's been paying tribute to little Miyu."

Ficus spoke as if we were still seated genteelly around the table. His teeth seemed unnaturally white.

Ginko did not cry, or make much of any sound at all.

"What would Miyu do if she were still with us?" Ficus asked. "What better way to honor her than to carry on her legacy? It's easy, isn't it? What would Miyu do here?"

He hit Ginko again with the cane. He didn't brandish it—no more theatricality. He brought it down faster than anyone could've expected, faster than anyone could react.

Inside Wist, something cracked like an eggshell. Overwhelming magic tumbled through the room, sapping my ability to breathe. Like getting somersaulted by a wrathful wave.

Then it washed out in the way of tides draining from a beach.

This was not a sign of mercy. Not a good thing. Water getting dragged back from the shore like a prisoner being dragged by their ankles—it heralded a devastating return. Time to run for high ground.

"Wist," It took conscious effort to move my tongue and lips. My inner voice had died on the vine. "Wist—this would be a good place to stop."

I said this before I grasped what she had done.

Cylindrical wooden dolls littered the floor and table like a flood of salt and pepper shakers. Ginko was still on her side, arms covering her head. Everyone else reeled as if they'd stepped off a roller coaster.

Nerium's cane lay snapped in two near Ginko's fallen chair.

A syrupy fluid filled the aquarium tanks embedded in all the walls. They'd been emptied of their dolls. Ficus floated behind the glass instead, eyes closed, longish hair rendered an unearthly hue as it lifted and spread. He curled in the fetal position, mirroring Ginko on the floor.

No breathing bubbles rose from his nose or mouth. The substance in the tank seemed more like an aurora given liquid form than anything resembling ordinary drowning water.

Old summer memories twinged through me. Ficus pitching a dead cicada at Wist. Ficus tossing steel-tipped darts at Tempus. That was nothing in the grand scheme of things, of course. He and the other Shien siblings had done much worse to Wist before I knew her.

13

Nerium rose, holding the table for support. With his left hand, he brushed dead flowers off his shoulders.

"Generous of you to leave him unconscious," he said to Wist, looking at Ficus through the aquarium glass.

"This is"—Tempus's throat sounded raw—"this is a serious form of assault."

Nerium shot an ironic glance down at Ginko. "Perhaps we can call it even. Doctor, are you waiting for something?"

Doctor Hazeldine jerked into motion, tripping over flat-faced dolls as he rushed to Ginko's side. He knelt, waving Danver out of the way, and extracted something from his long-tailed jacket. Magic flared near the carpet, a subdued pulse like the light of fireworks behind city roofs.

"I wouldn't have recommended going fully extrajudicial in front of an MP," Nerium said, "but what's done is done. Ficus brought it on himself."

For a fleeting moment, Wist wore a very small and mirthless smile. "You had nothing to do with this, did you. You've gotten better at judging the odds."

He sighed. "Ficus, unfortunately, has never cared about his odds of success. He measures victory by a different yardstick than the rest of us." He eyed Wist over the rim of his glasses. "Ficus would not consider this a loss."

"I'm sure he wouldn't," Wist said thinly.

I felt divorced from my own body. Wist's anger crawled on the underside of my skin, frigid and fiery and ferociously alive. More alive than the Void in the hollow of my eye.

How could these people stand it?

They didn't feel it. Not like I did. They had no bond with her, no conduit forcing them to understand how much she was still holding back. She'd expected him to go for me, and she'd been prepared for it. He would never have gotten close enough to harm a single thread of my clothing. She hadn't anticipated him targeting Ginko. Much of her fury was for herself.

Doctor Hazeldine brought Ginko to her feet and ushered her out of the room. They picked their way among knocked-over dolls and the crumbling dust of ceiling lilies.

Surely he had the resources to export patients directly to medical facilities. Guess this didn't qualify as a real emergency.

Danver started to charge after them. She hesitated in the entrance. The color was very high in her cheeks. Her eyes looked furiously damp behind her glasses.

"You care too much," Nerium said, as if she'd asked for advice. "I suppose you get that from your mother."

Lear shook flowers from her dark hair and slipped between them like a bodyguard. She coaxed Danver out of the dining room, saying something about Ginko and the doctor. That left me, Tempus, and three Shien siblings. Although Ficus didn't seem liable to participate in any subsequent conversations.

Tempus moved closer to the aquarium glass. Magic played across his face in the way of bright rippling shadows from a pool of moving water.

"So," I said. "Planning to arrest anyone?"

I could guess at the sorts of thoughts running through his head. Complications for the investigation. The political fallout of staining the Kraken's record. Grandmother Shien's displeasure. What Ficus might do to Ginko if he were the one who got arrested and later released.

Tempus cleared his throat. "You should—you should free him."

His words were meant for Wist. He spoke to me as if I were her translator.

"Why?" Wist asked.

Tempus took a shaky step back. Nerium removed his glasses and peered at them as if they would help with his hearing.

"Why not leave him?" Wist continued. "He'll be with family. No need to feed him. No need to clean the embalming fluid. He won't excrete waste. Months will pass before he atrophies."

"Embalming fluid?" said Nerium.

"A figure of speech. Consider this a gift. He'll never give you less trouble than he does in that tank. It'll be the most peace you've had in years."

"That does sound rather tempting," Nerium confessed to his glasses.

"Sir!" Tempus cried, alarmed. "My lord, you can't—"

"Don't *my lord* me, Tempus." Nerium's tone took on a note of fond exasperation. "Our families are of equal stature. If you use honorifics with me, then by rights, I'll be obliged to use them with you."

"I'm here in my capacity as an MP. Sir."

"A noble profession."

"In any case, you're older."

"I feel my age whenever I see how much you've grown. I certainly don't require any reminders."

"My apologies, sir."

Nerium extended a hand toward the tank trapping Ficus, palm up, as though pointing out a tourist landmark. "We returned to Follyhope because we thought you might wish to interview us again."

"Not to lament Miyu?" I said snidely.

"Oh, that goes without saying." His smile would have looked very merry if not for the fact that those glasses were back on his face, hiding his eyes again.

"We'll arrange for Ficus to be in a suitable state for questioning later this evening," he continued, addressing Tempus. "Just need to work out a few matters between us siblings first. Have you ever known me to break a promise?"

This was how he got rid of Tempus: with baseless assurances and softly voiced pressure. Afterward, he lowered himself into a nearby chair, which happened to be the chair originally used by Ficus. His gaze roved across the wilted flowers threatening to stain the tablecloth. He rubbed the top of his left leg, near the hip joint.

"It's a good thing Miyu isn't around to see the absolute mess you've made of her decor."

"Right," I muttered. "Good thing she's dead, huh?"

"You're putting words in my mouth, Asa Clematis. I would expect you to be the first to celebrate Miyu's death."

"Yeah. Get in line. But she wasn't always the worst of you."

"None of us ever liked to settle for second best," Nerium murmured. "Or worst, depending on how you frame it. We were quite a competitive lot."

"You shaped your brothers and sisters more than anyone."

"More than our parents?" he asked mildly. "More than Grandmother? I wonder what makes you think you know us so well. Were you there?"

He glanced up at Wist. "It occurs to me, Wisteria, that it would be a very kind gesture on your part to repair my cane."

"You have others," she replied shortly.

"None of them have been blessed by the Kraken's magic. I would value it very much. A rare and precious gift from my little sister. Have you ever given me a gift before?"

Wist made no move to retrieve the broken pieces of his cane. "How did Ficus disappear? What skill was he using?"

"And why were your glasses set up to see through it?" I added.

"Ficus dabbles," said Nerium. "There was a time when he considered joining the intelligence community."

"As a field agent?" I scoffed. "He'd spill state secrets just for the fun of it."

"Then you and he might, as fellow traitors, discover a whole new sort of camaraderie. How heartwarming."

As we sniped back and forth, I edged closer to Wist. I tugged inconspicuously at the threads of her magic, easing enraged knots.

"When activated," Nerium said, "that skill of his lends the user true imperceptibility. I suppose he first encountered it during his training."

The effects had parallels to Disappearance, the skill Wist favored for going around unnoticed, but the methodology seemed pointedly different.

Disappearance had more of a psychological effect, encouraging witnesses not to take notice of her. (Which, being a form of mental interference, meant it was essentially illegal. The Kraken could get away with a lot of gray-area hijinks.)

Ficus's skill might be closer to a powered-up version of classic invisibility, erasing him from the realms of sound and scent and magic perception, as well as sight. Also illegal? Probably. Like the Kraken, intelligence operatives got a lot of extra leeway.

"But he never finished training," Wist said. "He never became an operative."

"A sad tale. He couldn't hack it." Nerium's mouth pulled sideways in a facsimile of a smile.

Wist pressed on. "He would've been stripped of any sensitive or proprietary skills when they discharged him."

"Besides," I said, "if this imperceptibility skill is as powerful as it sounds, they wouldn't confer it on a trainee. Especially not on one with a shaky reputation."

"One way or another, he learned of the existence of that skill. How he acquired it is a different matter altogether." Nerium gave an elegant shrug. "There's a black market for everything under the sun, moon, and stars. Ficus has acquaintances from every imaginable cranny of society. I suppose he bought a skill or two off an underground dealer."

Ficus was not an originator. Imprinting a new skill on one of his five branches would require direct contact with a teacher already in possession of said skill. Like an intelligence agent betraying their employer to earn money under the table. Or a law-dodging mage with only tenuous connections to the bureau. A student of a student of a student.

Once a restricted skill leaked, leaping from mage to mage, the government would struggle tremendously to reel it back in. The more controversial or dangerous the skill, the less openly they could hunt down illicit possessors. They wouldn't want anyone to know it had leaked at all.

We could report this information to Tempus. Nerium wouldn't stop us. Tempus, in turn, might pass our story on to someone higher up in Public Security. There it would die an ignoble death. It'd take a lot more than hearsay to get them to crack down on a prominent member of the Shien clan. We'd witnessed Ficus using a suspicious skill, yes, but the whole sequence of events had ended with Wist violently taking him prisoner. All around, it'd be best to avoid pointed questions.

Nerium knew that. Which was why he'd told us. He wouldn't miss a chance to sound accommodating.

"What about my question?" I made circles with my fingers and held them up to my face like a pair of binoculars. "How come your specs could penetrate a restricted skill?"

He lifted his glasses off. His eyes were a lighter brown than I'd remembered, as if over the years they'd faded like wood exposed to sun.

"Would you like to try them on?" he inquired.

"Hah. I'm not touching those."

He contrived to look hurt.

"You already got me with that trick when I was naught but a delicate, innocent, trusting schoolgirl. A fragile young flower."

Wist remained preternaturally straight-faced, but I felt her laughter in our bond.

"I never make the same mistake twice," I finished with pride.

This was patently untrue, but Shien Nerium didn't call me out on it. He put his glasses back on, then passed me a black business card. It was light yet substantial, made of some material that vehemently rejected fingerprints.

Wist peeked over my shoulder, although she was trying to feign a lack of interest.

"Regalia Optics. Magic Imaging and Optical Equipment," I read. "Your company?"

"Yes."

"It's got a very highfaluting name. Well, I'd expect no less."

"Why, thank you. We have a growing line of consumer-oriented products—"

"Is this a sales pitch?"

"—but most revenue comes from defense contracts and industrial projects. We're part of the consortium working on the new SUPAS in northern Osmanthus."

"The what?"

"Supermassive Passive Scanner." He paused to gauge my understanding. "Like a giant telescope, albeit one exclusively for collecting data on natural magic."

"Right..."

"It'll be located in a remote mountaintop observatory. There's been talk of building another in Jace, but the complications seem rather insurmountable."

He tapped the bridge of his glasses. "These are a prototype produced under contract with the government. They're designed particularly to counteract the type of imperceptibility skills favored by intelligence agencies. Domestic and foreign alike."

"You're allowed to just walk around town with those?"

He glanced meaningfully at Wist. Then at Ficus, languishing in what looked very much like a watery grave. "All of us siblings bend certain rules here and there." He pushed his glasses up one last time. "They're a must-have for keeping an eye on Ficus."

"What does he *do* with himself?" I asked. "Aside from harass people."

"He was a duelist for a few years in his twenties."

"How'd he rank?"

"Not highly."

"Figures."

"But his matches were extremely well attended. Ultimately, he's a moneyed gentleman. He doesn't need to do anything except swan around and look beautiful."

"You're a moneyed gentleman, too," I said blandly.

"I can't pull off the *looking beautiful* part of that equation, so I find myself obliged to build value in other ways. Ficus does a decent amount of paid modeling."

"Runway jobs?"

"He usually turns those down."

"What's he model for, then? Ads? Billboards?"

"Not for the sort of brands you would patronize."

I took exception to this. "I have a highly sophisticated sense of personal style."

"Be that as it may, you have a budget, don't you?"

"Well—"

"You consider the price of your purchases?

"I mean—"

"Then you belong to a different target market."

Wist cut in. "You're in no rush to liberate Ficus. Shall I let him stew overnight?"

Nerium wore a pained smile. "I was simply enjoying a little carefree small talk with Asa Clematis."

"I could've left him conscious in there."

"I daresay you also contemplated leaving him dead."

Wist didn't reply.

"You can still choose to leave him dead," Nerium said, as if we were speaking of his SUPAS, or of Ficus's modeling gigs: anything but murder. "If Grandmother and I insist that you did nothing untoward, no charges would stick."

"Do you want him dead?" I blurted.

"Don't you?" Nerium inquired in turn.

I couldn't tell if his words were pointed more at me or at Wist. Our bond became constricted as if with a sudden unbearable muscle cramp. Reflections of magic from filled-up aquarium tanks washed blurrily across the freed crowd of polished columnar dolls, legless and armless and scattered about like a game of pick-up sticks.

"I'll clean this." Wist indicated the general state of the room. "Then I'll give you Ficus."

"No need to trouble yourself. That's what the household staff are for."

"Aren't a lot of them off the estate right now?" I said.

The servers who'd been coming by to refill drinks had, at some point, discreetly stopped appearing. Clearly they knew to stay far away during mid-dinner beatings, bursts of blinding magic, and the usual Shien sibling squabbles.

Wist picked up a crumbling flower petal and called all the other flower bits to it, forming a swirling spherical storm around her hand. Pressurized by her magic, the ruined oxblood lilies crunched down into a single dense ashen brick like a cinder block.

After debating briefly with Nerium about where to send the wooden dolls, she banished them into storage. I righted Ginko's chair, then got on my knees to collect Danver's plate and peafowl bones.

After that, the table looked more or less the way you might expect it to look (following a dinner attended by dissolute upper-class mages).

The pieces of Nerium's cane flew toward Wist. She touched the broken ends together and willed it to be whole again.

She used a very forceful skill, as though shaming the cane back into its original shape. She passed it to Nerium without a word.

I tried to give him back his fancy business card, too. He refused to take it.

Eventually I gave up. "Tell me this, then. When did you and Ficus arrive at Follyhope?"

"Today, you mean?"

"Today."

Cane in hand, he eased himself out of Ficus's chair. "Can't recall the exact time, I'm afraid."

"You came together?"

Nerium and his cane paused. He'd been working his way over to the wall, perhaps to take a closer gander at his pickling brother. "I can only speak for myself," he said ruefully, as if he were terribly sorry to be letting me down.

14

WIST EVAPORATED the mystical liquid in the luminous tanks. She ported Ficus out onto the floor. He lay there like Ginko had, curled up protectively. His lingering dampness darkened the white parts of the zebra-stripe carpet, forming an unpleasant yellowish outline like a shape drawn at a crime scene.

He would regain consciousness within a few minutes, Wist told Nerium. Unless he was extremely unlucky.

Leaving her brothers, she ported us—just the two of us—to the manor's main entrance hallway. A floating water sculpture gyrated in the massive open space overhead. The magic in the liquid produced a fuzzy bass thrum. Deep and disorienting.

Wist slumped sideways against the wall. Her pain came through our bond like a hissing through teeth.

Part of me worked on healing her magic. This required little conscious thought. Another part of me ruminated over Nerium's answer.

I can only speak for myself.

He was drawing a contrast between himself and Ficus. Between the reasonable brother and the unbalanced one. I'd given him an opening to nurture my suspicions, and he'd seized it.

With that illicit skill of his, Ficus might've been lurking around the manor all day. He could have lounged invisibly in the blue-floored room while we viewed Lear's painting of his magic core and branches.

He could have been watching when the Void came out of my eye.

The Void had detected five true branch-wielding mages on the estate. Wist, Tempus, Grandmother Shien, Doctor Hazeldine—and Ficus? Not Lear, who was after all just an ordinary subliminal mage, albeit one with a weirdly shaped core. Ficus's concealment skill had proven capable of deceiving human beings, but perhaps not the Void.

Why, though? Was he a voyeur? Had he prowled around without our knowledge solely to confirm that the skill would work on Wist, too? Then why reveal it so cavalierly at dinner?

I was instinctively wary of the dichotomy we'd been presented with. Rational, cooperative Nerium versus loose-cannon Ficus.

Nerium had always been the philosophical ringleader of Wist's old tormentors here at Follyhope. On the surface, Ficus seemed more frightening—but his was a spontaneous and shallow-rooted malice. He could lash out at anyone, at any moment, on a lazy whim.

Except Nerium. I'd never seen him seriously target Nerium.

Nerium might style himself as Ficus's warden, the only person with any hope of reining him in. He might receive pity and appreciation for continuing to play the responsible older brother (all the way into middle age). That just meant Ficus was a weapon he could point wherever he wanted, so long as he could stomach a certain degree of chaos along with the cruelty.

When Wist was well enough to get moving, we went to find Tempus.

Hidden melodiums piped scheduled music—refined, somber instrumentals—through open stretches of the manor. Outside the building, wires attached to bare flagpoles rattled madly in a rising breeze. The noise was bizarrely similar to blocky bamboo wind chimes.

Once we got hold of Tempus, Wist told him to mark Ficus as a person of interest, just as he'd marked Ginko. This devolved into a convoluted argument over the conditions under which he could deploy that skill, the maximum number of people he could mark at once, and various other technical limitations.

"This is not my only case," Tempus said bitterly. "Far from it."

And so on and so forth, but in the end Wist convinced him to do it anyway. With both of them marked by the same skill, she could apply protective magic to Ginko that would detect and repel Ficus, using Tempus's magic as a helpful key.

Tempus said grudgingly: "If he really has it out for her, this will only delay him. He'll find a loophole sooner or later."

"I know," Wist said.

"He's not that fixated on hurting Ginko," I opined. "No more so than he's fixated on hurting any of us. Raise the hurdles, and he'll scratch his itches some other way."

With exquisite sarcasm, Tempus thanked me for my expert assessment.

At my request, Wist contrived to sit in on his sessions with her brothers, Doctor Hazeldine, and Lear. He'd already done a second round of interviews with Danver, Ginko, and Grandmother Shien.

In the midst of this, we still managed to steal a few moments alone. For instance: Wist had to come rescue me when I got lost on my way back from one of many bathrooms.

As complex piano music rippled past us, I murmured to her that I'd been wondering if Grandmother Shien was actually still here, still alive, and still in her right mind. If not for Wist herself having met with

Grandmother several times today, I'd suspect the whole thing of being a farce.

"She's very much alive," Wist said, "and she's very much herself."

"Not just a corpse propped up by your brothers? Not a sophisticated body double?"

"No."

"Really?"

"Would you prefer for her to come out and socialize?"

I shuddered.

I wanted to shudder again when Ficus showed up in a fresh set of clothes. He walked around barefoot, holding a bowl of dry cereal, and seemed to be in an excellent mood.

"Never liked sensory deprivation tanks," he said to Wist, "but that wasn't so bad."

Wist, understandably, had no response for this.

While she and Ficus disappeared with Tempus, Nerium called for a maid to serve hot spica. We were in a sitting room with lush living walls covered in plants, and a fireplace that hung from the ceiling like a low chandelier.

"How nice of you two to stay over," Nerium said. "Care for some cinema? We have an excellent home theater."

"I'm more partial to live theater myself."

He spoke woefully of how Follyhope had been much more lively before the vorpal hole spawned, killing innocent gardeners, and Grandmother sent the majority of the staff and residents away for their own safety.

"There used to be a lot of children running around. And dogs. And decorative monkeys. And horses in the stables, and swans—oh, and of course our giant tortoise. He's several centuries old, or so they say. Most pets have been removed to other estates, together with their attendants."

He drank from his cup of spica. Steam coated his glasses.

"Miyu recently acquired a couple ostriches," he added.

"Ostriches," I said. "Of course."

"They're superb guard animals. I'm afraid you won't be hearing from them—they've been evacuated, too." His voice grew distant. "The last conversation I ever had with her was about those ostriches."

"Think she was killed?" I asked. "Or—"

"Whatever happened, it'll stay quiet."

"How convenient."

"Tempus might twist himself into knots attempting to divine an elusive truth, but when all is said and done, it'll be written off discreetly as a tragic accident. Grandmother wouldn't settle for anything less."

I finished my spica. It had been a mistake to drink so much. I was liable to get lost every time I went in search of a bathroom.

I considered asking whether he'd been the one to send me that anonymous letter.

Dearest Magebreaker...

"I was touched," Nerium said, "to discover our similarities."

I refused to feed him the obvious question.

"My missing leg." He patted his prosthetic left leg, concealed by beige fabric. "Your missing eye," he said to my eyepatch. "Wisteria took your eye, didn't she?"

"It wasn't Wist."

"Wasn't it?"

I would not discuss this with Shien Nerium. "Where are your parents?" I demanded. "Their daughter is dead. Why'd you come running, and not them?"

His eyebrows rose.

"None of you like me," I said, exasperated. "You'd like me even less if I tried to ingratiate myself."

"I feel more of a rapport with you than with Wisteria, actually."

"Think I'd be pleased to hear that?"

"Never. But I'm not trying to please you any more than you're trying to please me."

I could see the merit in Wist's strategy: her never-changing tone, her never-changing expression. Best not to react in any way that might entertain him.

"As for our parents," Nerium said lightly, "Grandmother won't let them set foot in Follyhope again, not as long as she lives. They disgraced themselves some years back. Financial crimes, you see. Insider trading, embezzlement, plus a few more technical maneuvers."

"Fascinating," I said. "Who reported them?"

Nerium smiled and gestured as if pulling a rope to ring an invisible bell.

The maid came back to collect our empty cups. Hers was more of a slim suit-based uniform, with little resemblance to Danver and Ginko's long skirt-like robes.

"Who's next in line to inherit?" I asked.

"You might be surprised. Regardless, I expect Grandmother to live an extraordinarily long life. Personally, I'm much too focused on my business to insert myself in succession conflicts."

"Yes. Your business." I took out the black card. "One you built from the ground up, I'm sure, without any help whatsoever. Three cheers for entrepreneurial spirit."

"That does make for a better story," he said, unoffended.

"And people eat it up, don't they? What a world."

He encouraged me to explore other parts of the manor. There were still small toxic songbirds kept in a climate-controlled aviary on the premises. There were game rooms, and the aforementioned cinema, and art galleries, and multiple pools and saunas, and—for music appreciation—the most bombastic high-end listening room in the nation.

They even had a collection of artifacts related to the original Kraken. This piqued my interest, but I elected to stay put.

With Ficus off getting questioned, I kept thinking of his imperceptibility skill. Was the interrogation—sorry, interview—already over? Was he here in the room with us, visible only through Nerium's twinkling glasses?

I wondered whether you'd leave traces of yourself detectable by forensics (magical or otherwise) when using such a skill.

If not, it would be an ideal tool for assassins.

Even Wist had struggled to locate Ficus when he was right there in the dining room, and she'd already noticed him gone from his chair. She lacked a skill developed as a targeted antidote to his particular brand of imperceptibility. She could engineer one on her own, but without his cooperation, it'd take weeks or months of steady concentration.

Doctor Hazeldine stopped by to let us know that Ginko was now in much better condition. This reminded me of how he'd aided Wist after the Void and I attacked her.

"Her hands looked good as new," I said. "Almost couldn't believe it."

I kept trying to thank him, but he demurred. "It was all her own magic," he said. "She already possessed quite a few applicable skills. The only thing I did was help talk her through which to activate, and in which order."

His voice changed. "The Kraken truly is—I lack the words to describe it. We're unbelievably blessed to have her as part of this family."

Good thing Wist wasn't around to hear this. Nothing made her quite so uncomfortable as reverence.

15

FICUS AND LEAR wandered into the green-walled room after Nerium went in for questioning. Lear wore fluffy house slippers, but Ficus remained barefoot. I shrank into a corner of the camelback sofa and feigned fascination with the hanging fireplace.

Ficus, in classic fashion, was toying with another knife. This one had some kind of hair-thin wire attached to it: the knife kept zipping back into his hand. I couldn't understand how he pulled it off without either stabbing or garotting his own fingers.

"A yo-yo knife." Lear watched my gaze go up and down and up and down together with Ficus's blade. "It's a Jacian thing. Maybe I shouldn't have told him about these."

"Too late for regrets," Ficus said.

He performed a whirling trick with his leashed knife that seemed extremely likely to make someone lose an eye. I put a hand up like a shield near the side of my face.

Ficus dragged over a gnarled wooden end table that I'd mistaken for a decorative sculpture. Then he claimed a seat on my couch.

"Let's play the knife game."

He was speaking to me, not to Lear.

"The knife game," I repeated.

In response he put one hand on the table and stabbed his knife swiftly in the open spaces around and between each finger. Left to right, right to left, back and forth, following some incomprehensible pattern as he jumped from gap to narrow gap.

He turned and held his knife out to me. Its mysterious string was nowhere in sight. The silent fire had warmed the room so thoroughly that it grew increasingly difficult to breathe.

I pointed at my eyepatch. "I don't join games where I'm at a severe disadvantage."

Lear sat on the sofa between us and plucked the knife out of his fingers. "I'll play on her behalf."

His face—as off-puttingly lovely in his forties as it had been in his twenties—took on a surly cast. "You'll win easily."

"But wouldn't it be hilarious if I didn't?" Lear said gently. "Watch. I'll even use my non-dominant hand. Just for you, Ficus."

Water trickled somewhere out of sight. Down through the roots of the greenery blanketing the walls, perhaps. The plants appeared to be thriving, their color so intense that they looked dyed. Would anyone know if the solid surface behind them had begun to soften and rot and decompose into soil?

Lear did win easily.

She played Ficus's knife game with her right hand, then her left hand. Sometimes, as though to appease him, she cut it extra close. One plunge of the knife opened a tiny line on the side of her index finger that took several long seconds to start weeping visible blood.

She explained a more complex variation of the game, one supposedly from her hometown in Jace. It involved playing as a duet, both knives moving at the same time, crossing seamlessly over to your partner's hand and then back to your own.

"This is how divers do it," she said. "Stretch your toes, and you can learn to stab between them, too."

Ficus raised one naked foot and showed her that, with no noticeable effort, he could spread those long toes of his nearly as wide as his fingers.

"You give it a try," Lear told him. "I'll pass." She dug herself deeper into her fuzzy slippers. Her accent thickened. "Winter here is much too cold for me to take my feet out."

I crept quietly away as they bickered.

In my twenties, I'd made one of the biggest mistakes of my life: trusting in Jacians. I'd wanted to believe that our interests aligned. I'd convinced myself that what was right for me was right for them, and in turn right for Osmanthus, and all the world.

My Jacian co-conspirators may indeed have agreed with me that healers deserve more rights in Osmanthus. But they had not traveled across the sea solely to facilitate my political schemes. They had their own lives, their own assignments, their own dreams.

They hadn't acted alone, either. They'd killed a Board member with the help of my Osmanthian allies. Few healer activists had been satisfied with the pace of my progress. We'd put in years of work since Wist ascended to the Board of Magi. We could boast of preternatural effort but had produced few actual reforms.

If some had seen me as a pet of powerful mages, a sniveling collaborator willing to talk big and performatively fling myself headfirst into the muck of bureaucracy, yet unwilling to change my approach when stalled, unwilling to extract so much as a drop of real blood from the ruling class—in retrospect, I couldn't find fault with them.

As for my Jacian friends, they did what had been their job all along. They'd perceived an opportunity to cause chaos abroad at little cost to themselves, and they took it.

If Lear had a secret mission here, it'd be something much along the same lines. Not to strap a bomb to herself and terrorize the Osmanthian populace. Not to assassinate anyone high-ranking in particular. She could be embedded for years, faithfully making art and collecting patrons, before she took any action.

The Jacians I'd worked with to kidnap a Board mage had only been carrying out a plan I'd prepared for them. Slight deviations ended up snowballing into violence. Deliberate sabotage? An unlucky coincidence? The end result was the same. I may not have meant for anyone to die, but I was always the chief conspirator.

Lear, I imagined, would follow suit. If she saw an Osmanthian digging their own grave, she'd hand them a shovel and offer helpful tips on efficient excavation. Then she would walk away, leaving the rest up to fate.

This was all an exercise in extreme extrapolation. My past acquaintance with Jacians had been fleeting. Individual Jacians would be just as different from one another as I, with my bizarre life story, differed from most other Osmanthian healers. Lear might very well be nothing more than a sinless pioneer of cultural exchange.

If not, there was a sizable chance that she'd had some sort of distant involvement with Miyu's death. Tempus could dig into that all he liked; I doubted he'd turn up anything sufficient to condemn her, legally or even morally. I'd stay out of it.

Lear didn't strike me as being a hardcore Jacian nationalist. Even if you stripped away all her outer pleasantries. I tried to keep an open mind, but I was inclined to think that she bore no personal enmity towards any of us—not me, and not the Shiens, and not even Wist the

Kraken. If she were here under assignment, it was just a job to her. Give her nothing nefarious to exploit, and she'd do us no harm.

I tried not to dwell on the fact that she'd seen my Void mindlessly eating Wist's magic.

That evening, I contacted my parole officer through an ear cuff. She was not overjoyed to hear of me staying on the same estate as a Jacian artist. She didn't order me to extricate myself, though. That would be tantamount to accusing the Shien clan of impropriety. Lear was, above all else, a Shien guest.

As were we. Nerium, acting as Grandmother's deputy, proposed that Wist and I sleep in the Sparrowhawk Room.

Despite its name, it would've been better characterized as a suite than a singular chamber. There was a boudoir with a weeping willow chandelier, a dressing room, a bathroom the size of a zoo enclosure for a large feline, and of course the bedroom itself.

A misty seascape painting dominated the wall across from the tub. It was so expansive that they could've only gotten it in here with porting. If this were a downtown theater, it would've covered the curtains from floor the ceiling, from stage left all the way to stage right. I looked blankly at the ocean scenery while Wist scrubbed my back.

We retired to a bed with a curtained frame. An ancient manservant insisted that we take a pot of elderflower tea. Wist fussed around with the hangings, tying them as far back as they'd go. She wouldn't like feeling trapped in an unfamiliar bed, in Shien clan accommodations.

I drank enough tea for both of us.

I didn't ask where she'd slept as a child.

Other members of Tempus's team would track down and question the Shien staff who'd been temporarily transferred from Follyhope to other properties. With Miyu's death all but confirmed, a forensics crew and a fully certified bond notary were supposed to show up first thing tomorrow morning. Once the crew finished their work, Tempus would be able to sign off on closing the vorpal hole. Then Wist could do her thing, and we could get out of here.

There was still the issue of that anonymous letter. And of Ginko's safety—not just from Ficus, but from suspicions of magicide. We could keep an eye on future developments from afar, though.

A strange and inflammatory cocktail of people had gathered at the estate tonight. Wist the Kraken and me, the Magebreaker. Grandmother, aka Lady Shien, the head of the clan. Wist's two oldest brothers—one of whom, with their parents currently in disgrace, might be the great lady's presumptive heir. Lear, a Jacian with an artistic eye for magic. Ginko, a healer bereft of her bondmate. Danver, a healer with a creepy resemblance to Shien Nerium.

Then there was Doctor Hazeldine, the only other family member at the manor. Plus a smattering of long-suffering staff, each forced to juggle a dozen workers' worth of tasks.

Tempus, at least, would head home for the night.

Ficus wouldn't be able to grab a stick and start cracking Ginko's ribs again. Not after Tempus reluctantly marked him, and Wist conferred her with a new set of protections. If Ficus were sufficiently determined, however, he could hire someone else to do it for him.

Automatic defensive magic was depressingly complicated to implement, even for Wist. The very best such skills remained prone to misfiring. How would they distinguish between someone trying to pat you on the shoulder and someone reaching for your neck? What if you were perfectly happy to get roughed up in bed?

Should the magic base its response on the intent of the potential attacker—which would require sophisticated, accurate, and lightning-fast mind-scanning—or on your interpretation of their intent? What about an ambush from behind? What about a purely verbal assault? What about a psychobomb, or an assassin with a mind cleared by meditation and not a spot of guilt on their conscience?

This was one of the treasures I'd lost when the Void melted away my prosthetic eye. Along with magic to summon Wist straight to my side, be she in heaven or hell, that eye had contained an entire system of her best protective skills. Each cutting fit together like the mechanism of a fine music box. She couldn't recreate anything nearly that scrupulous on short notice. Not for me, and not for Ginko.

16

THE SPARROWHAWK ROOM had been named for its wallpaper, which bore a pattern of multicolored finches and white-eyed warblers pecking at plum blossoms. Here and there lurked a sparrowhawk no larger than a pigeon, its gray hue blending with the plum branches, its white spots a perfect match for those small round flowers.

Wist came to bed together with a heap of packaged food diverted to her from the pantry. After all, she hadn't touched a bite of dinner.

The kitchen staff were glad to help. They understood that she didn't mean it as an insult. Some, remembering her from childhood, might know the reason she preferred sealed containers. Others might explain it as one of the Kraken's harmless eccentricities.

I was aghast to learn that if her requests went unheard, she'd have resorted to magically importing her usual canned food from the tower.

"Save your strength," I scolded. "Wanton use of magic ought to be a last resort, not your immediate Plan B."

She tore open a bag of kettle chips. I helped myself to a couple.

Once Wist had finished her arcane meal of chips, dried mango, prunes, canned baby corn, canned bread, and shredded cuttlefish, I reached for her magic. The dense strands convulsed like salt-sprinkled worms at my touch. She was still very much in pain from the Void.

"I'm sorry." It just slipped out of me. "I'm so sorry."

The unrepentant Void twisted at the back of my nonexistent eye.

After I'd done all the additional healing I could, and we'd picked crumbs off the duvet and finished our ablutions, Wist turned in bed and latched onto me. The Shiens' stock of exotic bath products made us both smell unfamiliar, as if we'd transformed into two strangers having an assignation at a luxury hotel.

I'd figured Wist wouldn't have energy to do anything other than sleep. But once she locked her arms and legs around me, she began filling me in on Tempus's interviews with her brothers.

Her voice tickled my neck. "On the last night anyone saw Miyu alive, they were both here at Follyhope."

They'd described having anodyne interactions with Miyu, and with each other. They'd taken bets on how long Wist would delay before showing up to close the new vorpal hole.

"I could see Ficus killing someone over a bet," I muttered.

Wist didn't disagree. "He told Tempus to get that thing off his face."

"What thing?"

She traced a finger along my upper lip.

"Oh." I laughed. "Watch—we'll see Tempus come in with a clean shave tomorrow. I guarantee it."

"He had trouble keeping Ficus on topic."

"What'd Ficus go off about?"

"The hole outside, and Grandmother's determination to keep it private. He cracked up over the futility of it all. He said..."

"Yeah?"

"He said, stuff like this makes you wonder if the Extinguishers have a point. He called them snuffers."

She was simply repeating him, not trying to reopen our own debate over it.

I caressed the bond thread on her wrist, still strung with the Church of the Kraken keychain I'd given her as a joke. Sometimes, while she slept, the metal edges and loops of thread would leave an illegible mark like an old rune on her skin.

"None of my brothers and sisters are full siblings by blood," she said. "Did I ever tell you?"

"What? No!"

News to me. I'd thought they started ganging up on Wist because she was the youngest, because she had the most magic—and because she was the only adoptee.

"They're all Shiens. Only I came from outside the clan. Nerium, Miyu, Pallas, Lilium—they got transferred to our parents after the downfall of other aunts and uncles. Our father brought Ficus from a previous marriage. Vier is the only child our father and mother had together."

Aside from Nerium and Ficus, I could no longer put a face to any of them. My mental image of Miyu was more recent, but still a caricature at best. I'd never be seeing her again, anyway.

I'd always assumed that Wist's parents had been obsessed with producing biological heirs. Six is a lot, especially with most of them coming two or fewer years apart.

Instead they were technically cousins. Or half-siblings. Or distant relations. All still born Shiens, in the end.

I could recall being surprised to think that Wist's mother, a well-off mage, would willingly spend a good chunk of her life either pregnant or recovering from childbirth.

These biological processes could be somewhat eased with magic—given unlimited funding—but they were never entirely without discomfort or danger. In a way, it made sense that Wist's parents had put together a brood of Shien children as if collecting chicks fallen from nests.

"Wait," I said. "Even Nerium got transferred from other parents? Their eldest son?"

"Even Nerium."

I remembered how he'd mimed tugging a rope—or pulling the release lever on a guillotine.

Financial crimes, you see. Insider trading, embezzlement...

Nerium was the perfect Shien son: capable of dispassionately eliminating any obstacle, up to and including his adoptive mother and father. They'd engaged in similar machinations in their time, too. Why had all those other aunts and uncles fallen out of favor in the first place, allowing the two left standing to consolidate control over the next generation?

"Any of your siblings have kids?" I asked.

"Some. Not Miyu."

"What about Nerium?"

"He sponsored the adoption of several mages into branch families. He visits them once a season or so. Showers them with presents and money for holidays."

"And Ficus?"

"Ficus has a lot of children—sired and abandoned, scattered to the winds. None on the Shien family register. Grandmother keeps it quiet."

"She keeps a lot of stuff quiet, doesn't she? What a headache."

"That's the Shien way."

We shifted to avoid losing feeling in various limbs. We both wore guest pajamas festooned with royal embroidery. Lined, thankfully—for winter warmth, and to keep the underside of the stitches from itching.

"I was wondering about Danver," I said. "Could she be Nerium's daughter?"

The moment I asked, I could tell that Wist had never considered this.

I attempted to defend my thought process. "They've got a weird resemblance."

"...Do they?"

"She wears fancy magical glasses—the same kind he keeps trying to press on you. Ginko doesn't."

Wist seemed unconvinced.

"I mean, I get that their physical resemblance could be coincidental, whether or not she's on the family register. She could just as easily be a child Ficus left with a servant. Or she could be a normal healer from outside the clan."

"Nerium didn't act like she was his daughter," Wist said eventually. "But he didn't act like she wasn't."

"Who do you think she's bonded to?"

Wist blinked. "No one."

"Huh?"

"Thought her bond thread was camouflage."

"Like wearing a fake wedding ring to deter suitors?"

"She speaks and acts her mind more than any bonded healer I've seen in the clan."

Wist would know. On the other hand, even without a certified notary on staff, the Shiens would have to be aware of whether a healer on their payroll was truly unavailable for bonding. If she falsely claimed to have a bondmate, they'd want a copy of the government records. Her lie would fall apart in a matter of weeks.

Unless, of course, she got special treatment as a secret darling daughter of Shien Nerium. Or some other equally influential clan member. Ah, nepotism.

"So you're betting she's not bonded to Nerium or Ficus," I said. "Or your grandmother."

Someone bound to Grandmother Shien would surely be more stifled. Quieter and subtler. Better trained.

Wist held out a hand. I sensed what she wanted through our bond. I groped at the bedside table until I found the business card Nerium had left with me.

Her mood darkened as she examined it.

"Take it," I said. "Or destroy it. I don't need it."

She passed it back. "It's not dangerous."

"Not very useful, either. No contact info."

She told me how to activate the subtle transceiver skill worked into the material of the card.

"Can't imagine wanting to call your brother for anything," I said honestly.

"Keep it on you. He gave it to you."

She could be oddly rigid about stuff like this.

"Let's have business cards made in the name of the Kraken. Something much flashier. Rainbow lights and precious stones and magic spitting everywhere. A great chance to one-up your brother."

"Yes," Wist said flatly. "That'll show him what's what."

I used my finger to underline the part that said *Regalia Optics.* "He always had a thing for magic perception enhancement. But isn't the Shien family business something totally different?"

"Vorpal insurance. Vorpal hole forecasting. Risk management. Construction," Wist recited. "But mostly insurance. Or reinsurance."

"Re-in—what?"

"Reinsurance. Insurance for insurers. I think."

All the more reason for Grandmother to keep a tight lid on news of the hole at Follyhope. It'd come off as more ominous and poetically humiliating than it would for any other clan. Especially if some subsidiary of theirs really had been offering vorpal hole prediction services—a sketchy business at best.

From the sound of things, though, Grandmother had a lot of experience with clan-related cover-ups. Perhaps recent events felt like just another long day at work.

We doubled back to the topic of the Extinguishers, and how Ficus had chosen to bring them up at a moment when Nerium wasn't there to shush him.

I'd heard plenty of rumors that the Extinguishers covertly received support and funding not just from Jace and other hostile nations, but also from certain segments of Osmanthian high society.

Some might view them as a justified counterbalance to the immense power of the Kraken. Insurance against a worst-case-scenario future in which Wist the Kraken went rogue. Or merely set her mind on purging the mageocracy of all its deep-rooted corruption.

The Shiens had ridden Wist's coattails to untold new heights of wealth and prestige, even when she attempted to have nothing to do with them. They might habitually undermine her in other ways, but they were the last mage clan in the country who'd invest in terrorists sworn to murder her.

Before sleeping, we spoke of Miyu, too. In part because it seemed like few others would. Not even tonight.

"Doesn't feel real, Miyu being dead," Wist said. "Doesn't feel any different from her being alive."

Considering how rigorously we'd avoided her, she could've died a year or two ago, and it wouldn't have changed much.

For us, that is. It would have made a world of difference for Ginko.

Wist slumped back down beneath the covers, boneless as a cat oozing to fit in some obscure corner. There was room for her to spread out, but she kept burrowing right up against me. Before I knew it, I'd been pushed all the way to the edge of the bed.

Her hair unbraided itself. Long and loose, it grew like a black river over the side of my body, down off the bed, and all the way across the room to the very distant bathroom door.

Someone had left the door ever so slightly ajar. (I was the last one who'd been in there.)

Wist's hair flowed up to the handle and slid the door shut.

"That's the most wasteful use of magic I've ever seen," I said. "Are you *trying* to hurt yourself?"

"At a certain point, everything hurts so much that it doesn't make much difference whether or not I hold back."

I decided to have another go at wrangling her damaged and Void-fearful magic.

"You could have asked me to get up and close the door myself."

Wist eyed the ceiling as if this had genuinely not occurred to her.

"I'm definitely the brains of this operation," I muttered.

The black stream of her hair kept growing and growing, circling the bed as though to form a whirlpool.

"Don't like having long hair here," she said.

"Looks like you're just making it longer."

By *here*, she meant Follyhope. Where the Shien clan had raised her like an old-school trainer breaking a horse. Which was not so different from how many elite mages handled healers, particularly their bond-mates.

Ironic that the greatest of mages would have an upbringing worse than the lowest of healers. At least we healers usually got to live as ordinary children for a time.

Wist reached for the back of her neck and gathered her hair in her fist. She pulled.

A glissando of magic played across my perception. The bulk of Wist's hair dropped away, shearing itself off near the nape of her neck. She held the cut ends as though gripping a live snake behind its head.

Then she let go. The excess length still lay piled up in soft rings around the base of the bed, like a highly nonconformist spiral-coil rug. It crawled ponderously up onto the mattress, shrinking and braiding itself thickly as it went.

"Um," I said. The disembodied rope of black hair was the width of my arm and looked about as long as Wist was tall. "Thought you would vaporize it."

"Might be good for something."

"Like what?"

She made a lazy shooing motion with her fingertips. The hair-rope climbed its way sulkily to the top of the bed frame and curled around the rod like a monkey's tail. It dangled among the bundled-up curtains, but failed to blend in: they were too gauzy and pale.

"Left a little of me in it," Wist said. "It'll protect you, if you let it."

I would've asked *when?* But the answer came to mind soon enough. Like when she finished closing the vorpal hole in the rose garden. Once that was done with, she might totter over and pass out for the rest of the day. Some vorpal holes were harder to seal than others, and she'd had no real chance to recover from the predations of the Void.

I sketched a mental image of myself tossing the braid over my shoulders like a ropey shawl, or tying it to a bag like a designer scarf. Wouldn't be the easiest accessory to incorporate in a casual outfit. Good thing I'd never worried about making the Shiens think well of me.

The part of Wist's hair still attached to her head formed a kind of tousled blunt bob. She shook herself a few times, like she had water in her ears.

"Must feel a lot lighter," I said.

She tilted her head from side to side as though trying to weigh it.

We battled silently to see who would end up holding the other once we finally dozed off. I think I won—I remember anchoring myself with a finger hooked through her bond thread.

I dreamt of going on an impossibly long journey with Wist like a shadow at my side. I dreamt of becoming like a shadow myself.

I also dreamt of being viciously and repeatedly murdered. But that was so common as to hardly warrant mentioning.

An earthquake rattled us awake some hours before dawn. A minor one, just enough to prompt us to stare into the dark and await another round of seasick shaking.

None came. It had been a sensation in the realm of magic, not a corporeal quake. Wist cast her awareness out around the manor like a fishing net—then, satisfied nothing more would happen, she turned back toward me and instantly fell asleep again.

I wanted to know what had happened. I wanted to know right now. But no assassins dropped from the ceiling. Wist's cut hair still hung sleepily from the upper part of the bed frame, unalarmed. Wist needed rest more than anyone else in this house. I wouldn't deprive her.

Besides, as much as I'd complained about setting foot on Shien land, Wist was the one with all the bad memories. As an adult, as the Kraken, she'd become untouchable, and they knew it. She'd never let them do us real harm.

17

The vorpal hole had undergone a growth spurt. Hence the intangible lurching we'd felt in the night.

Over breakfast in a room known as the Grand Salon, I gathered that there had been no casualties, nor damage to nearby buildings. In staking out new ground, the swelling hole had claimed several benches and trellises, the outer edge of a famed hydrangea garden, and a sculpture of a giant runny-looking creature alleged to be a melting rabbit.

The sheer scale of the Grand Salon meshed poorly with my humble bowl of granola. In the chair next to me, Wist bit off chunks of a sticky energy bar. We could've gotten a hot spread of cuisine from every corner of the continent, but all that late-night snacking had left us without much of an appetite.

Part of the wall bore an artistically arranged display of mounted canes. Another section held a similar display of empty gilt frames. I'd seen a warped echo of those frames in Wist's tower.

The sky wore a cover of clouds like cracked mud. Startling mirror-clad pillars reflected the clouds outside and the expanse of the room, as if it weren't already large enough.

Small black birds streaked across the mirror glass. Hopefully they knew better than to fly straight down into the estate's vorpal hole.

No sign of Ficus. He didn't seem like an early riser.

Nerium came by for a brief chat, already dressed for the day in gray and lavender. So did Lear, clad in embroidered pajamas just like ours.

They both complimented Wist on her hair. She seemed slightly happier to hear it from Lear.

Melancholy wind instruments piped out of high-end melodiums, making me wonder if someone—Grandmother?—had specifically chosen a suite of sad music.

Stay at Follyhope much longer, and they might make us don mourning colors. For now, the clothes we'd worn yesterday came back to us freshly laundered.

I proposed going to take a look at the clan's collection of artifacts from the first Kraken, but Wist shook her head.

The Void, she said.

According to Manglelander legends, the previous Kraken had also experienced at least one run-in with the Void.

My Void was docile now, as satiated as it might ever get, given how diminished it had become by taking root in me. But what if it remembered the other Kraken? What if reminders of her made it go wild in a whole new way, worse than how it had reacted near the Follyhope vorpal hole?

Wist was right. Best not to risk it.

Tempus and his forensics team arrived to an onslaught of criticism. Most of the complaints were, admittedly, not at all his fault. Everyone lamented how the vorpal hole had spread in the night, its border leaking irregularly as though an infected pustule had burst.

Ficus drifted through to share his opinion on how life at Follyhope had, thanks to staffing reductions, become unforgivably inconvenient. "No on-call masseuse? Might as well live out on the streets."

He stretched, showing skin where jogging pants rode low on his hips. He tossed out a startlingly cruel remark about Tempus's choice of facial hair. Tempus—a grown man in a pressed MP uniform—blushed.

Lear rescued him with a non sequitur. "Tried putting hot sauce on my buckwheat this morning. Didn't quite hit the spot."

"Oh, right," I said quickly. "Osmanthian fare must seem very bland to you. Jacian food is super spicy, isn't it?"

"Depends on the region. Different islands favor differing amounts of heat."

Normally I would've spun this topic around to take a dig at Tempus. I'd weaponized lethal-grade hot sauce against him during our first year at Guralta Academy. Like me, he'd probably forgotten everything from the names of peripheral teachers to the content of courses and the faces of classmates. But that capsaicin burn would remain an indelible memory.

Instead of further provoking him, I steered us back to the main point. "Whatever evidence your team could've gleaned has probably been swallowed."

"Maybe. Maybe not. The hole didn't expand equally on all sides."

Once Ficus got sufficiently bored and left to work out, I told Tempus how impressed I was that he hadn't dashed off to excise his mustache.

He flushed resentfully. Again. Good grief.

While Tempus's crew did their thing, Lear took me and Wist through a mirror to her atelier. It was in a standalone building far from the central manor complex, awash in natural light.

Lear seemed to be the only artist in residence. I voiced my surprise at the fact that she could so freely navigate the network of mirrors.

"Seems like a security flaw," I said. "No offense."

She didn't take offense. From what I'd seen of her so far, it was difficult to imagine her taking offense to anything, really.

"There are places in the manor that can't be reached by mirrors," she said. "You have to walk the entire way, following a particular sequence, or you'll never get there. There are other facilities and portals accessible only to those on the family register."

Which would make it even more helpful to have a portion of the staff comprise actual Shiens. Subliminals and one-branch mages and healers— perhaps like Danver. You wouldn't catch Grandmother Shien getting down on her creaky old knees to scrub the floor of the top-secret family archives.

Lear showed us a completed painting of Miyu's magic (three branches) and an in-progress work inspired by Nerium (six branches). Along with quite a few mages who were strangers to me: people who had come through as guests of the clan.

"I'd love to paint Inspector Minashiro," she said. "It's hard to meet a nine-branch mage. Both in Jace and Osmanthus. But he keeps turning me down."

"How about the Kraken?" I asked.

Wist moved behind me, which was about as effective as a wolfhound trying to hide behind a toy poodle. Lear let out a rueful laugh. "I know my limits. Which isn't to say I'm not interested in a challenge." She turned her gaze on my eye patch. "I've never depicted the process of mage maintenance. You call it healing, I think? Perhaps I could attempt a portrait of the essence that came out of your eye."

Wist stepped forward again. "You saw nothing that can be rendered in paint."

Lear lasted an unsettlingly long time before breaking eye contact. "I'm certainly used to behaving as if I've seen nothing. A key life skill,

I'd say." She showed crooked teeth when she spoke. The crookedness was mild enough to come off as charming, like her teeth had once been straightened but had with age begun clandestinely reverting to old habits.

Just when I thought our tour would come to an end, she pointed up a flight of floating wooden stairs. They led to a loft with a vaulted glass ceiling. "Can you keep a secret?" she asked.

"That sounds like a trap," I said.

"Nothing too serious. Just a few extra pieces in storage."

We followed her up the steps.

The loft was a lot messier than the workspace below. Rickety-looking easels. Pulled-out drawers stuffed with broken palette knives and pencil stubs. Buckets and bottles of solvent.

There were quite a few ways one might incur mortal injuries in an artist's studio. At a glance: drinking poison, breathing fumes, cutting yourself on damaged supplies. Downstairs, she'd shown us her glass palettes and the razor-edged tool she used to scrape paint off. Hand that tool to an assassin, and they'd invent a whole different use for it.

Lear pushed aside piled-up hazards and led us to the back of the loft. On the wall were tacked sketches in an entirely different style than her principal body of work. Pencil drawings of people stretching, of six-legged rabbits and various types of ocean waves. Quite a few faces, too, many in profile or turned away. Those that looked full-on at the viewer were visibly irritated. They were also pretty much all Danver.

She'd annotated Danver's pouting in Jacian characters, the strokes so slanted and truncated that I couldn't make out a single word.

"Not those," Lear said. "These."

She directed our attention to a pair of canvases propped up against the wall. They were smaller than her other finished paintings, but they'd still seem overlarge if you hung them in my little city apartment.

"Some pieces can't be sold or displayed to the public. It just wouldn't do. Some pieces I paint solely for my own satisfaction."

She ceased to elaborate. Wist and I lined up side-by-side in front of the two paintings—those condemned to never hang in a gallery or shine in the lights of an auction. Unlike her scrappy sketches, these would fit right in with the type of work she'd become known for. Like the painting of Ficus's magic in the room with the blue floor.

Except—

Wist caught it at the same time as I did, or maybe earlier.

The paintings both depicted mages, each with a magic core and a couple branches apiece.

But their branches were all wrong. Their branches were beyond healing. They'd grown in twisted from the start, rather than getting twisted over time. Virtually impossible to imprint with skills. The skills wouldn't take, or if they did, they'd be worse than useless. By virtue of their very shape, the branches would generate constant magical pain without offering any power in return.

Stunted mages had only come up in passing during my schooling. They were not a topic for polite conversation. They were extremely rare to begin with, and most would live in seclusion.

Their magic was crippled by a kind of incurable birth defect. A metaphysical immune disorder. No treatment existed except for frequent healing, and healers could never offer sufficient relief.

The canvas on the right felt inexplicably familiar. The one on the left was someone I'd never seen before. Although I shouldn't have recognized either of them: I'd never met a stunted mage.

Wist stared without blinking at the canvas on the left.

"You still remember?" Lear said.

Who is it? I asked without opening my mouth.

Wist answered out loud. "I barely knew her."

"But she's a Shien," said Lear.

"It's a big clan." Then, almost defensively: "I—they kept us away from her."

Lear nodded, unsurprised. "Yes. I suppose they did."

Whatever emotions Wist was having, she'd plated them in ice. I let our bond hang slack.

"That's you," I said to Lear, motioning at the painting on the right. "That's you—but you're a subliminal. You don't actually have any branches."

She raised her hands as if admitting defeat. "I'm the kind of artist who can't stand to do a straightforward self-portrait. I have to pervert it somehow. This one is a more surreal and fantastical piece than my portraits of other mages. A vision of another possible self."

"You see yourself as a stunted mage?" One with branches, unlike a subliminal. Vestigial branches that would only ever weigh her down.

Her mouth curved. I noticed, out of nowhere, that every fourth or fifth pearl in her necklace was an irregular lumpy shape. Like teeth without roots.

What did this vision of herself imply? Trauma, hidden agony, an inferiority complex? Perhaps that was the trick. The painting took the guise of a window to her inner self, when in truth it was a mirror. Why did the imagined magical anatomy of a stunted mage need to imply anything at all? Any conclusions you drew from this would shed light not on Lear but instead on you the observer, you the would-be analyst. Your assumptions, your prejudices, your ignorance.

A portrait of someone's physical shell might also reduce them to nothing more than a scarecrow made of meat, flesh put on view for an audience. But in most cases, you'd convince yourself you could see hints of the person within. A glint of soul in the eyes, or a whole story told by their pose and expression, by their clothing or lack thereof.

Reduce mages to their magic alone, and you couldn't fool yourself into thinking you perceived anything about who they really were. These were like paintings of brains embalmed in jars.

Lear must have gotten on well in Osmanthus because her work seemed flattering. A raw tribute to the naked power of great mages.

Maybe it was also a way of reducing them, flattening them into two dimensions, stripping away every nonmagical aspect of their humanity, shoving in their faces the fact that they valued their magical birthright over all else. Over physical beauty, over affection, over morality, even over empty costumes of status and wealth.

A mage could buy a penthouse at the heart of Osmanthus city, but they couldn't buy more branches.

Lear wasn't just diagramming the magic of individual Osmanthian mages. Her oeuvre formed a type of holistic portrait, a mosaic that no one would notice unless they stepped far enough away to reconsider how it all fit together. With each new piece she produced, she added to her portrait of the mageocracy as a whole. A visual compendium of mages stripped down to their basic taxonomy. Class 5-5. Class 6-3. Class 9-4.

Or maybe her art had no inherent meaning. She was a Jacian subliminal who'd paved her own unique path to getting by in a foreign land. A resounding success. All she had to do was ingratiate herself with and satisfactorily paint powerful patrons.

And I, fishing for some deeper intent, had just betrayed the innate bend of my own thoughts on mageocracy before a large and faithful mirror.

Dearest Magebreaker...

Could Lear have sent me that letter?

I couldn't imagine why. Nor could I figure out why any of the Shiens would've sent it, either. Maybe for a chance to lure us in and spring a trap. To cut the Kraken down to size. To reassert their mastery. If so, they'd been doing an awful lot of dilly-dallying and very little trap-springing.

I couldn't speculate much about the stunted Shien mage—apparently a relative that Wist had known at one point, though I'd never heard of them. Naturally I hadn't. It was the Shien way to keep shameful things quiet, regardless of whether or not the shame was deserved. Their giant vorpal hole would remain on a need-to-know basis, and they would hide away their stunted mage.

I packed up these thoughts of mine once we climbed down from Lear's loft. Wist wanted to leave the topic behind as quickly as possible.

I hadn't come to Follyhope to dig up Shien family secrets, anyhow. Shake a few loose, and more would tumble down to bury us, like some paranoid mechanism set in a king's rotting old tomb.

Nerium caught us when we returned from our tour of the atelier. Apparently having nothing better to do, he offered running commentary on the work of the forensics crew, as well as the professional bond notary that Tempus had brought over to get a second opinion on Ginko.

"They're both supplied with Regalia equipment," he said. "The forensic technicians as well as the notary. Although magic imaging systems for bond examination still have a long, long way to go."

"Business must be going great," I said dryly.

The conversation turned back toward Lear's atelier.

Nerium said: "If you'll permit me to brag—"

"I can hardly forbid it."

"—I'm proud to have had a role in recommending Lear for her grant. It's so important to create real-life examples of peaceful cultural exchange. The things we could learn from Jacian technology...."

"Why is Jacian magitech so advanced?" I genuinely didn't get it. "They're not a mageocracy."

"There's a lot more room for ruthless innovation when mages are considered a shared resource."

"Rather than being the ruling class."

"See? You understand perfectly."

That was around the time when I made the executive decision to stop asking him unnecessary questions.

A six-branch son of the eminent Shien family could afford to express any number of radical views. An ex-con healer like myself would manufacture endless trouble for Wist if I didn't know when to swallow my opinions and shut my mouth.

Tempus's forensic technicians had come specifically to search for traces of magic. A physical evidence team had already combed over wide swathes of the estate to no avail.

There were fewer experts on magic forensics available to join the search. That team only got called in now that Miyu was on the verge of being declared officially dead—and Wist was raring to close the vorpal hole. Doing so would flood Follyhope with Kraken magic, utterly wiping away any lingering magical vestiges left in recent weeks by other mages.

I made sure to stay far from the vorpal hole, but I did venture outdoors to watch the technicians wrap up their work. I had plenty of company: a long line of pale birds perched on the roof of a garden storage shed, starlings pecking at golden winter grass, and Wist, leaning on one of the manor's prodigious pillars with folded arms.

Tempus came up to us in a high-necked overcoat and said grimly that the most recent traces of Miyu they'd found were right by the vorpal hole.

"That's it, then," I said. "Grandmother Shien's going to ask you to drop it."

He started to argue, but immediately ran out of steam.

"She already has," he confessed. "It'll be kept as private as possible. It'll be filed away as—"

"A tragic accident," I said, quoting Nerium. "Find any traces of other mages?"

"Shien Nerium and Shien Ficus. They were both staying on the estate when she vanished, and both walked around to survey the vorpal hole multiple times. It's only to be expected."

"Miyu could've fallen in the hole on her own," I said. "She could've been clumsy. She could've been on drugs. She could've been ready to give it all up. Or she could've gotten help. A little push, as it were."

Mori had told me a story like that about his brother. With a vorpal hole nearby, all it would take to commit murder was a single fatal shove.

I went on. "There are people I can imagine doing it on impulse. Seeing her standing there watching the abyss, drawn to it for reasons of her own, too absorbed to look over her shoulder. A dark night with no witnesses. Or maybe witnesses wouldn't matter. Maybe it was someone who could go imperceptible. Who could walk by and bash her off-balance like a spiteful gust of wind."

"If I pursue that line of investigation," Tempus said, "you know what will happen."

If he cast suspicions on Ficus—or any other Shien mage—eventually the full weight of Grandmother Shien's political influence would bear down on him. If he didn't conclude that the incident was an accident, he'd be pushed by his superiors to settle on an acceptable scapegoat.

Ginko, who had lied about losing her bond, would be the obvious candidate.

Healers and subliminals might leave behind biological calling cards like hair and fingerprints and skin cells—but nothing magical.

With several storms having swept through the area over the past few weeks, there was no way to physically prove that Ginko had or hadn't followed Miyu right up to the edge of the vorpal hole. If they needed to declare that someone had pushed Miyu in, that someone would always be her lying bondmate.

"Guess I'm on Lady Shien's side this time, Inspector," I said. "Kind of an icky feeling. Icky or not, hope you do write it off as an accident."

He grimaced. Then he told us good riddance, and informed Wist that she could start sealing the vorpal hole.

18

TEMPUS LEFT to escort his forensics team and the bond notary off the estate. Wist left for the vorpal hole. I didn't accompany her: we'd decided not to tempt fate.

Instead, I tossed her disembodied braid around my shoulders and made my way up several floors to a glass-walled gym. Once it would have looked down on a wild sea of rosebushes. Now it looked down on the incomprehensible shape of a humongous vorpal hole.

I'd been here during a previous visit to Follyhope. It was impeccably clean, but today there were no trainers on duty.

We'd exercised caution, since this would be my first time facing the hole dead-on since the Void's feeding frenzy. First we did a test run, with Wist accompanying me to the gym entrance. We concocted an elaborate plan for what she'd do with me if the Void acted up.

Nothing happened. Both times—once with Wist watching me, and now alone—I walked uneventfully up to the glass wall.

Looking directly at the mass of the metastasizing hole made pain seize my head like an exercise cramp.

The pangs were sporadic, though, and eased when I shifted my focus to anything else. The gleaming gym machinery. A fringe of young bare trees. Some had white bark, and some—whether by virtue of magic or an astonishing feat of breeding—were translucent like frosted glass.

I clutched Wist's braid and tried to spot nests left in naked winter branches. Bird nests, squirrel nests, wasp nests.

Footsteps came up behind me.

"Nice pet." Lear eyed the braid. "Looks warm."

"Thanks."

It was, in fact, as warm as a living mammal. It slithered restively across the backs of my shoulders.

I hadn't expected company. Ginko and Danver were lying low, which was just as well. The Shien brothers had both left the estate, claiming to be busy with corporate work (Nerium) and magesports gambling (Ficus).

Maybe they also needed to help with funeral planning. Whatever they did for Miyu, the clan would keep it as private as possible.

First they'd have to go through procedures to get her declared legally dead. There was no body to burn, so they'd find some other way to represent her at the family mausoleum. Which was, conveniently, located on the Follyhope grounds.

Outside and below us, Wist walked up to the lower edge of the vorpal hole. Her trench coat, unfastened, flapped behind her like a vengeful cloak.

From one hand she dangled an incongruously cheap-looking lawn chair. The teal of the webbed chair and the blue of her bond thread seemed almost artificially vivid. Something about the air today painted the rest of her surroundings gray.

She set the lawn chair down and sat with her back to us, legs stretched out. She could've lifted her feet and stuck them in the vorpal hole, but only if she really stretched.

"Like camping out to buy concert tickets," Lear said wryly. "What happens next?"

"It's not that exciting."

"I've never seen the Kraken close a vorpal hole before. Might never see it again." She leaned sideways to look at me, hands in her pockets. "You're not just watching, are you?" she continued in Jacian. "You'll be providing support on the fly."

She'd known my identity and my background—right down to my rusty language skills—before I ever said a word to her. I hadn't announced that I was Wist's bondmate (as opposed to an unbonded healer or a personal assistant). But she'd seemingly known that all along, too.

She'd left her native country for a strange and hostile land. She'd make it her business to know things, if only for the sake of survival.

Wist's attention flowed in only one direction right now—toward the bottomless pit of the vorpal hole. There was no one else in the wide echoing gym, just me and Lear and so many silent machines.

I'd lost my prosthetic eye, Wist's magnum opus, together with its state-of-the-art mesh of protective magic. The Void lolled about, sleepy and full, oblivious to the frailty of human flesh. Corporeal matters were not its realm of expertise.

This would be the perfect moment for a true fanatic to step closer and saw my throat open. Using, say, one of those palette scrapers equipped with a razor blade.

"Might not be able to talk much," I told Lear. "Sorry."

"I'll let you concentrate, then. Hm, maybe I'll see if Danny and Ginko know what's happening."

"This isn't a spectator sport," I said tartly.

Lear grinned. "Best of luck to you and the Kraken."

She strolled off, waving without looking back.

It was a relief to be alone. I looked down at Wist, equally isolated in her lawn chair.

This is a difficult one, isn't it.

Her reaction felt like the mental equivalent of a groan.

Well, take your time, I said.

I narrowed my awareness to the roots of her magic. I closed my left eye. I cut myself adrift from my own hearing until I stopped picking up the incessant cawing of crows. Why did crows get so agitated on cloudy days, anyway?

As Wist's bondmate, I could perform long-distance healing. I could comb through her thicket of magic while she strained to shrink the vorpal hole. Still, both of us would've preferred for me to be down there with her, bundled up in the cold, my hands hiding in her jacket, or Wist's hiding in mine. She liked the warm pocket formed between my dangling hood and my upper back.

We really needed to figure out a way past the Void's aversion. Much of Wist's work involved dealing with vorpal holes. Would my original plan—gradually increasing exposure—be effective so long as we kept the Void fully fed?

Hosting the Void wasn't like buying a tank of rare fish. There were no experts I could consult, no handy guidebooks about its care and keeping, no store or breeder I could accuse of scamming me. I couldn't tell how long its satiation would last, or what might set it off next. Only time and careful observation (and terrible mistakes) would teach us anything more.

Wist worked on the vorpal hole. I worked on her magic, using our bond as a conduit. Until her branches stiffened—as if bracing for a fatal blow. My eye came open.

Below the window-wall, Wist was standing, her lawn chair abandoned. The vorpal hole had retreated a few meters, revealing the thorny stubs of shorn rosebushes. It was still shaped like a gradual cascade coming down through the air, a drawn-out frozen avalanche.

The surface looked lumpy ... insofar as mind-collapsing nothingness could possess qualities like depth or bumpiness. It wrinkled and puckered, resisting Wist's efforts. A new sound infiltrated the gym, a sound like a finger running around the rim of a wineglass.

Time for a break? I said. *You can do this in stages.*

Wist glanced back at the building. Her eyes found me immediately. I waved. So did the end of her disembodied braid. She reoriented herself toward the vorpal hole. *Would rather get it over with.*

I figured our exchange would end there. She wouldn't waste energy entertaining me.

Then Wist said: *There's a problem with this hole.*

She sounded more perplexed than alarmed. Like a mathematician puzzling over a false proof.

Isn't there a problem with every hole? I asked. *Doesn't the problem lie in the very fact that they exist?*

This one is different. Her voice in my head faded as she spoke, as if she'd begun walking away, drawn irresistibly toward some distant point on an imagined horizon. *This doesn't belong here.*

Doesn't belong here?

I let it go for the moment. Silence washed back up inside us.

Wist was at her most vulnerable when she sealed large and complex rifts. The rest of the world disappeared for her, and her reaction times would slow to a crawl.

Sometimes she said things that made no sense till she got a chance to explain herself in retrospect. Sometimes she'd have no memory of her mutterings, and no clue as to what she'd meant.

Cuttings she'd previously dispensed elsewhere—like whatever animated the hair draped around my shoulders—would still work. But she wouldn't dilute her strength while tackling a vorpal hole; she wouldn't attempt to sustain unrelated types of active branch magic. Not even to protect herself.

It was probably for the best that we'd decided to separate her from the opportunistic Void. If I were cuddled up right next to her, it might pounce instinctively at her moment of weakness. Even if it weren't starving.

Thank god that it hadn't worked out a way to consume Wist's magic through our bond.

I immediately regretted this thought. Why would I do that? Why would I give the Void ideas? I was already half-convinced that I'd unconsciously prompted it to feed on her yesterday. I'd considered various worst-case scenarios, as was my wont. What if my fear of the Void attacking her was the very factor that made it more likely to happen?

I'd drive myself mad if I kept thinking like this. Worse, Wist would know I'd been obsessing over it. I lacked her faculty for internal self-censorship.

Not that we made a habit of deliberately invading each other's private thoughts. She'd notice it bothering me even if I said nothing. She knew me inside and out.

How many days until the Void would need to feast again?

I'd considered feeding it vorpal beasts. If we got word of some aggressive monster wreaking havoc in the city—why not dispose of it and satiate the Void in one fell swoop?

Unfortunately, there weren't that many vorpal beasts on the rampage. At least not in Osmanthus. I also had a sinking suspicion that, like me, the Void would intrinsically prefer Wist to all other options. Once you tasted the good stuff, there might be no turning back.

A muscle twitched in my throat; an involuntary contraction.

I felt what happened before I saw it.

Something invisible grabbed Wist. Grabbed her by her left arm. Yanked or pushed her.

It all took place in an instant. She stumbled, tripping forward, her arm outstretched, her consciousness swimming murkily up out of its entanglement with vorpal complexities.

By the time she pulled back, her hand had already plunged through the hole.

19

THERE WAS NO BLOOD. She whirled, elbowing empty air with her handless arm. As if the air itself had grabbed her, and she knew exactly where to hurt it.

The lawn chair clattered, toppling head over heels like a tumbleweed. It was light enough to go flying when kicked, although nothing visible had touched it.

Barrier magic surrounded Wist in a column of light. Her own magic. She stood safe within it, the vorpal hole neglected behind her. She looked at the stump of her left forearm, and then I realized through the choking in my chest that it wasn't a stump at all.

Her missing hand flickered in and out like the guttering of a candle. She flexed ghostly fingers until they began to solidify. The vorpal hole had sliced her hand off well past the wrist, at a point halfway up to her elbow—but there it was again, her skin and tendons only a little transparent.

I crouched dizzily at the base of the glass wall.

This was Wist. My Wist was the Kraken. A vorpal hole would mean maiming or death for any other human being. It didn't have to mean that for her. In past times, she'd even jumped through vorpal holes to reach other worlds. As if hopping down into the maintenance chamber below a manhole.

That had all taken place before our reunion several years ago. Before she sacrificed her entire skill set. By now she'd regained enough key branch skills that virtually no one realized how the Kraken had changed.

She'd had no time to protect herself with anything but the most primal, thoughtless sort of magic. Whatever she'd done, though, it'd worked. The arm of her coat had been chopped shorter, but the hand and wrist that emerged from it were empty of scars. Completely unharmed. Completely bare.

Bare.

Someone wearing a guise of imperceptibility had thrust Wist's left wrist into the vorpal hole as though thrusting it in a molten furnace. Her hand had emerged intact, if rather flickery. Her fingers were all there.

Her keychain had vanished.

Her blue bond thread had vanished.

I couldn't breathe.

I couldn't breathe because that thick braid of hers, eyeless and brainless and confoundingly lively, had gotten a stranglehold on my throat.

The ambient magical sound of human fingertips caressing glass had long since given way, drowned out by a bone-deep thumping like meteorites hitting ground all over the estate.

I clutched Wist's severed hair, digging at the links of her braid to ease the pressure on my larynx. Nothing had actually come down from the sky. No craters pocked the garden. But the machines in the gym rattled as if the earth of Follyhope were being hammered.

I fought to form words. It was like whistling into the wall of a hurricane. There was too much magical noise, inside my head and outside it.

Bond or no bond, Wist couldn't hear me. She couldn't—wouldn't—hear anyone.

Torturous seconds passed as she contemplated her naked left wrist.

The world went dark—the red-tinged divine darkness of a total eclipse—except for where Wist stood in her round-walled magical spotlight.

The shield around her formed a brilliant shaft reaching all the way up toward the night-black sky. Like a tower without end. Like a well dug down from heaven. She stood at the very bottom of the well, trapped, the fingers of her right hand thoughtfully circling the part of her wrist that used to wear a bond thread.

Her cut-off hair trembled around my shoulders, scorching hot. It smelled as if it were starting to cook. The Void scraped desperately at the back of my eye socket as though seeking a deeper place to hide.

Clem's thread, she thought. *It's gone.*

She was not speaking to me. She was not calm: she was insensate.

It's gone.

I lost it.

No.

If he made me lose it—

I couldn't get through to her. I was on my hands and knees and furious about it, wet-eyed with impotence. The gym machines clacked their teeth behind me like a chorus of laughing skeletons.

What good was a bond if I couldn't use it to haul her back from the edge? My grip on our bond kept slipping. My grip felt much too weak, faltering at this most critical moment for no reason whatsoever. I couldn't have performed worse if the Shien brothers had marched up and kicked me in the stomach.

I wanted to scream ten times louder than I was already screaming at her. I wanted to put my head through the palpitating glass wall of the gym.

I have to get it back.

I have to get it back.

I have to get it back.

I have to get it back.

Wist's thoughts poured out into the atmosphere as if she'd begun to assimilate the entire estate, as if everything beneath the blotted-out sky were a rightful extension of her magic-flooded body.

I have to get it back.

She crooked her finger at the vorpal hole. It came to her like a pet. It wrapped around her, veiling her in nothingness. Her hair flashed white as it enfolded her, as white as death.

I have to get it back.

Her voice stopped throbbing through the soupy air, through the confines of my skull, through the vibrating floor. The vorpal hole sealed her in its cocoon, then deflated to a line as thin as a knife-scar.

Something snapped. I felt as if I were floating, unmoored.

Wist's braid constricted my right arm as though attempting to measure my blood pressure. My palms and knees still pressed at the rubbery gym flooring.

The moment Wist passed through that vorpal hole, our bond had snapped like a twig.

I would've expected it to ricochet when it broke. I would've expected the backlash to knock me out, to flatten me, to run me through like a murdering sword.

The sky lightened back to a milky sort of white. The vorpal hole had been reduced to a sprawling sliver, a crazed smile that stretched from end to end of the former rose garden. Wist's lawn chair had been blown out of sight.

A pile shaped like Shien Ficus lay motionless near the first thorny row of decapitated bushes.

20

I HAD ZERO thoughts to spare for Shien Ficus. He might be dead or alive. Or somewhere between those two states, mewling for mercy. Not my concern.

I have to get it back.

The same mad chant consumed me.

Our bond had snapped.

I have to get it back.

Wist had gone after a lost thread. A symbol. A goddamn accessory made of string. Here I was bereft of the real thing, and I couldn't stop shaking, and I couldn't follow her.

Once-silenced birds began vociferously voicing their opinions outside.

I ripped off my eyepatch, dropping it like a dirty tissue. Wist's braid snatched it out of the air.

I reached for my right eye. There was nothing to fill the hole behind my eyelid; nothing but the Void.

I couldn't summon her.

Our bond had broken. But she wasn't dead. If she were dead, the magic cutting animating this hair of hers would've crumbled to nothing. If she were dead, her tower would fall—but it would be easier for me to prove her alive with this squirming braid in my arms than with a distant tower that no one could see from here.

A raw ache filled the top of my throat. I got back on my feet. Why didn't I hear any shouting, panic, confusion? I hadn't been the only one watching her.

Maybe very little time had actually passed since she vanished. Maybe they were all shell-shocked. Maybe, battered though I felt, I was far more accustomed to the Kraken and her feats of magic than anyone else on the premises. Maybe I'd recovered fastest.

The broken bond didn't dangle in me like an aimless piece of string. It had evaporated the moment it snapped. I felt it missing under every inch of skin.

When we first came together, she'd planted her bond like a cord in my back. It had grown to encompass so much more. In the end, it hadn't been anchored to any one specific part of me, tied to a finger or rooted in my spine or my heart. It had interfaced with everything I was. With it ripped away, my everything had become the site of a wound, inflamed.

I couldn't get any thoughts together. I leaned on the cold glass wall. The machines had stopped jangling. The wall had stopped jiggling like a train window. The air outside was very bright.

She wasn't dead. She hadn't even lost her hand. With sheer instinct, she'd managed to salvage her own flesh and blood. But she hadn't saved the fabric of her coat sleeve. She hadn't saved her bond thread.

That blue string used to be my bond thread, not hers. Mine from another life, from a now-dying world. It was the only artifact she'd brought over from the world where we'd first been born, first met, first bonded. That bond thread had once made a miraculous transition across vorpal borders. From one world to another, from our first world to our second. Yet it had no unique properties to protect it from being annihilated by the space between.

It was, after all, just a beloved piece of string.

It had survived only because of Wist's superhuman resolve. Now it was gone because of a petty ambush.

In leaving to pursue that length of string, Wist had severed the very bond it was meant to represent.

For Wist, this would be the second time our bond had snapped.

Why had it snapped?

She'd been possessed by a rage of incalculable dimensions. Still, if she'd been through this once before, all alone, she'd have done anything to avoid the same grief again. She wouldn't have let the hole swallow her if she knew it would tear up our bond.

Wist hadn't traversed a single vorpal hole while we were bonded, had she? Not in our first lives, and not this time, either.

She'd sealed too many to count. She'd opened and closed them, played around with them, threatened the Void with them—but she'd never stepped through one. Not once since we bonded.

I wrung at her braid. I called her a vast range of unpleasant names. No one heard me.

Our bond hadn't broken when she sent me to the short-term past in Manglesea. Of course, I'd never gone to a part of the past where Wist herself didn't exist.

Our bond had stretched across the whole continent, too. She'd gone to all sorts of different countries without me.

But she hadn't ventured into other worlds. At first because she'd lost the skill for it. Later on, even if she reconstructed her old magic, she wouldn't have found much use for it. Our own world had plenty of troubles that needed tending.

Miyu's bond with Ginko had broken when she (allegedly) fell in a vorpal hole. It broke because the hole killed her. Had Wist and I inadvertently become history's first-ever case study of whether a living bond could span worlds?

No one else could've tested it. No one else could've warned us.

Wist would've felt it sever, too. Wist would turn back as soon as she could. Time worked differently outside vorpal borders, though. Last time she traveled to another world, she thought she was only there for a couple of hours. She ended up being MIA from our reality for months.

This line of thought was a crooked little staircase that could only ever spiral down toward darker places.

I forced myself to look outside the gymnasium.

Doctor Hazeldine knelt over Ficus, who stirred like a drunk on a city street getting pestered by a low-ranking MP.

Shien Nerium, cane in hand, studied the narrow line that remained of the vorpal hole.

It was still very much a vorpal hole. If he reached for it, the border would guillotine his fingertips like a bagel cutter. During her passage, however, Wist had diminished it to a gnarled vein of ore in the air, one that cut a jagged path to the other end of the rose garden. Almost as far as the eye could see.

This freed up large tracts of Shien land. If the hole had been a lake, she'd transformed it to a creek.

Nerium wore a long coat in a muted hue. The purplish equivalent of navy blue. Mourning clothes, I guess, although I wouldn't have called it lavender.

A certain pocket of my brain, one keen on escapism via irrelevant details, immediately seized on this. Did all Shiens have a full mourning wardrobe set aside for them, just in case? Did his coat smell musty from storage, or was it properly aired out? Had he known he'd be needing it? How had he gotten back to the estate so fast, anyway? Had Hazeldine called him?

Nerium moved his cane. He turned his body forty-five degrees back toward the manor.

He looked up at the glass-fronted gym.

The glaring magic on his spectacles found me. His expression seemed peaceful, sympathetic.

I stumbled away from the glass.

Before I knew what I was doing, I'd burst out through the doors of the gym.

My head rang. I told myself I was being hysterical. It didn't help that Wist's hair was being hysterical, too. It kept trying to do violent compressions on my torso, as if convinced I needed resuscitation.

"Looking for refuge?" said a voice on my right. Smack in the middle of my blind spot.

I wheeled and saw Lear. She stood like an idle sentry along the wall outside the gym doors.

"I thought—" I sounded breathless. Wist's hair kneaded at me harder, which only made it worse. "You—"

"Want to go someplace where no one will look for you?"

Wist was gone. I hadn't been the only one to witness her wrapping herself in the stuff of a vorpal hole like a corpse in a shroud. If her absence prolonged itself by hours or days or more, it would rapidly become an issue of national security.

Sooner or later, frenzied questions from the Shien clan would be the least of my worries. I'd fled Nerium's gaze, but I had no plan for where to go next. Of course I'd hide if I could.

"Sounds too good to be true," I said.

"They'll find you eventually. But it'll slow them down for a bit."

Between the remaining Shiens and a Jacian—hell, I'd try my luck with the Jacian.

She motioned for me to follow her.

Again, this was a prime chance for subversive foreign forces to kidnap or slaughter me. But even the simple act of temporarily making me difficult to locate would fit with my theory of Lear's mission in Osmanthus. To casually sow the seeds of disorder. To opportunistically amplify chaos and distress, but never in a way that would result in her shouldering serious blame.

Unfamiliar corridors passed in a blur. The parsimonious staffing made it easy to avoid people. We never saw another soul.

Lear kept glancing at the braid that crawled uneasily about my shoulders. "I take it that the Kraken is alive?" she said.

"Yeah. Sorry."

"I'd be much more disappointed if she died."

I could believe that. As a Jacian in the Shien household, as someone firmly established as being on the premises at the moment the Kraken erased herself, Lear would come under an uncomfortable degree of scrutiny in the event that the Osmanthian government declared their precious Kraken dead. Even if her personal record appeared faultless.

"Did you know Ficus was going to do that?" I asked.

"Do what?"

I stared until she gave in, or appeared to. "No. I didn't know."

"Really," I said, in Wist's flat voice.

"I'll tell you this: I found it odd that he announced his departure from the estate today."

"Why?"

"He usually comes and goes without a care for who might be inconvenienced by his appearance or disappearance."

"Does he have a death wish?" I demanded. "He's lucky Wist didn't—"

"Lucky?" Lear stopped walking. "The Kraken is renowned for her restraint. She has to be, doesn't she? She can't go around killing anyone who acts as a splinter in her side.

"Shien Ficus isn't just a creature of cruel caprice and wild luck. He must've been quite confident that your Kraken wouldn't destroy him in a fit of rage. Even a god isn't too scary if you know they won't smite you."

"But he made it so obvious," I said. "At dinner, and again today. He didn't take even the most elementary steps to hide his involvement."

"Obvious to who?" Lear inquired. "No one *saw* what he did to the Kraken."

"I—"

"You witnessed the effects of his actions. You didn't witness him doing it. He only became visible afterward. Lying there like a victim. Like any other innocent passerby who might've gotten swept up in the Kraken's spontaneous madness. People might start saying she went berserk."

"She didn't," I said sharply. "He lived, didn't he?"

"I know. Consider this: after he approached her, the Kraken's magic completely swamped the estate. No forensics team would ever discover the faintest trace of him skulking around undercover. He planned it out quite well, actually. He wouldn't need to guess at the specifics of her reaction in order to understand its general shape."

Shien Ficus had never struck me as being much of a plotter. Nerium, on the other hand—

"But don't let me keep you," said Lear.

She paused at a wide hallway that opened up past a heavy archway.

Unlike the pristine wooden moulding elsewhere in the manor, the arch consisted of unpainted white stone. Ornate though it was, it didn't depict anything recognizable. The stone had been carved into a throng of polyps and slender tendons, swellings like seed pods and other disconcertingly organic forms. Each time I thought I'd spotted a distended face, it turned out to be a trick of all those complex curves and shadows.

Lear pointed down the hallway beyond the arch.

"At the end, turn left. Keep going. If the next corridor is the exact same as the previous corridor, then turn right. If you spot even a single discrepancy, then turn left. Keep going, and eventually you'll get there."

I muttered under my breath until I understood what she'd meant. "What if I get it wrong?"

"You'll find yourself starting over. Just keep going." She indicated the hair clinging ropily to my back. "Might not take you long to reach the end. The corridors will be more lenient if they think you're a Shien."

I took a step toward the archway. "I should ask where you're sending me."

She thought for a moment. "To someone the Kraken hasn't seen since she was a tiny child."

She watched me steadily through hooded eyes. Her brief smile showed a thin glimpse of crooked teeth.

21

AT THE END of the first corridor, I turned left as instructed. This took me into a corridor that did appear to be the same as the first in every regard, including its curiously distasteful stone archway. At the end of that second corridor, I turned right.

And so on and so forth. No matter how far I walked, I remained blessedly alone.

Sometimes the differences between corridors were blatantly obvious. Snow and autumn leaves falling from magic chandeliers, for instance (a type of decoration I'd seen duplicated elsewhere in the mansion). A sound like rushing water, or the distracting scent of a cake baked to the point of charring.

When I didn't have to think much about whether to turn right or left, my mind drifted to Wist.

Wist was alive.

Wist would come back.

The problem, as always, was a matter of timing. What if her triumphant return happened as I lay on my deathbed, decades in the future? What if, in her experience, she'd only been gone half an hour? Oh, how bitter I'd be. Would I curse her?

In all likelihood, my Wist was still in one piece. She'd just gone out of reach.

It still felt like something had shattered. It still felt like something had died. This was not a sensation I could talk myself out of. It was a heavy thing, as concrete as a stomachache.

I gripped both ends of her braid as if using it to shoulder a burden twice my own weight.

Empirically, what was the difference between this and what had happened to Shien Miyu? What was the difference between this and Wist actually being dead to our world, dead to eternity?

Nothing but scraps of her living magic wriggling about my shoulders. Nothing but my own hole-ridden belief that it wasn't yet time to keel over against the nearest wall, wretched, inconsolable.

Did Wist really have any chance of retrieving her bond thread?

(Again, it had been mine in another life, but she clearly had way more attachment to it than I did. It just made sense for her to wear it as her own in this life, and she'd done so with a shy sort of pride.)

It might be salvageable—if objects that passed through vorpal holes got lost in liminal territory like stranded space junk. Not a bad metaphor. According to some folk beliefs, outer space and stars belonged to demons.

This seemed to me like false hope. A sports ball hurled through a vorpal hole wouldn't break windows in another universe. Vorpal holes represented erasure. A border of total elimination. A glimpse of the invisible ends of our world. A boundary that should never be exposed.

You couldn't just fall through the cracks into some strange and wonderful realm, or even into a terrible purgatory. Not without the power of a Kraken-class mage. The nature of those cracks was to filter out of existence all life and matter as we know it.

I'd heard alternate theories (especially regarding the origin of vorpal beasts), but why else would vorpal holes be so viscerally abhorrent?

After several trips through corridors where the solid-looking floor squished like mud, I reached a dead end.

No more branching hallways. No choice of right or left. Nothing but an unmarked door that seemed tailored to my height. It would've been painfully short for Wist, or most of the men of the family.

I was eager to leave behind the sonorous magic in those looping corridors. The lattice of cuttings formed layers as dense as something you might see in an archaeological dig. Dozens of mages had pitched in, presumably to reduce the likelihood of there being any single point of failure. They'd all contributed pieces of the same type of magic, but there were still tiny idiosyncrasies. My long walk had felt like being sung at from all sides by a mediocre community chorus, one where everyone either overshot or undershot their assigned notes.

I put my eyepatch back on. I took a fistful of Wist's braid in my hand, in hopes of seeming more like a Shien, and grabbed the knob.

It wasn't locked. Or if it was, it had yielded to the combination of my fingers and Wist's hair. I stepped inside and immediately pressed the door shut behind me.

The room felt cozy compared to most Shien suites. Even so, the ceilings were a good deal higher than the size of the door had implied. Airy bay windows pointed out toward a strangely sunny courtyard. One I was positive I'd never glimpsed before, though by logic it must've been visible from other angles of the house.

An elderly mage with very thick glasses sat in bed with her back propped up by embroidered cushions, most in fiery shades of red and hot pink. She wore a sparkly shawl over rounded shoulders.

She'd been doing something with her hands. She stopped. She regarded me with a faint and unhurried bemusement.

"Would you like to introduce yourself, dear?"

Her voice sounded strong enough to hold a good tune. Her hair was grayish-white, sure, but so was half of mine.

The light-distorting thickness of her glasses and her ensconcement in bed had made me jump to conclusions. I'd figured she was as old as Grandmother Shien—well past eighty, maybe past ninety.

Upon stepping closer, I rounded her age several decades down. She likely hailed from the same generation as Wist's adoptive parents. Midsixties or so; less than twice as old as me.

"I'm a healer," I said. Better keep it simple. "Asa Clematis."

There was a scarred sound to my voice. The price of swallowing that stabbing heat in my throat, again and again. I would not think of Wist.

"I'm a mage," said the seemingly bedridden woman. "Shien Riegel."

I noticed the following three details at the same time.

First, she had a coin-sized black mole near her jaw. Too large to be termed a beauty mark, but astonishingly round and perfect.

Second, the thing she'd been fiddling with was a tiny hat. Like a fedora sized for a cat, adorned with inexplicable growths of netting and feathery fluff. She wore a similar mini hat in her own hair, floating at an angle. Must've pinned it there.

Third, her magic core was in the wrong place. Not down near her lower back, but wedged high up between her ribs. Not only that, her branches—

This was Lear's second stunted mage. The one in the painting Wist had stared at. Wist had said: *I barely knew her.*

Possibilities exploded in my head like fireworks.

"Take your time," Shien Riegel said generously. "Look around. You came here to lie low, I expect. Did Lear the painter send you?" There was something oddly touching about how she phrased it as *Lear the painter* rather than *Lear the Jacian*.

"How'd you know?" I asked.

"Well, there aren't very many possible candidates."

She lowered her gaze to her little hat. The one she'd been busy decorating, not the one on her head. I took this as a silent invitation to familiarize myself with her quarters.

Every lamp—tall standing lamps, hanging lamps, table lamps—wore a heavy shade of old-fashioned stained glass. Floral patterns, mostly, interspersed with fruit and colorful insects.

On a side table between sets of windows, a dark porcelain vase held a mass of white chrysanthemums. For Miyu, I assumed. The room smelled of incense, as if someone had burned it to mask more vexing odors. The air felt several degrees warmer than the rest of the manor. I wouldn't have been surprised to see the window glass all fogged up.

The windows remained clear. We were in a secret room with a view of a secret courtyard, one that at other times of year would've been marvelously green.

I gave up on attempting to deduce where I was in the manor. Someone with keener architectural and spatial awareness might've had a better shot at it—but the magic obfuscating Shien Riegel's location would've rendered the whole effort moot.

Sliding doors opened onto what looked like a sewing room. Couldn't see much of it. Here in the bedroom, tiny hats and frilly fascinators covered tiered cake stands like a plethora of uneaten snacks. More headgear than any one person could possibly wear in a lifetime.

"If you don't mind me asking questions..." I began.

"I'm not busy," said Shien Riegel, "and I enjoy company. Go ahead, dear."

"Did you already know who I was?"

"I couldn't be sure without hearing it from you directly." She patted her hair meaninglessly, as though flustered. "Would you like a mini hat? A lot of people think it won't suit them. But it's all in how you wear it. There are tricks, you see. Certain angles. You don't need to be a girly-girl to make it work."

She peered at me hopefully.

"All the same," I said, "I'll pass for now. Kind of you to offer."

There was a growing distance in me, one reminiscent of the period after I'd first lost my eye. I couldn't do anything to stop it. Felt like looking out the back window of an express train as it hurtled down unchangeable tracks. The next stop wouldn't arrive for a long time to come.

The infinite frayed edges where our bond had torn apart began to seem like a tragedy happening inside an enclosure at a zoo. Some poor clumsy soul had fallen in and was getting shredded by carnivores. Horrible, but separated from my thinking mind by walls and railings and a very deep moat.

This made it both easier and harder to decide what to say next. There were so many things I could ask Shien Riegel and her army of tiny hats.

I pulled up a chair.

She had no obligation to give me refuge. But as far as I could tell, she hasn't raised any alarms, hadn't summoned other Shiens. For that alone, I'd better be grateful.

"Listen," I told her. "Dunno how much you know about me. Like I said, I'm a healer. A really, really good healer. If you're interested, I can…" I stumbled over how to phrase this. "I can take a look at your magic. Can't make any promises. But I might be able to give you a slightly different kind of relief."

She didn't stint at all when she smiled. "That's lovely," she said. "You're as lovely as I thought."

"Er, don't expect much. I've never treated a—" Would it be insulting to call her a stunted mage to her face? "—a mage like you," I finished feebly.

"That's all right," said Shien Riegel. "I'd love to say yes. It'd be a wonderful experience, I'm sure. Wisteria is such an extreme outlier that she's almost like a stunted mage herself, isn't she? Or the opposite of a stunted mage. An overgrown mage. One could argue that her magic's afflicted with a type of gigantism. So your understanding of how best to heal her might be quite useful for others suffering from anomalous magic.

"But there's nothing you can do for me, I'm afraid," she continued, apologetic. "Please don't feel badly about it. I'm bonded, you see."

A bonded healer could still act as a free agent of sorts. I could heal any mage I pleased. Bonded mages, however, couldn't be healed by anyone other than their bondmate.

The more I learned about the art of bond authentication, the more I'd come to respect the fact that—first and foremost—the bond status of random strangers was really none of my business. People's reasons for bonding or not bonding could be deeply complex and private and painful. Besides, you just couldn't know merely by looking. Your initial perception might mislead you. Better not to make assumptions.

I took a breath and decided to start with the hardest part first.

22

"THAT VINE." I kept my tone nonchalant. "It's a wisteria, isn't it?"

A climbing vine grew all over a wooden pergola in the courtyard. The old gnarled trunk had a density of texture like poured concrete.

"It's not blooming," Riegel said.

Indeed: the vine was naked, with wild offshoots ripe for winter pruning. Shriveled gray-brown seed pods dangled like bait strung on fishing lines.

I jabbed my thumb at a corner. "That floor lamp has a wisteria pattern, too."

"It's a common theme for works of stained glass."

I held my tongue, unsure of how to continue.

This was not a situation where I'd be happy blurting something I could never take back.

Shien Riegel was the fifth mage I'd felt in Follyhope. She hadn't materialized in this room overnight. And by extension—Ficus hadn't been creeping around the manor yesterday, hidden by his imperceptibility skill. At least not while the Void took over my senses.

I'd speculated that the clan was keeping Miyu locked up, and I hadn't been totally off the mark. They did have a secret captive—one a full generation older. Dunno if Riegel saw herself as a prisoner, but she might've been here a very long time.

Why hide her from the world?

A branch-bearing mage too crippled to wield magic might, in the eyes of the Shien clan, be an embarrassing abomination. But it probably wasn't just that.

Rightly or wrongly, stunted mages were thought to be a sign of inbreeding.

Magical inbreeding had its own parameters, ones quite different from genetic inbreeding. Blood-related mage lineages would magically fall apart over time, even if they remained healthy (and non-incestuous) in a purely genetic sense. The mechanism behind that remains poorly understood to this day.

Mage eugenics was a huge priority for Osmanthus in olden times, but it ended in disaster. The harder scientists tried to engineer multi-branch mages, the more brittle and berserk-prone they turned out. Long-dead generations of the Shien clan would've been among the worst affected. Most clans nowadays relied heavily on adoption to ensure sufficient dilution of the bloodline.

On the flip side—although I can't say if statistics actually bear this out—the children of stunted mages were much more likely to be blessed with powerful magic than children born to any other parents.

"I know what you're thinking," Riegel said.

"Then tell me. Please."

"I only met Wisteria a few times, when she was very young. She called me Aunt Riegel."

"Is that what she should've called you?"

"I quite liked it." Light from the window reflected off her bottle-bottom glasses. "Tell me, do you see a resemblance?"

"I don't know." I pictured Wist. "No. Not at all."

It all made too much sense. The lack of information about Wist's birth parents. Her aversion to learning more.

They could've disguised Wist's induction into the family as an adoption from strangers in order to obscure her parentage. To hide the fact that the prestigious Shien clan had spawned, and was now sheltering—or imprisoning—a stunted mage.

This might in turn also explain why the Shien clan, despite fierce competition, had been best positioned to nab the child who would become the Kraken.

Wist's braid lay across my neck and arms, breathing in and out like a sleeping animal.

"On the way here," I said, "I tricked myself. I'd see staircases branching off from one corridor. In the next corridor, I'd see the same thing, and I'd think the stairs' angle had shifted. But nothing had changed. Every time I turned the wrong way, I got punted back to the beginning, and I had to face a brand new set of corridors."

"I'm awfully sorry for the trouble." She sounded genuinely disheartened.

"Say, mind if I call you Aunt Riegel?"

She revived like a wilted plant in water. "Of course not! I would love that."

"I feel like I'm out in your corridors again, Aunt Riegel. Seeing things that aren't there. Thinking myself into a corner."

My revelation might be nothing more than a passing illusion.

"It would explain a whole lot if you were her mother," I said. "But life doesn't always come together that cleanly, does it? Anyway, if she'd secretly been born within the clan—no matter how convoluted it got, they would definitely have found some way to register her with her family name first. To mark her more strongly as a true Shien."

Her smile deepened. It was less sunny than before, but also more knowing. "Yes. Although I would've been a very proud parent if Wisteria were my daughter."

"Because she's the Kraken?"

"Because she drank all the poison this clan poured down her throat," Riegel said easily, "and never let it taint her."

"Sometimes a wisteria vine is just a vine," I said. "But..."

"Yes?"

"When she got adopted—I don't suppose you had a hand in naming her?"

She adjusted her glasses and said, not without a touch of smugness, "That's between me and Hosanna."

"Uh, who?"

"Oh—I'm sorry. Lady Shien. Wisteria's grandmother."

"And your mother?" I guessed.

"And my mother."

Although we'd tabled the question of Wist's birth parents, there were still a ton of other things I wanted to ask her. Before I could launch my next barrage, Riegel ordered me rather sternly to go to an adjoining room and fetch snacks.

I wheeled in a cart laden with a water pitcher and glasses and dainty foodstuffs. Fruit sandwiches full of sweet cream, carrot pudding, ramekins of citrusy mushrooms. The kitchen staff used a magical porter to send Riegel fresh-made provisions. A far cry from Wist's makeshift dinner—or the rations I'd eaten in prison, for that matter.

I drank a full glass of water in one go. Took a while to catch my breath afterward. Hadn't realized how thirsty I'd gotten.

"I was still a student the first time I came to Follyhope," I said. "Were you here in this room? Even back then?"

"Oh, yes."

"And Wist knew?"

"I suppose she did."

At the time, I'd been too preoccupied with Wist—and with dodging her Shien siblings—to do much exploring on my own. But it wouldn't have shocked me to learn that they had a whole basement full of chained-up prisoners, if not outright skeletons.

Riegel's face creased into a frown. "Now, don't think poorly of Wisteria for not mentioning it. I'm sure she was taught from a young age not to speak of me. She wouldn't fear the consequences for herself—she'd worry about what it might mean for me."

She might never have met Wist as an adult, but she certainly had Wist's number.

I took the anonymous letter out of my jacket.

"You wrote this."

I waited for her to deny it. I'd wanted to catch her by surprise.

"Ah," she murmured. "It's been a while since I sent that."

"I was going to ignore it," I informed her. "Even if I didn't, I could've stumbled around the estate for weeks without finding you. When I first looked around this room, I thought maybe you were going to come busting out with big claims about Wist's heritage. Well, apparently not. I'm kind of lost."

"However it happened, you're here now," Riegel said. "I was fortunate."

"Is it actually me that you wanted to see?" I asked, bewildered. "Not Wist? Why?"

I scanned her letter again.

Dearest Magebreaker... That stupid monoceros crest looked like a finger pointed to mock me.

...a chance to put your recent studies into practice. The best way to become comfortable with a new skill is simply to....

"I'm not Wisteria's mother, biological or otherwise. But I do have children," said Shien Riegel.

"Okay," I said, uncomprehending.

"They're adults. Perhaps I shouldn't worry. They tell me I'm in no position to get anxious about anyone else. It's bad for my health. But I dwell on it. I'm very good at dwelling on things; it's one of my great hobbies, second only to millinery. Millinery of a more diminutive sort."

"Your children," I prompted.

"I get especially worried about my youngest. Are all parents like that, you think?"

"I haven't the foggiest idea. No kids here. And I'm an only child, to boot. Bet you already knew that."

She looked down, flushing. She had a strikingly transparent face, as if the solitude of this room had eroded her ability to conceal her feelings. She wrung her hands weakly on top of the bed covers.

"The truth is, I'm a failure as a parent. Thank goodness I'm not Wisteria's mother. She can do better, really. Parents ought to never rely on their children. Parents ought to let their children go, set them free. I'd like to fix my mistakes, Ms. Asa. I really would. That's why I wrote to you."

The last thing she'd eaten was a buttery finger sandwich with a walnut filling that looked just like meat drenched in sauce. A few nut crumbs had tumbled into bed with her, but I suspected she couldn't see them. I leaned forward and plucked them away, one by one, without saying anything.

There was still a miserable heat in her face. She wasn't trying to be coy. She'd told me everything I needed to know.

Shien Riegel had a bondmate.

While I wasn't intimately familiar with the lives of stunted mages, it couldn't be terribly common for them to take bondmates. Bonding wouldn't cure them. Their healer partner would receive less reflected glory than they could from any other eligible mage.

I knew only one healer at Follyhope who appeared to be tied to a mystery bondmate.

"Danver," I said.

Riegel tensed.

"Is her full name Shien Danver?"

A small nod.

"She's not just staff," I said in conclusion. "She's family."

I'd pictured Danver as a covert Shien. Nerium's daughter, and maybe his bondmate.

I'd been missing a crucial piece of the puzzle. She was a Shien daughter, yes. Riegel's daughter.

Stunted mages were by no means guaranteed to exclusively conceive magical children. They could birth subliminals, too, and they could birth healers. Riegel must've had Danver very late in life, but the math just barely worked out.

Your recent studies...

Riegel hadn't been referring to my laborious efforts to retain more Jacian vocab. Or maybe she'd been alluding to that, too, but it had nothing to do with her primary purpose.

She knew—somehow—of my notary training. Of how I'd attempted to educate myself on the anatomy of mage-healer bonds, all for the sake of one day discovering a way to dissect and disassemble them.

I wanted to find out as soon as possible if I'd gotten this completely wrong.

"Danver is your daughter," I said. "And your bondmate. Since childhood?"

"Heavens, no!" Riegel shook her head so hard that I thought those heavy glasses of hers would go flying off. She cupped her cheeks, distressed.

"She's not your bondmate?"

"She is—she is, but not ever since she was little. I couldn't ask a child to…"

I waited for her to pull herself together.

When I got tired of waiting, I said: "Let's give you the benefit of the doubt. Let's posit that she came to you as a legal adult. She said something like, *Mom, I'm sick of seeing you in pain all the time. Mom, I'm a healer. Let me help you. I'll heal you better if we're bonded.*"

I stopped. "Or," I said, lower and slower, "or she came to you crying. Maybe Miyu wanted to bond her. Or Ficus. Or someone from a distant branch of the family, or a different clan altogether. Maybe she was scared of them, or scared of getting sent away from you. Maybe she needed an excuse to dodge other would-be bondmates, and a reason to stay forever at Follyhope."

Riegel dabbed at her eyes, bumping her glasses.

"Children can choose to care for sickly parents." Her voice cracked. "But they shouldn't have to. If they choose it, it shouldn't take the form of an ironclad lifelong obligation, one that no one can annul, no matter what changes, no matter what happens.

"I agreed to it, and so did Danny. I'd have done anything to protect her, with what little power I possess. Yet so much can change in just a few years."

"Let me guess. Miyu bonded Ginko instead."

She sniffled helplessly. "Poor dear Ginko. And look what's happened now. If Danny did bond her own mother to avoid getting trapped with—with someone like Miyu, well, what about after the storm passes? What if I live as long as Hosanna, or longer still? God forbid. I'm not healthy enough to last *that* long, I can promise that much, but every extra day, every extra week—it feels like time I've stolen from the rest of Danny's life."

If Riegel were indeed in her sixties, and she went on to live as long as Grandmother Shien, that'd be close to another thirty years (and counting—Grandmother hadn't kicked the bucket yet). Longer than Danver's entire life so far.

I mulled over the anonymous letter.

I folded it up and put it away again. My hands were unsteady.

I knew what she wanted from me.

Laughter burbled up in the incense-scented air. My own laughter, cold and unhappy. Tears stung the corners of both my eyes, full and empty alike.

23

Shien Riegel let me laugh my little head off. She leaned over and fished a clean handkerchief out of her nightstand. She didn't even try to interrupt.

"You want me to break your bond," I stated. "With your daughter."

She nodded unhappily.

Far too many mages were like Miyu. There were nevertheless some bondmates who—within the parameters of that inimitable closeness—managed to treat each other as valued coworkers. Or even as equals. In their own eyes, if not in the eyes of society.

A mother-daughter bond didn't necessarily have to be a disaster. But it would be unbalanced from the start, touchy and tender. Smothering on both sides, despite their best efforts.

They'd had their reasons for bonding, and those reasons must've been good enough for them at the time. Not my place to question it. But I could also see why Riegel might regret it, why she might resort to extreme measures to avoid burdening her daughter for the rest of her life.

Under different circumstances, I might've taken her plea as an invigorating challenge.

"My own bond just got broken," I said.

I'd expected this to shock and stump her. Instead she looked curiously at Wist's hair preening as it wound about my arms.

Lear had mentioned trying to get Danver and Ginko to watch Wist close the vorpal hole. If Danver had witnessed the tail end of it, and didn't completely block her mind off from her mother, then of course Riegel would already have some idea of what had happened. Why I'd fled here.

Although she couldn't have known my bond was broken until I confirmed it with my own traitorous mouth.

I bowed my head to her, clutching my knees. "Don't tell anyone. I shouldn't have—"

"Not even Danny?"

"Not anyone—please."

It was impossible to have a bondmate and maintain a wholly untouched mind. Even if you were both squeamish, even if you tried your utmost to be as respectful as possible, there would come times when you tracked footprints through each other's fresh-fallen snow.

It was impossible to remain unaffected by the human presence of your bondmate.

But you could still learn how to keep secrets.

Riegel patted my hand. "I won't tell. Raise your head."

Relief flooded me like adrenaline. I was ashamed at how readily I believed her.

"Given the way it feels so far," I said jerkily, "I have—I have some trouble recommending it."

"Being ripped limb from limb by monstrous forces surely feels different from being bisected by a clean and sharpened blade."

I felt neither clean nor sharp. "Am I a blade? Hah. You flatter me." I swallowed. "I've noodled away at the notion of bondbreaking for a couple years now. Today was my biggest breakthrough yet. Want your bond erased? Leap in a vorpal hole. That'll do it."

Which was same as telling her to go die in a fire. Only Wist had magic proven to stave off the total annihilation promised by vorpal holes.

Wist wasn't here now.

"I'm kidding," I added. Just in case. "I can't break bonds on my own yet. Might never discover how. Frankly, I'd give up the possibility in an instant if that'd be enough of a sacrifice to bring Wist back."

"She's only been gone for a few hours," Riegel said mildly.

I was sweating, the kind of sweat that takes you straight from high noon heat to midnight ice. I wondered if the abrupt loss of a bond could make you physically ill—if it could invite invisible infection in the same way as a vast open wound.

"It's impressive that you've guessed at what I've been trying to do," I said. "With studying bonds. Far as I can tell, you're the only one. A normal, sensible person wouldn't ever suspect me of attempted bondbreaking. It's just so far beyond the pale."

"I am thoroughly sensible." Riegel held her head a little higher. Then she looked down as if trying to scrutinize her own core like a crystal ball.

"Could be a side effect of being a stunted mage," she said. "I fall at the very end of the bell curve. Maybe I'm primed to think more seriously about strange possibilities."

She gave me an unexpectedly impish smile. "It isn't that enormous of a leap, is it? You're already known as the Magebreaker. Why wouldn't you try to break other things, too?"

"You know an awful lot about me."

"I'm not in solitary confinement. I get more visitors than you might think. Danver overhears a lot, too, and she asks questions on my behalf. Hosanna lets me keep up a certain amount of correspondence with the outside world, as long as I stay anonymous. I've written to many of the same academics you work with."

Her tone turned mournful. "As an intellectual exercise, mini hats leave something to be desired. It's important to have multiple outlets for one's energies."

"Uh-huh," I said emptily. I tugged at Wist's braid around my neck as though loosening a tie at the end of a long day.

I was tempted to ask Riegel for help with escaping Follyhope. I desperately wished I could port myself off Shien territory.

But I wouldn't leave even if I could—I'd stay in this den of vipers. Follyhope was where Wist had exited our world for vorpal realms. Follyhope was most likely to be the site of her return.

I just needed to hold out till then. Somehow.

"I can't promise to help you," I told Shien Riegel. "Can't even think about it right now. Maybe someday. I'm sorry, for whatever it's worth. This is a really bad time."

"*Maybe someday* is more than enough," she said. "It was always a fragile hope."

I looked at her anew.

A sweet old lady—okay, not that old. Right around the same age as my own parents. Being propped up in bed created an impression of decrepitude, but she had remarkably good skin. Her eyes were quite keen behind the distortion of those old-fashioned lenses.

"If I could break a bond like snapping my fingers—just like that—things would be different," I said. "Hey, I'd do it pro bono. But I've gotta wonder. Were you planning on offering me anything in exchange? Or were you hoping I'd be inspired to help out of the goodness of my heart?"

A smart knock sounded at the door before she could answer.

Riegel gestured at her sewing room. I shrugged to indicate that I had no intention of running off to hide in a crevice.

I'd known the other Shiens would track me down eventually. My reprieve could only last so long.

"Come in," Riegel called.

Nerium and his cane stepped inside. That deep purple coat still hung from his shoulders. My immediate instinct was to tell Wist who'd shown up. But my inner voice stayed trapped like an insect in tree sap.

There was no one listening.

There was no bond.

There was no Wist.

"Aunt Riegel," Nerium said. "So good to see you."

"You saw me yesterday, too," she said crisply.

"It's no less of a pleasure to see you today as well. Lovely hat." He touched the side of his own threadbare head, as though he too wore a tiny hat in the same place as her.

"You always say that."

"Because your hats are always lovely. May I borrow Asa Clematis?"

"Would you like to be borrowed?" Riegel asked me.

"Don't think I've got much of a choice."

Riegel gave Nerium a stern glare. "She's a guest. Don't you dare mistreat her."

"Of course not," he replied smoothly. He tipped his head at me. "Whatever anyone else may say or do, I'll look out for you, Asa Clematis. It's what Wisteria would have wanted."

"Don't talk like she's dead." I paused. "If you thought she were dead, you should've started off by offering proper condolences."

"If *you* thought she were dead," he said, matching my tone, "you'd be running after Ficus with an axe in hand, and I doubt any of us would be quick enough to stop you."

Wist's braid rustled about my shoulders. I knew for a fact that he'd taken note of it. His voice softened—a shift which did nothing to reassure me. "You know Wisteria best."

"Better than you lot, that's for sure."

"Indeed. Personally, I'm inclined to trust your judgment. But I'm afraid you'll find that not everyone is quite so optimistic about Wisteria's prospects. The longer her absence lasts—"

I got up. "You don't have to spell it out."

I made him wait while I poured Riegel another glass of water. I wheeled our leftovers back where they belonged.

"Are you ready?" he inquired. He'd been left standing with his cane all the while.

"Wish I had that axe you mentioned."

He smiled beatifically. "Come along, then. I'll defend you, and so will Wisteria's trimmings. There's no need for violence."

Wist's hair bristled like an angry cat.

We bid farewell to Shien Riegel. The ancient vine in her courtyard looked desolate, like it had never sprouted a single green leaf in its life. She and her sparkling tiny hats watched placidly as we left.

My legs moved as usual. Some other self in some other dimension seemed to be endlessly collapsing without anyone to catch her. I pitied her in the way you might pity an earthworm trying to cross a city sidewalk. Good luck not getting stepped on.

Wist's braid was still very warm. As warm as it would've gotten when soaking up sunlight. While we lazed together on one of her many tower roofs, for instance. I was grateful that I could close my fists around her hair as hard as I liked without hurting it.

I was also grateful, bizarrely enough, to sense the Void lingering in the unlit depths of my skull like some great eldritch evil lurking on the dark side of the moon.

Bond or no bond, the Void was always with me. If everything went to hell in Wist's absence—well, I wouldn't need to rely on Shien Nerium to protect me. I wouldn't need an axe to cause havoc.

24

WE STEPPED OUT of Riegel's room and into a luminous atrium. This space bore zero resemblance to the maze of corridors that had originally carried me to her door. Glistening water ran down the glass, blurring the scenery beyond into a blobby abstraction.

Nerium's cane echoed as it met the hard, gleaming floor. Sunlight bent sinuously wherever it hit the watery veil clinging to the inner curves of the birdcage-shaped ceiling.

"She's a bit prickly," he said once we were a few paces away from the door. "Perhaps only towards me."

"For good reason, I'm sure."

"I'm always on my best behavior."

"If you haven't fooled her, she must be an excellent judge of character."

He pointed at the bridge of his nose. "She does wear the glasses I gave her."

"With such old-fashioned lenses?"

"She won't let me update them."

I wavered. Then I said it anyway. "It was you, wasn't it."

He listened politely.

"You scared Wist off," I continued. "When she was still very young. You convinced her that Aunt Riegel would be horribly punished for showing her kindness."

Wist had been six when she came to the Shien clan. Nerium, the oldest of her new siblings, was already eighteen (followed by Ficus at fifteen, Miyu at thirteen, then three more). Despite all of Wist's raw malleable magic, she'd never stood a chance.

Nerium knew I wasn't done yet.

"All that energy," I said. "All that effort, just to deceive a tiny underfed child. You would've ordered her to prove how sorry she was for going in rooms where she wasn't allowed.

"You made her write apologies on herself with a box cutter. For visiting Aunt Riegel, and for other made-up transgressions. She invented a crude skill to wipe away surface-level wounds. You forced her to keep reusing the same patches of skin where no one would look.

"She was a little kid. Her magic couldn't completely cure all those cuts, could it? Turned out like trying to rub bad markers off a dry-erase board."

In adulthood, her scars were subtle. Only visible under certain types of sunlight. I couldn't make out individual words, or even letters. But the scars were still very much there. I'd seen them. I'd touched them.

It might have started as punishment for sneaking off to see Riegel. It might have started some other time. They'd invented so many ways to torment her. When she devised countermeasures, they upped the ante. Early on, they stapled paper fairy wings to the skin of her back—a mocking costume. Three years later, they nailed her to the wall of an unused shed.

Nerium slipped his glasses off and dangled them by their stems. "Are you the same person you were at eighteen?" he asked.

My answer: a bleat of laughter. Keep pursuing this line of inquiry, and he'd bring up my involvement with the death of a Board member.

I was perfectly aware of my own sins, including plenty he couldn't possibly care about. I'd turned my back on Ginko—without ever learning her name—the last time I left Follyhope. I'd crushed a brilliant healer to death inside a place of worship; she'd been a true generational talent. I'd invited the Void to take up residence in my empty eye socket. I could never evict it, and it would always urge me to feed on Wist.

What else?

"You don't have to believe me," Nerium said, "but I've always looked out for Aunt Riegel. I've always given extra consideration to those left vulnerable through no fault of their own."

From the moment he met Wist, he'd seen only her magic, only her future potential. He'd envisioned the Kraken in her before anyone else.

Never in a million years would he have viewed anything he'd done to her as punching down. She'd bounced back from all of it, hadn't she?

He'd fed her rat poison and paint thinner. Sometimes with *try this, it'll be delicious* and sometimes with *bad children need to take their medicine* and sometimes with *I'm only giving you what you deserve* and sometimes with *pass this test, and you'll never have to do it again.*

Her magic always bulldozed a path to survival, in the end. But she never passed his tests. She suffered too quietly, or not quietly enough. She cried or didn't cry in all the wrong ways. She never proved herself worthy of her extraordinary power—as if a child, or anyone, could ever do something to truly deserve it.

"So you warned Wist away," I said, "to protect Aunt Riegel's delicate psyche?"

"Imagine, if you can, being a stunted mage." He didn't sound tremendously confident in my ability to imagine this. "A stunted mage born into the Shien clan, no less. Imagine being hidden away like a leper—and only after enduring much worse. Seclusion at home is the compassionate solution."

"Compared to being institutionalized?"

"Compared to how stunted mages got treated in Aunt Riegel's youth." The brown of his eyes again gave me that sun-bleached impression, weary and faded. "Wisteria really latched on to her. Facing a child like that, being loved by a child like that—"

"A child like what?"

"A future Kraken. What could hurt Aunt Riegel more than the mere fact of her existence? The volume of magic given to one ignorant little girl—who could tolerate the sheer iniquity of it all?"

"You sure couldn't," I muttered.

"It was a dangerous situation," Nerium said. "The most fortunate mage in thousands of years, and one of the least fortunate mages ever born with the Shien name. Aunt Riegel might have been gripped by a compulsion to restore balance. To wound Wisteria. To bring her lower."

"You would," I said, "if you were Riegel. But would she?"

"I've known Aunt Riegel slightly longer than you have."

"*You* can't use the excuse of being a stunted mage born under a cursed star, or whatever you meant with your talk of good luck and bad luck. Wist's fortunes took a drastic turn for the worse as soon as she got tacked on to your family register."

"We understand things so very differently," Nerium said softly. "I believe in my heart that Wisteria ended up in the best possible place for her, the only possible place for her. We saved her from becoming a monster. We saved her from becoming a tyrant. Any other family would have coddled and worshipped and spoiled her beyond repair."

"I've heard that before," I said. "It was gross then, and it's gross now."

For the first time, I found myself glad that Wist had left. If she were still in this world, if our bond were intact, my disgust at him would've swamped her like light leaking through these watery walls. That light came from—from somewhere, anyhow, defying the physical shape of the building, and the fact that we were supposed to be staring down the improbable halls of Riegel's maze.

"Anything else?" Nerium put his glasses back on. He tapped the floor with his cane as though making a call to order. "Let's clear the air, shall we?"

Simple insults and recrimination would zip past him like mayflies.

"Maybe there's another reason you kept Wist away from Aunt Riegel," I said. "You know what they say about stunted mages."

His thin-lipped smile began to look bloodless.

"Maybe," I went on, "you suspected them of being related. You and I do think alike at times, don't we? Maybe that's why you had to tear them apart. Why you worked so hard to keep Wist beaten down. You feared that she was a legitimate Shien child, after all, behind all the secrecy of her supposed adoption."

The creases around his mouth still looked taut. He answered with a measured air of indulgence. "No part of you truly believes that Wisteria is Aunt Riegel's daughter."

"Merely a passing fancy. Bet you had the same idea, though. You wouldn't have taken it lightly."

Nerium clasped his hands atop his cane.

"All these years later," he lamented, "and still you misjudge me."

I wondered if he would move closer. We were very much alone.

So what if he did? I didn't regret speaking frankly. Any damage he'd ever done to me had been collateral in nature. A way of getting to Wist—who was now far out of reach.

I felt almost freakishly unafraid. I had Wist's hair wrapped warm around me. Inside me lay the Void, like the dark dregs at the bottom of a bitter drink. Inside me lay the burning sheared-off edges of a broken bond, and a detachment that stretched far, far beyond the horizon of all my senses. Without Wist here, no other Shien could disturb my waters.

25

MY INDIFFERENCE would soon be tested.

We convened in a grand office. By we, I mean me and Nerium and Ficus and Doctor Hazeldine. And—behind a great desk—the head of the clan. Everyone's grandmother. Lady Shien Hosanna.

Lear and Danver and Ginko had been excluded from this meeting. They'd gotten lumped in with the rest of the Follyhope staff, who were already sworn to have seen and heard nothing. Didn't matter even if they tried to go rogue—Grandmother would keep a tight rein on attempts to communicate outside the estate.

The Shiens took seats. Ficus, wearing ragged jeans, had a scornful look that would've fit well in an ad for designer cologne. The dandy doctor glowed with an appreciation for vitamins, sunlight, exercise, and beard oil. Then there was Nerium, who on his best days still appeared distinctly froggy. No matter where they went, the other two would overshadow him. Which, I suspected, was exactly how he liked it.

I stood off to one side, in a place with a clear path to the exit. I wouldn't actually be able to make it out of here by bolting like a rabbit, not with four mages watching me. But it gave me an empty sort of comfort to mentally simulate my escape route.

Wist's braid curled into a tight spiral shape like a turtle shell on my back. A futile attempt to hide from probing eyes. I remained as still as possible, radiating all the life and vivacity of a houseplant.

Grandmother was in a familiar-looking office chair. The kind that wouldn't seem like anything special unless you happened to know a thing or two about luxury furniture. In that case, you might recognize it as one of the most expensive chairs in the world.

Wist owned the same model—although hers was a bootleg; she'd conjured it out of thin air. I saw no observable difference between this legit brand-name piece and Wist's magically manufactured fake.

Grandmother was separated from the others by her huge curved desk. The surface tilted toward her like an architect's drafting table, fitted with living scrolls angled so only she could read them.

Wall panels around the room were painted with larger-than-life renditions of previous family heads. They all wore mage robes, though the length and hues and layers and embroidery varied from era to era.

Up above, a spacious triangular skylight illuminated a choir of small birds, some vividly colored and some dull. The space below the ceiling must've been connected to the aviary Nerium had mentioned.

Toxic birds, he'd said. How toxic? Could they kill you by touching you? By pooping on you? The birds rarely stopped moving and never stopped chattering. Speaking of poop, I saw one casually drop a gift for us—but a magical force field vaporized it mid-air. Whew.

Nerium claimed to have received word that Wist's tower still stood tall in its usual place. No one outside Follyhope had any notion that something might've happened to the Kraken.

"It's not unusual for Wisteria to make herself briefly unavailable," he said. "She might disappear to complete a classified mission in a distant country. She might collapse from exhaustion after a marathon of vorpal hole extermination."

I didn't like Nerium knowing this much about Wist's habits.

Then he looked at me, which I liked even less. "Does Wisteria often put herself through vorpal holes?"

"Dunno about often," I said, "but she's done it before."

"And she came back unharmed."

"Obviously. Unless you think the Wist you saw today was a revenant."

"How long did it take?" he asked.

My throat clenched. Doctor Hazeldine glanced at me through his monocle (not unkindly). Ficus stared up at Grandmother's collection of toxic birds like a cat torn over which to kill first.

"Might've been a few months," I said at last. "I was in prison at the time."

It wouldn't take Nerium long to dig for intel about the most notable of Wist's mysterious absences. Better save my lies for something they'd have a harder time disproving.

Now everyone had their eyes on me. Including Grandmother Shien. She'd shrunk a little, these past few years, but otherwise appeared much the same. Buzz-cut hair, small black eyes, lightly powdered brows, skin like crumpled brown paper, and never a smile.

"Call her back," she said.

Oh, god. "With all due respect," I answered, cringing, "bonds don't seem to transmit anything across vorpal borders."

"Call her back," Grandmother repeated.

"I've tried. Believe me."

I'd put myself in the same untenable position as Ginko: lying to cover up a broken bond.

I suddenly had no idea whether my acting skills were up to snuff. Could I really trust Riegel to keep her mouth shut? Did I have any hope of pulling this off?

The birds under the skylight sounded high and mocking. They lined up on horizontal beams that resembled entire tree trunks stripped of bark. I'd never seen beams like those, round and tapered, retaining all the curves and imperfections of a living tree. Would be great if one could come crashing down to end the conversation.

"Your bond is useless," Grandmother said. "Yet you claim she'll return."

"She came back before."

"Let's hope that Wisteria sees fit to reemerge in a timely manner."

As she spoke, she flicked a look at Ficus. He shot her a rare grin.

I couldn't tell if she already knew of his involvement. Either way, I had no intention of lobbing accusations. Grandmother might decide that he was more trouble than he'd ever been worth. But if he were going to get excommunicated from the family anyway, he'd take me down with him. The safest approach would be to say nothing.

"Ten days," stated Grandmother Shien.

No one asked what she meant.

She regarded each of us in turn, and appeared to find each of us wanting.

"Ten days is the longest I can reasonably hold off any inquiries about Wisteria's whereabouts."

So we were here to give a vow of silence. To pray that Wist would pop back up before her absenteeism became impossible to ignore. Before government bodies got antsy about national security risks. Before rival families began attacking the Shiens for mishandling their Kraken.

Doctor Hazeldine asked tentatively what would happen ten days later. Grandmother moved her head at Nerium. Her neck seemed to possess a very limited range of motion.

"In the absence of decisive evidence, it would normally take years for a missing person to be declared dead," Nerium said.

"Dead?" I demanded. "Why even say that? You know she's not—"

"In this case, of course, the powers that be will be deeply invested in uncovering all available evidence. One doesn't always need a body to serve as incontrovertible proof of death. Consider what happened just yesterday. You yourself provided that proof for Miyu."

"That's totally different. You can't compare Miyu with the Kraken."

"It would be best for all of us if Wisteria shows up again before people start asking questions. Should there still be no sign of her, we'll have to explain her disappearance. The government's next obvious step—given the circumstances—would be to order a formal examination of her bondmate."

My voice came out as a squeak. "But her magic—"

"Yes. It would be utterly unprecedented for a mage to go missing, their bond confirmed broken by a notary, and yet for any cuttings they've left behind to remain functional." Nerium spread his hands. "Who can say where the law would come down on that?

"In some ways, it's a moot point. You said that she previously went missing for months. It doesn't matter if she's gone for years—the Board will stop at nothing to cover it up for as long as humanly possible. Poor Lear won't ever be allowed to return to Jace."

"I'm still bonded," I lied. "She's alive. I can feel it."

"If a notary comes to examine you, I hope you'll face them as calmly as Ginko," Nerium murmured. "I wonder—will you still be bonded then?"

Grandmother spoke. "If you're unbonded, your bonding rights will pass to the clan."

"To me, specifically," Nerium said.

"As per request," said Grandmother.

"I'll fight you for it," Ficus announced. He'd produced his yo-yo knife again. It dangled from his fingers and minced about in the air like a marionette.

"Ficus," Nerium said patiently, "you don't want Asa Clematis. You just want a fight."

"So give me one."

A shadow passed over the skylight.

"Don't be greedy."

The moment Nerium said this, even those poisonous little birds recoiled into silence. The only sound in the office came buzzing from the magic-woven thread on Ficus's knife.

I should've protested, should've kept insisting I was still bonded. But every permutation of those words died at the back of my mouth. Nothing I could say would further delay the moment when a notary would come to expose my lies. The only reason I'd been given ten days of leeway was because the Shiens would so greatly prefer for no one to know that anything had gone awry. If Wist came back in time, they could pretend she'd never been missing.

Grandmother Shien informed us that, for the foreseeable future, no one would be permitted to leave Follyhope. Communication with outside parties would need to be routed through her or Nerium.

I didn't listen closely to the rest. There was nowhere I could run if I fled, and no one anywhere on the continent who could offer meaningful help. I was so alone that it felt almost wondrous to contemplate—a staggering natural vista, too big for words. Like the sea off Guralta Isle, or the midnight sky over a desert.

I was more alone now than I'd been in prison. If I'd known how much bonding would alter my brain and my body, if I'd known how losing it would ruin me, maybe I wouldn't ever have been able to reach for her. I couldn't even bring myself to think her name.

26

AFTER GETTING RELEASED from the family meeting, I spent the rest of the day rigorously avoiding every Shien.

Except for Danver. I ambushed her outside Riegel's corridors, right below the stone arch carved with shapes like cross-sections of a cancerous gut. I didn't bring up the fact that I'd met her mother. Although she must've guessed it, based on our current location.

I told her that I wasn't looking to bother anyone. In fact, nothing would make me happier than if everyone on the estate forgot me. But I'd need tips on sourcing food, clothes, and so on for the foreseeable future. Preferably with as little fuss as possible. The last thing I wanted was to be feted as an honored guest.

"Do I look like a maid?" Danver snapped.

"Er, yes."

For some reason, this seemed to deflate her indignation. Cool professionalism descended over her like a set of blinds snapping shut.

She told me succinctly about which pantries and closets I could raid, and how to find them.

I thanked her warmly. I didn't mind her ill humor. I'd have turned out much more warped than her if I'd been raised from birth as a Shien healer. She definitely didn't harbor a single speck of camaraderie toward the likes of me, but if anything, that just went to show that she had decent survival instincts.

That night, I retreated to the Sparrowhawk Room once more. Wist's hair tried to come with me when I bathed; I had to give it a good scolding to scare it away from the tub. Afterward, I found it waiting by the door like a lonely cat.

I sat heavily on the floor next to the bed, back in embroidered pajamas, a damp towel around my neck.

By now that long severed braid should've come unraveled from the friction of rubbing up on clothes and skin and carpet, but it still looked as sleek as ever. Maybe it had rewoven itself during my bath.

It wriggled up onto the bed and beckoned at me as though wondering why I wouldn't follow.

I didn't want to climb in bed alone. A skein of shorn hair didn't count as company. Although it was lively, warm, and had plenty of personality. It also beat my grip strength by a mile, and could probably out-lift me if we started a competition in the gym.

Hardening itself like a flexed muscle, Wist's hair prodded persistently at the backs of my shoulders. Not bad for an amateur massage.

I wondered if this was our punishment for time traveling in Manglesea. Getting our bond hacked in two, I mean. Not getting poked by an animated rope of human hair.

There was a tempting gleam to the notion that we'd lost our bond as a form of fateful payback. It would lend some meaning to this desolation.

I held that thought close, and then I released it. The very temptation of it meant it was wrong. Our real punishment would be something much worse—which was, at the moment, rather difficult to imagine.

That punishment wouldn't come when we were braced for it, dreading it. It'd come many, many years in the future, when we'd all but forgotten our old unpaid debts. We'd never get through it if I fell apart now, after such a brief sundering.

Would it really be brief, though?

Wist's braid gave up on luring me to bed. It pulled the big wet towel off my neck and—in a series of astonishing flying leaps, enough to do any gliding snake proud—went to hang it in the bathroom.

I wrenched my thoughts in a different direction. Shien Ficus swinging his knife like a pendulum. The chirping of toxic birds. (Still didn't know what made them toxic. If I'd seen them out in the wild, I wouldn't have been able to tell the difference.)

In Grandmother's office, I'd had a lot of time to study the oversized portraits of her predecessors. Mostly because I'd been dead set on avoiding eye contact with anyone living.

Even accounting for differences in age, historical customs, et cetera, few of the paintings bore much resemblance to any Shiens of my acquaintance. Much less to each other.

The monoceros was the one element that connected them. All the family heads' formal mage robes bore the official Shien crest. It might appear as a repeating pattern, or a single large design broken up into incoherence by elaborate folds of fabric, or as part of dangling hair ornaments.

The entire concept of Shien blood was a social construct, now that I thought about it. If they'd ever tried to preserve their old bloodline, they'd have abandoned the effort as soon as they encountered the end result of magical inbreeding.

They couldn't afford to value genetic loyalty. It would turn them into a clan of stunted mages. Being a purebred Shien mage simply meant being born with the right to put your family name first. Even if one or both of your parents were adoptees brought into the clan from distant lands.

The great mage clans invariably poached their strongest members from lesser families. Maybe that was why relatives jockeyed so viciously to secure their positions.

There was a difference between being born as a Shien and becoming one later. But your origins might matter little compared to your magical power, and your cleverness, and your willingness to trample anyone who got in your way.

A remembered tapping echoed in my ears. Nerium's cane.

I felt sick at the prospect of him waiting for my bonding rights to fall in his lap.

I could've felt sicker. The one good thing I could say about Shien Nerium was that, despite occasional attempts to butter up my intellect, he'd never looked at me with physical covetousness. All he saw in me was a chance to take Wist down a peg.

Nerium had to be behind this, however distantly. I'd believe it even if no one else—not even Ficus—recalled who'd planted the seed that led to him attacking Wist in that particular way, at that particular time.

Ficus hadn't attempted to push her all the way in. He hadn't slashed her face with his knife. From the start, he'd gone straight for her bond thread—which, again, was just an ordinary thread—as if he'd known exactly how to deal out maximum damage with minimum effort.

The funny part of it was that if I'd never met Wist, Shien Nerium wouldn't have been the worst of all possible bondmates. He wouldn't needlessly raze his healer's psyche like Miyu. He'd save that sort of warfare for those he perceived as threats. Like young Wist.

He considered himself a rational man. Not a wasteful man. Under different circumstances, I suppose we could've gotten along grand. I'd have taken a certain clinical satisfaction in meeting whatever challenges he set me, regardless of their morality.

If I were in my right mind, I'd be plotting revenge. But my anger was a dying furnace. I'd been sliced open, exposed to the elements; I couldn't retain any urgency. Only self-pitying ashes remained, stale and rapidly cooling.

I got up to bury myself in bed. Wist's braid had snuggled in a lumpy pile on top of the covers.

Without warning, it shot up like a garden eel, nearly knocking me back to the floor. A bell like a wind chime rang, muffled, inside bundled-up bed curtains.

The birds printed all over the wallpaper—predators and prey alike—glanced simultaneously at the door. Then they froze in place again, as if they'd always been facing the same direction.

27

I held Wist's braid stretched in my hands like a whip as I crossed the bedroom and boudoir to answer the door.

It was Lear, holding a lit candelabra. Wist's hair squirmed in fear. I quickly stepped back.

In doing so, I gave her just enough space to edge her way in.

"Wasn't planning on receiving visitors this late," I said.

She looked around for a place to put her candles down.

I motioned at a table. I'd never gotten much of an education in upper-class etiquette, but I was pretty sure the boudoir was meant to serve as a receiving room. Better than bringing her back to the bedroom with that avid audience of two-dimensional birds. Their eyes had started glittering as I slipped past.

So we stayed beneath the gigantic willow-shaped chandelier: me decked out in royal embroidery, and Lear wearing a long hotel-style flannel robe with a dizzying pattern of interlocking monoceros crests.

The candlelight flickered as if to mark the beginning of a diabolic ritual.

"Be careful of fire," Lear said.

"Wasn't at much risk of setting stuff on fire before you came knocking."

She reached across to pinch out one flame, then another. Like a gardener picking weeds.

The last candle guttered nervously. It could read the writing on the wall. But she let it live; she lowered her hand.

"I was wondering how you've been doing," she said.

"Why?" I asked warily. If Danver was unnecessarily abrasive, then Lear was unnecessarily amiable.

"Your bondmate vanished."

"Temporarily."

"Right."

I tossed Wist's braid over my shoulders. "She didn't abandon me."

"Of course not," Lear agreed. "Did you find refuge beyond the trick corridors?"

I belatedly thanked her for giving me a chance to meet Shien Riegel.

"My pleasure."

We sat in silence, observing her final candle, as I grew increasingly confused about why she'd come.

"Got anything you can turn to for comfort in troubled times?" she asked obscurely.

I pulled Wist's braid from side to side as though scrubbing the back of my neck. "Like what, drugs?"

"Religion, for instance."

"Don't tell me you're here to proselytize."

She grinned without humor. "Lord, no. I'm not trying to get deported."

I racked my memory. "Who's your god in Jace? The Lord of Orbs?"

"The Lord of Circles. But not all our islands follow a single religion."

She leaned back, legs crossed, her feet hidden in furry house boots. "In my hometown, we pay tribute to the Lady from the Sea. Our heaven is deep in the ocean. A paradise where magic grows on underwater trees."

"Sounds nice."

"In paradise, magic is always ripe for plucking. It's pain-free and abundant."Her smile turned crooked, and out peeped those crooked teeth of hers. "A good number of us die by drowning. It helps to have nice stories about the bottom of the sea."

The Lady from the Sea. That sounded like the first Kraken. She'd crossed unknown oceans to menace Jace and the continent. She'd certainly killed enough islanders to reign over their heaven or hell.

Although I'd always thought that Jacian national mythology had more to do with how they'd defeated her. They took justified pride in being the only country on this side of the world to succeed in making the historical Kraken turn back.

"Want some conversation practice?" Lear asked in Jacian. "No one's listening."

Her voice changed the moment she switched languages—higher and softer in Jacian, lower and blunter in Continental. Her pronunciation was nonstandard either way, which made it difficult to tell when she was being sarcastic.

"Better not risk it," I answered in Jacian, cringing at my own accent, then switched back. "It's in my interest to avoid undue scrutiny. Especially with Wist out of the picture. I should kick you out soon."

To my surprise, she concurred. "From tomorrow onward, I'll keep my distance. Gotta keep up appearances, right? If the Kraken takes her time coming back, it'll be safer not to seem chummy. Anything you want to ask me while I'm here? Might be our last chance to talk frankly."

I was about to give a flat no. Unfortunately, curiosity got the best of me. "Why'd you send me to Shien Riegel?"

"She's wanted to meet you for a long time."

"Aren't you a do-gooder."

"I try," Lear said modestly.

I drummed my fingers on the table between us. The willow chandelier emanated an ambient watery rustling like the sound of old wind stirring a thousand leaves. If I were alone, it might've put me to sleep.

"You're well acquainted with Ficus," I said.

"As well as anyone can be."

"How? He's not the type to pour you a beer and have heart-to-heart talks."

"I only paint mages who agree to sit for me," she explained. "I make them stand the whole time, actually. Gives a better view of their core and branches. I don't work from any form of magical imaging. Although Nerium keeps offering all sorts of tech support. I don't work from memory, either."

"Seems like that'd rule out a lot of possible subjects."

"All those sessions give me a chance to get to know them. Even if they don't say much out loud."

My honest response: "I'm surprised Ficus didn't set your studio on fire."

"I kept him sufficiently entertained." She shrugged. "He's not that complicated. He never really feels anything except for when he plays the knife game, or its equivalent. And for him it evokes something closer to the calmness of belonging than raging adrenaline. It's a bloodletting, a release of agitation, a brief and total serenity."

"What I don't get," I said, "is why Lady Shien puts up with him. He's a massive liability. A headache at best, and a time bomb at worst."

From my perspective, the bomb had already gone off.

Accusing him wouldn't do much for me, but I knew it was him. He'd clothed himself in a shroud of imperceptibility. He'd strategically obliterated Wist's single most prized possession. She wouldn't have cared if only he'd targeted her right hand instead.

Lear touched the pearls at her neck—she wore them even with her night robe—as though trying to ascertain if any were fake.

"You don't understand why Lady Shien hasn't cast Ficus out yet?" She made it sound like a question so simple that she couldn't see why I'd asked it. "He's famous."

"I've gathered."

"He has very passionate fans. He's the best-known Shien at the moment, aside from the Kraken. I thought all Osmanthians—"

"Doesn't his fame include loads of nasty rumors?"

Lear nodded. "Those who love him—they love him despite that, or because of it. Sleazy stories give them something to fight against. They fight for him with every scrap of influence they possess, while he never lifts a finger on his own behalf. He does come across very differently when seen from far away at banquets, or in portraits or ads."

Seven years of prison hadn't done much for my pop cultural awareness. I'd followed that with several years of hanging out with Wist, who was generally oblivious to fellow celebrities.

I didn't care to know what the public really thought of anything. I especially didn't care to know what they thought of me in my various guises as a traitor, as a scheming murderer, as the Magebreaker. (None of which was widely available information. But skewed whispers had a way of sneaking past government censors.)

Grandmother Shien hailed from a generation of elite mages who'd preferred to cultivate an air of mystery. Their cachet came from their cloak of untouchable privacy, not from being seen or known. The power of Ficus's type of fame might have been utterly foreign to her.

She would've dismissed it as gauche and frivolous until she could no longer dismiss it at all.

To ardent admirers, Ficus was the face of the Shien family. Not the nigh-anonymous clan head. Not the Kraken, who was the Kraken before she was a Shien, and who'd purposefully distanced herself from all mage clans in the name of impartiality. (Also—just between us—because she couldn't stand any of them.)

In short, Lear thought Ficus was too beloved for Grandmother to write him off, no matter how many headaches he'd caused her. His fame must also have been a useful distraction from scandals like his parents' financial misconduct. Not to mention Miyu's withdrawal from public life, as well as her more recent disappearance and death.

Ficus and Nerium had both been present at Follyhope when Miyu vanished.

Wist might not have been the first person Ficus pushed in that vorpal hole, partially or fully. He could've called Miyu out to the edge of the old rose garden. Using the same imperceptibility skill as always, he could've crept up behind her and shoved her through.

Much of the hole was positioned like a horizontal floating oil slick, with large stretches rippling at waist level or higher. He'd have needed to give her legs some help to tumble in.

Still, it'd be much quicker than holding her head underwater till she drowned. No kicking, no flailing, no need to keep forcing her down, and—minus any initial startled yips—almost absolute silence.

The moment her head dipped below the surface of the hole, it'd be gone, brain and eyes and tongue and memories and identity and all. An instant kill. Quite humane, actually. For just that reason, I'd heard of countries that used vorpal holes to carry out capital punishment.

Only the Kraken had ever returned alive after immersing herself in the nothingness between worlds.

My chitchat with Lear meandered over to the subject of duelists. She very much wanted to paint my old friend Fanren. Personally I thought the chances were low—he'd avoid anything that would result in the exact shape of his core and branches coming under close public scrutiny.

Fanren had his own reasons, but he was hardly the only one to feel that way. Some mages might take pride in having a unique map of their personal magic exposed in a gallery. Others might consider it little different from blowing up a garish print of their own colonoscopy.

"Speaking of which," I said, "you painted Miyu, too."

"She wasn't terribly pleased with it."

Must've been why her portrait sat in Lear's atelier, instead of getting hung in the manor.

"How'd she and Ficus get on?" I asked.

Lear gave me a sly look. "You already know the answer."

"It's been almost twenty years since I last saw them in the same room. Your impressions will be more up-to-date."

"Ficus is—was—indifferent to her. Miyu hated his guts."

"Sounds about right."

They'd ganged up on Wist, as had her other adoptive siblings. They didn't need to like each other to band together in the face of an obvious threat: a quiet younger child, brought in from outside, with immeasurable quantities of magic.

Once Wist grew old enough to opt out of the family business (savagely undermining each other in an eternal scrabble for the upper hand), her brothers and sisters would inevitably start infighting. But perhaps Nerium and Ficus had never perceived the rest of them as true rivals.

Ficus effortlessly won people to him by not caring what they thought. No amount of desperation or diligent work could ever have earned Miyu the same cultish approval. There was a strange alchemy by which it only blessed those who seemed not to need it.

Everything he gained came with ease and in spite of his vigorous self-sabotage. His looseness with money. The fatherless children he'd apparently seeded in every major Osmanthian city. His unpredictable temper. Random episodes of violence that had little correlation with his actual mood.

He didn't even try to hide it. Other scrambled to do all the work for him. But not, somehow, for Miyu. She would've felt that everything she gained had been clawed to her against all odds, and was still less than she deserved. Never mind that she'd been born to one of the wealthiest families in the country.

"You seem smart enough to want to stay out of things," I said to Lear.

"And you aren't?"

"I'm bonded"—the lie stuck in my throat—"to a Shien. I was prepared to get deep in it as soon as we set foot on the estate. I'd rather have stayed far away, of course."

Lear looked up into the light of the willow chandelier. Then she snuffed the last lit candle on the table, again using her fingers.

"Well, best of luck."

She stopped on her way out, half-turning. "Think you'll be able to break bonds one day?"

I stared.

I didn't trust myself to open my mouth.

"I've spent a lot of time around Shien Riegel," she added. "Maybe more than I should have. What can I say? I really like her hats. Whoever got to decide that painting is a higher art form than tiny hats, anyway? I've lived in quite a few different countries, and she never leaves this house, but she's got more imagination than I've ever mined from the depths of whatever soul I've got left. She's got no ulterior motives—she'd keep doing crafts without anyone watching her, and without any hope of personal profit."

"Yeah, her hats are nice," I said automatically. "She told you about me trying to...?" I gave up on subtle phrasing, and instead chopped the table with the side of my hand as if dicing vegetables.

"Just wondering," Lear said.

"Because of Danver?"

She didn't flinch. "Think what you like."

"Can't think about any of this while Wist's away," I replied. "Thought you were trying to stay out of all that family stuff. I gotta say, I don't think Danver would thank you—or anyone—for inserting yourself in her personal affairs."

"Oh, I'm already the sand in Danny's oyster. I've got a terrible soft spot for snippety young fools."

"Tell her to her face," I said. "She'd love to hear you say that. In fact, do it while I'm there. I want to enjoy the show."

Lear laughed under her breath. Immediately afterward, her smile disappeared. "If you ever do work out a way to, you know"—she mimed taking a twig in both hands and breaking it—"please tell me. That's all I ask."

"Fair enough," I said. "Just don't get your hopes up."

This had the distinct ring of telling a passing acquaintance *Let's hang out sometime!* and then never seeing each other again for the rest of your lives.

Once Lear departed the boudoir, I found myself alone with the fading scent of her finger-snuffed candles. She hadn't taken the candelabra when she left.

28

If I were a detective, I'd be convinced that Ficus had attacked—murdered—Miyu before he ever attacked Wist. Same type of victim (one of his sisters), same location, same methodology.

Ficus didn't require much of a reason to attack anyone. Look at how he'd whaled on Ginko in the dining room. She'd done nothing that could be construed as remotely offensive.

Still, would he really start shoving relatives in a vorpal hole just because it happened to manifest in the gardens of his childhood home?

Early in the morning, I turned to Wist with a start. But there was no one else in bed with me. Nothing but the warm breathing mass of her impeccably braided hair. The ends fluttered softly as if threatening to snore. Did the hair make itself swell and fall like lungs just to comfort me? What thankless work.

Ficus had said to Tempus: *Stuff like this makes you wonder if the snuffers have a point.*

Snuffers. Extinguishers.

My mind looped fragmented images of Lear pinching out candle flames.

We'd come to the estate in winter. No one would go around baring their forearms. Anyone might look like a secret Extinguisher, smoke tattoos hidden demurely beneath long sleeves. Maybe Lear's candle-snuffing had been a simple surface-level message, as straightforward as a confession could get without using actual words.

This one is different, Wist had uttered as she locked eyes with the Follyhope vorpal hole. *This doesn't belong here.*

Come on, Wist. What was I supposed to make of that? No vorpal hole belonged anywhere. That was the whole point of them—their inherent wrongness. Wherever they appeared, they violated the integrity of our reality.

If I were a detective, I might've spent more time thinking through the implications. But it wasn't my job to winnow out the truth, was it? No one would pay me, much less praise me. If I had a job, it was to survive my stay here until Wist found her way home to me.

Over the course of the next week, snow fell on Follyhope, but it didn't stick.

I dreamt of dying alone. I dreamt of Wist murdering me, and I was so stupidly joyful to see her. I dreamt of someone handing me a pill bottle with no cap. I kept dropping it and spilling the pills everywhere, scrambling to collect them.

I began to worry about Wist's cat back at the tower. I pleaded with Danver and Lear to help me appeal to Grandmother, and thus managed to speak briefly with Mori. Just long enough to work out arrangements for pet-sitting.

No idea what I would've done if he weren't available. We needed a better system to cover unexpected stays away from home.

That was the only time I got in contact with anyone outside the estate. Meanwhile, I evaded the resident Shiens at all costs—with the exception of Riegel and, by extension, Danver.

Riegel was not wholly bedridden, as I'd originally thought. But she was easily fatigued, weighed down by the incurable deformities in her magic, and she disliked straining herself in front of strangers.

I helped dust her vase of chrysanthemums, which was so rife with preservation magic that no one ever needed to change its water.

When I made up excuses to hang out in her quarters—which felt safer than anywhere else in the manor—she sent me into her sewing room to fetch scrap fabric.

We crafted all sorts of patterned eyepatches. She gave me fabric pens to doodle with, and the first thing I drew was a ferocious snail. I was trying to be that snail, I guess. Hiding at the heart of a magical spiral of mischievous corridors.

"You won't take credit for Wist's name," I said as I considered whether to give my snail a pair of angry eyebrows. "But someone came up with the idea. And Lady Shien approved it. Why couldn't she just as easily have been named Tulip"—I glanced at the dark vase filled with white flowers—"or Mum?"

Riegel coughed. I passed her a drink and a lozenge.

She didn't request any of the other medication lined up on her nightstand: a mix of pill bottles and paper-wrapped powder. Plus an open glass jar of honey sticks.

The pills were for her blood pressure. The mysterious honey and some of the powder packets had the iridescence of magic. The cuttings on them might've been concocted in-house by Doctor Hazeldine.

The Shien clan had taken everything from Wist when they adopted her. Her original name, her original family, and her clearest memories of family life before adoption. Maybe Doctor Hazeldine's predecessor had given her a honey stick to sip at. A bit of magic-imbued sweetness to make it easier to steal from her.

True memory erasure would've been deeply illegal, but there were milder types of memory-suppressive magic available in certain therapeutic contexts. Which included uses that the mageocratic elite would find convenient. Like pacifying the minds of mage children slated for induction into an unfamiliar clan.

Such magic did not delete young memories per se; it faded them to incoherence, bleach applied to a stain. The only other saving grace was that it couldn't reach back far enough to touch what Wist had carried over from her past life.

Riegel's coughing fit wound down. She still sounded hoarser than usual. "Can a wisteria vine grow without support?"

"Maybe? I always see them crawling up something."

I indicated the wisteria-infested pergola in her courtyard. Wist's hair stretched out and pointed at it, too, for good measure.

"The answer is no," said Riegel. "Even if you train it to grow in a freestanding pot, you've got to start it off with a pole or stake, something for the trunk to form around. The biggest and strongest vines grow on trellises or walls. They can rip apart shoddily built structures, actually, if you don't watch out. Wisteria thrives when it's got something to hold."

Wist's braid wound in corkscrew loops up and down my arms. I capped my pen.

Perhaps Grandmother Shien had envisioned Wist becoming hopelessly entwined with the clan like a vine inextricably binding itself to a trellis, year after year.

One might think she'd just grown tangled with me instead. But it hadn't stopped her from shunting me off to prison for seven years. (You'd keep bringing that up, too, if it had happened to you.)

Once I saw Grandmother stumping into Aunt Riegel's room. I shrank back and decided to visit another time.

Grandmother walked with a cane like Nerium, although hers looked better-suited for use as a weapon.

Riegel had told me, quite without guile, that she was the only person to whom Grandmother had ever shown real affection. As a stunted mage, she would never be a threat.

Unlike other aunts and uncles. For a while Wist's parents had been the last two left standing, but eventually they too had schemed themselves into disgrace. All the rest—tripped up by their very eagerness to inherit—disqualified themselves from the race much earlier.

I also stayed away from Riegel's room on the day I heard voices as I reached to let myself in. Danver pleaded for Riegel to exercise more with her walker. She pleaded so intently that she didn't notice me slinking back out the door.

Another time, Danver caught me below the sickly welcoming arch of marble flesh. I glanced down the magic corridor beyond, then back at Riegel's daughter. She was pinched and pale and looked as if she'd never laughed in her life. Limp lavender ribbons hung from the rolled-up buns of her hair.

Her expression grew even more humorless when she saw my new eyepatch: gaudy pink with green palm trees. Maybe she recognized the pattern from Riegel's bin of scraps.

"Don't even think about it," she said.

"What?" I asked, baffled.

"Whatever Lady Riegel tried to request from you. Don't do it. I don't consent."

Ah.

"First off, I can't break a bond like a wishbone. Even if I wanted to. No one can. So…"

So relax, I tried to tell her, but my voice stopped.

I'd never broken someone else's bond. For all my theorizing, I didn't know how.

Didn't I?

Wist's hair rubbed anxiously at my throat. This felt very much like being strangled.

Danver glared, suspicious of my silence.

I made the sort of noise you'd expect to hear from a dying hamster. Then I recovered.

"You're not scary," I said, "so stop trying. I can't fulfill Aunt Riegel's request. It's literally impossible. No need to harass me."

I left the manor to escape her. I took shelter on the far side of the nude giant reclining artistically out back.

Near me sat a placard with the name of the piece and its artist, and a few details about the materials used and the installation process. I stared as though I'd forgotten how to read.

My head buzzed. Cold cramped my fingers. I'd begun to harbor a horrible suspicion that I did, contrary to all my denial, have an inkling of how to untwist the fibers of a mage-healer bond. And I don't mean by telling people to go jump in the nearest vorpal hole.

I'd labored for years to construct a theory of bondbreaking. I'd never gotten anywhere.

Now that I'd stopped trying, stopped caring—now it came to me against my will. It stewed morbidly at the back of my brain while I averted every conscious thought to things like the high winter sky and the eerie cleanness of the statue towering at my back.

Now that the roots of my lost bond had been laid bare, now that I could examine my own vivisected self—now, at last, I started to understand. I saw what the vorpal hole had done to us, and I saw how I might replicate it. Wouldn't know for sure until I did a hands-on experiment.

But the revelation had the same undeniable truth to it as when I'd first worked out how to hobble mages, and how to drive them berserk, and how to hijack their magic.

I couldn't celebrate. This burgeoning knowledge promised to be a real pain in the ass.

The cleaving of my bond with Wist had, at least temporarily, cut my head down to size. I felt nothing of the usual intellectual triumph. No joyous megalomania. Which was a shame, really, because what was the point of being a genius if you couldn't even lord it over people in the privacy of your own mind?

I reminded myself of my original goals. I could be a hero. I could sneak around strategically freeing select healers, freeing birds from cages.

Of course, the two healers within immediate reach needed none of that. Ginko's mage was dead. Danver wanted to stay bonded, no matter what her mother might say.

Leave Follyhope, and it wouldn't take long to find more bonded healers stuck with mages like Shien Miyu. What then? I didn't have a network capable of helping severed healers seek asylum in foreign countries. Even if I did, I'm pretty sure that'd be a parole violation. Wist was too much of a public figure to openly offer assistance, either.

Wist, I said. *There's only a few days left. Your grandmother can't smooth things over forever. People will start wondering. If you don't come back...*

Her braid wound miserably around my chest, tightening like a python. It knew my heart: I kind of wished a great big snake would come along and swallow me.

29

THE VORPAL HOLE was now more of a vorpal line, a thin dried-up river in the air. I watched it from a grove of aged hydrangeas. Most of the flower heads had dried to a light tan hue, although some were mottled mauve and dark green, the colors of a bruise.

I'd tried speaking to the vorpal hole, believe it or not. I'd cupped my hands around my mouth and whispered as if it could carry my voice to Wist. I'd chucked lucky coins in, treating it like a wishing well.

I wasn't littering. The coins wouldn't go anywhere, or turn into anything useful. They'd just get vaporized. Like Shien Miyu.

That's where Ginko found me, muttering foolishly to myself, lurking like a hunter in a forest blind.

Wist had been gone for eight days now.

Ginko came up diagonally behind me. On my left side, not my right.

For about a thousandth of a second, I mistook her for Wist. This was more a sign of how badly I wanted to see Wist than an indication of any legitimate resemblance. She had black hair, yes, and she was taller than most other women on staff, but she wasn't even a mage. Besides, as much as Wist slouched and hid in corners, she had some real muscle beneath her clothing. Ginko was a waif.

"Hi," I said as she hovered.

She greeted me with a little bobbing bow.

All this time, we'd both been suspended in a peculiar sort of limbo. Wist had disappeared right after Tempus's notary confirmed that Ginko had blatantly lied to hide the loss of her bond. (That made two of us.) Which was definitely a crime in itself—obstruction of justice, I suppose.

Grandmother Shien had been holding Tempus at bay ever since, trying to buy time for Wist to reemerge without incident. It'd be funny, in a way, if Ginko and I ended up getting arrested at more or less the same time, for more or less the same crime.

With all the fuss about Wist, Ginko might actually have a chance of getting off the hook. Miyu's death had been deemed an accident—just as the clan desired, for the sake of propriety. For the same reason, they'd shelter Ginko from any related accusations.

Before, Grandmother might've gladly offered her to the MPs as a sacrificial pawn. But now there were bigger issues that needed covering up. Now there was some Kraken-sized drama to contend with. Grandmother would shield Ginko: not out of concern for Ginko herself, or as belated penance for Miyu's abuse, but simply for the sake of closing the case as dully and inconspicuously as possible.

It was early afternoon, but the sun had already traveled so far that the day felt almost over. Ginko wore a quilted patchwork coat over her drab robes.

She must've approached me for a reason. Right? She said nothing for so long that I began to doubt myself. Maybe she'd just wanted to view the remnants of the vorpal hole from an alternate angle.

"What'd you feel when your bond broke?" I asked.

Abrupt, yes, but I was currently too braindead to finesse my way through delicate topics.

"Nothing much," said Ginko.

"Nothing—"

I realized I was just repeating her. I stopped myself. I stopped talking, period, for a good minute.

Ginko's bond had been a source of torment, not comfort. But it had been part of her all the same.

Even a necessary operation—like getting cancer cut out—would have aftereffects. An amputation could be incredibly justified and still feel terrible. You'd still have to learn how to cope with it.

Through the medium of their bond, Miyu had infested Ginko like an acute illness. Such an illness could leave you drained for years, long after doctors deemed you fully recovered.

The destruction of their bond might've come as an unspeakable relief. It might've saved Ginko's life. Still, it could never have been just a pure joyous release, just a bright new beginning.

She'd been injured by her attachment to Miyu, and again by her violent detachment. Except that no one would see her limping, and no one would offer her a cane.

A broken bond was its own sort of burden. I felt that with every waking moment.

I regrouped. "You're ... very stoic," I said weakly.

I meant it, too. She was made of stronger stuff than me. Despite giving an impression of extreme breakability—the sickly beauty of poor nutrition, damaged lungs, and old-fashioned poetic melancholy. That babyish whispering voice of hers didn't help, either.

"It isn't me," Ginko said after a moment.

"What isn't?"

"I'm not stoic."

Was she trying to be humble?

She touched her head in an odd, proprietary sort of way. As if petting a flighty animal. "I've had help."

"From who?"

"The doctor," she said, as though wondering why I needed to ask. "Lady Miyu told him the problem was on my end. She told him to do something about me. He did his best."

I thought of the doctor. I thought of holding Ginko's hands while he blabbered at my back about being a Guralta alumnus. About sending his daughter there, too.

I thought of meeting Shien Nerium and Shien Ficus on campus. They'd just been visiting; they'd graduated years before I enrolled.

Seniors at school used to pass around psychoactive cuttings. Go to an off-campus party, and just about everyone would be on mind-altering magic. Illegal, obviously, but so were a lot of things. No mage students got in real trouble for it.

I'd always figured that Nerium knew where the older students got their supply. Heck, he could've been involved himself, could've set up a tidy little side business. But he was neither an originator nor a working-class mage. Nerium couldn't have invented that magic on his own. Besides, he'd have considered beneath him to personally churn out cuttings for sale like a one-man factory.

"Doctor Hazeldine prescribed you magic," I said to Ginko. "What kind? For how long?"

She lowered her eyes. "I still take it. Had fits when I stopped."

"Fits?"

"Panic attacks?" She made it sound like a question.

I probed further, but she wouldn't directly describe the magic that Hazeldine produced for her. And only her, it seemed—Danver didn't need any. If I had to guess, it seemed vaguely like a sedative. Or a mental anesthetic.

I could understand her reluctance to go into detail. Those cuttings might be highly restricted. If not outright illegal. Maybe he had permission to manufacture them, and maybe he didn't.

Of course, the question of legality would fly right out the window if Doctor Hazeldine had helped incubate the culture of magical psychotropics at Guralta Academy. Whether as an underage student, a young graduate, an aging alumnus—or through every stage of his career.

Aristocratic Guralta grads would be highly motivated to help protect that sort of secret. A lot of mages thought the law was meant for everyone but them. Frankly, they weren't entirely wrong.

I noticed belatedly that Ginko still wore a bond thread around her neck. "You can cut that off, you know," I said.

She tried to look down at it. She made a noncommittal noise.

I asked what had happened to her after our first brief meeting a couple years ago. After Miyu got hauled away for berserking.

They'd been separated for months, she said, but Miyu was still always there in her head.

In fact, everything got much worse after Miyu lost her job at the Ministry of Justice. She never left Follyhope anymore. She had no career, no rivals, no reason to direct her attention outside the estate. She stayed closer to Ginko than ever, physically and metaphysically. That inescapable closeness only multiplied her humiliation, her vindictive frustration.

When Miyu had a job, she'd been intermittently distracted by workplace politics and events in the city. After she got fired, taking her stress out on Ginko became her primary occupation. It stayed that way right up until her death.

Miyu's malevolence remained confined to the estate—and, for the most part, to a single target. Whatever happened inside their bond would go unseen and unheard by others. Nothing she did outwardly would be considered newsworthy, either. Berating your healer bondmate was hardly unusual enough to give rise to interesting rumors.

When I made Miyu go berserk, I'd meant to punish her for mistreating her previous bondmate.

I hadn't intended any of this, but ultimately I'd forced her and Ginko into closer proximity. I'd removed her other outlets. She could bolster herself only by constantly trampling Ginko, an endless stream-of-consciousness voice finding everything wrong with her. Screaming at her to shut up when she hadn't said a word. Criticizing her for the thoughts she had and the thoughts she didn't have, for sleeping and for waking, for the frivolity of eating and bathing, for breathing air and taking up space.

If Ginko shoved Miyu in a vorpal hole, you could call it self-defense. You could argue that I'd set it in motion years ago. I'd put them on that path.

In the eyes of the law, she would still be a murderer.

I'd pitied Ginko, trapped on the estate as Miyu's bondmate. But my own actions had plunged her into a deeper hell than ever before, one she could survive only by pickling her brain in Doctor Hazeldine's magic. And I'd barely looked back.

Maybe Ginko saw some of this on my face. We were completely alone among the withered hydrangeas.

No apology could ever be adequate.

"The day your bond broke," I said. "Miyu went out at night, didn't she? Someone must've asked her to meet—or vice versa. Near the vorpal hole."

She looked back at me with incurious eyes.

I caved. "You don't know who Miyu was going to see?"

"She didn't tell me."

But an observant bondmate might be able to read between the lines.

"No guesses?" I asked.

"Might not be the same person."

"Hm?"

"Who she thought she was going to meet. Who came to meet her."

"Was it Ficus?"

Ginko blinked slowly. More than anything, this lag in her reactions reminded me excruciatingly of Wist.

"...May I ask a question?" she said.

An obvious dodge, but I didn't have the heart to point it out. "Yeah?"

"How can I leave here?"

"Get arrested."

She patted the pockets of her coat as if wishing she'd brought a pad of paper for taking earnest notes. I wanted to slap myself.

"No," I told her hastily. "Look, forget I said that. Slip of the tongue. Didn't mean it. Now I'm being serious, okay? Don't get arrested. Really."

Her silence made it difficult to put the brakes on. I said the same thing several more times, with only a minimum of rephrasing.

My experience of incarceration had been highly atypical. Wist—unobtrusively, and from a distance—had exerted pressure to make sure I wouldn't be severely mistreated. I hadn't known about her efforts at the time. If I'd known, I'd have been ferociously ungrateful.

Thankfully, Ginko offered me a change of subject. Kind of.

"You and the Kraken." She shyly laced gloved fingers together in front of her face. "You're ... are you...?"

Wist and I weren't much inclined toward public displays of affection. Around strangers, I might pretend to be her executive assistant.

Even when we weren't deliberately putting on an act, people might doubt whether we were more than ex-schoolmates, more than practical-minded bondmates. It was safer to let them view me as a hard-nosed social climber than as someone who actually mattered.

I waved at the central building of the manor. Wist's braid mimicked me.

"They put us in the Sparrowhawk Room," I said. "One bedroom. One large bed. Does that answer your question? She doesn't make me sleep on the floor, for the record."

Acting as if I owned the place, I invited Ginko in for spica. Or any other drink of her choice. Instead she took me back to the staff boarding house—which was admittedly a more comfortable environment for both of us.

Through things said and unsaid, I learned that she'd spent years cloistered with other healers before Miyu chose her. They'd lived in a Shien property out in the countryside. She expected to get sent back there once things calmed down at Follyhope. (Assuming that she didn't get herself arrested.)

Only big-name mage families had healer cloisters. It was a practice that allegedly dated back to the Osmanthian monarchy. In olden times, they'd maintained a special court where top healers lived in luxury, walled and protected. Never leaving the premises, but also wanting for nothing. You could call it a Court of Healers, or you could call it a harem.

Modern-day cloistered healers didn't reside in an extravagant inner palace. They weren't swarmed by valets and ladies-in-waiting. They weren't adored as living saints.

Life in the Shien cloister might nevertheless be preferable to life at Follyhope. I could only pray that they'd have enough sense not to make Ginko bond another mage.

I almost asked her what she wanted for herself. But in the aftermath of years with Shien Miyu, would she be capable of longing for anything?

I wasn't in a position to grant wishes, anyway. Without Wist, I had no power to make anyone heed my demands. For all I knew, I might be heading straight back to prison next week.

Ginko got up to empty a few sparkling dust traps.

She told me quietly that she'd only spoken to Miyu once or twice before they bonded. Miyu would occasionally visit the cloisters, sometimes with a sibling or two in tow.

"I admired her," Ginko murmured. "She was always so nicely dressed."

She would've been. Everything fitted to her body just so, not a blond hair out of place, slim and attractive in an uptight sort of way.

Most healers could only dream of being swept away by such a rich and distant mage.

Ginko said she'd been curious about me and Wist because she couldn't imagine loving a bondmate. Or anyone at all. She'd been reduced to just a few alternating states of existence: she cycled through them like a light flashing from bright to dim. A dazed and empty serenity from Hazeldine's magic. Numbness as the magic wore off. Then a sensation like looking into a vorpal hole—a visceral wrongness in need of righting.

Even then, the magic held her at arm's length. These moods crossed her as intangibly as clouds covering the moon. Her despair crouched on the opposite side of a thousand-mile gulf. Whether because of the doctor's cuttings or lingering traces of Miyu's brutal control, she'd been rendered incapable of contemplating self-destruction. She would live on no matter what anyone did to her.

This was way above my pay grade. I listened, but there wasn't a thing I could find to say in response.

If Ginko asked me to break a bond for her ... well, now I had a decent chance of pulling it off. Too bad she didn't need that anymore.

Once Wist returned, once the trouble at Follyhope settled down—was there really nothing else I could offer her?

After we washed our mugs, Ginko retrieved a steel bowl from a ground-level wooden deck out back. She cleaned and refilled it; the water threatened to spill as she carried it outside again. I held the door for her.

"For fairies?" I asked.

"There's a garden cat."

I looked around. Maybe her cat was shy.

"It's been missing ever since the vorpal hole showed up," she said, almost inaudible.

"Didn't all the other pets and livestock get sent away?" I said. "Like those ostriches. Your cat might've gotten rounded up with the rest of them."

"He's not my cat. He just lives out here."

Wist's braid squeezed me in sympathy.

"Okay," I told Ginko. "Whatever you say."

30

I WAS SO, so tired of this place. Tired of fake fire glowing in nooks. Reflective floors and doors like black water. Walls paneled in stainless steel and painted silk. Pendant lights hanging on showy chains. Marble-clad everything.

Similar features appeared in Wist's tower. Sometimes an exact replica, sometimes a visual rhyme. But that was different. Wist's magic infused the tower: it could wear all the trappings of the Shien manor, and it would still feel like home.

If I were fully myself, I'd have plotted out what to do in the event that Wist took too long to return. But my mind balked like a dumb beast of burden. No amount of whipping could make it move.

I couldn't cobble together to-do lists predicated on the notion of Wist being gone for longer, and longer, and longer. Planning for it threatened to make it real. Like how my fear of hurting her might've steered the Void's gaze toward her, a burning spotlight. The very act of thinking about it seemed heavy enough to tip the fragile scales of probability.

Intellectually, I believed that of course it'd be best to ready myself for the worst. Regardless of how I spent my time, Wist would return when she could, and not a moment sooner.

That knowledge sank deep into the mud at my feet. It couldn't stir me. My stomach rebelled at the prospect of a future more than an hour or two in the distance. I dragged myself from one foggy day to the next without any will to prepare for what might come at me later.

Until Tempus showed up again on the ninth day without Wist.

I couldn't seem to get him alone. I wanted to give up and sit down on the floor and laugh. Imagine telling my teenage self that one day I'd be frantic for a chance to speak with Minashiro Tempus in private.

Nerium stuck to us like a tick to a deer. Lear quite reasonably kept her distance. It wouldn't be fair to ask Danver or Ginko to run interference. Even if they tried, Nerium wouldn't fall for it.

I should've explored my options sooner. I should've done more than wallow in loss and wring fretfully at Wist's hair. I'd been irrationally determined to stay in place—as if leaving the site of Wist's disappearance would somehow make her less likely to return at all. As if I needed to hold vigil in enemy territory to prove my devotion.

The truth was that, yeah, Wist might turn up here first. But she could find me back at the tower just as easily as she could find me at Follyhope. No Shien mage could get to me there. If I shut myself up in Wist's tower, even the government would struggle to do much more than vigorously request my cooperation.

"Where's the Kraken?" Tempus asked. Not for the first time.

"Still occupied," Nerium said from his corner. "She sends her regrets."

We were in a palatial two-story library with more space devoted to scrolls than to books.

"It was incredibly difficult to get an appointment," Tempus said in a tone that stopped just short of blatant accusation.

"My grandmother has many other concerns to attend to."

"But this is…" Tempus shot me a baleful glare, as though willing me to get a clue and give them some privacy.

I didn't budge an inch. I kept pretending to browse boxes of scrolls that I had no real interest in reading. Something about the grand history of the preeminent Osmanthian mage clans.

Tempus stalked closer to Nerium. As he resumed speaking, though, Nerium interrupted him and beckoned me over. "This is relevant to her, too. Wouldn't you say?"

I took up a position by Nerium's armchair. Even with malaise dragging at my heels, I couldn't pass up a chance to get under an MP's starchy skin. Tempus—together with the fuzzy black caterpillar of his mustache—scowled at me, right on cue.

"Always good to see you, Inspector," I said. "We've been feeling neglected."

He didn't comment on the mass of borrowed hair writhing decoratively about my shoulders. He looked at Nerium's impenetrable glasses and said: "It's about your brother."

"Which one?" I asked winsomely, although the answer was obvious.

Tempus's voice dropped. "This isn't a formal warning. I wasn't authorized to bring backup. All I can say is that they've been showing unusual activity this past week."

"They," I uttered.

Nerium pinched the air, miming the act of snuffing out a flame.

"Please," Tempus said. "Be careful."

"Follyhope is remarkably well-defended," Nerium replied. "Even with our current paucity of bodyguards. As for Wisteria, she's her own best protection. No need to worry—we're rather used to this."

"To being targeted by terrorists?" Tempus asked harshly.

"To Ficus acting out." Nerium lowered his glasses and gazed my way with eyes like muddy water. "Do you know why he's between bondmates? Ah, *between* might not be the best way to put it. He's now been un-bonded for much, much longer than the length of time he spent with his previous bondmate."

Tempus cut in. "I don't mean to cast aspersions. Just—for the time being, it'd be best to exercise caution. If the Kraken can make a show of departing from Follyhope, all the better. She's always been the Extinguishers' main target. Ficus's bonding history has nothing to do with—"

"But Asa Clematis wants to hear about it," Nerium said.

I nodded. Gossip can be a sharpened weapon, or a key to closed doors, or at least a set of lock picks.

Nerium continued. "Ficus's previous bondmate was an elderly gentleman from the cloister. An eccentric choice. People"—he glanced sidelong at Tempus—"found it quite charming. Like a young prince keeping a creaky old butler as his closest companion.

"Ficus hadn't grown up around that healer at all, though. Never laid eyes on him before picking him out from the cloister. All Ficus wanted was someone frail. You see, he went through a phase of being absolutely fascinated by placebo effects and nocebo effects and so forth. Especially in regards to magic."

Tempus squirmed in his crisp-collared suit. "I ought to excuse myself. I said what I came to say."

"No, no." Nerium smiled fondly. "You've always been keen on Ficus. Do listen.

"He was curious about the effects of the emotional pressure it's possible to exert through a bond. He was curious if, with thought alone, one might give one's bondmate the illusion of—say, of having a stroke. Or a heart attack. If you convinced them you were using magic to induce cardiac arrest, could you trick their heart into stopping all on its own? Without actually using magic. Without actually doing anything objectionable."

"Did it work?" I asked.

"Ficus hasn't been bonded for a long time now."

Out of nowhere, Tempus said—to me, not Shien Nerium—"Is there anything you want to tell me?"

Wist's braid stilled. I shook my head.

If Nerium weren't listening, I might have said something. I might have turned to Minashiro Tempus, of all people. I might have swallowed my pride and asked him for help. Help getting out of here and back to Wist's tower, if nothing else.

But how could I convince Tempus to stick his neck out for me without explaining what had happened to Wist?

If he guessed at the unspoken context, he'd take it seriously. However he had or hadn't changed since our school days, Inspector Minashiro didn't come across as a slacker.

At minimum, he'd insist on reporting about her to the highest levels of government. The general public still wouldn't hear of it—witnesses would all be marked and sworn even more strictly to silence. I'd get whisked away into protective custody.

All of this would happen soon enough, anyway. As soon as tomorrow, if Wist remained MIA, and Lady Shien decided to come clean about it. Throwing myself on Tempus's mercy seemed unlikely to accomplish much aside from hastening my incarceration.

Nerium smoothed the cover of the heavily bound volume in his lap. He opened it once more, inviting us to look.

It was a printed album, with colors richer and pages larger than a coffee table book of fine art. The entire tome was devoted to childhood images of the six Shien siblings. Seven, once Wist showed up. They all wore gloriously colored mage robes for formal occasions.

Wist was so much smaller than the rest of them. A dull-eyed doll surrounded by gangly children and adolescents.

The eldest three stood out the most. Miyu, who attempted a smile, although it gave an impression more of effort than of joy. Ficus, who seemed not to possess a single bad angle: it was as though a secret host of angels followed him around with reflectors to ensure he always appeared in the best possible light. Nerium, who was almost unrecognizable minus his glasses and cane and self-deprecating posture, and with a sweep of startling dark hair crowning his tall forehead.

I wanted to reach in and pluck Wist out of there. I wanted to slam the book shut like a bear trap on Shien Nerium's placid middle-aged fingers.

The room rocked beneath us as if buckling under the violence of my thoughts. Enough to make me grab the nearest shelf for balance, though nothing fell out. Tempus said something, swift and urgent.

My ears were closed to him. To everything.

Wist? I thought.

Her braid stayed still and watchful.

31

Scroll boxes rattled on their shelves. The floor shook again, longer and less overtly. Queasiness bloomed in me.

I tried to ask if this were an earthquake. Tempus pointed at something, his voice rising.

Nerium set aside the album in his lap. He collected his cane. No rushing. As he rose, his eyes seemed to linger on an empty chair by a curtained window.

Tempus was almost screeching. "Sir, we've got to—"

"Patience," Nerium said. "I can't move as quickly as you."

The shaking had settled down to a kind of sporadic vibration. Like being trapped in a thin-skinned building next to heavy construction.

Nerium touched the temple of his glasses and uttered a few portentous phrases at the nearest wall. Layers of embedded magic flashed high in the air and low underfoot.

"Was it you, Tempus?" he inquired.

"What?" Tempus sounded bewildered.

"You urged caution. Yet we've been exceedingly cautious all along. You're the first outside visitor we've welcomed in over a week. You were so desperate to warn us of the Extinguishers' movements. How strange. There was no sign of them encroaching on our territory until the very day—the very hour—you came."

Tempus gasped and sputtered to defend himself, choking on his own spit.

Nerium, unconcerned, leaned harder on his cane. He still had one hand to his glasses. The next time he spoke, his voice side-stepped the air between us. It brushed up directly against my eardrums.

"May I have your attention. May I have your attention. Subliminals and healers, please remain calm and shelter indoors. There is no immediate danger."

Tempus squawked an objection to the notion of there being no immediate danger. Nerium looked past him and, this time in an ordinarily audible voice, said: "That message applies to you as well, Asa Clematis. Shelter in place."

While I clung to the nearest shelf, he and Tempus had already moved far out of reach.

I stared at the depression left in the armchair he'd vacated. Then at the other silent chair he'd been keeping an eye on, over next to a bank of funereal curtains.

"Wait." My voice came out thin and breathless. "I—"

He tapped his cane on the floor—twice, thrice—and took Tempus firmly by the arm. I leapt at them much too late. Nerium's cane lit up like a red-hot poker. Porting magic erased them both from the library.

No more shaking now. Or else I'd become so used to it that I could no longer sense it. The scrolls and books were excruciatingly quiet.

I watched the empty armchair.

Not Nerium's. The other one, further away. I watched it even though there was nothing to see there. I watched it as I backed away toward the nearest door. What the hell was Nerium playing at?

Wist, what do I do?

Something touched my right cheek.

Piercing pain came a second later, delayed. Blood smudged the fingertips I'd pressed to my face. A shallow vertical slash ran from the bottom of my eyepatch to my jaw.

"Why stare so hard at that chair?" asked Shien Ficus. "I already moved."

He stepped right between me and the door. He'd lifted his veil of imperceptibility. His yo-yo knife dangled from his fingers like a pocket watch swinging at the end of its chain.

I pressed at the skin around the leaky cut on my cheek. It leaked harder.

"Wist will skin you alive if this scars." Speaking made it sting worse.

He squinted at me. "No," he said with confidence. "She'll like it. I know what flatters a face."

Dear god.

"If you didn't want it, you should have avoided it," he added. "Didn't you learn anything in basic training?"

"I'm a civilian!"

"Oh?"

"Training wouldn't make a difference, anyway. You were undetectable."

He stilled his knife. I refrained from making any sudden moves.

"The Extinguishers," I said. He seemed to be in a bizarrely good mood—good enough, anyhow, to risk asking questions. "Did you call them?"

He wore a shapeless black shirt that would've looked like a trash bag on just about anyone else. He pushed his left sleeve up and turned his forearm to expose the veins of his wrist.

A colorless tattoo of a melted candle sprouted just below a stack of dark bracelets. Black smoke billowed from the wick, meandering up to the crook of his elbow.

"Could've called them," he said. "But I didn't."

He twirled his knife.

When it stopped moving—pointed at me again—it didn't resemble a yo-yo knife at all. The silvery string had vanished. The handle split and clacked in his fingers like the sort of butterfly knife you'd whip out in a back alley.

"A blade is a blade," I said, pretending not to be afraid. "You already cut me. Why change it?"

"This one's a substitute," he said cryptically. "Left the real thing with Aunt Riegel. No safer place on the entire estate." With his free hand, he waved at the monoceros-logo carpet. "We go this way. Hold your breath."

The magic on the house might not welcome the Extinguishers, but it hadn't turned on Shien Ficus.

Wist's braid shivered against me as if fighting the urge to leap across and tackle him.

I held her braid close. And I held my breath as instructed. Didn't even dream of making a break for it. I'd consider myself lucky if the only part of me he sliced open was the side of my face.

I didn't know much about the rest of his skill set, but that imperceptibility magic was bad enough on its own. No healer or subliminal—and few mages—would stand a chance.

I could boast of a couple tricks unknown to other healers, though. Maybe I could hobble him—or even hijack his magic—before he filleted me like a trout. But stripping Ficus of his magic wouldn't necessarily stop him from running faster than me, or hitting harder. It wouldn't make him forget how to use a blade.

Ficus traced the monoceros pattern on the carpet with his toe. The floor turned to quicksand beneath us. He grabbed the back of my borrowed blazer as magic churned us downward with the violence of a poorly regulated waterslide.

This was a form of accelerated phasing, not porting. We lurched through wood and steel and concrete and stone like cannonballs fired through a pool of jelly. I wasn't practiced at holding my breath, but the sheer dread of accidentally drinking down a smoothie of beams and plaster kept me from gulping for air.

We came to a halt by a wine cellar about three times as large as the magnificent library. I doubled over, gasping.

"And now," said Shien Ficus, "you get to vanish, too."

He cast his imperceptibility skill on both of us.

His magic applied itself like a coating of insect repellent: a moist tickle that soon dried and vanished. I could still see and feel myself, and I could see and hear Ficus. His knife clacked again in his hand, a whirling blur of metal.

He ordered me to keep walking. I obeyed without question. My face still bled sluggishly, and that knife sounded very persuasive.

The tunnels down here were grander and cleaner than some of the biggest subway stations in the capital city. Ficus prodded me past mysterious vaults and security bunkers, and many deep echoing crenelations of stone.

We emerged aboveground right by the art installation made to look like a train crossing. A limp body lay in the middle of the tracks.

Ficus went over to the body and poked at it, pulling up the sleeves to expose smoke-tattooed forearms.

"Won't leave visible evidence while we're outside human perception," he said. "No fingerprints. No skin cells. No trailing mage dust. Might want to stop pulling your hair out."

I sheepishly lowered my hand from the back of my head.

He seemed unable to detect a pulse. "The snuffers won't be happy about this." He kicked the unresisting corpse this way and that until it flopped into a position perfectly perpendicular to the tracks. "That's what they get for barging onto Shien land. Could've warned them. Morons."

I wasn't dressed for the cold. Wist's braid, twining tensely inside and outside my blazer, felt like a portable heat pack. Ficus's butterfly knife clicked as industriously as a woodpecker.

The statue of the sprawled-out titan behind the manor had shifted. It rested on one knee now, alert, as though poised to start running. It was taller than any building in sight: even only half-risen, the naked figure loomed like a muscle-bound construction crane.

The art mobiles I'd previously seen floating over Follyhope appeared to have fled like migratory birds. The afternoon sky was a shredded melange of blue and gray.

Ficus tapped a few outdoor lights as we headed down a path through the hills. Magic crunched like gravel underfoot. The flagstones carried us forward faster than a moving walkway, so fast that the scenery on either side whooshed past like something viewed from the window of an accelerating train.

By the time our pace went back to normal, I had to crane my neck to catch a glimpse of the giant sculpture. Then the hills sloped lower, funneling us toward some kind of wide green valley or overgrown crater. I lost sight of the giant altogether.

Flurries drifted past us, slow and irregular, melting the instant they touched anything solid. They fell like the last few grains of sand dribbling down through the neck of an hourglass.

The estate contained enough untouched wilderness to rival any number of public nature preserves. Great for dumping bodies.

I asked Ficus where he was taking me.

"The family mausoleum," he said, like I ought to have known from the start.

Well, that didn't sound promising.

"What do you need me for?"

He gestured with his blade. "Keep moving."

In lieu of breadcrumbs, I'd attempted to sprinkle a feeble trail of my own plucked-out hair. I'd stopped once Ficus alluded to the futility of it all by the trompe de l'oeil train tracks (although apparently something about that art piece was real enough to brutally run down unauthorized intruders).

Still, this didn't mean I'd just been blindly stumbling around ever since. I'd learned a lot, these past few minutes. I'd concentrated on the sensation of Ficus's magic veiling us from the physical world—and on the shape and composition of his core, his five branches.

Picture someone lunging close enough to stab you. Picture being defenseless, unarmed. If you were a skilled martial artist, you might know of some clever way to parry the thrust. Or knock the knife from their grip. Or grab their thrusting arm and yank them off-balance. Look, I have no idea. I'm not a martial artist.

And yet. In applying his magic to me, Ficus had done the metaphysical equivalent of lurching close enough for me to slip inside his reach.

Right now I could hobble his magic with barely a twitch. I could do it painfully enough that it might delay him for seconds—or entire minutes—while I sprinted off like a rabbit into the woods.

"Don't think," Ficus advised. "What good has thinking ever done you?"

"Excuse me?" I blurted.

The butterfly knife flipped across his knuckles again. When it stopped moving, it was no longer a knife at all. He was holding a gun.

32

FICUS AIMED his gun at me. One-handed. Nonchalant. Like he did this every day. The gun was a watermelon-esque mix of neon pink and neon green. Only the density of its magic cuttings kept me from laughing.

"Which is it?" I said. "A yo-yo knife? A butterfly knife? A squirt gun? You didn't squirt open this cut on my face."

"Maybe I did." He tilted his ridiculous gun like an actor posing for a poster. "I'm the best shot in the clan."

He could shoot at my back even if I managed to debilitate him, even if I ran for my life. How good were my odds of escaping unscathed?

"You're my insurance policy," he said. "Won't hand you over if the snuffers never catch up."

"I'm supposed to believe that?"

"Wanna go try your luck with the snuffers instead?"

The hills shook again. Far away, the hidden giant must've risen to its feet. I saw its dark shoulders silhouetted against the half-stormy sky.

It took another earth-thumping step. Hopefully not straight into the manor. In terms of sheer scale, it felt like an imitation of legendary Jacian war machines, although I couldn't tell if it were capable of anything more than angry stomping.

"Why the mausoleum?" I asked.

"Snuffers respect dead people. They won't just blow up the whole place."

The Extinguishers weren't a monolith. Just look at Ficus. He bore their mark. Like the rest of them, he would hurt Wist without a second thought. Unlike the rest of them, he wouldn't hesitate to blow a mausoleum sky-high. Even one that guarded generations' worth of Shien ashes.

I hadn't been letting myself think about his invisible hand on Wist's arm. The nauseating shimmer of the vorpal hole that spread out flat like a floating mirage. The jackhammering of her heartbeat when she saw that the blue thread around her wrist was gone.

If Wist could speak to me, she'd urge me to focus first on my own survival. Her braid felt the same way. It stuck to me like a leech, passing up every possible chance to lash out and whip Ficus, to exact a semblance of revenge.

The Shien mausoleum filled the valley ahead of us like a rain-gorged river swelling to fill a canyon. The complex centered around a dome that looked more like a half-sunken planet than an architectural point of interest. It dwarfed the rest of the sprawling building.

Even if I mentally edited out that domineering dome, the mausoleum as a whole seemed considerably larger than the manor itself. This made a kind of sense, I guess: the all-time deceased population of the Shien clan must far outweigh its currently living membership. Of course the dead would require more housing.

Gun in hand, Ficus pointed me through a series of stony gates.

"You're here to take shelter," I said by way of confirmation. "To hide from the Extinguishers. You really think they're coming after you?"

"Who else would they come for?"

"Their entire organization is built around snuffing out Wist."

"Not here now, is she?"

"No thanks to you," I said. "I don't get it. They should be praising you. They should be kissing your feet. You've made more progress toward their sacred mission than they've made in years."

Ficus didn't elaborate. He heard me when he felt like it; he heard nothing when he didn't. Evidently he'd had a falling-out with the Extinguishers. But if I were him, I wouldn't flee. I'd tell them what I'd done to Wist the Kraken. A tricky thing to prove, yes, but the mere possibility ought to calm their ire.

Maybe he was supposed to have brought them her head on a stick. Maybe Wist's disappearance represented a form of failure. But it wasn't like the rest of the Extinguishers had been any more successful. They would understand and sympathize with the sheer futility of going up against Wist.

Ficus lifted his imperceptibility magic once we were inside the mausoleum. It felt like a layer of dried glue peeling off my entire body.

Our footsteps echoed dryly. The space within was styled like a gallery, not a crypt. The dimness made me think of museums archiving material so delicate that it couldn't withstand prolonged exposure to light. We wound through room after room of placards and sculptures and art panels, shrines in ornate alcoves, tablets listing obscure accomplishments, human-sized urns.

My thumb worried at the hard unbending edges of Nerium's business card in my pocket. The end of Wist's braid slipped inside that same pocket, too, and pulled my fingers open as though begging me to reconsider.

Loath though I was to rely on Nerium, I might've been able to use his card to hint at our location. To send a covert plea for rescue.

Then I thought of the library, of how Nerium had calmly kept watch over Ficus's chair. His glasses could pierce the veil of magic. He'd known Ficus was there. He'd known Ficus was listening. He'd known who he was leaving me with when he ported out of the room.

Some things had changed over the past few decades, and some things hadn't. If Ficus was not to be trusted, then Nerium was to be trusted even less.

The mausoleum appeared to have been built out in a spiral, or a series of concentric circles. The outermost portion housed the ashes of those who'd died most recently. The names and trappings of the dead grew increasingly dated as we ventured deeper. The mosaic-laden ceilings veered higher and then lower and then higher again as architectural tastes shifted across decades, or maybe centuries.

"It's a water gun," Ficus said. He sounded as though he were giving a perfectly ordinary answer to a perfectly ordinary question, although I hadn't uttered a word in ages.

"What'll you do if the Extinguishers come?" I asked. "Squirt them?"

He turned and shot one of his ancestors in the back of the head.

A painted statue of a robe-clad ancestor, that is. Their stone hair had a neat round tunnel like something drilled by a hard-beaked bird. Liquid dribbled out, coursing down to pool where the sculpted nape of their neck met layer upon layer of mage robes.

"A water gun," Ficus repeated. "Turns stuff to water."

He pointed the hot pink barrel of the gun at my forehead and winked.

The room that we'd stopped in displayed multiple stone caskets—possibly just for decoration, possibly housing bones and ash. He sat on one of them as though plopping down on a bench at the park, then crumpled a stick of gum into his mouth. He chewed very loudly.

"Gum?" he offered.

I declined. He shot a flawless circle of holes in the wall as though sketching out the shape of a dartboard. Then, apparently bored, he tossed the gun and caught it in his hands like a ball. I fought not to wince. The only good reaction was no reaction at all.

"Wanna know why the snuffers have it in for me?"

What I really wanted was for him to forget I was here, but that seemed like too much to ask.

"I'm a hero." He was grinning, but he sounded dead serious. "Terrorists hate heroes."

"Huh," I said feebly.

"It all goes back to that knife."

"The one you turned into a gun?"

"The real knife. The original knife. The one I left with Aunt Riegel." He made a yo-yo motion with his free hand. "Stole it from the Extinguishers. They'll step over any number of corpses to get it back."

I couldn't help myself. "Why?"

"It's priceless. Got their hands on a bit of Jacian technology. A whole system, you know. The knife is the key." He mimed turning a key in a lock. "The rest is worthless without it. With that knife, they can move vorpal holes."

"They can *what*?"

"I helped run a demonstration. Then I kept their precious knife for myself."

There's a problem with this hole, Wist had told me.

"The hole that ate the rose garden." My voice felt as if it were coming from one of those immobilized caskets. "It didn't spawn naturally on the estate. The Extinguishers—you—you transferred it."

"Yep," Ficus said readily. "From out in the southern marshes. Was a pretty fresh hole, too. Didn't exist in any records before we moved it."

I knew why the Extinguishers would kill to get that knife back.

Most of them had radicalized after experiencing some manner of irreversible loss. A child, a spouse, a workplace, a house, a hometown. A vorpal hole could swallow any or all of those.

Extinguishers blamed the modern prevalence of vorpal holes on Wist. On the Kraken. By their logic, the irreconcilable weight of her magic had tipped the world out of balance, tearing holes along its seams like rips in an overloaded shopping bag. Empty the bag of its burden, and new holes would stop appearing.

They were half right and half wrong. But a long time had passed since Wist officially got declared a Kraken-class mage. Eighteen years, maybe? And the Extinguishers' assassination attempts had never made much headway.

With the ability to shift vorpal holes from place to place, they'd have a real chance at turning the tide of public opinion.

The continent overflowed with vorpal holes large and small—more than one person could ever visit, much less seal. VorDef and local leadership advised Wist on which to prioritize. As a result, rifts in wealthy areas often got tended to first and fastest.

Wist did her best to stay on top of things; still, she couldn't be everywhere at once. Sometimes no one told her about dire vorpal holes out in the sticks until months or years after entire villages gave up and abandoned their ancestral lands.

Reclaim Ficus's secret knife, and the Extinguishers could make those vorpal holes a real problem for the Osmanthian elite who hid behind the shield of Wist's peerless magic. They could take holes from neglected regions and launch them like heavy artillery into the heart of the capital, over and over, until core members of the mageocracy had no choice but to make vorpal holes everywhere a top priority. Until more people started wondering if maybe the Extinguishers had a point.

The cut on my cheek started smarting whenever I'd been just about to forget it.

"Why steal their knife?" I asked. "You knew they'd hunt you down for it."

"Not this soon," he said evenly. "Could've dragged it out another month or two. Could've kept them anxious, wondering about my loyalties. Someone ratted me out."

"You kept it to spite them? What—got sick of rubbing shoulders with zealots? Then you shouldn't have gotten their tattoo in the first place."

He looked at me as if I'd started rambling in Jacian. He raised his garish gun again—my arms went cold—then swung to face his makeshift dartboard. He shot a bulls-eye three times in quick succession. More water leaked out, tracing a wan line down to where the wall met the floor.

When Ficus turned back to me, he was smiling brilliantly. "You fell for it, too."

He nudged up his sleeve again and traced his smoky tattoo with the end of his gun. (Water gun or not, he definitely wasn't following recommended safety practices for deadly weapons.)

"I've been undercover," he said. "I get paid to mess with the snuffers."

"Your brother said you got kicked out of..."

I trailed off.

How had Nerium put it?

A sad tale. He couldn't hack it.

He'd smiled wryly, inviting Wist and me to chuckle with him. Not that we ever would, but the invitation was there. In his tone and demeanor, he'd fully agreed with us: Shien Ficus wouldn't last a day as an intelligence operative. Ridiculous.

"Officially, only my org knows I'm an agent," Ficus said. "Unofficially— who could've guessed it, hm?"

He might be bullshitting me out of sheer boredom. On the other hand—an overweening need for secrecy might explain his current lack of a bondmate.

"You've barely done anything to hide it," I said. "You say things sympathetic to the Extinguishers. Everywhere you walk, you sow colorful rumors. You're an even worse fit for stealth work than Wist."

"Yeah." He showed unearthly white teeth. "It's a great gig. Being myself is the best damn cover that money can buy."

I felt sicker than ever. "I don't like knowing this. I *really* don't like knowing this."

"Relax. You won't snitch. Who would believe you?"

Wist would.

"Unmask me, and you'd be making yourself a traitor all over again," he went on. "I'm a loyal servant of the motherland. Or hey—maybe I'm telling you because no one who matters will ever see you alive again."

He gave me another practiced smile.

"You think Nerium outed you to the Extinguishers," I said dully.

"Couldn't have been anyone else. They must've slipped through at the same time as Tempus. Our security only weakens when you admit a visitor. Gotta know precisely how to work that loophole to break in."

"...You don't sound angry."

"Angry? At who?"

"Your brother."

Ficus leaned forward, gun dangling lightly from his fingers. The more I saw of it, the more it seemed like a toy.

"You're all alone in the world, aren't you." His tone had gone skin-crawlingly intimate. "No brothers? No sisters? Nah, you wouldn't understand."

"Wist won't be forgiving," I said. "She won't give you any final warnings."

He shrugged expansively. "She's not the one coming to execute me right now, is she?"

I threw caution to the wind. "Did you kill Miyu?"

"Miyu? Why?" he asked, all innocence. "Little Miyu never did a thing to hurt me."

33

WHEN WE FIRST entered the mausoleum, I'd felt the echoes of distant eruptions—magic, physical explosives, or both. Now, waiting like rabbits in a warren, we'd gone too deep to feel anything at all.

"So if the Extinguishers barge in, you'll hand me over," I said. "You'll tell them you can't give back their knife, but you can give them the Kraken's healer. You think your org would authorize that?"

"The Magebreaker isn't universally loved," he replied. Talk about an understatement. I was a sty in the eye of most Board members.

He held his translucent gun up in the sepia-toned light that seemed to seep from nowhere in particular. "That's half of why I took you."

I understood instantly that I didn't want to know the other half. Cold air closed around my throat.

"Will she come if you cry for her?" He still handled that stupid gun of his like an actor in a stage play. Broad elegant movements meant for an audience. "What would she do if she found you dead?"

I could say what Wist had done, once, when she found me dead in the past. No one knew what she'd do if it happened again.

"Won't be much use as a bargaining chip if I'm in pieces," I said thinly.

"Then I'll veil myself with magic. I'll bet on the snuffers getting apprehended before they find me. There's an MP already on the grounds, you see."

"Nerium could help the Extinguishers perceive you. His glasses let him look straight at you. Like in the library. Your stealth magic means nothing."

"Nerium and me, we've always loved games," Ficus said. "Victory isn't worth much if you never take risks."

He was more capable than anyone could've thought—anyone except, perhaps, Shien Nerium. And maybe Lear the Jacian.

But Ficus was also exactly what he appeared to be. Callous, capricious, impulsive. A mage could get away with his particular brand of derangement if they were rich and well-bred and good-looking. If they had sufficiently powerful backing.

Ficus rose from his seat on the closed stone casket.

"What's that in your pocket?" he asked.

I took my hand out. Empty. "Nothing that matters."

The end of Wist's braid stayed tucked in my pocket, gripping Nerium's card like a fist.

"I've always been good with fire," Ficus said thoughtfully.

Getting sound past my throat felt like squeezing dry hardened paint from a near-empty tube. I named the first skill that came to mind. "Pyro?"

"When I was fifteen, maybe."

He lowered his gun. Flames shaped like crawling hands rose from the marble floor. They jostled together, tumbled over one another, scuttled about with wavery fingertips.

I jumped up on the nearest casket like a cat on a kitchen table.

"This variant's called Incinerator," Ficus said helpfully. "An industrial-strength skill. No heat. No scent. Minimal ash. Can still make enough smoke to kill you. Won't even realize you're breathing it."

He could've been making me breathe it already. This whole time, he could've been kindling a hidden fire behind one of the caskets. There was enough sundry magic floating around in the mausoleum that I might not have noticed. Not till after invisible smoke clouded my head and choked my lungs.

The hands shot forward like fireworks launching, sprouting toward me on impossibly long arms with too many joints. Arcs of flame curved down with outstretched fingers.

I tripped backwards off the casket. The flaming hands could already have caught me. They'd slowed their approach, mocking me. They probably didn't need to masquerade as hands at all.

Ficus watched me scramble with half a smile. It was the most genuinely friendly look he'd ever pointed my way.

"It'd be so sad if she let you burn," he said.

The flames surged closer, backing me against the wall. The lack of heat made them seem less real than my many dreams of death.

I might have flinched and thrown my arms up. I might have involuntarily shut my eye. But I could perceive this fire even when I couldn't see it. An eyelid was no barrier to magic.

Terror, on the other hand, was very much a barrier to thought.

Wist's braid leapt off me and parried the curving arms of flame. It immediately caught fire. It kept twisting anyway, roping away those reaching fingers. Its twisting looked like the writhing of something dying in horrible pain.

I was still. Like how I'd been shocked to stillness when Ficus beat Ginko. I quailed as if he stood over me with the same cane. As if I were a healer who'd never been bonded to the Kraken. Who'd never earned the title of Magebreaker.

Ficus wasn't even looking. He'd turned away. He had his head cocked as though listening for something other than the hiss of fire eating Wist's hair.

If I launched myself at his back, couldn't I seize hold of his magic? I could puppeteer him into marching out there and executing every last lurking Extinguisher with his ridiculous water gun.

He'd never faced hobbling or hijacking before in his life. Unlike Wist, who'd practiced resisting me, he wouldn't know how to defend himself.

Somehow I'd convinced myself that I would only ever get one chance. That I had to time it right, or lose everything.

The truth was that horror jolted every bone in my body at the prospect of venturing even half a step closer to his golden head and relaxed shoulders and cheap-looking gun.

He would kill me not out of hatred, nor warped bigotry, nor as the first step of some convoluted political scheme. He would kill me on a whim. He would kill me because he had a little too much time on his hands, and there was no one else here to distract him with the knife game. He'd kill me, and he'd forget the whole thing in a matter of weeks.

Yet the heatless flames folded down into nothing once they'd finished consuming Wist's braid. They bowed gracefully out of existence.

Ficus looked over his shoulder as though curious to see what remained of me. He showed no surprise at the fact that I still stood there, shamefully alive, holding the wall like a jelly-legged novice at the edge of an ice rink. He crossed the floor in a few swift ringing steps that echoed nastily through the weakest parts of my teeth.

He gazed at the ash left by Wist's braid.

There was very little of it. Less ash than would've been deposited by a single incense stick. The room was devoid of the reek of burning hair.

He plucked Nerium's black business card off the black floor. He blew a coating of ash off it as though blowing smoke in my face.

"I sent my fire after his calling card." Ficus spoke as though letting me in on a secret. "Not after your flesh. Someone—something—understood that, and grasped how to protect you. If it was a bet, then these ashes won big. But I don't think you had much to do with it, did you?"

He crouched again and dragged an idle fingertip through Wist's trail of ash. He put that same finger on the tip of his tongue, then made a face. He pocketed Nerium's card. He nimbly flipped his gun from hand to hand.

"They're coming," he said. "Hear those footsteps?"

He grimaced as, for no apparent reason, he pinched more floor ash and sprinkled it in his mouth like a dusting of dirty powdered sugar.

A fist-sized knot hardened in my stomach.

The Extinguishers' footsteps were so distant that I couldn't be sure I hadn't imagined them. But they sounded inhumanly rapid.

Ficus began to straighten up. I pitched forward as if tripping over my own feet. I swiped at his back—not even grabbing anything, just dragging splayed fingers through the air by his shirt.

Close enough.

He moved at the same time I did, pivoting away from me, gun rising. He moved much more smoothly than me. He was never fully in reach.

He shot too late. I'd seized the reins of his magic. I borrowed his imperceptibility skill as though spraying myself with a hose. I vanished, hidden from his senses, and I was still in control.

He must've barely grasped what was happening. He could neither use nor revoke his own magic.

He didn't shout. He didn't whirl. His water gun bored a near-silent series of holes in the far wall, and then in a nearby casket. Right where I'd staggered half a breath ago, shortly after going imperceptible.

I hurtled into the next gallery as a squad of Extinguishers broke in to surround him.

I didn't get more than a fleeting impression of the Extinguishers. There were eight to ten of them. I didn't see any faces. I didn't look back.

I only made it through four more rooms before I hit the limit of my ability to run while simultaneously hijacking his magic.

I collapsed on a mezzanine overlooking a forest of tall pipes. Like a wind organ, except that there wouldn't ever be wind in here. The urn mounted in the alcove behind me looked like a water barometer.

I covered both eye sockets with my fists. I maintained a death grip on Ficus's magic. Scraps of sound came through it like noise transmitted along a string stretched between cups. The muted magical pop of his water gun. Stone cracking. A confusion of fighting.

With every passing second, the Void stirred more and more awake. It wasn't yet starving, but it was bottomless. It could always find room to consume. When I commandeered Ficus's magic, I may as well have thrust a bloody steak into the mouth of a lion. The Void slavered.

I held it off, somehow. It was like wrestling with my own shadow.

What would the Void do if I stopped breathing long enough to pass out? Would that contain it or liberate it? I couldn't remember if I knew the answer.

The sounds of combat petered out. Ficus had lost.

Whatever they'd done to him, he was still coherent enough to talk.

They asked him where the knife was.

A premonition palpitated through the threads of his magic. I knew what he was about to say.

He'd tell the Extinguishers that he'd brought me here. He'd tell them which direction I'd fled. He'd tell them *I* had their knife—the one he'd hidden with Aunt Riegel.

I rotated his branches the wrong way with a sharp, vicious twist. Like dislocating an arm.

He only faltered for a moment. Then he resumed speaking, steady through the pain.

My mouth came open as if I were about to scream. Panic poured in like drowning water.

The Void slipped through the increasingly rickety fence of my self-control. It leaked out from around the edges of my eyepatch—a useless fabric lid, incapable of holding anything in. It spilled out in an inky torrent, an avaricious flood.

I felt myself tip over sideways. It was akin to watching someone knock a glass off a table at the other end of a banquet hall. There was no one to catch me.

Through it all, I never let go of Ficus's magic.

I blacked out as the Void filled the mezzanine like poisonous mist.

34

THE FIRST THING I felt was the Void curled back inside my right eye socket, all but purring with contentment.

I was balled up on the floor. I contemplated—and promptly dismissed—the idea of trying to move. My left eye stayed closed.

A long time later, timid fingers pushed at me. Wist, I thought. I reached, sight unseen, to pat her arm or shoulder or side.

All I touched was empty air.

I caught at those familiar fingers, confused. Definitely her.

I squinted my eye open.

I was holding a disembodied left hand. Wist's hand, yes. Minus the rest of her, and minus her blue bond thread.

The hand tried to tug free.

I wouldn't let go. I was too drained for astonishment. This was part of Wist. So I latched on grimly, and with the same tenacity I'd shown toward Ficus's magic. I'd let the rest sort itself out later.

Ficus's magic?

It was gone without a trace. Either I'd lost my grip on him after losing consciousness, or the Void had devoured his magic right down to his core. Most mages needed much more time to regrow lost branches than Wist.

Either that, or he was dead.

Wist's hand gave up on trying to slither away.

From some angles, its severed end appeared like the clean chopped-off limb of a mannequin. From other angles—or if I blinked—it trailed a tadpole tail of mist.

I set the hand like a pet bird on my shoulder. My throat made a sound that I refused to acknowledge.

I'd lost her braid. Getting a bit of flesh in exchange was better than nothing, but what about the rest of Wist? What would show up next, her big toe? Her left knee rolling in like a coconut?

Wist, I'm here.

The severed hand awkwardly squeezed the side of my neck, though it couldn't have heard me. It felt comforting simply because it was so very her.

I crawled to my knees. The glass urn ensconced beside me—the one shaped like a water barometer—bore a fatal-looking crack. At least it hadn't spat out its contents.

The colossal organ pipes were badly skewed now. They leaned on one another like trees uprooted by a typhoon. Though there was still no indoor wind, they'd begun to generate a deeply unpleasant hum, the low grumble of a brooding machine. The sort of noise you'd use to scare off pests.

It certainly worked on me. With Wist's hand riding my shoulder, I felt my way along the frigid wall as if navigating a cave in the dark. I had vague memories of how I'd gotten here, and no clue how to get out.

My mental map might've been wildly off, but I had nothing else to rely on. I was so focused on following it that I almost walked straight into Wist.

I stared up at her, wordless.

We stood at the open threshold of a gallery, Wist on one side and me on the other. On the pompous walls behind her hung moody paintings that may or may not have been composed partly of dead Shien ash.

Her hair was white, and noticeably longer than it had been when she vanished. The ends stopped around her collarbone.

Her left arm stopped at her wrist.

The hand hitching a ride with me pressed apologetic fingertips into a stiff spot between my shoulder and neck. Then it launched itself like a flying squirrel. It snapped to Wist's stump as though drawn in by some secret magnetic force. The skin of her rejoined hand and wrist melded together, seamless.

Throughout this, her gaze remained fixed to my cheek.

"Was it Ficus?" she asked.

I'd completely forgotten about him cutting me. It seemed like small potatoes at this point.

"Yeah," I said, "but it doesn't matter. Have you seen him? What happened with the Extinguishers? How'd you come back? Is your hand okay?" My voice hitched. "The bond. It—"

I couldn't continue.

"I forced my way back through the hole in the garden," she said. "Walked into a contingent of Extinguishers attacking the manor."

"You stopped them?"

She nodded. Just once. "There aren't any left in the mausoleum. They might have escaped."

Or they might have gotten swallowed by the Void, shipwrecked sailors sinking to the bottom of an unforgiving sea.

"I meant to port to your exact location," she said abruptly. "I missed."

"Only by a couple hundred feet, no?"

"That's too large a margin of error."

"It's been a long time since you've had to find me without using our bond for coordinates."

Her face didn't crumple. I don't know if Wist's face was capable of crumpling. I'd forgotten how unfeeling she could appear. When we were bonded, I'd been able to sense so much more of her without looking.

The bond had given me constant reassurance. Something like walking along side by side, looking forward. Feeling for her hand without saying anything. Knowing it would be there. Anticipating every immeasurable subtlety of how she would respond to my touch. The bond was that times a million—whether we were together or apart, weary or rested, furious or placid.

"Ficus burned your hair," I blurted. "The hair you left with me. He burned it to nothing."

I didn't mention him licking the ashes. He'd done that exclusively to get a rise out of me. He hadn't derived much pleasure from the taste.

Wist blinked at me, bemused. "I can always grow more."

There were so many questions I ought to ask her. They came to me in all the wrong order. Like: why hadn't she reached for me yet? Why hadn't she pulled me to her, pulled me across the threshold? What was she waiting for?

She kept rubbing her left hand. It looked mostly solid, but occasionally the light of the mausoleum would pierce it as though filtering through muddy water.

"When I saw the thread gone." She ended it with the finality of a complete sentence. "I've never felt anger like that. Not in this lifetime. I would have killed him. I would have killed everyone on the estate except you. I felt their lives like a pile of squirming larva in my palm." Her left hand cupped the air. "It would've been easy."

"They lived," I said.

"I redirected myself. Something had built up in me almost to the point of berserking. Like a cannon already in the process of being fired. All I could do was wrench it around, change its aim at the last second. My rage drilled a path between worlds."

She stopped moving. She held her wrist as though taking it prisoner.

"If I'd been able to think a second longer, I would've understood the risks," she said. "I felt our bond tear as soon as I entered the passage. But it was too late to reverse. I couldn't turn around. Couldn't come back.

"The thread I went looking for—long gone. Vorpal space unmade it. Not a single molecule left. I protected my hand, but I couldn't protect one small—"

"It's your *hand*," I said. "It's part of you. Of course that's what you'd protect. You're lucky you managed to save it."

Unlike me, Wist didn't raise her voice. "That thread felt like part of me, too. Our actual bond was undeniably part of me. Part of both of us. And I—"

Apologies were coming. I didn't bother telling her to shut up. I threw myself at her, which ought to have worked just as well.

She caught me without staggering. It felt so right that I almost laughed. She smelled like Wist, not like alien worlds.

I was in her arms when the pain came. Blinding pain, as abrupt and unfair as a lightning strike.

It neatly sliced off my ability to think analytically or make noise, my understanding of where it came from or even where in my body I was suffering.

It didn't seem to originate from my body at all.

Wist didn't drop me. Before I could comprehend anything, I'd flung myself back.

Once again, the threshold of the room divided us.

35

I MET HER EYES. My skull tightened. Wist hadn't so much as winced, but she'd felt the same thing. I've known her long enough. I could tell.

"What?" I said dumbly, several seconds delayed. "What was—what...?"

The agony had drained from me as soon as I stopped touching her. Still, a long time seemed to pass before its ripples subsided. Only then could I think clearly enough to try to define it.

It was neither physical in the same way as a broken bone nor mental in the same way as a broken heart. It was phantom pain in a body part I'd never possessed, in a dimension I'd never experienced.

"Your face," Wist said. "It's bleeding."

As if that were somehow more important. It was just the same old cut from earlier.

"Well, sorry to inflict this terrible sight on you, but we've got to—"

Her magic caught the light like motes of dust. The sliced edges of my cheek knit together; the skin turned smooth and whole.

"I fixed it."

"Wist. Stay focused." I was proud that I'd managed to sound as detached as she did. "We have to experiment."

I got off my knees and stepped into the gallery where she waited. The paintings on the walls were a turgid slosh of dim ugly colors. Unusually depressing, even for a mausoleum.

I told Wist to hold out her hand.

"Which one?"

"Your left hand," I said. "I was fine when it touched me earlier."

She offered her hand as instructed. I gingerly touched one of the lines on her palm.

Skin met skin. Just the very tip of my finger. Not even enough to discern if her hand was warm or cold, dry or moist, steady or shaking.

It was like being electrocuted. My finger froze, welded to her. Then, with spasmodic effort, I broke contact. My arm windmilled back.

My breath cascaded out in ragged pants. Wist was unchanged, her eyes shadowed by the ominous overhead light. She'd had more than one lifetime to get accustomed to various types of magical pain.

"Maybe—maybe it'll be different through clothes."

Even to my own ears, I sounded desperate. I pulled my jacket sleeve up around my fist. Before I could lose my nerve, I prodded her arm.

That … might've been a few percentage points less awful? But it was like trying to weigh the difference between getting stabbed once in a vital organ, or multiple times in less fatal locations. As more seconds ticked by, I grew less sure about which time had actually been worse. I'd torn myself away from her just as quickly either way.

"I don't … I don't understand what's happening," I managed. My voice had climbed higher than usual. I despised it.

"Neither do I," said Wist.

"Never heard of anything like this."

"Neither have I."

"So we're both useless."

Normally, if your bond broke, it'd be because your bondmate had died. You might still be able to touch them, but only as a corpse. Post-separation, you'd never come together again as two living beings.

In other words, we had no way to tell if this were some sort of natural backlash—or a curse unique to the two of us.

"...For now," Wist said, "do you want to keep my hand?"

She detached her left hand as if pulling off a glove. It flickered in and out of solidity, sometimes so faint that I could've held it up to my eye like a magnifying glass and still seen every detail of the nearest gloomy painting. Most of the art here depicted battlefields.

"It's unstable," she added as an afterthought—the fingers of her disconnected left hand wiggled for emphasis—"but not in danger of dematerializing."

I imagined her standing on the other side of a busy room while her hand stowed away in my jacket. Ready for secret hand-holding at any moment. I imagined going together to a VorDef meeting—then me stumbling, sending her hand flying out of my pants and onto the table. I'd crack inappropriate jokes about it to stone-faced officials.

Then I imagined Wist looking on like a micromanaging supervisor while her detached hand had its way with me in the privacy of our bedroom. Maybe she'd leave her hand to ravish me while she went on tours of duty in faraway countries.

I hiccuped with laughter. Crazed laughter, if you must know. I laughed until Wist began to seem faintly worried. She reattached her left hand to the misty stub of her wrist.

It was as though our now-missing bond had infiltrated the entirety of my self with invisible roots. As though the bond getting ripped out like a weed had left me riddled with ghastly tunneled wounds.

Images of vines crowded my mind. The ancient wisteria outside Aunt Riegel's window. The way wisteria vines could dismantle old walls. They'd topple any inadequate form of support. They couldn't help it. They hadn't chosen to grow powerful to the point of destruction.

My vocal cords squeezed as if there were a hand on my throat. "How will I heal you?"

"Try it without touching me," Wist said.

Okay. Fair. Bonded or not, I had more than enough skill to heal her magic without physically massaging her flesh.

I hovered my hand over the small of her back. Like we were teenagers out on a first date, and I hadn't figured out how much physical contact made sense. My heart thudded unevenly—a beat better suited for a swaying bridge.

I knew Wist loved me. She loved me more than was right or reasonable. I knew that, but I missed how intensely palpable it had been through our bond.

Guess what happened the very instant I attempted to exert my influence on her magic.

That same raw pain exploded in me, worse than ever. My next impulse was to grab at her, to seek refuge. But I didn't. I restrained myself. I stopped placing any pressure whatsoever on her branches.

The pain abated.

I wanted to holler and cry and scream to the heavens. An empty, shapeless, ghostly want. Even if I had it in me to scream, I wouldn't have known what to say.

Then—though I hadn't been thinking about it in the slightest—I understood something. The gears in my head clicked impeccably into place. A hidden window opened, and merciless light poured in.

I couldn't have explained it to anyone for the life of me. With a disturbingly fierce clarity, I grasped not just how to break bonds all on my own—I'd already had that unsought-for epiphany—but also how I could do it more cleanly. So cleanly that severed bondmates could cuddle up together afterward without the slightest discomfort.

(Although there were cases where it'd be better to leave them with this messy, double-edged pain, to make physical contact with each other all but impossible. Like a built-in restraining order.)

I started laughing again, though little sound came out. God, I'm brilliant. My sudden understanding was a perfect diamond, unbreakable and unwanted.

I lurched over to a poorly lit corner of the gallery. I vomited.

Wist's footsteps followed me.

A hand rested on the back of my head. Her left hand—broken away from her body again, liberated like a bird from a cage. It must've been that hand, and it must've been disconnected from her, because there was no new wave of all-consuming pain. Nothing to send me pitching forward into my own vomit.

Needless to say, it smelled horrid. My stomach heaved again at the stench of acid. Wetness dripped down the side of my nose. Would've liked to call it tears of laughter.

A cool breeze blew past me. The puddle vanished, and so did its smell, although the taste in my mouth persisted.

"Don't waste your magic," I said automatically.

"Someone would've had to clean that up eventually," Wist replied.

I pulled off my eyepatch and wiped my face with it. This didn't accomplish much except for spreading the wetness around more evenly.

Every instance of magic use would make Wist's tangling worse. No way around it.

I couldn't heal her. Well, maybe I could. But forcing myself to work through that pain—and forcing Wist to endure it all the while, too— didn't seem like it would lead anywhere good.

We weren't bondmates anymore. She could accept treatment from any competent healer, although most would have no clue how to work on a Kraken-class mage.

I got up. Wist's left hand seemed to have discovered a comfortable perch right around the nape of my neck.

Realistically speaking, there was only one possible solution, and we both knew it.

I set my emotions aside. This was not difficult, to be honest. Didn't have much left to set aside in the first place. Just a papery shell like the withered husk of a lantern plant.

"You'll need to go to other healers," I said briskly. "Let's start by asking Mori."

"It can wait a day or two."

I shot Wist a skeptical look. She appeared unmoved. But out of her sight—and mine—her severed hand tensed against the back of my neck.

"I was in the old world," she said.

"Our old world?"

"I had to get healed over there, on the other side."

"Yeah, I kind of figured—"

"I needed healing to regain control of my magic. To come home."

Her hidden fingers pressed fitfully at the knobs of bone at the top of my spine, as if trying to play a broken instrument.

I genuinely didn't know what to say. This was not a betrayal. I'd never demanded that she refrain from seeing other healers. It had merely occurred as the simple and inevitable consequence of becoming bondmates.

Healing would've been an unimpeachable necessity, if only to prevent her from going berserk in another world. The world that she (and therefore I) had once abandoned. So I wasn't jealous per se. Jealousy wouldn't have made any sense.

But I didn't like it, okay? I really, really didn't like it.

I cleared my throat. "How soon can we try to bond again?"

Wist remained silent. Well, it's not like I couldn't understand her hesitation. Bonding would no doubt be just as painful as—as whatever happened whenever we touched now. Bonding would be worse, actually, if such a thing were even possible. With no guarantee of the pain ending once the splintered ends of our bond wove back together.

We might end up locking ourselves together for a lifetime of torture. A lifetime that might turn out to be pretty short, frankly, if it got bad enough.

I've got a decent head on my shoulders. But I didn't have much confidence in my ability to calmly unravel our bond again while mind-erasing pain thundered through both of us, multiplying as it reverberated back and forth, liquefying our senses like silty ground in an earthquake.

"Let's leave Follyhope," Wist said at last. "Then let's decide what comes next."

36

"I closed the vorpal hole," Wist added.

"The what—? Oh. When? How?"

"As I came back through. Sealed it off behind me."

"And the Extinguishers are all taken care of? One way or another."

Wist nodded.

"So we can get out of here," I said. "Job done." Rarely had I tasted a hollower triumph. "But where's Ficus?"

The moment I uttered those words, I knew in my bones that she was about to use a scanning skill to find him. With heroic effort, I stopped myself from reflexively catching her arm.

"Don't," I said. "We can do a little legwork. Conserve your magic. On that note—" I reached back and prised her left hand off the nape of my neck.

I tossed the hand to Wist. She fitted it to her arm. A brief dark mist seeped out of the vanishing seam. She didn't shake her wrist or flex her fingers or test it in any other way: it was immediately and utterly hers again.

We hadn't been whispering discreetly in the shadows. If Shien Ficus were still in the mausoleum—and if he were in any state to be active—surely he'd have shown up to interrupt us.

"Might be nothing left of Ficus to find," I said. "The Void might have taken him. His magic, and then all the rest of him. I felt it slipping out of me. Then I fainted."

I opened my right eyelid and asked her to take a look.

Wist bent closer. About as close as she could get without touching me. She peered, absurdly, into my empty eye socket. As if it might be possible to see a tiny Ficus (or his fading corpse) stowing away inside.

Well, I'd wanted this. My mouth still tasted awful. I kept my lips pressed shut.

You know, it's not like we were kids wondering how a kiss would feel, or fretting over whether a kiss would even be welcome. I knew precisely what would happen if I stretched a little to kiss her—not that I actually would have, in this case, without rinsing my mouth first. But you get the point.

My mind wouldn't even have gone there if not for the fact that there was no safe way for us to touch. There was an extremely high chance that I'd just killed one of her brothers. Not a beloved brother, but still. This was not a situation for making mopey eyes at one another, or starting anything remotely risqué.

The thing is, there was something very specifically infuriating about being unable to kiss her or squeeze her or lovingly head-butt her the way I always would. Isn't it human nature to want to do the exact things you're told not to? The absolute worst itches are the ones you can't scratch.

"The Void seems no different from usual," Wist pronounced.

"Which doesn't prove it didn't eat your brother," I finished. "We just don't know."

I fumbled my eyepatch back on. It was still disagreeably damp. My hands felt weak with thwarted desire.

"If it's swallowed him, there may not be any evidence left," said Wist. "Either in the Void or outside it."

Yeah, I wasn't too worried about getting prosecuted. No one knew about the Void. They wouldn't be able to deduce its existence from circumstantial evidence, either. Wouldn't be able to wrap their minds around it. I had a hard enough time wrapping my mind around it, and it lived in me.

"Where did you last see Ficus?"

I looked around. "Uh...."

She asked if I would rather search for him or leave without looking.

Think what you like about me, but I wouldn't be particularly devastated if it did turn out that the Void had taken him. I had a feeling I'd get away with it, too—the Extinguishers would make an easy scape-goat. They'd been openly hunting him.

So on the one hand, I couldn't care less about what had become of Shien Ficus. My last memory of him would be how he'd grimaced after tasting incinerated hair.

On the other hand, I did want to know what the Void might have done to him—and to anyone else in the mausoleum at the time. The Void had changed after coming to roost in me, and we still had so little concrete knowledge of its habits.

"Let's look," I said. "Help me retrace my steps. I'm kind of lost."

If we uncovered no clues, I'd make up my own end to the story. We could tell the Shiens we were done with them. We could port back to Wist's tower and nurse our wounds—far from the clan, and far from their troubles. I couldn't wait.

We backtracked to the mezzanine where I'd awakened. Wist silenced the low-whining pipes with a look.

From there, she translated my garbled explanations into a route back to the room with stone caskets. (There were many other rooms housing stone caskets, but only one had recently played host to high-level incineration magic.)

"That way," I said, "except it felt like going forward. The door was more on the left." I pointed at a wall without any visible doors.

Wist didn't use magic to parse what I meant. Nor could she rely on our bond. She nevertheless displayed a remarkable knack for reading my mind.

Along the way, I gave her a blow-by-blow account of everything that had happened since Nerium and Tempus abandoned me in the curtained library.

Eventually we ended up at the entrance to the chamber of caskets. An undefinable miasma hung about the room, something heavy and metallic that mingled poorly with the rawness of my nose and mouth.

Water gun holes riddled the walls like a complex game of connect-the-dots. Columnar wax candles stood on several caskets, naked and unlit. Their wicks were black.

A reddish-black stain ran down the front of one central casket like a tattered altar cloth. It ran all the way down to the floor. The casket was much more generously sized than seemed necessary to fit a single ancestor's sacred ashes or honorable effigy. The casket equivalent of a king-sized bed, you could call it.

On top of the heavy stone lid rested Shien Ficus's sawed-off head.

I swayed. Wist didn't.

My body reacted as if I were seeing double. Part of me looked at the plastic shine of gore and thought it seemed like a cleverly crafted prop. Only the smell suggested otherwise.

Another part of me realized with glittering clarity that despite my contempt for Wist's siblings, despite my fear for my own life, despite my spurts of fury and occasional fantasies about hacking off the heads of hated foes—I wouldn't have done it.

There was an impassable gulf between the catharsis of violence in the back of my mind and the palpable reality of his leaking ragged neck, his slack bloody mouth, his livid bruised cheeks. Someone had struck him before killing him. Maybe almost as hard as he'd struck Ginko in the dining room.

I wouldn't have done it.

But I had—in a way—hadn't I? If the Void muffled his screams like a cocoon ... if the Void held him down....

Wist kept half-reaching for me as I mastered myself. It must've pained her not to be able to catch me when I staggered.

Blood darkened the ends of Ficus's golden hair, the sort of hair that would've gained a bewitching beauty by firelight.

There was no firelight left now. Snuffed candles flanked him. So did his own severed hands, chopped off right at the forearm, rotated carefully so they rested palm-up, giving a full view of the Extinguisher tattoos that ran from his wrists to just below the remains of his elbows. One arm still wore a fashionable cluster of dark masculine bracelets.

No sign of the rest of him. Nor of his precious water gun. Nothing remained but his head, his hands, congealed blood, and taunting candles.

Bloody bootprints tracked wild circles around other caskets. They were difficult to make out against the dark floor. None seemed to lead back outside the room, anyway. If the Extinguishers had managed to flee the premises, their escape route must've been magical.

"He's definitely dead," I said, somewhat unnecessarily. "Unless that's a—a wax replica. Guess he *is* the sort of celeb who'd end up in wax museums. They'd pose him side by side with you, wouldn't they?"

"There's a reason I don't go to wax museums," Wist said blandly.

She floated off the ground and wafted like a ghost over to Ficus's decapitated head.

"They used his own gun to do it," she said.

"What, sever his head?"

"One watery shot at a time."

"Inefficient, to say the least," I muttered.

I wondered what they'd done with the rest of him. They'd left behind the most obvious (and most portable) trophies. What use would the Extinguishers have for his headless and handless corpse? Without that famously captivating face, his body could've belonged to any well-kept man north of forty.

"Clem," Wist said.

"Hm?"

"They stuck Nerium's card in the back of his head like a cleaver."

I skirted the edges of the chamber, trying not to tread on any drying footprints, until I reached a position where I could sort of see it.

"Might be the card Nerium gave me," I said. "Ficus took it after he burned your braid."

Someone—very likely the Extinguishers—had confiscated Ficus's water gun. They'd shot off his head and hands. They'd killed him while I lay on the floor in an oblivious swoon. The moment he died, the imperceptibility magic I'd stolen would've vanished, exposing me. Maybe by then, with a fresh corpse on their hands, the Extinguishers would've been more focused on getting the heck out of there than sweeping the rest of the mausoleum. Especially if they got word from their colleagues over at the manor that Wist the Kraken had returned to remind everyone why she was widely considered invincible.

Both Wist and I had killed before. Few Extinguishers had ever made it out of her tower alive. There were other incidents, too, that she liked to talk about even less. As for me: there was the time with Larkspur a couple years ago, and (albeit less directly) the tragedy of Magus Gwindel, back when I'd had political aspirations.

The Void—still somewhat sated from its tryst with Wist—may have miraculously settled for gnawing at Ficus's magic rather than gulping down his whole body, heart, and soul. So the Void and I may not have murdered him in a literal sense.

Then again, I'd hijacked his magic and left him vulnerable, unable to use his own imperceptibility skill to hide from deadly foes. For that matter, the Void might have torn so vigorously into his branches and core that he went into a fatal state of shock and never had a chance to recover.

Let's say he keeled over as if he'd gone into cardiac arrest. Let's say he didn't respond to any attempts to rouse him. The Extinguishers might've assumed that he'd pulled the stereotypical move of a spy activating an instant-kill cutting buried in a convenient back tooth.

The Void eating him to death made more sense, honestly, than the Extinguishers slaughtering him on the spot. They still wanted their knife back. No matter how much they might loathe him for being a spook, surely he'd be more useful alive than dead.

If they were going to cart away the bulk of his body regardless, might as well let him live. They could hold him for ransom, or pry agency secrets out of him, or at least force him to help recover their knife.

Wist guessed at what I was thinking. "His death, his decapitation ... could've happened in either order."

"That's something for Tempus to puzzle over," I said. "Did you see him during combat at the manor?"

Apparently the answer was yes.

"Could you call him here? The longer we wait, the more suspicious he'll get."

37

WIST HAD BEEN hovering above Ficus's chopped-off head and hands as we spoke. Now she floated over to the edge of the room to join me. I'd found a spot bare of blood—whether splattered or tracked around—and with fewer damp gun-holes.

As she alighted, I realized I'd gotten things all out of order. I'd vomited *before* witnessing the sticky aftermath of a vicious murder. Coming face-to-face with a severed head had left me comparatively unmoved.

Not a great omen for the state of my psychological landscape, huh? But I wasn't interested in delving into that at the moment. I carried a literal Void in me. I'd be here all year if I performed a sincere self-examination of every last blot on my soul.

Call me shallow if you like. I was just glad I'd gotten away with only throwing up once.

A black tide went through Wist's hair, eradicating any hint that it had ever gone white. So much for avoiding gratuitous magic use.

But that white hair had made me wonder. "You didn't do it again, did you?" I asked, not without trepidation.

"What?"

"Borrow strength from your future self."

"No," she answered. Not quickly, but quicker than usual for Wisteria Shien. "This time it was just … stress. Or the shock of foreign magic."

"Or the Queen peeking out to say hello."

I almost reached up to brush her newly black hair off the side of her neck. I huffed out an irritated breath and moved half a step away. Not even under the threat of torture could I be trusted to keep my hands to myself.

"Didn't people already see you with white hair over at the manor?" I said.

"Briefly. They'll think it was an illusion, or a passing side effect of battle magic."

"Still, why rush to change it back?"

"To avoid extra questions."

If I were her, I'd rather field distracted questions about my hair—as opposed to questions about where I'd been and what I'd been up to all this time.

Then again, no one from outside Follyhope (not even Tempus) had any idea that she'd vanished to the other side of a vorpal hole. As long as the Shiens kept their mouths shut, she could pretend she'd flitted off to some classified location on urgent Kraken business.

"I'll summon Tempus," Wist said.

True to her word, she ported him in. Except—perhaps still disoriented from her travel to other realms—she ported him to a spot high up near the shadowed crevices of the frieze-adorned ceiling.

Tempus made a noise like three different barnyard animals rolled together into a single shrieking chimera.

He fell fast, then more slowly, cushioned by Wist's magic.

Wist put out her arms and caught him like a princess.

This lasted for about a tenth of a second. Tempus sprang free of her with the superhuman agility of an insulted cat. He brushed invisible dust off his uniform with such vehemence that he had to be hurting himself.

Wist would've caught anyone who dropped from the ceiling at her. In this case, she'd used her arms as a form of magical frugality. She'd whipped out a modest skill to temper his fall. Without any physical intervention, it would've made for a jarring reintroduction to solid ground. A praiseworthy example of corner-cutting.

Anyway, she hadn't intended to humiliate him. It just came to her naturally.

Thankfully, Tempus wasn't the type to get off on being embarrassed. Not by a woman, at least.

I did find myself more than a little aggravated at the fact that Wist had been able to touch him without a second thought. If I fell from the same place this very instant, it'd hurt less to belly-flop into one of the nobly arrayed caskets than it would for Wist to catch and hold me.

But of all the people in all the countries on the continent, I knew better than to waste time being jealous of Minashiro Tempus. Who, thanks to Wist, was now thoroughly out of sorts. He kept obsessively checking his clothes, as if expecting to find that we'd stolen one of his precious spare buttons.

"Inspector," I said. "Turn around."

I'll give him this: he reacted with unassailable professionalism to the sight of Shien Ficus's gory leftovers.

I don't know if they'd ever had the kind of relationship he'd longed for back when we were all much younger. I don't know if his view of Ficus—as a human being, I mean—had changed over the years.

Maybe Tempus's fixation had never expanded beyond the territory of a youthful crush. Whatever the case, it couldn't have felt great to see that once-alluring face gone all vague and sagging and listless—lids low and languid, showing only a sliver of the whites of dead eyes.

Tempus immediately unleashed a skill that sent fine particles of magic fanning out to coat the room. A way to preserve the crime scene in every detail. It reminded me of using setting spray on a made-up face.

"You aren't surprised," I said.

"I had him marked," Tempus said shortly. "You insisted."

Ah. Yes.

"You could tell he—"

"I knew something drastic had happened." Tempus stopped. He pressed the side of his fist to his forehead. "I couldn't drop everything to come find him. The Extinguishers back at the manor—I had to stay there till—"

"You did right," Wist said. Tempus bristled.

We answered rapid questions about the overall sequence of events. Tempus paced between caskets, sometimes pausing to mutter at a transparent scroll. Afterward, it rolled up to the thickness of a cigarette. He tucked it angrily behind his ear.

We stayed out of the way in a corner, since he wouldn't let us leave yet. As the acidic burn in my mouth receded, I picked up more nuance in the muddled smells around us. Dirty blood. Stale old smoke. The body odor of strangers. Burnt-out magic.

I had thoughts of my own, though I'd chosen not to voice them. Whether Ficus's life had been snuffed out by the Void or by a bloodthirsty crew of Extinguishers, it seemed odd that they'd gone to the trouble of laboring over his corpse, creating a lurid display with his head and hands.

A warning to other traitors in their ranks? A savage personal insult aimed at the Shien clan—the clan they blamed for raising a monster?

Or did they believe that showily brutalizing Wist's brother would be the best shot they'd had in ages at landing an unseen blow on Wist herself?

The risk of enraging one of the most powerful families in Osmanthus seemed proportionately much greater than any potential reward. The Extinguishers had their own continued survival to think of. They hadn't lasted this long without some notion of what they could and couldn't get away with.

Which brought me back to the question of how they'd penetrated such a well-defended estate.

To Ficus, it hadn't been a question at all. He'd concluded immediately that it must have been an inside job. And if it were an inside job, it must have been Nerium.

I couldn't find many holes in that argument. The only part of it that bothered me was—why now? By all appearances, and despite tremendous differences in looks, career, and personality, Nerium and Ficus had gotten along better than any of Wist's other adoptive siblings.

This couldn't have been the first time that Nerium grew weary of cleaning up his brother's messes. More like the thousandth time. Besides, Nerium was too cold-blooded to have been stirred to vengeful righteousness by Ficus's capricious attacks on Ginko and Wist. The most profound emotion I could imagine that provoking in him was a well-tamed annoyance.

Summoning terrorists to take out a bloody hit could hardly have been Nerium's only remaining option for getting Ficus under control, either. It might make more sense if it wasn't really Nerium's decision at all. If he'd been acting under orders—or a strongly worded suggestion—from someone higher up.

Who (other than double-crossed Extinguishers) might benefit from Ficus's death?

Lear had given me the impression that Ficus was too publicly popular to eliminate. But Grandmother Shien might've changed her mind after his antics with the hole in the garden and Wist.

Despite being essentially estranged from the clan, Wist remained—at least in name—a central pillar of their influence. They never hesitated to make use of their assumed association with the Kraken.

Grandmother might tolerate all sorts of petty pranks, no matter how cruel. She might turn a blind eye to healers being so harangued and abused that they needed semi-legal numbing magic just to function. She might let her grandchildren tear each other apart in the name of growing up tough. She might lock up and all but erase the existence of her own daughter—a stunted mage—to avoid unwanted scrutiny.

No matter what Ficus and Nerium did to Wist as a child, Grandmother Shien had never once intervened. Wist had survived all that to become a new Kraken. Now, perhaps, Grandmother thought Ficus had gone one step too far. A threat to the life and health of the Kraken was a threat not just to the Shien clan, but to the stability of the entire continent.

Or maybe she'd made up her mind about Ficus a long time ago. Maybe she'd been waiting and waiting for a handy excuse to get rid of him.

38

It wasn't my job to solve murders. Especially not ones where I might bear a significant share of the blame.

I answered Tempus truthfully, minus a few key details about things like the Void. I didn't volunteer any further opinions.

PubSec would have to conclude the obvious. That a contingent of Extinguishers had murdered Shien Ficus. That the Extinguishers had exploited a little-known security vulnerability to trespass on the Shien estate—and that their insider information about Follyhope might have come from none other than Ficus himself.

There was, after all, the matter of his tattooed arms.

"It was the guard ostriches," Nerium said gravely.

I took the bait. "What'd they ever do to you?"

"There's a suite of defensive cuttings around the estate perimeter. It had to be modified to allow for the presence of Miyu's ostriches."

"Aren't they all gone now?"

"They were on active patrol up until recently, and they'll be back again soon enough. The accommodations made for those ostriches ended up introducing a temporary security loophole. One that would surface each time a guest enters Follyhope."

"Should've fixed it."

"Clearly. It's a very complicated and sensitive system—one can't rush changes, sadly. We're still working to confirm the loophole's parameters."

I got tired of acting like neither of us knew what had really happened. "Then there's no way some random Extinguisher could've figured it out on their own. A Shien told them."

"Not necessarily," he said with a smile. "An intelligent observer might have witnessed the vulnerability when you and Wisteria first arrived, for instance. This proves only that they were having the estate closely watched."

It was late afternoon. Flurries had stopped falling after briefly dampening the unreceptive ground. Nerium and Wist and I waited in the blue-floored receiving room while Tempus spoke at length with Grandmother Shien.

The scintillating colors of Ficus's magic loomed over us, giving me a troubled sense of deja vu. For being rendered in only two dimensions, the painting was a remarkable likeness.

It seemed a tad morbid to have convened beneath a murder victim's portrait, especially given our notable lack of weeping or even token sadness. But here we were anyway.

At least none of us felt obligated to perform grief. I might've expected it from Nerium, soulless though he was. Perhaps he knew better than to waste his efforts on his current audience.

Tempus had brought a couple Extinguishers into custody, though none seemed liable to say much. Wist had tried very hard not do them direct physical harm. She may have overcompensated: apparently she'd slipped up and turned them into gibbering fools. She was their mortal foe, after all, the subject of untenable levels of primal hatred, primal terror. She'd appeared on the scene like the magical equivalent of the sun rising from a fresh-dug grave—not up in the sky where it belonged.

Not all of the Extinguishers at the manor had lived. Nerium informed us that Grandmother's toxic birds had taken out several attackers.

This astonished me for a number of reasons. First, the fact that those itty-bitty birds hadn't been left at Follyhope solely for decorative purposes. Second, the fact that they could kill a grown adult.

Did all they have to do was rub their feathers on you? Would they peck you like small woodpeckers, or inject venom like a snake? Were toxic birds in the wild just as deadly to humans, or had these been specially bred for it?

I was enormously curious, but I was also making an effort to engage in less frivolous talk. Wist had done her duty in closing off the vorpal hole. Everyone could see that.

We were well on track to escape the estate before dinner. Just needed to wrap up a couple last loose ends.

So far, no one had questioned our lack of physical contact. (One of the benefits of habitually being discreet.)

In this whole household, only Aunt Riegel knew our bond was broken. I hadn't confessed to anyone else, although Nerium might be harboring dark suspicions of his own. Wouldn't put it past him.

I trusted Riegel despite the fact that she had no particular incentive to keep her mouth shut. Despite her being the least powerful mage in the entire clan.

They'd sequestered her away for years in a sort of genteel captivity, just like how they sent excess healers off to the cloister. Perhaps it was her very powerlessness and insignificance that made me trust her. She seemed more human than other Shiens.

They would overlook her, trapped by complex magical corridors. Fiddling patiently with her intricate tiny hats. Marking the passage of the seasons by how the wisteria vine outside her window grew and shed flowers and seed pods and leaves. It'd send out wild antennae-like tendrils, seeking new structures to cling to, only to have them sternly chopped back to bristling stubs.

No one would expect Shien Riegel to know anything of importance.

I guess that's why I'd blurted it out to her. I'd been caught in a moment of weakness, yes, but my instincts had been on point. Some part of me must've considered it safe to blabber one of the biggest secrets I'd ever kept, even though I'd never met her before in my life.

At the moment, Wist's return seemed sufficient to quash further questions about our bond. The clan had far more pressing concerns. For starters—something would have to be done about Ficus's head and hands, if not the rest of him.

If anyone traced him back to the org where he'd worked as an agent, I suppose they'd disavow knowledge of him. Such was the way of things.

I'd spare no melancholy thoughts for him—no more than I had for Shien Miyu. Ficus himself wouldn't have been particularly torn up by that sort of abandonment. It'd be beyond ridiculous for me to waste energy furrowing my brow on his behalf.

Especially since it was quite likely his closest family who'd decided that he needed to die. Nerium—one hand relaxed on the end of his cane, gazing affectionately up at the radiant portrait of Ficus's magic—didn't exactly seem wracked by guilt.

Proper Shien mages would possess little capacity for remorse. Follyhope had a way of squeezing out that sort of vulnerable human emotion as if emptying a fruit of soft pulp. To this day, it astounded me that Wist hadn't emerged from the chrysalis of her Shien upbringing as a finely honed sociopath.

I didn't ask Nerium why the clan had condemned his brother. Whether he'd been behind it from start to finish, or his grandmother had made the ultimate decision, they would've been careful not to leave traces. No one would be able to prove that they'd had contact with the Extinguishers. Any such accusations would sound downright histrionic.

I was satisfied with my hypothesis. Shien Miyu and Shien Ficus: when all was said and done, these two deaths represented the surgical elimination of two potential liabilities to the family. That's what they had in common.

Grandmother must've written Miyu off years ago. As soon as that one time I made her go berserk. Grandmother must also have seen that Ficus, who so relished risky games, would keep upping the ante over and over. All the rest of his life. Without any care for who else might have to deal with the fallout.

Didn't this fit with established patterns, too? Virtually everyone in the generation above Wist and her siblings had one by one become nonentities. Like their parents, exiled for seedy financial crimes.

I'm not a biologist, but I've heard of animals that slaughter their young at the slightest provocation. In humans, maybe this was a sickness of the rich and powerful. Grandmother had found her descendants to be unforgivably deficient.

I'd offered Nerium a few rote words of condolence. He accepted with off-putting graciousness. Only Doctor Hazeldine seemed genuinely shaken up about Ficus getting butchered. I hadn't seen him for more than a couple brief minutes, though.

The statue of the titan behind the manor returned to its original lazy position, stretched out flat on its belly like an overheated dog. The Extinguishers had left other scars on the manor grounds. But the damage outside wasn't as shocking as I might've expected. No giant smoking craters.

Overall, it paled in comparison to the now-sealed vorpal hole that had annihilated the glorious rose garden.

The Extinguishers' much-coveted yo-yo knife had remained safe with Aunt Riegel throughout the attack. The clan had already turned it over to authorities. Come to think of it, I'd noticed quite a few strangers (wearing uniforms marked by varying degrees of militancy) prowling the estate.

As we spoke of this, Nerium's pensive smile slipped.

"Shouldn't have done that." He spoke half to himself, in a curious flat tone that reminded me chillingly of Wist.

"The Extinguishers, you mean?" I asked. "Shouldn't have beheaded your brother?"

"That, too. Quite uncalled for." He had both hands clasped on the end of his cane. "No, I was thinking of Ficus. He shouldn't have left the artifact with Aunt Riegel."

"He said it'd be safest there."

"Tell me, how would she defend herself if terrorists broke down her door?"

"Uh—"

"How would she call for help if they hurt her? They might not charge in there intending to wound an innocent old woman, but she's very frail. They'd have been jacked up on adrenaline."

"It was Ficus's plan, not mine," I ventured.

"Forgive me. I've become overheated."

"Might want to tone it down," I said. "For your own sake."

"How so?"

"You sound very angry at him. Your freshly dead brother. Your tragically, cruelly murdered brother. We found him with that fancy business card of yours buried in his skull like a hatchet."

"The very same business card I gave you, if I recall correctly."

"Yeah," I said. "Sorry. You're all about optics, aren't you? It's in your company name. Anyway, the optics aren't great."

"If I were to murder someone, I'd make at least a cursory attempt not to leave my business card with their corpse."

"Right. No one's going to accuse you of being dumb enough to put it there yourself. It just seems like a message, you know? One simple message can get interpreted in many different ways. Not all of them look good for you."

I knew I'd gone too far. I knew because he turned his head with the mechanical smoothness of an owl.

"Nerium," Wist said.

She'd been occupying a corner of the room, arms crossed, blending in with a stand of dark luxuriant houseplants. All of which matched or exceeded her in height.

She didn't even look our way, but her voice came from so close that she seemed to be seated right between us, so close that it was like a physical thing on me.

Weakness went down my spine (tempered somewhat by the fact that she'd uttered her brother's name, not mine).

"Why, that's another point we have in common," Nerium said to me. He smiled again. "The optics are rather undesirable for both of us, aren't they? Ficus was found with my business card, yes. You found him—and he was closer to you than to anyone else when he died."

"Don't remind me," I said. "I'll have nightmares."

He didn't believe this for a second. "It must have been dreadful, what they did to him. I'm glad you weren't awake for it. I'm so very glad you weren't forced to witness it, whatever hell they made in our mausoleum. The lack of witnesses might prove troublesome for PubSec—but you win some, you lose some."

"Nerium," Wist said again.

"I'm being facetious," he told her. "It's my natural instinct, I'm afraid, in sorrowful times such as these. Unseemly, I know. But please do lower your hackles. Let's avoid setting a record of two murders in one day."

"It's already been set." Wist hadn't lowered her hackles at all. "Multiple Extinguishers died."

"You know quite well what I meant. Don't split hairs."

He took out another business card—just as fine as the one that had gotten buried in Ficus's brain matter—and handed it to me with a self-deprecating flourish.

I pocketed it. I wondered if this new card would end up sticking out of some other cadaver like a festive candle in a cake.

<h1 style="text-align:center">39</h1>

At last Tempus showed up and told us we were free to leave. I could've hugged him (for both our sakes, I refrained). PubSec would contact Wist if they needed anything further.

I waited while she ducked in for a few parting words with Grandmother Shien. I tried and failed to picture Grandmother wailing from loss. Whether or not she'd personally played some part in arranging Ficus's murder, big displays of grief didn't seem to be much of a Shien specialty. Nerium paid tribute to his siblings with mourning colors, not tears.

Once Wist emerged, Nerium said he would see us off. I waved him away and told him to give us an hour. The Sparrowhawk Room had a bath better than any five-star hotel—not that I'd seen many myself. I'll enjoy one last soak at your expense, I said.

We did not, in fact, go take a bath. After getting Wist alone, I pulled her aside without touching her, a feat that involved tugging haplessly at the air by her arm. "I met your aunt while you were away," I said in a whisper.

"Who?"

"Aunt Riegel. Shien Riegel."

Wist still looked blank.

"The stunted mage."

At this, her face changed more than it had upon spotting Ficus arrayed bloodily among burnt-out candles.

"Let's go see her before we take off," I said. "She was good to me."

Wist didn't argue. But she moved slowly as we went through the corridors, as though dragging an unseen weight. Her left hand—safely separated from her arm—clung like a limpet to my right hip.

Sometimes, even with her hand properly attached, the shadow of her left arm stopped at the wrist. Right now, conversely, the fingers holding my waistband cast no shadow of their own at all.

"You feel everything your hand feels?" I slid my fingers between her knuckles.

"Of course," Wist said. "It's mine."

We had three eyes between the two of us. You'd think this would make it easier to accurately spot the differences between corridors. You'd be wrong: we messed up several times and found ourselves forced to start over.

It didn't help that I was trying to simultaneously get Wist caught up on everything else I'd learned in her absence. Like the fact that the mysterious letter inviting me to Follyhope had been sent by Aunt Riegel. Who was bonded to Danver, her own blood daughter. And who, unlike Danver, hoped for a way to someday break that bond.

"Danver's her daughter?" Wist seemed stuck on that part.

"Stunted mages don't always birth S-class progeny."

"They don't?"

"It's just a matter of probability. They can have healers and subliminals as children, too."

I stared at a stretch of wallpaper depicting a life-sized forest. Looked like you could walk right into it. "Has this changed at all?"

Wist eyed it with me. "No."

We went right. In the next corridor, the forest turned black and white. We went left. And then we were at Riegel's door.

She sat on the edge of her bed with her hands on her thighs and her feet on the floor, facing the window. She wore soft shapeless pajamas with a tiny floral pattern that came out looking like faint, well-scrubbed food stains.

Upon hearing us, she felt around for her heavy glasses. She greeted us both with real pleasure.

"Wisteria, my dear," she said, as if Wist came here all the time.

Wist's eyes were on the vase full of flourishing white chrysanthemums. She hung back behind me like a gangly child. She'd reclaimed her left hand before we entered, but I could almost sense its ghost tensing fitfully at my hip.

"There was some trouble at the manor earlier," I said to Riegel. "Anyone bother you?"

"Oh, no," she said at once. "No one came by. It's rather difficult to get here if you don't know the trick. Sometimes it's difficult if even if you do know the trick."

"Ficus gave you something for safekeeping."

She bobbed her head. "A little knife. Nerium said he'd pass it to that nice MP."

I imagined Nerium pocketing the knife and not telling anyone. Or switching it out with some lesser artifact. But no—I'd discussed this with Tempus. The government had definitely taken custody of it. Which made for one less thing to worry about.

"You heard about Ficus?" I asked, trying (and failing) to be delicate.

Her face collapsed. "That poor boy." Then she put a wavery hand to her lips. "Oh, I'm so sorry. He treated you terribly, didn't he? I don't quite understand what he—did he *abduct* you?"

"Yep," I said. "At gunpoint."

She almost teetered up off the bed in her rush to apologize. Only when she clumsily took out a handkerchief did I realize she'd worked up actual tears. For me or for Ficus, or maybe both of us. There was something marvelously refreshing about hearing a Shien mage cry and tell me how very sorry she was, over and over.

I murmured to Wist. She poured room-temperature water from a pitcher; Riegel preferred not to drink it cold.

Riegel held the glass with both hands. She shook so much that I feared she'd spill it all in her lap. But when she drank, and breathed, and hiccuped, it was as if the years came off her.

She wasn't truly all that elderly. At least not compared to Grandmother. Just as many years lay between Riegel and Grandmother as between the Wist of today (in her mid-thirties, like me) and the Wist who'd first come to Follyhope (a child of six).

Of the entire generation that fell between Grandmother and Wist, Riegel seemed to be the only member still permitted—or forced, rather—to live at Follyhope.

As her siblings and cousins fell into disgrace or were otherwise disinherited, she alone remained. But she'd never been a candidate to succeed Grandmother in the first place. As a stunted mage, shame and stigma had marked her from the start.

The mini hats arranged on the cake stand by the bed were all done up in shades of dark purple and lavender. Mourning hats. There were more than I could easily count at a glance. She must've been working on these since well before Miyu's passing.

"Wisteria," Riegel said, her voice growing steadier, "I remember when you were small enough to sit on that chair without your feet touching the floor."

We looked at the chair in question. She'd probably break it if she sat in it now. It appeared to be sized more for teddy bears than for people. Either Riegel was exaggerating for effect, or Wist had been astonishingly tiny for a six-year-old.

Wist didn't seem to know how to respond. I was about to intervene when Riegel beckoned me over, closer and closer.

"I have a surprise," she said in my ear.

She directed me to her sewing room. I got up on a step stool and pulled baskets down from shelves. When I started sneezing, Riegel twittered a bunch of apologies about the dust. She sounded oddly faint, though there wasn't much distance between here and the bedroom.

I returned with my prize: a square tin colored in arching bands of pink and yellow and turquoise, like an exaggerated sunset. I offered to open it, suspecting that Riegel might lack the strength.

As things turned out, I lacked the strength, too. Should've guessed from all the dust. This tin hadn't been opened in years. Wist ended up doing the honors.

"It's really nothing too exciting." Riegel sounded like she regretted making me fetch it. "Just a little—well, I thought—"

Wist looked around for a place to set the lid. She ended up putting it on the same table as the vase of chrysanthemums.

All three of us peeked inside the tin.

It smelled only of dust. It was filled with layer upon layer of something wrapped in preservation paper. The kind you'd use to keep food from going bad. The paper bore a modest oily sheen of magic.

"They're quite old now." This was the fastest I'd ever heard Riegel speak. "Quite inedible. Rather silly of me to keep these around for so long, to be honest. No one else ever liked them. I'm sure you wouldn't—"

"I remember these," Wist said.

Riegel's voice shrank. "You do?"

I held the tin for Wist while she picked up one little packet and twisted open the preservation paper. It let out a soft static crackle of resistance as the magic gave way. Inside lay a small, flat cookie shaped like a cartoon sun.

Wist held the cookie out as if displaying a badge. "You gave me these every time I came to visit."

Riegel deflated in relief. "You ate so many. Especially for such a small girl! You wiped out my entire stash in a single afternoon."

"Wow, Wist," I said. "Must've been hungry."

"Or greedy," Wist muttered.

"After that, I always made sure to keep extra packs in stock," Riegel said nostalgically. "I'd have them special-ordered from a bakery over in the Old River district. Oh, but the bakery closed down maybe eleven, twelve years ago. I learned about it too late—didn't get a chance to request any more. Had to make do with what I was already keeping in storage."

"You kept this tin for eleven years?" I asked.

Her fair cheeks colored. "Closer to twelve years, I think. Or thirteen. Or fourteen."

"You don't eat them yourself?"

"Not good for my health," she said primly, although I seemed to recall us sharing fussy sandwiches stuffed with caramel and cream.

"I was only six when I stopped coming to see you," Wist said. "All this time, you—"

"I had the space," Riegel said. "It was nothing. What's a few sun cookies? I kept them on hand just in case." She smiled apologetically.

"Of course, they're much too old to eat now. I'm sorry I didn't have anything fresher to show you. It's such a shame about that bakery closing. No one else makes them quite the same way."

Wist took a large bite. The cookie snapped with a sound like knuckles crackling.

Riegel gasped high in her chest. "Oh! Oh, you really can't. They're over a decade old. Please!"

She swatted at my arm, all but begging me to do something.

I watched Wist chew expressionlessly and then swallow. Also expressionlessly.

Riegel had only ever met Wist as a small child. She might not know what to make of the adult Kraken. If Wist's eyes had to be compared to windows, they were windows permanently boarded up and draped with blackout curtains, for good measure. No traitorous light could creep through to illuminate the self within.

"Tastes the same," Wist said.

Riegel stopped weakly pummeling me. "Does it ... does it really?"

Aunt Riegel was rather gullible, wasn't she? I unwrapped a second sun-shaped cookie and—pretending not to hear her high-pitched protests—sank my teeth in it.

The cookie tasted like lightly sweetened beach sand. I dutifully ate the whole thing.

"Delicious," I said hollowly.

Riegel had her hands cupped around her glasses, trying to cover her eyes without smearing the lenses. "You'll get sick," she moaned. "Both of you. I ought to call Doctor Hazeldine."

Wist, meanwhile, was already plowing through her third or fourth cookie. She finished at least six before she put the tin aside.

"That's top-quality preservation paper." She patted the sides of her lips to check for crumbs. "We'll be fine."

Riegel reluctantly lowered her hands, as if being forced to witness untold carnage. She peered up at Wist through her owl-like glasses.

"Preservation paper is only guaranteed for a maximum of five years," she said sternly. "You really ought to be more careful. Food-borne illnesses are no joking matter."

"I'm very good at treating food-borne illnesses," Wist said, straight-faced. "It's the one type of medical magic I've always excelled at."

She was self-taught, too. Growing up, the majority of her meals had been laced with some kind of rot or poison or laxative. No wonder she'd been so small and skinny when Riegel first saw her. No wonder she'd devoured those sun cookies.

I guess I could cut the bakers some slack. Preservation paper could only do so much: a decade-plus in storage must've severely degraded the cookies' taste. But even taking all that into account, it made sense to me that the bakery had been forced to close.

I raised my arms, fingers spread, as if I'd just finished a sleight-of-hand trick. "No one's sick yet," I told Riegel. "Luckily enough. Might have trouble keeping Wist away from the rest of those cookies."

At last her distress seemed to ebb.

"Did I ever explain why I offered you sun cookies?" she asked Wist.

"No."

"You were like a little sun to me." Riegel looked at her dotingly. "Such bright, plentiful magic. You hadn't yet learned how to dampen it. All the time, everywhere you went, you shone with such light and hope. With infinite promise."

"I was a dour child," Wist said dryly.

"Not at all! You were just a bit shy. Who wouldn't be, thrown in the middle of a strange new family in a strange big house? It's a bit simplistic, I know, but your magic made me think of a sun come to live among us. I was so glad you liked the cookies."

A literal sun descending to mingle with humanity would mean the end of the world. I'll admit, however, that it was rather sweet to imagine Riegel happily doling out cookies to a tight-lipped and cautious little Wist.

"Aunt Riegel," Wist said.

"Yes?"

She sat on the edge of the bed next to Riegel. The mattress dipped visibly. "You held those cookies such a long time for me. I never gave you anything in return. And I never came back."

"Why, you're here now," Riegel said. "What more could I wish for?"

"I'm sorry."

"You were a child. You were frightened into staying away."

"I haven't been a child in a long time."

"You had your reasons," Riegel said gently. "I remember what happened even after you left for the academy. Those on staff who'd shown you kindness got used against you. Banished from the clan, in the end. It was terrible."

Yes. Banished by Nerium's scheming. Not by some unavoidable act of god.

That aside, Riegel sure knew a lot, for someone who seemed to have lived out much of her life enclosed in the loneliest part of Follyhope. Maybe knowing things was one of her hobbies, like decorating mini hats. Despite her limitations, she'd found a way to make it happen.

"You couldn't have known I was still here," Riegel added. "Years passed. You didn't want to raise questions by prying. You didn't want to impose."

Wist nodded, though it wasn't clear how much she agreed.

"I know Follyhope isn't your favorite place. I would never ask you to visit." Riegel took a breath. "But if you wish to come—I would gladly welcome you in any season."

I discreetly retreated over to the window while they caught up. I was envious when Riegel took Wist's hand without flinching, admiring the length of her fingers, reminiscing about how her six-year-old hands had struggled with stacks of sun cookies.

There were other matters I wanted to raise before we left, but I could wait. It was so rare for Wist to spend time with a relative who'd never hurt her.

40

THE WHITE CHRYSANTHEMUMS by the window were unusually lush. Really packed in there. I wondered why Riegel crammed them all together. Did she have no other vases handy?

Once the pace of her chatter with Wist began to slow, I turned back and said that I had a better idea of how to break bonds now. "I'd be willing to experiment," I told her. "But only if Danver agrees to it."

"I could say that Danny changed her mind."

"What would she say if I asked her myself?"

Riegel sighed. "Oh, dear. Well, I do respect your stance."

"Sorry about that—after you went to the trouble of writing to me and all."

"Regardless, I'm glad we met," she said.

"Same."

It was hard not stare at the coin-shaped birthmark near her jaw. Not because it was unsightly. It drew the eye like a piece of statement jewelry.

Wist got up and closed the tin of sun cookies. She wiped sticky traces of dust from the lid with the care of a lapidarist shaping a gemstone.

I dragged a red chair over to the bed. One larger than the child-sized chair once used by a younger Wist, and now used by no one at all.

Riegel fiddled with her glasses for a moment. Then she looked up.

"You won't break our bond because Danny doesn't need rescuing," she said meditatively. "Would you change your mind if I hurt her?"

I blinked. For the first time, winter cold touched this cozy room with its secret view of bare-branched wisteria. But the cold was only beneath my skin. I felt Wist watching us, saying nothing.

"You're not serious," I asserted. "You couldn't do that."

"I could," Riegel said. "Physically, no. But in other ways, yes. Miyu spent years demonstrating how to systematically break a healer down into nothing."

"You wouldn't do that to your own daughter."

"You've got me there," she said after a beat. "I suppose I wouldn't."

Her tone hadn't changed. Not when she spoke of how cute Wist had been as a child, not when she spoke of hurting Danver, and not now. She had a warm and burbling voice, completely unselfconscious, unafraid of sounding silly. An unguarded voice that might easily break apart into laughter or sobs.

"You're awfully eager to send her away," I said. "I don't get it. You bonded her so she wouldn't get tied to the likes of Miyu or Ficus. Well, she's safe now. Can't you just enjoy your life together? If she really wanted to run from you, wouldn't you feel it through your bond? Not all adult children leave home."

"I want her to have a life of her own," Riegel answered. "One that doesn't revolve around me. I want assurance that she'll live well, no matter what becomes of me. Is that so unusual? I'm not getting any younger."

She reached for her hair as if expecting to find a mini hat there, but today she wore none.

"Or perhaps that's an excuse," she said slowly. "Perhaps driving one's children away runs in the blood."

"In the blood," I repeated.

She glanced up at Wist, silhouetted darkly against the courtyard window.

I told Wist to come closer. As we gathered around the bed, Aunt Riegel said: "There's a reason I call her Hosanna."

"Lady Shien?"

"Yes. My mother." She nodded at Wist. "Your grandmother. I used to call her Mother, or Mama, or something along those lines. Not anymore. Not since she sent me off to be a brood mare."

Stunted mages were a sign of poor breeding. A badly planned and stifled bloodline. A horrible shame. And yet—statistically speaking—they had a reputation for birthing unusually powerful mages.

At last I uttered the name of her daughter. A healer, not a mage. Statistics could not guarantee a specific outcome in individual cases.

"Danver," I said. "Was she—"

"No. I chose to have Danny. Long after returning to Follyhope." She lowered her gaze. Those thick glasses made her eyes look distorted. "Stop me if you don't wish to hear this."

Neither of us said a word.

She explained matter-of-factly that she'd grown up here in seclusion. Virtually unknown even to her siblings, not to mention all sorts of cousins.

She was a dirty family secret. Worse than a child born out of wedlock.

If she went out in public, people would make unfair assumptions about the clan, and especially about her mother. They might suspect incest, though that really wasn't how it worked at all. The parents of a stunted mage didn't need to be related closely by blood. It merely meant there was some kind of subtle entanglement further upstream—harmless in the eyes of society, all but undetectable. Just enough to cause issues on a magical level.

That was the going theory, anyhow. Did anyone know for a fact what caused stunted mages? Plenty of ignorant people certainly thought they did. The innocent existence of a young stunted mage could make the clan suffer an unforgivable loss of face.

Riegel had learned much later that stunted mages were born occasionally to other clans as well. Everyone invested a great deal in maintaining the polite public charade that they'd been all but eradicated. A triumph brought about by several successive generations with a heavy emphasis on adoption and careful diversification of clan bloodlines.

"After I..." Riegel swallowed. Wist offered her another glass of water. "After I had my first menses..." She lowered her gaze as if she'd said a bad word. "...I went to a government facility. Hosanna signed some papers. I signed others. I agreed to live there. No one dragged me away in handcuffs. But at the same time, there really wasn't much choice."

A squalid premonition rose in me, a feeling like motion sickness.

Riegel's cheeks pinked unhappily. She'd correctly interpreted the look on my face. "I had one child there. A few years before I turned twenty. I thought I remembered them taking him away. Afterward, everyone told me I'd been completely out of it the whole time. Couldn't have remembered a thing. I suppose my mind invented something to fill in the gaps. I knew all along that the clan would come collect him. He turned out to be a mage, luckily for them, although not nearly as powerful as anyone hoped."

"The father," I said. "Did—"

"Oh, it was very carefully planned. Artificial insemination," she said evenly. "They told me exactly what they would do, and then they did it by the book. Being a Shien helped protect me, you see. There were other patients—inmates—there were others like me—"

She faltered, then steeled herself. "There were others who ended up conceiving children the natural way. Whether they liked it or not. Although I really don't think there's anything *natural* about corralling stunted mages and forcing them to—forcing that on them."

"You were a prisoner," I said. "Worse than a prisoner."

"They treated me extra well because of my family name," Riegel said. "I have to say, though, they made it seem like a very reasonable trade. They gave us a lot of sunlight, and green space, and quiet. They gave us access to incredibly skilled healers.

"They reminded us constantly of how fortunate we were to be lavished with such extravagant resources. Especially considering that our magic could never truly be cured, and the pain would seek every chance it could take to resurge, and we'd never be able to contribute to society like proper mages.

"The implication was that we could instead earn our keep by attempting to produce great new mages for the future. No one ever laid it out as an explicit obligatory tit-for-tat. They were just very, very good at making us feel like the only right thing to do would be to go along with their plans.

"And what would be the alternative? Run away from good food and leisure and unlimited healing? Run to families that didn't want us? Run—without any money or life skills or common sense—into the embrace of unspeakable magical pain?"

"Did you run?" I asked.

"I never even tried," she said distantly.

She pulled a cushion into her lap and traced its florid embroidery with her fingertips. It looked as if she were trying to find a path through a maze.

"When I was around twenty-four, Hosanna met the child for the first time. My son. He'd been tossed off to one of the most distant branch families. Far from Follyhope. She never even attempted to go visit him as an infant. He was five or six when she saw him. I think it might've been an accident. But at any rate, she laid eyes on him. Her first grandchild.

"Something about that made her decide to drag me back. She spent political capital she couldn't afford to spend. She pulled strings, and made private apologies—she never does that—and eventually she got me out of the facility. I've been enjoying my retirement at Follyhope ever since."

She said this last part with a bitter twist of her lips.

Wist sat very still, head bowed.

I considered the resemblance between Nerium and Danver. A resemblance so close that at first I'd suspected Danver of being his daughter.

He and Riegel had been rather cold to each other, at least in my presence. He called her Aunt Riegel.

And yet—the company he'd founded was named Regalia Optics.

That must've been why Ficus left the knife with her. This wasn't the safest place on the estate because of Riegel's seclusion. It was the safest place on the estate because Nerium would protect her at all costs. On paper, he had other parents. But he still considered himself her son.

Riegel leaned toward the nearest of her tiered displays and plucked off a little mourning hat. One with a cascade of purple flowers much larger than the hat itself. She turned it about critically in her fingers.

"He was always a sharp child," she said. "He knew when he was being lied to. I suppose he figured out his origins much sooner than anyone could have guessed.

"He was six—almost seven—when I came back to Follyhope. When I met him properly and learned his name. Right about the same age you would've been when we first met, in fact."

She held the mini hat up to the side of Wist's head. It suited Wist much better than I would've guessed, considering that she wasn't usually one to wear flowery accessories. The soft violet hues of grief stood out exquisitely against the implacable black sweep of her hair.

"Perhaps I was never fair to him," Riegel murmured. "I must say that the world was never quite fair to me, either. I felt a lake of ice in me when I looked at him. I saw a proper Shien mage in the making. He'll do quite fine on his own, I thought.

"Years later, I saw you—my perfect opposite. A mage with more magic than any Shien. You were so small, and so terrified, and so lonely.

"Maybe he was, too, at that age. But I couldn't see it in him. Because of some defect within me, most likely. Not because of anything he did wrong as a child. I could see it in you, though. My little sun. For the first time in maybe my whole life, I could imagine being a mother. I was in my thirties." She grinned at Wist. "Three whole decades ago. I looked very different, didn't I?

"That's what got me thinking about trying to have another child. I've never seen Hosanna look so astonished as when I told her. She didn't say no, of course—difficult to discard the possibility of me birthing a mage for the ages. Or maybe she saw it as a chance to make it up to me. To let me have a do-over. To let me breed on my own terms."

She kept holding out the flowery mourning hat until Wist took it with a whisper of thanks.

"So then you had Danver," I said.

"Close to a decade later. With seven miscarriages along the way. Doctor Hazeldine did all the fertility treatments. They could hardly entrust me to anyone outside the family, you see." She gave me a wry look. "I'm surprised you haven't asked about Danny's father."

"Oh, you know," I said. "Just trying to scrape together the last few ashes of my decorum."

Her lips twitched. "The father of my first child could have been anyone. I didn't want to know him. And I didn't want to hear about Danny's father, either. Knowing Hazeldine, though, there's an extremely high chance that he used his own seed for her."

"Eurgh."

"Indeed." Riegel's face softened. "But Danny was worth it."

"Weren't you worried about how Ne—how your son might react?"

"I was too slow to understand why Wisteria stopped coming by. I swore I wouldn't let the same thing happen twice." She put her hands together as if protecting something in the soft space between them. "To tell you the truth, he's treated Danny much better than I could ever have hoped. Maybe because she's a healer—because she could never be direct competition.

"I wasn't involved in naming him, you know. I was never able to do anything motherly for him. I didn't have it in me. Just once, he asked if he could call me—" She shut her eyes. "I made him call me Aunt Riegel instead. He did always respect that. I suppose that's part of why I still call his grandmother Hosanna, and never anything else."

Perhaps, for a time, he'd suspected Wist of being his biological sister. What would make more sense than an S-Class (and future Kraken-class) child born from a stunted mage?

Perhaps he'd been consumed by the thought that it should've been him blessed with all those branches.

"You can't make me feel sorry for him," I said.

"That's fine," Riegel replied. "My greatest flaw—aside from being a stunted mage, I suppose—is that I don't feel particularly sorry for him myself."

As Wist and I made our way here through the spot-the-difference maze of corridors, she'd filled me in on why she'd stopped visiting Riegel before turning seven.

Nerium had told her very kindly that Riegel resented her, hated being forced to play nice with her. They were magical opposites, after all. Wist had everything, and Riegel had less than nothing: magical pain without anything of value to show for it. He'd viciously punished Wist every time she tried to sneak back there. He'd implied—with a tragic look on his face—that Riegel would be punished as well.

Sometimes I wondered how much of this Nerium even remembered.

The truth is, there was no world in which eighteen-year-old Nerium's inferiority complex would reasonably result in him leaving a six-year-old at the bottom of an old well.

He and Ficus—and Miyu and the others, to varying degrees—had made her pierce her own hand with forks and pens and kebab skewers. The pincushion game, they'd called it. They'd sickened her with moldy meat and worm-laced cake, brown puddle water sipped from straws, rice seasoned with broken glass. They'd knocked her down staircases, locked her in the cellars.

They'd taught her how magic could conceal bleeding and bruises and oozing burns. They'd taught her how to hide injuries, but not how to repair them. She had to learn that all on her own, and she learned it badly.

Through it all, they'd told her she was the one liable to hurt *them*. They told her she was explosive, uncontrollable, a dangerous menace. If she was, it came only in response to things like getting pushed down and held underwater in the bath. But the order of events didn't matter. Her Shien siblings systematically pushed her past her limits. They produced real factual evidence of the accusations that they kept beating her over the head with. However paradoxically, however forcibly, they proved their point about her volatility, her inadequacy.

No one else had magic like Wist—and they meant to show that she was not nearly enough of a god or a saint to deserve it, either. This wouldn't have been a terribly difficult project. She had no chance from the start.

She was only a child.

And the architect of it all had been Shien Nerium. No amount of motherly neglect could justify that. What an insult to those—like Wist herself!—who'd grown up without ever knowing parents they could trust for unconditional love and protection.

He'd tortured his little sister because he liked it. On some level, it really was that simple.

Time might have modulated the self-righteous sadism of his late teens and twenties. But it had never taught him repentance. I still saw an unbroken line—like a lifelong bond between souls—stretching from the younger man he'd been back then to the older man he was today.

Aunt Riegel told us to take the rest of the sun cookies when we left. Apparently she'd changed her mind about them after observing that neither Wist nor I had developed a crippling stomachache.

She tried to give me a tiny hat to match Wist's as well.

"Very cute," I said, "but I'd rather admire Wist wearing hers. Actually..." I shooed Wist over to the door, then dropped my voice and told Riegel what I'd prefer to receive as a present instead.

"Ah." She set the second hat back with its brethren. "Of course. Gladly. But—"

"Not today." I still spoke in a whisper behind cupped hands. "We'll—I'll come back for it some other time. In a few weeks, or maybe months. Whenever you're ready. Follyhope may be a den of monsters, but that won't stop us from visiting. She's the Kraken, you know. Sometimes she even acts the part."

Wist studied me from across the room and said: "It would be harder to keep secrets if we were still bonded."

In all the world, only Riegel knew we weren't.

I laughed, though it hurt. Like laughing with a broken rib. "Harder," I concurred, "but not impossible. I could surprise you."

41

Nerium knew where we'd been. As he escorted us off the estate, he warned us to take Aunt Riegel's stories with a grain of salt.

"Her imagination is a bit on the wild side," he confided. "An inevitable byproduct of being cooped up for so long, I think."

"That's a fine thing to say about your own mother," I replied.

One doesn't often get a chance to hit Shien Nerium where it hurts.

We'd been away from the tower for less than two weeks. Yet the distance between before Follyhope and after Follyhope felt almost as long as our autumn trip to Manglesea.

Wist detached her left hand and let it run free, sliding down long banisters and skedaddling across curtain rails. Her cat (named Turtle) prickled and arched upon seeing it.

"You're going to traumatize her," I warned Wist.

At last the hand came rushing home. Not to Wist, but to me. It held my wrist as if offended to find another hand already attached to my arm. It kept trying to butt my own hand out of the way. Eventually it settled for grabbing a fistful of my shirt, swinging lightly as I moved around the kitchen.

Despite all the space available in the tower—a magical thousand-layer cake—and the overwhelming variety of rooms, we ended up in a cramped glassy turret that protruded from the outer wall like a stack of mushrooms from a tree trunk. We settled on opposite sides of the U-shaped window seat.

The floor, too, was pure glass. Not my favorite, but cushions and blankets overflowing from the benches helped mask it.

We didn't touch, of course. Except for her left hand. It moved to my bicep, latching on with the comforting snugness of an arm ring.

Outside and below, the tower's shadow stretched to the far end of the blue prairie. It looked like a natural land formation: an unmoving dark canyon.

Almost as soon as we ported back home, Wist had said: "I have things to show you." She didn't meet my gaze. Her eyes followed her runaway hand and her increasingly agitated cat.

If we were still bonded, I'd have a sense of whether the things she had to tell me were things I'd dread hearing. But our bond was gone. All I could feel was the hot-and-cold fluttering terror that haunts the space between not knowing and knowing.

I'd suggested that we change to house clothes and settle down first. Now here we were, me in sweats that dragged on the floor and Wist in leggings that had unraveled to show provocative swathes of her inner thigh. Not that I could do anything about it.

Turtle the cat settled in Wist's lap, eying me with wary triumph. She wasn't usually so needy. Mori would've made sure she wanted for nothing, but perhaps the tower didn't feel the same to her without Wist here. I could sympathize.

Wist had brought a few sun cookies. She untwisted the ends of the preservation paper. Turtle made a stifled noise of complaint.

"I know what happened to Miyu," Wist said.

I don't know what I'd expected. Definitely not that.

"How? Since when?"

"Since before I came back."

I caved to the impulse to respond flippantly. "What happened over in the old world? You take a course in detection?"

She regarded me with eyes too dark to make out the shape of her pupils. Her right hand ran along the ridge of Turtle's back. I heard purring. My arms tightened around my knees.

"There's not much to say about the old world," she replied.

"Really."

"Of all the worlds I could've landed in, there was no reason it had to be that one. I plunged into the vorpal hole without any coherent sense of direction. Maybe I got thrown there because I used to watch it so much. Because I've been there before."

I held my tongue and let her continue.

"Last time, I did what I could to stop vorpal holes from eating everything."

"So you got to take a look at the world you saved."

"I saw that my saving it didn't matter much," she said. "It was already too far gone. Now it deteriorates in other ways.

"Some beings—some people, they know it's dying. They seem unconcerned. Time in the old world passes faster and faster as it wheels toward destruction. Maybe *faster* is the wrong word? More and more time goes by even as the world's lifespan dwindles. It's constantly verging on death. But its final moments will spool out almost long enough to reach infinity. Enough to hold countless more generations, the rise and fall of eras."

"Like taking the distance between us." I stretched an arm out without brushing her. "And dividing it in half. And in half again. And in half again. Getting closer and closer and never touching."

"They healed my magic," Wist said.

"Good."

"I also told them to try to kill me."

"Typical."

"Even with healing, I was in really bad shape. Couldn't break out—make it back home—any other way."

"Except under a genuine threat of death. Nice little shock to the system. Bet you thought if they succeeded in killing you, then you'd deserve it," I said coldly. "Bet you pictured yourself fertilizing their world. Curing it with the sweet rain of your blood and flesh and sacrificed magic. Well, you're alive, and you're here, so I'll spare you my lectures. You already know what I want to say."

"I wondered about that," Wist said.

"What part of it?"

"If I'm really alive. If I'm really here."

Turtle's eyes had narrowed to slits. Wist's right hand stilled. Her severed left hand kept its stubborn grip on me.

"There was a decapitated head in the other world, too. Not like Ficus. A living head that talked to me, recognized me for what I am. Strange things happen as a world nears its end. Even if it'll take close to forever.

"When I saw Ficus—I saw an echo of the old world. An imitation. Like I'd caused his decapitation by crossing back over, my feet tracking pollution from one world into another. Or like I was dreaming—like I'd never really returned at all."

"I'm real," I said.

"I know."

But I couldn't reach across and squeeze her knee to prove it.

Her left hand clambered up the side of my head, twining itself in the white parts of my hair like a flower secured behind my ear.

She took a hard-sounding bite of her sun cookie. After swallowing, she said: "It wasn't just in the other world that time stretched out beyond its ordinary length. It first happened on this side. On the event horizon of the vorpal hole. Before I passed through, but too late to back out."

"When you felt our bond start to break."

"I saw memories of the vorpal hole. The moment of its formation—how it ruptured like an earthquake releasing tension. I saw the Extinguishers using magical tools to transfer it to Follyhope. Ficus helped."

"And you saw the moment when Miyu died," I said.

"I can show you. But—"

"Will it hurt?"

"Probably," Wist said, muted.

"Oh, what the hell." I threw up my hands. Turtle squinted resentfully. "Unless we plan on being chaste roommates for the rest of our lives, at some point we'll have to work through this."

It might not be as bad as touching, anyway. It hadn't hurt when she ported me.

So far, only physical contact and healing attempts had grated unbearably at the empty site of our bond.

Wist shifted Turtle gently to a cushion. Outside, wind pushed at the protruding glass facets of our little nook. The skinny scar-like shadow of the tower had faded as the defined orange light of sunset yielded ground to twilight gray.

Discarded preservation paper rattled like a dry leaf when her magic closed the distance between us. It wasn't as bad as physical touch, although that became harder to remember with each ticking second. It was just this side of bearable.

I hunched over myself. Her magic set a fire in my mind, and I saw a shadow play of puppets performing at the fringes of its raging light. First the vorpal hole had witnessed this. Then Wist. And now me.

Late in the dark of night, Miyu and Ficus argued at the edge of the Follyhope vorpal hole.

Muted caution lights ringed the perimeter. Subsequent jerky expansions of the hole had swallowed repeated attempts at creating a barrier.

Ficus looked amused. Not really listening. Miyu was enraged, jabbing her finger at him. Beheaded rosebushes formed a peculiar matrix of shadows low to the ground beside them. The stingy sky showed precisely two stars.

No matter how heated Miyu got, it wasn't quite cold enough to see anyone's breath. She said something about the vorpal hole, about the Extinguishers, about dead gardeners. How much did she know, and how had she found out? Had she threatened him before he called her here under the cover of night, or was it the other way around?

Some distance away, past where the vorpal hole curved in and out like the winding shore of an ancient lake, two other people whispered angrily in the shadow of a hedge.

Lear had thrown on a heavy-duty coat over flimsy silken pajamas. She grabbed Danver by the arm.

It was my first time seeing Danver without her maid-healer robes, without those tight-wound buns on the back of her head. Without the big spindly glasses that Nerium had given her, either.

"Who put you up to this?" Lear demanded.

Danver said nothing. She was deathly pale in the dark.

"You aren't a Shien in the same way as they are," Lear said, as if explaining to a child why they shouldn't go swimming with sharks. "You can't play games and get away with it."

Her grip on Danver's arm looked painfully tight.

Danver stared across at Lear as if they were both the same height. "You're a foreigner. A Jacian. You can't afford to interfere, either."

The haughtiness of that cultured voice aged her at least a decade. If I hadn't known any better, I might've thought I was hearing Miyu.

"Think your friend will be pleased?" Lear asked. "Think she'll thank you? It's too late, Danny. She's a shattered shell."

"She has a name."

"If you wanted to save her, you should've started killing Shiens years ago. Don't ruin yourself just because you're desperate to do something meaningful."

The light along the path they'd diverted from was too far away to reveal much. Lear's pearls were the brightest part of her, glimmering like the whites of agitated animal eyes.

"Let *go*," Danver said, suddenly younger-sounding, tugging helplessly.

Lear released her.

Danver glared, her teeth briefly bared, her small lips a dark drowned-looking hue.

"Your mother needs you." Lear's accent had thickened. "Isn't that why you...?" She traced the air with her index finger, mimicking the shape of the bond thread at Danver's neck. "Don't do this. It won't satisfy anyone but you, and the satisfaction won't last."

"You come leech off us for a few months, and you think you see through us," Danver grated out. "You think you know everything. And we're supposed to be the arrogant ones? Back in your own country, you'd be less than nothing. Not even a proper mage. Don't think for a second that anyone actually values your art. You're a political tool to both sides. A useful chump. Or a useless one, if you insist on wasting your time harassing—"

"I know what I am," Lear said pityingly.

"Then get away from me."

They'd kept their voices low and tight, low enough not to be heard by Ficus or Miyu even in the midnight hush of the depopulated estate. Danver shivered as if sickened by the strength of her urge to slap, to claw, to shove.

To be fair, Lear probably wanted to give Danver a good hard smack, too.

Instead she glanced up at the two feeble stars overhead and said, bitterly, "Oh, to be young and selfish and absolutely convinced of your righteousness. Those were the days."

Danver let out a hiss of breath. Lear had already turned her back. She strode briskly toward her far-off atelier, avoiding the safely lit path. It was the stiff-shouldered walk of someone who felt much colder than they looked.

42

WIST POURED this vision into me like water into a narrow-mouthed vessel.

Now we returned to Ficus and Miyu. Ficus stood with one hand in his pocket. If he got tired of getting harangued, he'd walk away—or he'd put a blade through her larynx. Which would it be?

Halfway through barking more of the same old accusations, pointing with futile fury at the vorpal hole, Miyu stopped. She whirled. She stared into the night with wide paranoid eyes.

Ficus's hand stayed in his pocket. He clicked his tongue. Might've been too quiet for anyone to notice except the vorpal hole itself.

"Show yourself," Miyu said. This time it sounded like she actually expected to be obeyed.

Ginko stepped forward, hugging her arms. She wasn't dressed for the cold. She didn't have to step far. She was only seven or eight feet behind Miyu.

She'd appeared out of nothingness. But she'd been there all along.

"What a waste," Ficus said, disappointment heavy in his voice.

Miyu glanced between them. Her gaze stopped on Ginko. "Ah," she breathed. "You little whore."

She sounded more wondering than angry. She almost didn't sound angry at all. Like she loved nothing more than being proven right.

"Lose your nerve?" Ficus asked Ginko. "People would kill for that cutting I gave you."

She didn't give a direct response. Not to him, and not to Miyu. She stared down at her toes—she was wearing gardening clogs—and said, as if reading off a script she'd practiced in private, "It's dangerous here. We should leave."

"Dangerous," Miyu repeated.

"We should leave."

"You were going to shove me in," Miyu said. "You were going to sneak up on me with my brother's magic and shove me in that hole. Did you think you could get away with it? Did you think you could bond him?" She crowed with laughter. "Why would Ficus ever bond *you*? He's got no use for anything weak, ugly, or gutless."

"You should praise your healer. Applaud her," Ficus said in a tone that suggested he was rapidly losing interest. "She double-crossed me. She came to warn you. She squandered her golden chance."

Miyu grabbed Ginko's hair as if grabbing a dog by the collar. She hauled Ginko closer to the vorpal border.

Ginko's feet scraped the pavement, but she barely resisted. She didn't cry out. She stumbled after Miyu as if weightless and boneless, already rendered a ghost.

Ficus lamented her lack of nerve, sighing dolefully.

I too was a ghost here. My nonexistent body seized up. I couldn't stop them, couldn't look away.

Miyu let go at the last moment. Ginko almost stumbled into the razor's edge of the hole on her own.

They were in a spot where the fringe of the vorpal hole skirted a stone lantern surrounded by boulders.

"Climb up," Miyu ordered. "Time to take out the trash."

Ginko got on the rocks. She looked back at Miyu as if unsure of what to do next.

"Put yourself in the hole," Miyu said, expressionless. "Step in on your own. Feet first."

The vorpal hole simmered beside them; in some places it rose up past Miyu's shoulders. I couldn't decide if it was more or less horrible at night. It gave off no light of its own, not even an ordinary aura of magic. I couldn't tell if I were seeing it with imaginary eyes or magic perception or another unknown sense.

Bondmates did not inherently possess the power to issue suicidal commands. But Ginko had been conditioned to listen.

No, more than that—Doctor Hazeldine had fed her a steady diet of mind-massaging magic. Maybe the original intention had been to bring her relief. It didn't work by stopping Miyu's abuses, though. It worked by making Ginko herself more suggestible, less of a person, less capable of fearing or caring.

With obvious effort, she turned her head to see Ficus. He looked away at the ominous hulk of the manor, whistling indolently into the night wind. He might as well have been alone. For all he knew, she and Miyu could've already tumbled through the hole together.

"Go in," Miyu said to Ginko. "Just go."

She sounded profoundly tired. I wished I could've been there in person. I wished I could've pushed her.

Ginko's body faced the vorpal hole. The cruel dark sea of it—although it was the opposite of both darkness and light, and had no qualities I would compare to water—spread out before her. She seemed more concerned with rubbing the cold off her bare arms than with trying to save her own life.

Someone came running.

Their approach was not subtle. The sound of far-off wind provided only a flimsy mask. Miyu must've been too preoccupied with her own aggravated thoughts, with the tension of Ginko's brittle form poised on the precipice. She hadn't heard footsteps slap the flagstones. Or she heard their echo too late to understand what they meant.

Ficus stepped neatly out of the way. Danver barreled past him. She barreled straight into Miyu, nearly launching both of them into the maw of the hole.

There was a peculiar silence as they grappled. They had no breath to spare for anything but stifled grunts of effort.

Between the two of them, Miyu seemed more sinewy, more rabid. Like she often made use of the glass-fronted gym. I could only imagine this going one way.

Ginko clutched her head and half-collapsed at the foot of the stone lantern.

Miyu tripped on her, tried to catch herself—accidentally released Danver, who pushed her on reflex—and went toppling into the eye-smarting horizontal edge of the hole.

It was like a body meeting an industrial sawblade. Her top half, separated at the waist, sank into the vorpal hole as fast as a statue dropped in a lake. Gone before anyone could blink, or glimpse the last expression on her face.

Her legs—abandoned, already lifeless—dropped among the thorny remnants of rosebushes below the vorpal hole. There was no glistening or gushing or stench of blood, or of her last meal, or anything else. I don't know if vorpal holes always cauterize open flesh like infernal fire, soundless and smokeless, but something had happened to leave her fallen legs as clean as the legs of a doll snapped in half.

Ginko, hands over her face, made a sound as if she were dying. Danver was on the ground with her, rigid with shock.

Ficus came over. He bent to eye Miyu's severed legs like an elder fisherman assessing an unusual catch. He chuckled deep in his throat. A convulsive shiver went through Danver's shoulders.

"So not all healers are cowards," he said with approval. "Must be the Shien blood in you." He smacked her rousingly on the back. "Guess I'll go have a couple drinks to forget this. Never saw a thing."

He shook his head in amusement. He sauntered away into the shadows, unhurried.

On his way out, he passed Lear. She'd circled back around, unseen. Now she watched them from near the wall of the manor. Ficus caught her eye and winked, then sailed off without a word. No one else detected her presence.

Danver turned abruptly, retching.

Ginko moved like a snake striking. She clamped both hands over Danver's mouth. As though blocking a pipe to stop a flood. Danver heaved visibly, but for the time being, it actually worked. Her eyes shone wetter and wetter as she struggled to hold it in.

Eventually Ginko lowered her hands. Without saying a word, she began tugging at Miyu's right ankle. Danver quickly got up to help.

They hoisted Miyu's eerily bloodless legs and sheared-off hips up to shoulder level. They heaved their burden feet-first toward the vorpal hole as though pushing an empty canoe toward open water.

The legs plummeted out of reality. Leaving nothing of Miyu except, perhaps, scuffed footprints in the garden dirt. A prick or two of blood. Scraped skin cells where her hacked-off lower half had abraded itself on woody thorns. There was plenty of evidence, if you knew what to look for. If you dared venture close enough to the vorpal hole to perform a search.

But Ginko would claim that her bond remained safely intact. That she still felt Miyu somewhere out there, alive and well. Enough time would pass for storms to sweep across the estate, and for the vorpal hole to shift and breathe and eat away at the last ignominious traces of Shien Miyu's two halves.

Perhaps—without ever knowing it—Danver and Ginko had received help from other corners, too. Ficus might've been sufficiently entertained to come back and casually tidy up the crime scene.

Lear still watched from the shadows, stone-faced. An ordinary artist might not know much about how to cover up a murder (or, depending on how you looked at it, a deadly accident). But Lear the Jacian had never been an ordinary artist.

Ginko tugged at Danver, pulling her back from the brink of the vorpal hole. Danver wiped her face and tried to say something. She gave up halfway through. They hurried away until the night swallowed the sound of their feet.

43

"THEY'RE VERY LUCKY that Grandmother just wants to move past this," I said.

Wist rubbed her head as if she'd just emerged from a boxing match. I felt much the same way. Echoes of her magic crackled excruciatingly in a unreachable part of my ear.

Despite my discomfort, and eager though I was to forget about the Shien clan for another couple of years, I was grateful to have seen the truth of Miyu's death. Wist knew me well.

Philosophically speaking, the question of who had killed Miyu might be answered in any number of ways. Danver had shoved and grappled with her. Ginko had—deliberately or accidentally—collapsed in just the right place and at just the right time to fatally trip her. Ficus had thought himself quite generous for giving Ginko an initial opening to attack her; he'd even lent Ginko imperceptibility magic. He'd looked the other way when Danver joined the fray.

Ginko and Danver were young healers, not trained assassins. If the final moments of Miyu's life had ended up looking like a two-bit slapstick routine—well, what else could you expect from a bunch of amateurs?

And yet there was a pocket of my mind that remained decidedly unsatisfied.

Wist and I laid out floor beds in the room where she usually slept. Her big bed with a mattress stayed empty. We knew better than to argue over who would take it, and we couldn't risk sharing it. We had to keep our mats and bedding far enough apart that there'd be no danger of rolling into each other or unconsciously cuddling.

I looked blearily at the salt-colored stars outside her window.

The familiarity of the tower made me realize how tense I'd been at Follyhope.

Some aspects of that tension had yet to leave me. The only part of her I dared go near was the disembodied left hand that snuck up onto my pillow, all but wagging its long misty tail.

What a gift it had been to be able to touch her without any thought or calculation. I missed it. I missed her all the more when she was right across the room from me, a beloved shape entombed in fuzzy blankets.

I used to feel her thoughts pressing up against me like a pack of protective animals as we fell asleep together. I wouldn't know precisely what she was thinking, not unless I went looking—tomorrow's groceries, the beginnings of an intricate new magical skill, vague memories of other countries, a renewed fascination with my hipbone. Could be anything.

No, I wouldn't know the exact content of her thoughts, but I would sleep better surrounded by their comforting weight. Like the difference between floating on an inflatable raft, and treading cold bottomless water all on your own.

Look, I do realize that most people never have a bondmate. Subliminals can't bond, and that's already the majority of the population right there. Besides, for a lot of healers (and some mages), bonding is not at all a positive experience.

Life without bonding ought to be perfectly bearable. Such a life was, in fact, the true default for humanity. Nothing to complain about.

I flipped noisily from side to side. My toes were still little icicles. When I tried not to think about what might become of us, my thoughts slid back downhill to the death of Shien Miyu.

She'd become increasingly suspicious of Ficus's involvement with the Extinguishers. Maybe she'd glimpsed his tattoos. Maybe she'd glimpsed some other sign pointing to the fact that the vorpal hole hadn't naturally spawned in Follyhope. Whatever the case, she'd probed too deep. Ficus called her out. Or—she'd demanded an audience, and he'd suggested a time and location.

It didn't matter how they'd come to meet there. Only that it had been planned far enough in advance—earlier that day, perhaps?—for Ficus to tell Ginko. For him to offer her an imperceptibility cutting. For him to offer Miyu up on a platter.

I doubt he had much personal animosity toward Miyu, no matter how she may have felt about him. If he wanted to get rid of her, it'd have been because her (not unjustified) paranoia was starting to make his life less convenient.

But how had Danver known to show up when they met in secret?

Ficus had invited Ginko: he'd lent her some of his rarest and most precious magic. It didn't seem like he'd done the same for Danver.

Ginko could've let her in on it. Could've asked her for help—either to kill Miyu, or to spare her. In that case, why had they been so unco-ordinated? To me, it appeared as though Ginko hadn't known she would be there.

As for Lear, she'd obviously been keeping tabs on Danver. She could've confronted Danver after noticing her acting weird all day, sneaking out at strange times, et cetera. They didn't seem friendly enough—at least not on Danver's side—to habitually go on midnight strolls together for no particular reason.

I just didn't get why Lear and Danver had spoken from the start as if they shared a mutual understanding that this was a set-up for murder. They hadn't noticed Ficus and Miyu arguing next to the vorpal hole by pure happenstance. They'd been watching and waiting for it.

Danver knew how bad Ginko had it. She knew and cared more than anyone. Had she been stalking Miyu, constantly seeking a chance to off her? Or had she known in advance—quite separately from Ginko— that the perfect opportunity was about to present itself?

Agent Shien Ficus had been in a conundrum. Harassed by his rightfully mistrustful sister. Accused of flirting with terrorists, of sabotaging the estate at the very heart of the clan. Once Miyu decided you were an enemy, she wouldn't shut up about it, and she wouldn't back down. That's why he began exploring other solutions. Like getting Ginko to do his dirty work.

Everything Ficus did was on his own terms, from roping in Ginko to walking away from the scene of the murder with laughter on his lips.

Miyu, too, must've thought that she was acting entirely on her own. That she was the only family member sharp enough to see through Ficus's facade. She wasn't, though, not by a long shot. And she hadn't really seen through him at all.

What if someone else had fanned the flames of her suspicion? What if they'd proceeded so quietly and unobtrusively that even Miyu didn't realize she hadn't thought of it all by herself? What if they'd subtly leaked information to set the stage for an inevitable clash with Ficus? What if they'd looped in Danver just like how Ficus had looped in

Ginko? Look: here's your chance to rid us of that evil woman. No one will miss her. No one will stop you.

No point, really, in framing it in my mind as *someone*. I'd immediately thought of Nerium.

It wasn't an airtight plan. Too many people involved. Too many unpredictable elements. If this were indeed a situation that Nerium had deliberately engineered, then his main priority must've been to create a small window of opportunity—and to ensure that he himself had zero involvement in whatever happened next. Lucky for him if Miyu died. No sweat off his back if she didn't. The casual homicidal equivalent of buying a fistful of lottery tickets.

Ficus's murder had been rather more—pointed, you could say. Fewer elements left to chance. It was still similar in the sense that it had taken place far outside of Nerium's purview. He hadn't been anywhere near the scene of either death.

This lack of control would've been unacceptable if his primary objective were to get Miyu and Ficus killed at a certain time, in a certain way. It could be perfectly acceptable, however, if his primary objective was to keep his own hands clean. If he didn't mind trying again and again, rolling more rocks down the slope of the mountain just to see where they went.

Call me prejudiced, but if someone accused Shien Nerium of countless other murders, I'd believe them in an instant.

Look at it this way. If I died in some freak weekend accident—if, say, I got trampled by a runaway horse—he might mourn the loss of my healing talent. He might mean it from the bottom of his heart.

He'd also smile to think of how my death would ruin Wist.

Nerium playing the part of a diabolical hands-off mastermind was one hundred percent believable. Nerium arranging the deaths of his own (semi) blood-related siblings was, likewise, one hundred percent believable. To be totally frank with you, I wanted to believe it. Sadly, I remained unconvinced.

Sure, he might not have been heartbroken over losing Miyu and Ficus. But what did he stand to gain from their deaths?

What did he want for himself, anyway? Was he trying to grow his company? If so, fratricide could hardly be anything more than an irrelevant and counterproductive distraction. Miyu and Ficus had nothing to do with his industry. They weren't corporate competitors.

Was he attempting to position himself as the best candidate to succeed Grandmother Shien? If anything, he'd have been better off keeping Miyu and Ficus alive and close for as long as possible. Just by being themselves, they made him look saner. More moderate. They made him seem like the only logical choice.

I guess I'd have to stick with my earlier suspicions. The idea that Grandmother had come to view Miyu and Ficus as boils in need of lancing. The idea that Nerium had meddled—ever so lightly—with their respective fates in order to please her.

Perhaps she believed that the clan demanded periodic purging. A culling of the weak. The parental generation sandwiched between her and Nerium had been pruned back so ruthlessly that only Riegel—whose very existence was a dirty secret—remained close to the seat of family power.

I knew nothing of Grandmother's own siblings or cousins, for that matter. It seemed quite likely that none remained in any position of relevance.

In the midst of confusion, Danver had shoved Miyu one last time, and that shove had been fatal. It would not normally be this easy for a healer to get away with murder. Or manslaughter. Danver had been blessed with a dearth of evidence, as well as friendly (or at least untalkative) witnesses.

Such trappings would matter little, however, if a mage of sufficient status demanded that you be held culpable. The desires of those in power would ultimately determine your fate. Everything else was malleable: the truth of Miyu's death, the presence or lack of compelling proof.

Danver owed thanks to Grandmother's aversion to embarrassment. Miyu had already fallen from grace by going berserk. Afterward, she'd become a recluse at Follyhope. Grandmother would not compound the scandal of Miyu's life with a whole new scandal surrounding the sordid circumstances of her death.

If Grandmother herself had wished Miyu gone—whether privately, or in such a way as to encourage others to grant her wish—that would be all the more reason to discourage further investigation. Even if doing so meant passing up a chance to use a very convenient healer scapegoat.

I couldn't celebrate Nerium's potential involvement. I had little sympathy for Grandmother's hypothetical motives. But I was glad that Danver had gotten away with it.

I wondered if, in retrospect, it had felt like an accident. She'd run at Miyu with every apparent intention of knocking her into the hole. Yet the actual final seconds of it—Miyu losing her balance, a belated push— had been chaotic. Not very purposeful.

Hopefully Danver wouldn't be haunted by memories of Miyu's fallen legs. Hopefully she wouldn't crumble under pressure and blurt needless confessions.

If she did, though, it'd be none of our concern.

I'm sorry if that sounds cold. The recent deaths in the Shien clan were distracting in the way that other people's problems are always distracting. Something I could mull over from a safe remove, especially now that we were back at the tower. From here, Follyhope felt as distant as the country of Manglesea.

44

MORI WHIRLED into our room at dawn the next morning. He was one of very few people who could freely enter the tower.

"Ms. Asa!" he cried. He hadn't called me that in ages. "You're ... alive?"

"Alive," I replied groggily, "but less than awake."

"The Kraken said you—you—"

"What'd I do?"

"She asked me to heal her. I thought...."

I rubbed crud from the corner of my eye. Wist, unusually, appeared to have already slipped away. She'd folded her floor bed and blankets into a stack by the wall.

I suppose she'd requested that Mori come heal her as soon as possible. If we were still bonded, she wouldn't have been able to receive healing from anyone other than me. The very fact of her request would imply that our bond had been shattered. Under ordinary circumstances, this would in turn imply that I was verifiably dead.

Mori hadn't jumped to conclusions: he'd simply put two and two together.

"Wist didn't really offer any context, did she," I said.

"Er..."

"Well, I'm not a ghost. But she does need healing. Thanks for taking care of Turtle, by the way."

"Oh. That was nothing."

I got up, kicked my floor bed aside, and gave Mori a rough explanation.

He interrupted before I reached any of the dramatic parts.

"You've been interested in bondbreaking," he said, hesitant. "Did you—did you actually pioneer a way to do it? Did you break your own bond?"

"What kind of mad scientist do you think I am?" I demanded.

"The kind who would rather test a new technique on yourself than on strangers."

"Look at you," I said. "You've learned to talk back."

Yeah—if I'd worked out how to break bonds before my bond broke all on its own, I might indeed have volunteered myself (and therefore Wist as well, with her agreement) for a two-person human trial. Surely we could bond again right afterward. No harm done.

In reality, it couldn't have happened in any other order. My current state of brokenness had given me a whole different way to perceive bonds and their hidden fragility. If—when—we rebonded, I'd never be able to work up the nerve to break it myself. Not in the name of science. Not in the name of anything.

Anyway, I finished getting Mori caught up on our adventures. We joined Wist in one of the tower's kitchens—an industrial-style space that looked like it was missing about twenty busy cooks. The gleam of steel and white tile made me suspect that it had never been used. Quite different from the sunny main kitchen where she kept most of her food.

Locating her had taken an embarrassingly long time. We'd resorted to checking the tower floor maps. It had been a lot easier to cope with her wandering when I could find her by following the pull of our bond.

Wist was in the process of heating pots of spica, coffee, and cinnamon-scented tea. Her left hand separated from her arm and floated across the room to offer Mori an empty mug, which he accepted with equanimity. (I'd told him to watch out for runaway body parts.)

It was weird to see Wist in such a well-equipped kitchen, considering that she liked eating straight from sealed cans. I made a comment to this effect.

Mori said: "You cook a bit, don't you?"

"When the mood strikes."

"The Kraken probably made this kitchen for you."

"Did you?" I asked Wist. I'd never used it.

She feigned ignorance. I would've needled her more, but then she brought out Aunt Riegel's tin of cookies.

"Those are over a decade old," I warned Mori. Wist and I really needed to work on our hospitality.

He poked the preservation paper a bit, and apparently decided that it passed muster. He unwrapped a sun cookie and dipped it in his cup of coffee before biting down.

"What's it taste like?" I inquired.

"Mmph."

Once the three of us had been adequately fed and watered, Mori started working on Wist's magic.

I perched on a barstool and strove not to make unnecessary comments. He knew what he was doing.

Wist's left hand stayed with me, resting possessively on my knee. It clung tighter when I spun around on my stool, trying not to stare at the exposed skin of her back.

Today Mori's hair was the sublime pink of wet fallen cherry blossoms. Must've gotten it touched up recently. Wist's hair still looked damp from her morning shower. My greedy one-eyed gaze fondled the contour of her shoulders, the hard hidden strength of her arms. The stool's faint whine of protest felt like a noise emitting from deep within my own organs.

This wasn't good: this was like picking at an open sore.

In a somewhat desperate bid to take my mind off all the ways I couldn't touch Wist, I asked Mori about his research.

Fortunately, he was a practiced enough healer that he could chat while he worked. And Wist had so much magic to get through that there was plenty of time for chatting.

"Actually," he said, "you inspired me."

"Me?" I was clueless. "How?"

"Back when you were starting to investigate bonding more deeply—you got me to look up a lot of studies. Remember?"

"Oh. Yeah."

I'd made him run all over the place. In my defense, he was a proper scholar. He had access to resources that I couldn't touch without raising uncomfortable questions.

"I began to develop my own interest in studying bonds."

"But why?"

"It's a highly underdeveloped field. Legally and ethically, it's impossible to conduct controlled experiments. At least not when it comes to the formation of new bonded pairs."

"So it's hard to get funding?"

"No," he said. "No—money isn't the issue."

This spun off into a discussion of funding sources, and NHRI versus lesser research institutes, and assorted other topics that made me grateful not to be a researcher myself.

During a stretch break, he told me how in very rare cases, bonding could transform a regular mage into an originator.

"That's what you're studying?"

"In my spare time." He looked pensively into the bottom of the cup he'd long since finished drinking from. "It's fascinating. I can't help but have mixed feelings, though. The implications—"

He didn't need to go on. There were already plenty of cases of quasi-forced bonding. The sort of situation where the healer in question might technically have the right to say no—but no one would risk it. They would think of their future, their family, the prospect of retaliation. They'd accept the offer if they knew what was good for them.

Let's say someone figured out a way to make bonding reliably convert mundane mages to originators. It'd be highly likely—no, inevitable—that this would lead to bonding becoming legally mandated. Not a matter of choice at all. Like back in the old days. By which I mean less than a century ago.

When I was young, I could never have imagined conditions getting worse for healers over time. That just wasn't how civilization worked, was it?

I'd been born several decades after the last of the old bonding lotteries. If I'd been alive back then, I'd have gotten raffled off, too. Same goes for Mori, also a top-tier healer in his own way. We were lucky to live in more civilized times. Of course healers would win more liberties over the course of my life, I'd thought—and I'd wanted to be the one credited with winning those liberties for everyone else.

Nowadays I had fewer grand aspirations. I had a harder time imagining anything about this country fundamentally changing. Not for good, anyway.

I'd become real skilled at thinking of how healers' rights might slide backwards, further and further, faster and faster. If we didn't constantly run full speed up that hill, didn't constantly sacrifice ourselves to fight the state, it felt like there was nowhere to go but down. Like rights getting peeled away from us was the ordinary way of the world.

But hey. I could try to be positive.

"Depends on what decides the outcome," I said to Mori. "Would those mages have become originators no matter who they bonded? Or was it unlocked in them by bonding a specific healer?"

"Sometimes I think it might be better not to know."

An odd statement, coming from a scholar. I understood what he meant, though.

Origination abilities aside, bonding often led to mages growing more branches. To date, no one had succeeded in elucidating why certain mages gained more from taking a bondmate than others. Some thought it depended on the mage; others thought it depended on the healer they chose as their bondmate.

If a mage knew how to calculate which healer would give them the greatest boost in power, what force could stop them from claiming that healer as their mate?

If the government knew how to consistently produce more originators, why wouldn't they go to unimaginable lengths to increase the originator population?

Originators—like Wist, like Doctor Hazeldine—were the only mages capable of inventing new magic. They alone could expand the library of skills that might ultimately be passed around to other Osmanthian mages, or traded to other nations.

If healers turned out to be the key, then the artificial appearance of choice would get torn away like a cheap curtain. Healers would get algorithmically paired with mages in order to make them originators— and would be punished, no doubt, if the results of bonding failed to meet expectations.

Mages, too, would lose the ability to choose a bondmate for their own reasons. At least they'd get something priceless out of it. Who'd say no to becoming an originator?

At any rate, I could see why Mori—one of the smartest people I'd ever met—might be simultaneously intrigued and apprehensive. He'd find joy in making revolutionary new discoveries. He'd have no control over what came next. And he was too soft-hearted to pretend it had nothing to do with him.

"We understand very little about ourselves as healers," Mori said later. "We know some mages are originators, and most aren't. We classify mages according to their number of branches. We have all sorts of ways to measure their potential. We're a lot more limited when it comes to measuring healers. In that sense, we could stand to learn a thing or two from Jace."

I shushed him on reflex. He gave me a quizzical look.

"I'd love to visit someday," he said. "I know relations are nowhere near normalizing, but there've been a lot more overtures lately. From both sides."

"Have you been studying?" I asked in Jacian.

He responded at once, then glanced away guiltily. I sighed. His accent was already miles ahead of mine. Why did some people have to be good at everything they put their minds to?

"Just be careful," I said.

Mori had a lot to be careful about, it turned out. Corporations and universities trying to headhunt him. Mages courting him for bonding despite his protective association with the Kraken. Fan mail and hate mail from correspondents—many of them anonymous—who either praised or condemned every single paper he put out.

Such small-scale fame was nothing compared to being known on the same level as Shien Ficus, or my duelist friend Fanren, or Wist the

Kraken. But even within niche fields, popularity and acclaim came with its own share of headaches.

"Leave society," I said. "Stay in the tower. Become a permanent pet-sitter. And plant-sitter. Then you can study Jacian as much as you like."

We chuckled together. But I knew he wouldn't do it.

By the time he finished giving Wist's magic a through workup, I'd wiped the shining steel counters so many times that I was making them worse. Adding smudges in places that hadn't been smudged before.

Mori left with a promise to come check up on Wist in two days or so. He did, after all, have a life and a career and interests outside the tower.

Wist and I spent the next few hours making the rounds of her houseplants. As was tradition, Wist did all the actual work. I just hung around to provide commentary.

What sort of commentary? For starters, something about the loss of our bond seemed to have unleashed my inner matchmaker. I asked Wist for her thoughts on Lear and Danver.

"Thoughts?" she said. "I have no thoughts. Except—"

"Yeah, I get it. I know better than to stick my nose in whatever's going on there."

I watched her mist deep green leaves with far more love and care than she'd apply to moisturizing her own face.

I tried again. "How about Tempus and Mori?"

"Have they ever met?"

"Surely not."

Wist contemplated this for a few prolonged seconds. It felt like a moment of silence to commemorate a tragedy.

"Poor Mori," she uttered.

"Tempus and Fanren?"

"Poor Tempus."

To this day, Wist tended to be rather hard on Fanren. Not that he minded. I couldn't argue: Fanren was as much of a heartbreaker as Ficus. Worse, maybe, because he gave his paramours actual hope. Many an older man had gotten all tangled up with him, convinced that they were the one in control—only to be proven devastatingly wrong. Fanren was kind, in his way, but he never looked back.

"You never think of pairing men and women romantically, do you?" Wist asked.

To anyone else, she would've sounded unimpressed. To my ear, she sounded amused.

"My brain doesn't work that way," I said. "I'll leave that stuff to the experts."

Wist pivoted. She sprayed me as if I were one of her plants, gentle as ever. I plucked her free-roaming left hand off the top of my head and—showing equal gentility—slapped her across the face with it.

Luckily, no one collapsed to the floor in a fit of agony. We chased each other around the sunroom with the unhinged energy of wild kids, Wist shooting mist about like a deranged perfumer. Her hand was quite cooperative, staying stiff-fingered to jab at her when I thrust it like an assassin wielding a stiletto.

I saw Wist laughing soundlessly. My heart felt as wrung out as weak legs after a long run—not, I think, in a bad way.

We pretended to be trying our utmost to catch each other. Even though we couldn't afford to ever get there; even though we couldn't afford to slip up. The second I touched her with anything other than her own fingertips, the game would end with an ugly jolt.

45

I WASN'T traumatized by Ficus's head. Nor by Miyu's legs.

In Miyu's case, I had an excuse. I hadn't actually been there to watch the vorpal hole slice her in half. I hadn't been present for Ficus's decapitation, either, but I'd smelled and gawked at the aftermath.

I waited for the true horror of it to sink in, but it never really did. I began to wonder if this were yet another thing I could blame on the Void. As it settled deeper in my body, would it change me in ways I could neither control nor detect?

In my more petulant moments, I wished I could forget how to break bonds. My new knowledge weighed on me. I didn't want the power to help anyone. I wanted my own bond back, and that seemed unlikely to happen anytime soon.

"I was fine before we bonded," I said. "I never needed it. Never wanted it! Now—"

"You never wanted it," Wist echoed. Not a question.

A couple years back, I'd consented to bonding her. Right here in her tower. I'd volunteered of my own free will. But there had been extenuating circumstances. She would understand what I meant.

"You've felt it before," I said, squeezing the palm of her pliant left hand. "A broken bond. Was it the same when I died?"

She didn't want to talk about it. She carried herself as if she had a broken rib floating around inside her, digging at parts of her that weren't meant to be dug at.

Over the next few weeks, the Shien clan put out a statement about their recent losses. They offered no details about how either Miyu or Ficus had died.

There must've been loads of theories flying around about Ficus in particular, but the clan maintained a stance of adamant privacy. They acknowledged no rumors and answered no questions.

Wist took this opportunity to hide out in the tower as much as possible, leaving only for emergencies. No reporters would be able to reach her here.

She wasn't lacking for things to take care of, anyhow. I don't just mean her aquariums and her greenhouses and her snooty cat. Years ago, not long before we bonded, she'd undergone a total wipe of her skill set—a calamity that would prove much more devastating for Wist than for any other mage. She had such an absurd number of branches to fill.

Now, in her spare time, she finished the tin of old cookies from Aunt Riegel and worked on relearning old skills. She painstakingly imprinted them back on her branches. Or she invented and imprinted brand new skills. More than anything, she poured hours into recreating my lost prosthetic eye.

We made multiple attempts to touch each other (without using her broken-off left hand). Each attempt ended with us on opposite sides of the room—Wist silent, me heaving as if I'd been kicked by a horse.

In a metaphorical sense, we weren't licking each other's wounds. We were needlessly jabbing fingers in them, tearing open sloppy stitches.

We tried to bond again, too. Maybe not the smartest decision. We hunkered down at opposite ends of the marriage coffin she'd imported from Manglesea. And we tried. We really gave it our best.

The wound turned raw and new again. The bond wouldn't take. I felt myself reject it as though yanking my hand back from a flame. The Void rejected it as though appalled on my behalf.

I started laughing as if ordered to laugh by a mad and murderous tyrant, the sort who'd chop your head off for the slightest infraction. It took a long time to stop.

"This is worse than when you stabbed me," Wist said meditatively.

"I won't say it's worse than when you sent me to prison." I thumped emphatically at the lacquered side of the coffin and hurt my hand in the process.

We went out on a terrace to feel the wind. I asked for rocks, which Wist provided. I flung said rocks off the side of the tower until my arm ached.

"We can't keep doing this," I told her.

"Throwing rocks?"

"Trying to touch," I said. "It'll give me a phobia of going anywhere near you. Like a lab animal getting shocked till the shocks wear down new grooves in its brain. I don't want to get in the habit of flinching."

Wist could've commented that I was already in the habit of flinching. That I already gave her a wider-than-usual berth when we maneuvered around each other to get to the sink.

She could've brought up the fact that I was the one who'd insisted on trying, who'd pretended that maybe it hurt one percent less each subsequent time—an awful lie. But it was not in Wist's nature to rub things in.

Normally, I might've been curious about how the Shien clan would handle the deaths of her siblings. I didn't know much about funerary practices among the Osmanthian elite. Would people send them flowers, condolence money, packaged gifts? Would any events be held off-site, or just at Follyhope?

Questions crossed my mind and vanished. I couldn't seem to care for long.

Wist went back to the estate on her own to attend various private ceremonies. By the next time we arrived at Follyhope together, no evidence of these rites remained.

It was late in the year, and we'd come to keep our promise to Aunt Riegel. Wist wore the tiny hat that Riegel had given her, plus a chore coat and high-waisted trousers. A deadly combination on her, if you ask me. Everyone she walked past would look hopelessly short-legged in comparison.

Despite the fact that we'd be inside soon enough, I'd bundled all the way up to my nose. The grounds were dotted with ridges of melting snow that lay about in the shadows like sleeping reptiles.

A platoon of landscapers worked on something mysterious in the ruins of the old rose garden. An intimidating throng of ostriches loomed in the distance, peculiarly unperturbed by the winter cold.

The rest of the estate staff had returned, as had livestock and exotic pets and distant relations and their children. Ginko, meanwhile, had gone off to stay in the countryside cloister of Shien-affiliated healers.

Danver seemed lonely, from what little I saw of her. I suppose Ginko had been her closest friend. Couldn't imagine her getting on very well with the rest of the staff.

Technically speaking, Doctor Hazeldine occupied a similar position. He was a family member on Grandmother's payroll. But he was also a mage. An originator, at that. As Grandmother's personal physician, he could boast of much greater prestige than a young healer stuck wearing robes like a housemaid.

Well, Danver might be isolated, but she still had her mother here. We kept our distance, and we kept mum about the fact that we knew what she'd done to Miyu.

Unsavory secrets seemed to be something of a Shien family tradition. In that sense, Danver would fit right in. I would, too. I still had a terrible Void hiding at the back of my eye.

Since we were really just there to see Riegel, we slipped in and out as discreetly as we could. Riegel welcomed us with a smile so huge that it looked like it hurt. I wondered what she'd think if she knew her daughter had—clumsily yet decisively—put Miyu in a vorpal hole.

Did she know? How good was Danver at walling off her private thoughts?

Riegel had bonded Danver in order to ensure that Miyu couldn't get to her. Now Danver had attacked Miyu, with remarkable success, to free the friend who'd ended up tied to her instead. I kept such thoughts to myself, of course. We hadn't come to speak of murder.

We gave Riegel a basket of gifts from the city: lace, ribbons, feathers, silk flowers. She exclaimed in shock, eyes glistening behind her glasses, as we pulled out more and more.

Once she'd recovered enough of her composure to provide coherent instructions, we put all the materials in their proper place. We spoke of trivial things—the slight accumulation of snow from a few days ago, and how in the city it had melted away almost as soon as it touched ground. The grass by Wist's tower, and how it stayed blue all year round. No one addressed the topic of bonding or unbonding.

The next time we came to see Riegel, right at the very end of the year, Lear was there too. She wheeled in a spread of imported breadfruit— roasted, mashed, fried, baked into sweet pudding.

"I'd have given you snakeskin fruit if I could," she said. "You'll have to come to my island for that."

I asked her if this were a special occasion. She pulled a face.

"No need to be humble, dear," Riegel said to her. "You've met with astounding success—and in a foreign land, no less. You're planning for another solo exhibition next year, no?"

Lear made a series of self-deprecating sounds. "Mm. And I owe it all to the tragic demise of Shien Ficus." She turned to me. "Remember my painting of his magic?"

"The one in the room with the blue floor," I said.

"Over the past month, I've sold a disgusting number of reproductions. And posters. And postcards. Not to mention various other types of merchandise. Fancy scarves, printed dresses, reusable bags and graphic tees and such."

"Good grief."

"The family gets a licensing fee. That painting was always one of the most popular pieces I've produced in Osmanthus. But it only really took off after they formally announced his death. I suppose my work is the closest his fans will ever get to seeing inside him. In a rather literal sense."

She smiled drolly. "I've become a financial success of such dreadful proportions, in fact, that I'm liable to get summoned back to Jace by the end of next year. Or maybe sooner. They won't want it to go to my head."

"You've earned your acclaim," Riegel said firmly. "Savor it."

"I intend to. Of course, one might also view me as a foreign leech dangling off the flank of the Shien clan, milking young Ficus's death for all it's worth."

"He was older than you or me," I remarked. "Young to die, yes, but not *that* young, really."

"You all seem terribly young to me," Riegel informed us.

I turned this around on her. "I'm sure you seem terribly young to Lady Shien."

"Leeches don't drink milk," said Wist. "Do they?"

"They suck blood," Lear acknowledged. "My apologies."

On our way out, Lear caught me and asked quietly if I would take a look at her.

I scanned her from head to toe. I saw only Lear the Jacian.

"Like how you looked at Ginko," she clarified.

My examination of Ginko felt like an event of the prehistoric past.

"A full bond assessment?" I said, flummoxed. "But you're a subliminal."

She had no branches. She couldn't bond. She did have a core; she could call herself a mage, although she'd need to use the *subliminal* modifier to avoid drastically misleading people. She wasn't a true mage in any strict sense of the word.

"A futile effort, no doubt," Lear said agreeably. "Would you do it as a favor? Or would you prefer to be paid? I don't mind. I'm about to come into more money than I've ever had in my life."

"I'll do it as thanks for feeding us," I told her. Wist had surprised me by polishing off an entire baked breadfruit on her own. She must've liked being able to peel off the black-charred skin herself.

We took a winding route to Lear's atelier, passing several stone dovecotes. There were a lot more people on the estate nowadays, and Wist would prefer to be seen by as few of them as possible.

We went to the loft, which was just as chaotic as last time.

"I've exceeded expectations in every possible way," Lear commented.

She'd waited till we came all the way up here to say this. She sounded too rueful to mean her recent spike in sales.

When dealing with her Jacian handlers, she'd probably had no choice but to implicitly assume credit for all the recent Shien turmoil, including the deaths of two possible heirs. She'd seem awfully ineffective if she admitted to having nothing to do with it. If it were indeed her work, though, then she'd done almost too good a job.

No one had come to arrest her as a foreign agent. Perhaps she was working for both sides—which would go a long way toward explaining the closeness of her acquaintance with Ficus—or perhaps the powers that be didn't mind having the occasional foreign element installed within their grasp. She was more of a pawn, after all, than a player.

"Success can be as tough as failure," I said, though I had more personal experience with the latter.

Lear grinned. She beckoned us closer. "On that note," she said conspiratorially, "I asked Danny to run away with me."

"She turned you down?" I guessed.

"Obviously."

"What'd she say?" I asked. Mostly out of morbid curiosity.

Lear drew herself up and recited—in a near-flawless imitation of Danver's usual prissy tone—"You want me to be your *mistress?*"

I choked a little. I decided not to inquire about how Lear had phrased her invitation. I could imagine her hinting darkly about Miyu's last moments, and Danver immediately interpreting it as a blatant attempt at extortion.

"For the record," I said, "there are other steps you should go through before you jump straight to eloping."

"Such as?"

I felt Wist watching us as though we'd begun speaking rapid-fire Jacian. I took off my winter hat and fluffed up my hair.

"You don't need lessons in flirtation," I told Lear. "If you made a serious effort to win Danver over, she'd already be yours. You're going easy on her. You don't plan on sticking around here much longer, anyway.

"You know how to spice up your days with the scent of the unattainable. You know how to make it easy to slip away. You like to think that years later, when she looks back and sees everything differently, you'll have become a beautiful lingering mystery, a pleasant memory about what might have been."

Lear was still smiling. "I'd love to hear you talk to Danny like that. Oh, she'd really lose her cool. You'd keep going till she screeched to make you stop."

"I try not to make a habit of bullying young people," I said waspishly. "Unlike some of us. Hurry up and give me your hands."

This was, as Lear herself had admitted, an exercise in futility. I assumed she'd asked for a bond examination as some sort of weird pretext to speak with us in a private setting. Now that we were up in her loft, I'd expected her to call the whole thing off.

She placed her hands in mine. She looked me trustingly in the eye.

For a moment I felt immensely sorry for Danver. She had more pride than she knew what to do with. She had enough self-control to conceal her knowledge of manslaughter. Perhaps even from her own mother and bondmate. But she didn't have nearly enough life experience to know what to do with a woman like this foreigner, slippery and easygoing and virtually impossible to hurt—and, beneath it all, possessed of a fatal sincerity.

I began going through the motions of a bond examination, scarcely paying attention. What was the point? We all knew I'd find nothing.

Still, I stopped seeing the easels pushed into corners, the rolls of unstretched canvas, the wooden bones of disassembled frames. Instead, I saw Lear grabbing Danver and asking, *Who put you up to this?*

Couldn't Lear have guessed quite easily that it all went back to Nerium? Or did she not actually care—or even want to know—whose machinations had propelled Ficus and Miyu and Ginko and Danver to the edge of a vorpal hole in the middle of the night? Maybe she'd only cared about yanking Danver out before she went in too deep.

She'd given up on that soon enough. She'd resorted to observing coolly from a distance.

I considered asking Lear why—back then, in the dark—she'd been convinced Danver was about to do something irreversible. Insider information? Mere instinct? But she was above all else a Jacian. I'd be safest not knowing her secrets.

"I thought you'd try to talk me into breaking Danver's bond," I said. "You heard about it from Riegel, didn't you?"

Lear flashed a hint of crooked teeth. "Boy, I could really fluster you. I could pretend I hadn't heard anything."

"Let's not waste each other's time. Aunt Riegel hasn't fully given up yet. Isn't that why you got us in private?"

"Not at all," Lear said readily. "Should I be flattered or insulted? You seem to think me downright lovesick. No, I'm not that much of a do-gooder. If Danny wants her bond broken, she can ask you herself. If she doesn't want it broken, then no one should break it. Her mother may know what's best for her, but she can't force Danny to feel the same way. My request for an examination was purely selfish, and purely for my own purposes. Don't you see it, Bondbreaker?"

She was joking, but I couldn't respond in kind.

I looked at Wist, who tipped her head as if trying and failing to read my mind.

I refocused on Lear's branchless magic core.

A minute later: "You're bonded," I said scratchily. I released her hands. "That's not even possible. You're a subliminal. But you're bonded."

There was a smile in Lear's voice, though not on her face. "You know what they say about Jacian technology."

"You need at least one branch to bond." I remembered Wist with a red light in her eyes, long black hair on a white carpet, Fanren bleeding. *I offer my bond.* "You have to hold a branch out to your healer."

"Healer?" said Lear. "Always thought that was a funny term. We call them operators in Jace. I'm sure you already knew that, though. Go on—guess how I ended up like this."

46

WIST MOVED toward the wall at the back of the loft. She stopped by the pair of stunted mage paintings that Lear had previously shown us.

The one on the left was Aunt Riegel.

The one on the right was an imaginary version of Lear herself. A what-if rendition of her magic core growing branches. She'd painted herself as a mage with power—albeit a stunted mage, her magic too congenitally warped to be of any real use.

I pictured my own hollow eye socket. Which was maybe not so hollow anymore, with the Void having taken up residence.

I pictured Shien Nerium's mechanical leg.

I pointed at the painting of Lear. "That's not a flight of fancy. It's a genuine self-portrait." My voice came out slower than usual. "You really did paint your own magic. You had branches at one point. You had branches when you bonded."

"Then where are they now?" Lear asked softly.

"You hid them."

"How?"

"No ... you lost them. You weren't born a subliminal. You were turned into one after the fact. After your bond took root." I groped for words. "You were a stunted mage. Like Aunt Riegel. But in Jace, they cut your magic out. They neutered you."

"They cured me," Lear said. "I don't envy Riegel her discomfort. The pain really is crippling. It corrodes you physically and mentally, not just magically. It ages you faster. It drastically shortens your lifespan."

"Aunt Riegel isn't doing too bad, is she?"

"That's debatable. She struggles to walk a full circuit of her own room." A pause. "When I first met her, I was very surprised. In Jace, uncut stunted mages rarely live past forty."

Wist might have thoughts of her own about chronic magical pain. For my part, my mind stuttered over the fact that Jace knew of a way to permanently amputate magic branches.

If Osmanthus had access to that sort of technology, there'd be less need to rely on my hobbling skills to tame dangerous mage criminals and dissidents. Certain factions of our government (and elite society in general) would be thrilled for a chance to demote the Magebreaker from essential to expendable.

On the other hand: whether as a punishment for lawbreakers or as a cure for stunted mages, the surgical removal of magic branches might lie far outside the realm of what modern Osmanthian culture would deem acceptable.

To mages of the ruling class, such neutering might not seem much different from chopping off the genitalia of convicted rapists. Or lobotomizing troublemakers of all stripes: mentally unbalanced subliminals, anger-prone mages with a history of berserking, overly outspoken healers.

Magical mutilation was by definition different from physical mutilation. To a mage, however, it might come across as equally abhorrent. Worse, even, since it was supposed to be impossible.

Everyone understood that legs sometimes broke, and appendices sometimes ruptured. That human flesh was squishy and frail, vulnerable to the predations of disease and bullets and malicious magic alike.

You weren't supposed to be able to uproot magic branches, to ravage them so badly that they never grew back. No Osmanthian mage would know to fear that. Things must be very different in Jace. Or else Lear was an extremely unusual case, a rare experiment in cutting-edge science.

I let out a breath. "I assume you've got a request for me."

Lear turned her necklace of lumpy pearls until the clasp came to rest right at the back of her neck. "Will you make me say it?" she asked slyly.

"Uh, yes."

She bowed lightly to Wist, then to me. "If you ever come to Jace, will you break my bond there?"

This was not what I'd been expecting to hear. I rubbed the upper edge of my eyepatch, the part that rested against my brow.

"That's an insurmountable *if.* Like asking Danver to run away with you—without any hope that she might actually accept. What's the point of even bringing it up? I ought to give Riegel a piece of my mind for telling you I can break bonds on command."

"Don't be angry with Riegel," Lear said, abruptly earnest. "I've told her my history. She feels a great kinship with me. Although her feelings might change if she knew I tried to lure away her Danny."

"Dunno about that," I muttered. "She'd rather have her daughter swept off to distant lands than live forever stuck in Follyhope. She'd cheer you on. Jace might be a little too far, though."

"I wouldn't take Danny to Jace."

This statement sank into the flotsam littered about the loft.

Wist eyed the vaulted glass of the ceiling as though guarding against a sudden attack from above.

"You're bonded," I said to Lear. The Void hummed thirstily against the bones of my eye socket.

"Indeed."

"In other words, you're never alone. You're being watched. And so are we."

"Is that what a bond means to you Osmanthians? Constant surveillance?" Her hands rested easy in her pockets. "Right—maybe I'm here as a human periscope. A harmless-looking subliminal. A frittering artist. Meanwhile, another foreigner looks out through my eyes. Hears what I hear. Transcribes all my thoughts. Reads my lowest desires. Pinches me from across the ocean if I tiptoe too close to subversive ideas."

She said this as if it were completely absurd, but we all knew it wasn't. Not entirely.

"Not that you need to believe me," Lear went on, "but if it's any comfort, operators in Jace really aren't much more advanced than continental healers. They know some extra tricks, yes. They're more confident in their dealings with mages. They call all the shots. But people are still people."

She raised her shoulders. "I'm not nearly so important as to merit a valuable operator wasting their time to remotely monitor the inner workings of my heart. I put up good walls, and I've done good work."

"Have you?" Wist asked.

Lear's lips quirked. "Either that, or I've got the good luck and good sense to graciously accept kudos for events I had absolutely nothing to do with."

"Respectable," I said. "I do admire that. So why don't you want me to break your bond right now?"

"What's your price?"

"A painting of the Kraken."

Wist whipped around to stare at me.

"Hah," said Lear. "Impossible."

"I mean a painting of the non-magical parts of her." I swept a hand at the sketches she'd pinned at uneven intervals all over the loft. Danver, faceless athletes, deep-sea creatures. "Wist won't be able to sit for long, so you'll have to work from memory. Or other pictures."

Lear wore a fluffy vest that went down past her hips. It gave her a somewhat kingly appearance. She'd commented about the cold even in Riegel's room—which was, if anything, overheated.

She strode over to Wist, somehow not tripping over any stray buckets or wooden debris despite not once glancing where she stepped. She lifted her face to give Wist a searching look.

Wist gazed back at her, as devoid of expression as the clear cold sky beyond the ceiling. It was very dry today, the kind of dry that would make healthy people start coughing.

Lear stepped back. "This breaks every personal rule of mine," she said over her shoulder, "but my most important rule is that I do what I want, to the extent that I can. Sure. I'll take your commission. Consider it advance payment. If we ever meet again, in other lands—like I said, that's when I'll ask you to break my bond."

"Very generous of you," I said. "Why?"

"Practical considerations."

"Let me guess. You—"

She did not, in fact, let me guess.

"When my bond breaks, I'll need to fake my death," she said levelly. "I've got unfinished business in Jace. With a broken bond, I'll never be able to risk going home again—and I'll never be able to show myself anywhere in Osmanthus, either. My best hope would be to flee somewhere far to the east of the continent, or maybe up north."

"Manglesea's a nice place," I offered.

She smiled knowingly, a quick and narrow compression of her lips.

Lear would trade immediate freedom—which would take the form of a permanent exile—for the ability to fantasize about first wrapping up all her loose ends. In her homeland, and maybe back here.

As long as she didn't yet break her bond, as long as she didn't yet fake her death, there might still be someone waiting and wishing to see her once more. In Jace, or in Osmanthus.

Or, on the opposite end of the spectrum, maybe there was someone she wanted to destroy before she vanished. Maybe, as she primed canvases, she dreamt of redemption or revenge for things that had happened decades ago, in a country whose sand and soil rarely got marked by Osmanthian footprints.

Lear was similar to me: she wouldn't put much stock in that sort of hope, whether it painted a picture of a grand reunion or pitiless vengeance. She'd prefer not to gaze at her buried dream head-on. She might find it all rather pathetic.

But it was the kind of morsel that could sustain you through long grim stretches of life where the tunnel you dug only ever went in one direction, and only ever took you deeper.

I indicated her self-portrait. "Does Danver know?"

"That I was a stunted mage? And now a—how did you put it, a neutered mage? Yes."

Lear bent and briskly cleared a narrow path along the side of the loft, making it easier for Wist to rejoin us. A drawer packed full of thin wooden wedges clunked in protest as she hip-checked it.

"Riegel hasn't spoken with other stunted mages in years," she said. "She loves my stories. Probably the only reason Danny tolerates me."

"Cultural exchange," I said innocently. "That's why you came here, isn't it?"

"Oh, yes. Shared quite a few choice tidbits about my upbringing. I actually learned to activate a skill or two before my surgery. Does that surprise you?"

"Branch skills? But—"

"Nothing productive. Nothing of value. Merely an exercise in proving that a stunted mage with sufficient willpower can use limited magic."

Wist's left hand moved at her side like a small animal twitching tenderly in its sleep. I edged away to avoid accidental contact.

Lear's gaze fell into the gap between us. She knew about my self-proclaimed ability to break bonds. She couldn't know what had become of my bond with Wist: that was the one secret I'd begged Riegel not to betray.

"They didn't modify you to make magic use possible?" I said, trying to distract her. "Like how they chopped off your branches later."

"Not at all. But I get why people call it impossible. It's like getting sliced open without anesthesia. Like taking a hammer to break your own bones. Inhumane, really, to make any stunted mage do it. They frowned on it even in Jace.

"In the end, some very nice men and women came and cut out my pain forever. Such angels they were! I'm not embarrassed to say that I wept all over them. What a relief—like excising a tumor. But they only did it after making sure I'd been bonded. Very practical of them. Some dogs are most useful on leashes."

Plenty of government entities must've felt the same way about Wist—and about me. They needed to believe that they could exert some meaningful degree of control over the Kraken and the Magebreaker. A knife pointed in the right direction could be a helpful tool. Pointed in the wrong direction, it'd be a liability.

"Nice hat," Lear said to Wist as we came down the stairs from the loft. "Riegel has remarkable taste, doesn't she? It all seems very froofy and fussy and frivolous in isolation. Way over-the-top. Works perfectly once you actually put it on, though."

I had to agree. Wist would never have chosen that purple-inflected mini hat for herself. (I wouldn't have, either.) For all that, it looked inexplicably good on her.

We came back to Follyhope a few more times after the beginning of the new year. Riegel was always so overjoyed to see us. It felt weirdly like coming home to a relative who'd known me since I was a little kid, too.

Lear followed through on our agreement, although I told her not to treat it as a serious obligation. She'd perch on a stool and sketch us whenever we sat to chat with Riegel. Wist, who had never been fond of portraits, tolerated it only because Lear cleverly offered to add me in the composition, too.

Danver became even snippier than usual when she spotted Lear drawing us.

"What," Lear said, "can't I sketch my friends? It's a nice change of pace from the usual. You have to admit that the Kraken makes for a very striking subject. Just look at those eyes."

"But you never—" Danver stopped and pulled herself together as though yanking at the strings of a corset. "You never make art of people. You only paint their magic."

"I am replete with hidden depths," Lear said smoothly. "I've trained in a variety of styles."

She sketched in silence for another agonizing minute, then lowered her charcoal. "Sorry, Danny," she said—suddenly contrite, almost stricken. "Have I been neglecting you?"

"She wanted to slap you," I said afterward, when we were no longer in a position to be overheard by either Danver or her mother.

Lear cupped her own cheek. "I rather wish she had."

"You could've just told her why you're drawing us. Advance payment and such. She's fully aware of the topic of bondbreaking. Her own mother started it."

"I could have told her," Lear agreed, "but I won't."

"Does she know you've covered your loft in sketches of her like some kind of maniac?" I asked tartly.

"You have a statuette of me in your apartment," Wist said from my left, too low for Lear to hear.

"Oh, Danny knows," Lear said with glee. "Haven't done much to hide it, have I? No locked doors to close off the loft. No curtains covering the walls. Still, she thinks I've hidden my drawings up there like some sort of shameful secret shrine.

"She doesn't realize that I know she knows—isn't that sweet? She was never so nice to me as in the days after she first discovered it. She marched around the estate in a hilariously good mood. She looked at me with such pity, such understanding and condescension, such superiority. Took all my self-control not to crack up. A truly delicious time for both of us."

I regretted ever asking. Which, to give credit where credit is due, had probably been Lear's intention.

"Don't toy with her too much," I said, feeling unbearably pompous. "She's only—what, twenty-four or twenty-five? She's never lived off Shien property. We healers lead very different lives from your operators."

The smile dropped off Lear's face. "I know," she said. "Trust me, I've wormed my way in just deep enough to be a temporary irritation. I understand the importance of cleaning up after myself. Won't leave any unnecessary traces."

Might be too late for that, I thought.

I'd tested Danver in passing. Just out of curiosity. I'd muttered a phrase or two in Jacian when she wasn't prepared for it, and when I knew she could hear me. Simple, innocent remarks, clear and easy to catch. Her head would snap up. If I'd been speaking of the weather, she'd glance at the window. If I mentioned a sound at the door, she'd wait for a few fidgety moments and then go to check if we had another lurking visitor.

She understood more than any Osmanthian should. More than any Osmanthian could grasp without serious study. Jacian had little in common with our mother tongue. The basic sounds differed, as did our writing systems. Most grammatical structures were completely backwards.

She must've gotten her hands on restricted texts. Pilfered them from the family library, perhaps. She must've been teaching herself Jacian for quite a while now. Since before the day we first met, when she'd lectured Lear for speaking it and pretended not to know any.

She'd struggle greatly with uttering words in a foreign language. She had too much pride to risk getting anything wrong. And she'd rather burn down the whole mansion than admit to having any interest in Jacian. She certainly wouldn't tell her mother about it. She'd hide it from Lear at all costs.

But she was learning Jacian all the same. Without any intention of putting her skills to practical use. She'd take all knowledge of it to her grave, together with the sensation of the first and last time she'd shoved Miyu. Her cousin. Her superior. A rotten and hateful mage.

Danver's pride would protect her. I just wasn't sure if it would protect her enough.

I knew how much motivation it took to teach yourself a language in secret. To wrestle with the searing frustration of starting from zero, being slower than a child, having no one you could ask for help. If she kept going anyway—well. That spoke for itself. But it wasn't my business to stop and listen.

47

Snow fell several more times early in the new year. Sometimes we saw it at the tower, and sometimes we saw it at Follyhope.

I became so familiar with every line on Wist's left palm that I could call up a detailed map of it in my mind. Just like how I could summon a precise recollection of every mage I'd ever touched. Might've been a handy little party trick, if we ever went to parties. (We didn't.)

I'd hoped that time would heal the split-open edges of what used to be our bond. I'd hoped that with time, I could touch more of her than just her detached hand.

Nothing got better. Worry dug a hole for itself inside me, settling down with the weight of a second Void.

The Void had finally grown accustomed to me, like a plant getting attuned to new soil. It felt less skittish around vorpal holes, although I didn't dare push it too far. The cycle of its hunger slowed to a crawl, as if its figurative metabolism had lapsed into a state of hibernation.

Still, I'd have to feed it again at some point. That point seemed likely to come before Wist and I could even think about rebonding, much less sleeping in the same bed at night.

I grew increasingly brittle, irritable. My thoughts veered in grisly directions. When strangers meandered too slowly—taking up the entire city sidewalk in front of me—my brain sketched out elaborate scenarios that ended with me feeding them to the Void.

Ficus had said his fire-based skill was called Incinerator. Well, the Void would be much more effective at making things vanish. The Void wouldn't leave any ash. If only I knew how to control it. I couldn't even control my own lurching angst over each new morning that proved nothing had changed. I could no more readily embrace Wist than I could embrace an electric fence.

On the surface, Wist maintained her equanimity. Objectively speaking, this had to be better than both of us falling to pieces. But the distance between us felt as if it ran deeper than anything physical.

I couldn't complain. She carried all that magic, and she carried all the ensuing pain. Even when we weren't touching. If you started measuring our burdens that way, though, then I'd never have the right to complain about anything. I'd have to sew my mouth shut for the rest of my life.

Mori came by to heal Wist whenever he could. I battled my worst urges and somehow managed not to snap at him—for visiting too often, or not often enough. For healing her too well, or not as well as I would.

I clung to the shreds of my self-awareness. I tried to comport myself like a grown adult. Everyone went through periods of being laid low, of being scraped bare, of seeing a future blocked by wreckage. There was nothing special about my misery, however peculiar its cause.

It was late January when Wist held out cupped hands and showed me the new eye she'd finished crafting. It looked very much like my lost prosthesis, with a mesh of magic interlaced more finely than the inner workings of a top-tier mechanical watch.

"I made some changes," she said.

"Like the summoning passphrase?" I asked hopefully.

"That's still the same."

"Should've known."

We were in one of her rooftop rock gardens, shaded by pine trees with trunks like cracked red mud. We sat with our pants rolled to our knees, ankles soaking in a sunken stone-lined foot bath. (It would've been large enough to use as a regular shared bath, or even a shallow swimming pool.)

Steam rose tirelessly off the water's surface. After I popped my new eye in, Wist leaned closer to watch me blink.

Her left hand had demurely married itself to the end of her wrist. I glanced at her fingers resting curled on the flat wooden slats of our bench seat.

I was jealous of the very water that swirled around her feet. I was jealous of the bond thread she'd chased to another world.

"It'll provide insulation," Wist said.

"Come again?"

"Between the Void and vorpal holes. It'll help tamp down the Void's reaction."

My new prosthetic eye. Right. "Sounds extremely advanced," I said. "How'd you work that one out?"

"Got some ideas from the other world."

The shattering of our bond had given me an epiphany about how to break bonds myself. And here Wist was getting inspired by violently diving through vorpal holes. At least we'd gotten something out of it, but the payout felt meager compared to the cost.

Wist appeared satisfied with the fit of my eye.

"I've made it more resistant to destruction. There'll be warning signs if the Void becomes a threat again."

"Warning signs? Like what?"

She didn't answer.

"Wist?"

She stirred her feet back and forth in the steaming water, which dimpled with agitated waves. She didn't meet either of my eyes. "It'll start weeping blood. Or ink. Or both."

"Nice and inconspicuous," I said. "Just the way I like it. You've certainly got a hidden flair for drama."

Her shoulders folded inward.

"The eye feels great," I added quickly. "Better than ever. But as far as warnings go—couldn't you just make it vibrate?"

"In your eye socket?"

"Would that be weird?" I asked.

"You tell me."

"On second thought, I've always wanted to be able to weep blood on command."

"It won't be on command." Wist sounded almost doleful.

"That's fine. Still a chance to drip red and black tears without any worry about serious medical issues."

"You won't have to worry about serious medical issues. You will have to worry about serious Void issues."

"What comes after the tears of blood?" I inquired.

"If all else fails, your eye will eject itself before the Void destroys it."

"Does it get a little parachute?" I asked, delighted.

"It'll bounce on the ground. It'll run away on foot." Wist blinked as though she'd confused herself. "So to speak."

I cackled at the image of my false eye rolling away at top speed, fleeing for its life.

No matter how foul my mood, no matter how deep my rut, Wist always found a way to get to me. So much for my plans to spend the rest of the month wallowing in well-earned gloom.

I kicked hot water at her. I tried to scoot out of the way before she could retaliate, but Wist was much faster.

The foot bath turned into a full-body bath, and then into a litany of cursing and dripping as we squelched and shivered back inside the tower. I thumped the wall with my fists because I couldn't thump Wist. Where did she get the audacity to make me laugh so long and so hard? The gall of that woman—it defies belief, I tell you.

My stupid face hurt from smiling. I told Wist as much. I told her I'd file a claim with her supervisor. She looked back after struggling to peel off her wet shirt—thoughtless of her; was she trying to make my mouth drier?—and her face was the softest I'd ever seen it. Almost completely unguarded.

I wanted to kiss her. I wanted to kick her. Guess what: I couldn't do either. I crouched down and put my head in my arms. I didn't get over myself until I glimpsed her stray left hand scuttling across the water-darkened carpet, approaching me as tentatively as a stressed-out pet. Oh, Wist.

48

It wasn't snowing anymore, but it might as well have been. Billowing gusts of old white powder blew off rooftops as I walked up to my city apartment.

This wasn't exactly normal. Most years, Osmanthus City barely saw a single snowflake.

Wist had nipped over to the Palace of Magi for a series of meetings. I could've huddled back in the tower, but I hadn't checked up on my apartment for a couple of weeks now. I needed to run the taps, switch out old tubs of desiccant, check ill-ventilated corners for mold, and so on. I clipped on an ear cuff and forced myself to venture out in the cold.

I unlocked the mailbox. Didn't find any new anonymous letters written on Shien stationery. Aunt Riegel now knew how to reach Wist at the tower, after all. I tramped up concrete steps and let myself in.

My bedroll hung over a pole to air out. In the middle of the small kitchen table presided a one-fourth scale figure of Wist in mage robes.

I'd have brought it to the tower, but she still found it acutely embarrassing.

By now, the apartment was more of a home for this statue than it was a home for me. I gave my miniature Wist a quick affectionate dusting, then went to crack open a window.

Between me and the window, right in the spot where I'd usually lay down my floor bed, rested a large hard-shell suitcase.

It stood upright, with the handle on top pulled out like a stiff pair of antennae. The shell was robin's-egg blue—all one color—covered in a repetitive embossed pattern.

I halted with my back to the kitchen. I gaped at the luggage, which appeared ready to roll towards me all on its own. Like a marble on a slanted floor.

It didn't move.

It didn't make a sound.

I couldn't perceive any obvious magic on its outer surface. Nothing that would explode if I touched it. But there were cuttings woven deeper inside it, magic like the sterile light you'd see when opening a refrigerator door late at night.

I touched my ear cuff. I kept my eye on the suitcase all the while, as if staring down a cockroach so it couldn't go skittering out of sight.

Maybe Wist would welcome an excuse to skip the rest of her meetings. I wouldn't poke at the suitcase on my own—but it might not be safe to turn my back and leave the apartment, either. I had no idea what I'd walked into, no idea what any further actions might trigger.

If Wist couldn't come over right away, I'd be reduced to huddling timidly in a corner until she managed to extricate herself from the Palace. What fun.

Wist ported in fifteen seconds after I started speaking. I was midway through a sentence when she just about landed right on top of me.

I felt her brush me. The lightning crack of anguish blew open every nerve. Then I realized that—no, actually, I'd felt nothing. Just a searing flash of horrified anticipation.

I'd shrunk against the wall, and she'd caught herself with her hands braced by my head. Her lips came very close to my hair. But no part of us touched.

"Maybe you should've just come through the door," I said shakily.

Wist's arms were taut on either side of me. She pushed herself away from the wall, careful not to graze me.

She hadn't bothered dressing up much for the Palace of Magi. The second she materialized, a puffer coat had slid off her shoulders and hit the wood veneer floor behind her. Beneath it she wore a dark sport dress, long and plain.

She twisted to see the luggage. She put one arm back up against the wall like a barricade to keep me out. Not that I had any intention of making mischief.

"This apartment should be one of the safest places in the city," she said. "In all of Osmanthus. It should be one of the safest places on the entire continent."

Wist—who never boasted about her magic, who never cared about being disparaged in foreign tabloids—that Wist of mine was taking this as a personal insult.

"It's still safe," I said. "My new suitcase hasn't harmed anyone yet."

She was not amused. I ducked to rescue her coat from the floor, bundling it up in my arms.

She'd previously planted magic all over the apartment. Most of the time, it called little attention to itself. It waited like cicadas in their wingless form living for years underground, sucking on tree roots for sustenance. Now her buried magic thrummed on all sides, boxing us in. I hugged her coat closer.

A hard, strange, penetrating light swept the walls and ceiling and floor. It had no obvious source. The shadow of the suitcase shortened and stretched and twisted. So did Wist's shadow; her left hand guttered like a candle. The sound of wind battering the windows grew muffled, then sharpened until it was loud enough to make me jump.

"The suitcase won't hurt you," Wist said.

She didn't sound pleased. If it was indeed harmless, inside and out, that was probably the crux of how they'd slipped it past her. Neither a pipe bomb nor a psychobomb could've threaded a way in through all Wist's defenses.

"What's in it?" I asked.

She flicked a look at the teal suitcase, then at the naked elm trees swaying outside the apartment balcony, then back at me. As if performing some manner of rapid calculus.

She touched the right side of her face. "Your eye," she said.

It was wet. Bloody, I realized, looking at my fingertips. Just the right side, the false side. The blood didn't come out of my tear ducts. It beaded up on the surface of the prosthesis like condensation on a cold bottle. It welled and overflowed and trickled down my cheek. I'd been so intent on Wist and her magic that I'd stopped feeling my own skin.

"It's been a while," Wist said. "The Void must be hungry."

"The suitcase—"

"Won't be going anywhere. Feed the Void while you still have control."

"I'm not about to lose control," I said. But I understood that the eye she'd crafted might be able to detect danger signs I couldn't consciously notice. Like a seismograph recording earthquakes too subtle for our senses.

Wist passed me a tissue box from the kitchen.

"I got the warning." I held a wad of tissue to my right eye. "Can't I make it stop dripping blood now?"

"Didn't think of that," Wist admitted.

I shooed her down into one of my gray floor chairs. I crouched before her and popped out my slippery eye. The Void felt like a sea of choppy water, foam-laced and opaque.

Wist's left hand decoupled from her wrist. It stole across the floor and climbed up to clasp my forearm, burrowing inside my sleeve.

When she looked up at me, she'd see nothingness behind my right eyelid, and a face smeared half in blood. I wondered whose blood it was—mine? Would it match my blood type? But it hadn't leaked from an open wound. I couldn't tell if it had the exact chemical composition of living blood, or if it were just an imitation with the same odor and color.

I didn't want to let the Void feed on her when I couldn't even rub her back afterward. All I could do was kneel beside her and watch like an inquisitor as she endured it.

With our bond, I'd been aware of some small fraction of what she went through when the Void ate her magic. Now I would experience it solely through the Void. I would be reduced to a predator. And I was so afraid of how much better it might feel. I was afraid of how sweet it might taste.

Her right hand clamped down on her truncated left wrist. Hidden inside my jacket, her left hand held me with a bruising grip. Her eyes lingered on small imperfections marring the cheap floor: a dent here, a missing strip of wood there.

"Wist," I said, "you understand that I don't want this, right? If we didn't have to make concessions to the Void—if we didn't have any other choice—"

"Please," she squeezed out, still fixated on the floor.

I was making it worse by making her wait. I relaxed a muscle that was not a muscle at all. It certainly wasn't part of my body. I just don't know how else to describe it. I opened a sluicegate in the middle of nowhere, and the Void came out.

The Void poured down her throat. I poured down her throat together with it, but it didn't hurt me. Not like touching her with my own skin. It didn't hurt at all.

I'd meant to kneel next to her in solidarity. Somehow I found myself standing over her, looking down at her while she curled in on herself and the shapeless Void drank from the tender roots of her magic. It burned her pitilessly from the inside out, leaving injuries invisible to human eyes, and in my body I felt only the hideous crackling leaping flames of hunger and pleasure and satisfaction.

I couldn't tell when the Void had eaten its fill. It could've kept going. I could've kept going. Maybe I waited too long. When I pulled away, its tentacles readily left her. It had gone all weak-limbed and sleepy with satiation.

I numbly fitted my prosthetic eye back in place, plugging the Void. Took me four tries to get it right.

That feeling of invading her, flowing into her together with the Void—it was the most deeply enmeshed we'd been in over a month. Two months? I was too shaken to count.

I couldn't see Wist's face. Her posture reminded me of Ginko folded up on the floor while Ficus caned her. My arm ached dangerously under the tourniquet of her left hand.

Eventually Wist lifted her head. She scraped the hair out of her face and gave me a dry-eyed look. Her hand eased its punishing hold on me. It wiggled out from the end of my sleeve like a fruit ripened to the point of falling.

The Void wasn't human. It lacked human sensation. But I'd certainly tasted something when the Void ate her magic. Guilty satiety pooled in me.

"Believe me," Wist said, "it was worse in Manglesea."

"For god's sake," I snapped, "don't try to *comfort* me." I was blazingly and unfairly furious. "I don't need comfort! Don't send your severed hand over like an emotional support animal. You were the one being eaten alive, you—"

"The suitcase," Wist uttered.

"The suitcase can wait."

I got her a glass of water, watched critically while she drank her fill, then poured her more.

If—as Wist claimed—the suitcase posed zero danger, then we could open it after I finished my chores. I'd come here to freshen up the place, not to throw Wist to the mercy of the Void. And certainly not for the purpose of investigating mysterious packages.

I washed the itchy stains off my face. Once the apartment was in good order, and well ventilated (albeit freezing cold), I went to close the windows I'd shoved open with a vengeance.

"Don't shut them yet," Wist said.

I eyed the unclaimed luggage with growing trepidation. It was forebodingly large. Wouldn't fit too well in my closet.

"Whatever's inside—is it smelly?" I asked.

"It's ... organic."

"Should we be in hazmat suits?"

"The suitcase is lined with all sorts of sterilization and preservation magic. It won't pose any immediate health risks."

"All right, then," I said. "Do the honors."

She swayed to her feet. She held her stomach and lower back—the parts closest to her magic core—as though she'd been stabbed there.

I backpedaled. "Wait, no, sit down. Goodness. Now it looks like I'm tyrannizing an invalid. Let me do it."

"I'm not that decrepit," Wist said steadily. She waved me off.

She examined the suitcase from above, one hand resting on the tall protruding handle.

She pushed the handle all the way down. She tilted the suitcase to lie flat on its back. Magic from her fingertips ran a rapid circuit of its seams. I heard a brief buzzing like flies. The wind outside withered to nothing.

She never fiddled with the zipper or lock or any other form of obvious fastener. The suitcase opened on its own, lifting its lid against gravity. This felt—as it should—so much like exhuming a casket.

49

THE SUITCASE held a trim male body, light-skinned, with no head and no hands and no forearms.

It was perversely devoid of scent. It was also devoid of clothes.

Neither of us gasped.

"Is it real?" I asked. Couldn't hurt to be sure.

Wist looked at the mutilated body without a ounce of compassion. I don't mean her default dismissive expression—there was something more in the set of her mouth. A hint of disgust. As if she blamed the body for having the audacity to invade my apartment.

"It's human," she replied.

"Is it Ficus?"

I had no idea what he looked like naked. I couldn't judge based on his magic, either.

This corpse might've been a mage; if so, his core and branches had already vanished. The cuttings lining the suitcase had flawlessly preserved his physicality in death, but they couldn't preserve his magic. Magic was always the first thing to go. Like how Riegel's paper-wrapped cookies had kept their color and texture for years, but hadn't kept very much of their taste.

"It's him," Wist said after considering my question at length. She turned from the open luggage. "You need to move."

I stepped over to one side. "Sorry."

It was a small apartment—all too easy to get in each other's way. Especially when we needed to avoid touching.

"You need to move," she repeated. "To another building."

Mystified, I glanced out the window.

"The Extinguishers know where you live."

"Well, hold on," I said. "Nowadays I'm at the tower more often than not. They can't touch me there. You already said yourself that this—this delivery isn't hazardous. It's just Ficus."

"Part of him."

"Most of him. Maybe they got tired of hauling him around. Maybe they figured that if they had to dump him somewhere, might as well dump him in a place carefully calculated to cause you maximum insult."

"Do you realize how difficult it would have been to port a single grain of sand in here without my explicit permission?"

"No," I allowed, "not really, but I can take a guess based on your reaction. I mean, the Extinguishers are nothing if not highly motivated. However they did it, they got it done. That isn't the problem. The problem is that—"

"This is a message to us. A statement of some kind. But it doesn't make sense."

Right. The Extinguishers didn't need cutesy new ways to declare war on Wist. They'd had it out for her for decades.

Why else would they leave Ficus here?

To frame me for murder? That might've worked if I were a different healer, someone with zero connections and no way to defend myself. But I had Wist.

I circled closer to the open rectangular suitcase. The body lay crumpled into a fetal shape in order to fit. The ends of the severed neck and forearms had taken on the hard white-ashen texture of crumbling concrete. An artifact, perhaps, of hasty and forceful preservation. His wounds looked more like fossils than flesh.

It would be interesting if this were a total stranger. Someone that some other shadowy faction wanted to pass off as Shien Ficus. Nothing to do with the Extinguishers. I trusted Wist's diagnosis, though.

If the Extinguishers wanted to show that they knew where I lived, that they knew how to get to me—they wouldn't mince around the subject with morbid pranks.

Wist's magic may have prevented them from attempting to, say, blow up the entire apartment as soon as I stepped through the door. In that case, they'd have even less reason to reveal their hand by depositing a murdered body, wholly unprompted. A needlessly dramatic gesture.

Planting the body here could only lead to them losing any informational advantage they'd temporarily gained. Look at the results: Wist was already trying to convince me to move.

Was the Extinguishers' goal to make me go apartment-hunting? Would they pop up in the guise of real estate hustlers? Had sleeper agents secretly infiltrated my apartment management company?

Ridiculous.

"Can you tell how long he's been here?" I asked.

"Not with precision."

I'd been by the apartment a few times in December, but this was my first visit of the new year. Ficus could've been languishing in my bedroom for weeks.

The thought of that made me suddenly feel inclined to drop everything—to seek out a brand new apartment and never look back.

The Void sprawled in me, heavy and sated and utterly lacking in urgency. Without its anchoring presence, I'd have been wired with anxiety. I'd have reacted more appropriately, I think, to the physical fact of a beheaded dead body stuffed in a suitcase.

I wracked my brain for a way to rouse the Void again. The necessary next step seemed quite plain to me. I just wasn't sure how to make it happen.

"Clem."

"Yeah?"

"Why are you taking your eye out?"

"Nothing good will come of tangling with the Shiens," I recited. "Ergo, nothing good will come of reporting this. He's dead either way. You owe that family nothing—and regardless, they've got his head and his hands. They can live without the rest of him."

I scrutinized my prosthesis in the light from the balcony. The white parts still looked awash in shades of pink. Better give it another thorough cleaning later.

"What are you trying to do?" Wist asked.

"What good is the Void, if not for making things vanish?"

She swiftly stepped between me and the remnants of Shien Ficus.

"The Void is bottomless," I said. "It can fit any number of bodies."

As if she needed a reminder. She'd taken on the full punishment of its unrestrained appetites back in Manglesea. In a vessel like me, the Void was but a thin gauzy shadow of what it had been in a vessel like the Kraken.

"I know you won't let them send me back to prison," I continued. "I don't like how this looks, though. I've found part of his body not just once, but twice in a row. Why not make it all disappear?"

"And forget we ever saw it?"

"And forget we ever saw it. I'm willing to move, by the way. Don't worry about me squatting here to battle a bunch of Extinguishers."

Together we contemplated the garish bruising on his torso and side.

"If this is a message to us," said Wist, "you want to ignore it."

"Tear it to shreds. Burn it. Like how Ficus burned your hair."

"You're still holding a grudge over that?"

"Sure am."

"He's dead."

"And now he can enjoy eternity in my Void. Headless and handless."

I cupped my prosthetic in my palm like a lucky charm. It was starting to feel decidedly sticky.

"The Void might be able to take an unlimited number of guests," Wist said slowly.

"Convenient, right?"

"I don't like it."

"It'll be less troublesome than reporting this to authorities. And less work than moving the body elsewhere. Well—you could just port it over to some vorpal hole out in the woods and be done with it, couldn't you?" I ran my fingers over the stylized pattern embossed on the slick outer shell of the suitcase. It didn't bite.

"The Void is a cleaner solution," I said. "You won't have to compromise your own ethics. I'll just whisk him away into nothingness. No tasty magic in him anymore, but maybe the Void will digest him anyway. If not, he can float at the back of my eye forever. I won't feel it."

"That's what I don't like," Wist said.

"Illegal corpse disposal?"

"You carrying his naked chopped-up body around inside you."

"Inside the Void," I corrected, "which just happens to be inside me. In a matter of speaking."

I got her point, though.

"This pattern." I rapped the suitcase with my knuckles. "Seems familiar."

"The monoceros crest," Wist said.

It had taken me a while to notice because the raised ridges of the design were all one color—the same eggshell blue as the rest of the suitcase—and because the crests interlocked like links of chain mail.

"Bit on the nose, isn't it?" I asked.

"You almost didn't recognize it."

"Yeah, thanks for telling me," I said bitingly. "You'd have let me breeze right past key evidence."

"You seemed pretty set on erasing all evidence with the Void."

"I still am."

But I didn't coax the Void into swallowing Ficus and his Shien suitcase. I went to clean my hands and my prosthetic eye, then reinserted it. I made Wist sit back down and put her coat on. I wrapped a blanket around her shoulders for good measure.

With both my balcony doors and a window cracked, icy air came through in a constant stream, unflagging. My heart sank at the notion of attempting to find a new apartment. I'd never get another corner room at a price this good, that's for sure.

If the body were an implied message, it wasn't a message from the Extinguishers. They might've gone through the literal motions of planting him here: a remarkable feat of magical engineering, and one that would demand the use of extraordinarily expensive resources. I really did have to applaud them for getting Ficus past Wist's barriers.

The Extinguishers themselves didn't have much to gain from all that labor. They weren't interested in denting Wist's pride. Their overarching goal was the same as it had always been. To destroy her. They wouldn't bother launching a mildly irritating campaign of harassment.

If they thought they could hurt Wist by hurting me, they wouldn't merely inconvenience me by dumping a dead body in my room. The dead body, I might add, of someone I'd never even liked.

No—the Extinguishers would jump straight to beheading me. If they knew this to be logistically impossible, they wouldn't settle for half-measures. They'd go quiet, maybe for years, and regroup till they had a better chance.

But the Extinguishers were an organization, and a positively ancient one at that. Most such organizations have an innate drive to survive and perpetuate their line.

Whether you were a gang of terrorists or a guild of nonprofit do-gooders, the fundamental needs of any organization—like the basic physiological needs of any human—were more or less the same. Membership: a healthy mix of the jaded old guard and idealistic fresh blood. Funds: the raising and management thereof. Resources. Knowledge. Structure. Goals.

I went to a satchel I'd left hanging from a chair in the kitchen. I fussed around until I found Nerium's business card. The second one he'd given me. No need to handle it with special care. I could toss it in beneath my coin purse, train pass, keys, and pens—nothing would make it crumple.

I held it between my finger and thumb and imagined flinging it at Ficus's corpse like a throwing star. The first business card I'd gotten from Nerium had been left embedded in Ficus's head.

"Do you always carry that?" Wist asked.

I gestured with the card. "This?"

"That."

"Just threw it in my bag and forgot it," I said. "Don't give me that look. It's not like I had it lovingly tucked away in my bra, right over the skin of my heart."

Wist scanned me as if she could see through my clothes. "Are you wearing a bra?"

"Not under all these layers. I'm not in desperate need of extra support." I glowered back at her. "Unlike certain other people."

Normally, I'd prove my point by diving headfirst into her chest. Or she might offer hopefully to give me the support I'd just declared I didn't need. She'd reach around from behind me and demonstrate what she meant with her hands. Now we were reduced to a repressed exchange of smoldering looks.

Granted, there was a dead body resting where I usually laid down my bed. Kind of a mood-killer.

"Will you use it?" Wist asked, eyes on the business card.

"No." The black surface refused to reflect light, just as it refused to dirty itself with my fingerprints. "I'm sure it was him. I can live without hearing confirmation—or smiling denials—from his mouth. Why play into his hands?"

50

To be quite truthful, I felt ... disappointed.

It had to be Nerium. He'd already proven that he could get the Extinguishers (or at least one faction of them) to do as he asked.

I doubt he'd funded them in any obvious way. But for some fleeting span of time—perhaps just these past few months—their interests had aligned. He'd handed them an opportunity to reap a traitor. An undercover agent. His own golden-haired brother.

This body-dumping prank might've been the Extinguishers' final act of repayment. They would never have done it without prompting. It didn't adequately serve their own interests. As a favor to their temporary patron, though—one last effort to ensure nothing further would be owed—yeah, I could see that.

It was Nerium himself who'd disappointed me. There were countless other ways he could've tried to get our attention. How had he convinced himself that pulling a stunt like this would make us any more likely to respond? He'd left us alone for years and years now. (As had most of the other Shien siblings.) After all that time, had he extended his illicit cooperation with the Extinguishers just to make me panic at the sight of a headless man in my bedroom?

I could believe it of him. Underneath it all, he and Ficus were far more alike than they might seem at first glance. Still—this was how he'd chosen to use the already-desecrated corpse of his own closest brother? It just seemed kind of sad, really.

He knew nothing about me and Wist if he'd thought this would perturb us in any lasting way. Had he forgotten how he and Ficus used to treat her? He wasn't even fifty yet: was he suffering from early-onset senility? Or was this the privilege of the well-rested perpetrator, some innate ability to let the tides of time file the jagged edges off old transgressions?

Then again, why in the world would I have expected anything better? Don't tell me that I'd been taken in by all his comments about our similarities. Ugh.

"You don't think I should use the Void," I said to Wist.

"For concealing dead bodies? No."

"And I don't want to confront Nerium. Let him stew. So what should we do instead? Zip up the suitcase? Keep Ficus's corpse as a pet?"

"What do people usually do when they find a dead body?"

"Scream?" I said blankly.

"They tell the nearest MP."

I made a face. "If you want to get MPs involved, you'll have to do most of the talking. They'll try to arrest me the second they learn who I am."

"Let's start with Tempus," Wist said.

I let Wist figure out how to reach him. Meanwhile, I used my ear cuff to speak with Manatree.

"Hey," I said perkily. "I've got exciting news."

"Oh, no."

She'd been my parole officer for years now. She could tell from my tone that this was something she would very much prefer not to hear about. Not that she had any choice in the matter.

I proudly told her I'd found a dead body.

The parole thread hidden around my ankle barely served a purpose anymore. It was largely thanks to Manatree that the restrictions on me had eased to the point that I could (if accompanied by Wist) travel across international borders.

So although homicide investigations were pretty far outside Manatree's department, I figured I'd better keep her in the loop.

Our conversation was, as usual, exceedingly cheerful on my side and semi-despairing on hers. By the time we finished, Wist had gotten hold of Tempus. She requested that he come alone—the sort of request that would only be honored when it came from the Kraken. If I asked the Mage Police for special treatment, they'd just send even more goons in pursuit of me.

While they were talking, I interrupted with an extra request of my own. And Tempus followed through. He showed up at my door with a shopping bag.

He removed his boots roughly at the entrance, then dropped the bag on the kitchen table.

"Anything else I can get you?" he asked through his teeth.

"A very happy New Year to you, too," I said.

"It's almost the end of January."

"We haven't spoken since last year, have we?" I peered inside his bag. "Don't suppose you brought any drinks?"

The ensuing silence made me wonder if I'd gone too far. Wouldn't want to give him an aneurysm. Tempus dropping dead here (just one open-plan room away from Ficus) would make me look extremely suspicious.

I lifted out two prepackaged lunch boxes. I'd asked him to get us something to eat from the convenience store down the street. We could've gone there ourselves, but it seemed more responsible to stay together, and to keep standing guard over Ficus.

"Thanks," I said. I did mean it. "Awfully kind of you. Mind if I pay you in change?"

I jangled my coin purse. Tempus lowered his eyes to it as if I'd held out a dead rat.

"I'm sure the Kraken can arrange a transfer sufficient to cover both of you."

"Already done," Wist told him.

"That was fast." My admiration was genuine.

My kitchen table was more of a small desk. The statue of Wist, which Tempus had glanced over with wordless disdain, took up so much real estate that there wasn't room left for two people to eat. I made Wist take a seat instead of me, although she was less than enthused about dining face-to-face with a miniature sculpture of herself in mage robes.

I stood with my lunch box resting on top of the fridge, which was only about as tall as my chest. We picked at rice and saucy fried chicken and cold rolled omelettes.

"Want some?" I said to Tempus. "You didn't get any food for yourself."

"I don't eat around cadavers."

"I don't, either, but you kept us waiting an awful long time."

"You have only yourself to blame if you were starving. This is *your* kitchen. Stock it better."

I had no comeback to that one. Anyway, huddling in the kitchen to nibble a semblance of lunch helped us avoid getting underfoot while Tempus inspected the body and suitcase.

From time to time, the resident in the room next door unleashed a painful-sounding sneeze. Passing voices dribbled in from the tree-lined street. My neighbors upstairs went through their daily routine of industriously pushing around furniture.

All such noise came to us as if through a one-way mirror. Wist had assured us that it was safe to speak freely. She'd put magical insulation on the room ages ago: our voices wouldn't leak.

At last Tempus finished up.

"Well?" I said.

He brushed off his uniform. "We'll have to go through the usual routine identification procedures. I expect it'll be quick. The body will be released to Lady Shien upon request."

"That's it?"

He looked judgmentally at Wist's half-empty lunch box. "I can bring a team out to confirm that the Extinguishers smuggled him in."

"Won't get you any closer to pinning down who told them to do it."

"No," he said deliberately. "It won't. Nothing will. If I were foolish enough to make another attempt, I'd be stopped."

"Another attempt?"

Tempus raised his head. The bitterness in his face startled me. I almost fumbled my lunch off the edge of the fridge.

"Do you think I haven't been trying?" he asked.

My view of him skewed, blurred, resharpened. Was it the same for Wist? She closed the lid of her lunch box. She held it two-handed as though weighing her leftovers.

Maybe I knew Minashiro Tempus only about as well as Shien Nerium knew me. We'd all come a very long way since our academy days.

"You care," I said curiously. "You care about the truth. You're genuinely upset that it won't be possible to investigate further, and we all know it. Why? Because it's your first love lying dead over there?"

He reared back. His anger was so palpable that I almost apologized on reflex. "I'd feel the same way if it were a stranger. Or if it were *you* with your head chopped—"

All sound in the room vanished, as if an explosion had blown out our eardrums. Tempus's mouth stopped moving. Wist turned her face toward him. No one sane would've described the look she wore as a smile, and yet I couldn't think of any other word for it.

My neighbor sneezed again. Slowly, other sounds came back. The fretful breeze. Shrill brown birds.

I harrumphed with all the delicacy I could muster. "She doesn't like hearing talk of me dead," I told Tempus.

"Quite," he replied meaninglessly. At least he hadn't pissed himself.

I found myself inordinately eager to fill the quiet that followed. "Not to sound patronizing—"

"You already do," Tempus muttered.

"What I mean to say is that you've changed more than I'd have ever imagined."

"Oh, shut up."

A small cracking sound came from the box in Wist's hands. Getting chewed up by the Void must've shortened her temper.

"I—" He glanced nervously at every corner in the room except for the one where she sat without moving. Wist didn't need to frown to look foreboding. "I apologize," he said in formal tones.

I pointed at myself.

"Yes, you—yes. To you. I apologize to you."

"For what?" I pressed. "Which incident?"

"Shall I list them?" he asked, sardonic. "You probably remember my teenage misdeeds much better than I do."

I waved him off. "My memory isn't that great, either."

"Then ... no, never mind."

"What?"

"The healer who died," Tempus said. "When we were students. Your classmate. Do you remember him?"

"Not his name," I said. "Not his face. But the fact that he was there, and then he wasn't—yeah. I remember that."

It had been sometime after our first year at Guralta Academy. A boy disappeared over the weekend. He never sat at his desk again, and they never told us what happened. Not in a way that any of us would find satisfactorily conclusive. He'd been torn apart by vorpal beasts. Or he'd been sacrificed by a secret society of mage students. Or he'd slipped and fallen off a seaside cliff. Or he hadn't slipped: he'd been pushed. Or he'd gone and drowned himself all on his own.

Someone had crowned his desk with a vase of white chrysanthemums. The most common symbol of grief and separation, remembrance, unchanging feelings, a longing for eternity.

"Were you close?" I asked Tempus.

"No."

No surprise there. He'd had little association with healer students. I bet he'd spoken to me more than any other healer at the academy— usually for the express purpose of ruining my day.

"We weren't close," Tempus amended, "but I would've liked to know him better. We'd been partnered for an assignment around the time when it happened. I was one of the last people to see him alive."

I met Tempus's gaze.

"You weren't involved with his death," I said. A statement in the tone of a question.

I saw outrage spark in him. It was short-lived, vanishing like a flame in winter wind.

"I knew nothing," he said plainly. "I did nothing. I'd thought of asking him to stay after class. If I'd held him back longer, then maybe—but my pride had a death grip on me. I watched him walk away. I thought there would always be another chance. At that age, you think life is a neverending series of chances."

Sure—if you're a mage.

"You don't remember the MP who took his case?" Tempus asked.

"Not at all."

"You might have liked her. As much as you've ever liked any mage. I'd been raised to think most MPs were—"

"Beneath you?" Wist interjected.

Tempus nodded jerkily.

"That's who inspired you to become an MP?" I said, intrigued. "Ever end up working with her?"

"Never had a chance. She got discharged before I joined the force. Eventually she was murdered by a perp with a grudge. Or so they say."

A wan smile ghosted across his face. He indicated the suitcase in the other room. "The higher-ups would've been desperate to take her off a case like this one. She would have pretended not to know when to stop."

"Unlike you," I said. A bit of a low blow, perhaps.

I stacked my lunch box on the table with Wist's. She appeared to be finished. I took out Nerium's business card again and wordlessly flipped it about in my fingers. Tempus regarded it without comment.

In short, he'd only started caring about injustice when someone he had a crush on got killed. I wouldn't rag on him for it, though. I only object to the plight of Osmanthian healers because I'm a healer myself. If I'd been born a mage, I'd be happily preoccupied with other ambitions. Selfish, yes. The best you can say of me is that I've got a pretty clear view of my own vices and virtues.

Two other MPs came by later to scope out the scene and help retrieve the body. Tempus, who far outranked them, squeezed his way over to the balcony with me and Wist. So he could stand back and survey their work, I guess. The apartment was scarcely large enough for three people, much less five (plus a corpse).

For lack of anything more productive to do, I kept toying with Nerium's card. We were not a talkative trio.

It came as something of a relief when my downstairs neighbor started blasting rural dance tunes from what must have been an industrial-strength melodium. I explained to Tempus—who had started in alarm—that this was just one of my building's many amenities. The guy on the third floor who, no matter the season, played music loud enough to hear it from the sidewalk.

A few minutes later, both Tempus and Wist had begun bobbing unconsciously to the beat.

I bit back a grin. Imagine attempting to describe this scene to myself at fifteen. Shien Nerium's fancy business card in my hand. Shien Ficus's decapitated dead body in the middle of my room. Wist with shockingly short hair—compared to our school days, anyway; right now it just touched the tops of her shoulders. Minashiro Tempus in an MP uniform. Wist and Tempus idly swaying to the same obscure song. Me with a parole thread tucked away under my sock and a Void tucked away at the back of my eye, enjoying the show.

How absolutely bizarre. But also: how delightful. It really was worth living just to see where life might take you.

Of course, that was easy enough to say in retrospect, knowing that Wist had loved me for two lives in a row. I'd had a very different perspective during my years in prison. I'd have a very different perspective if I were the body in the suitcase.

"That healer at Follyhope," Tempus said, only just audible through the music.

"Who?"

"She confessed to murder."

It was bleakly wintery out here on the balcony, but now a different kind of cold took hold of me. I saw Miyu falling. Danver pushing her. She'd been poised to get away with it—against all odds—if only she kept her stupid mouth shut.

"Whose murder?" I asked cautiously.

"Both of them."

"Miyu *and* Ficus?"

"It's an impossible confession," Tempus said. "For a number of reasons. But difficult to ignore." He heaved a sigh.

My mind turned like a whirligig. He'd brought this up as an aside—casually, as if something had jogged his memory. Surely not my neighbor's music.

The card pinched in my fingers? He did keep glancing at it. Had his thoughts leapt to Danver because of her resemblance to Nerium?

He—like me, once upon a time—might've suspected her of being Nerium's daughter. Even if he had some awareness of Aunt Riegel's existence, he might not know that Nerium and Danver were blood-related siblings. Half-siblings, rather. The family hadn't let Tempus in that deeply, had they? He hailed from an allied clan, but he was also an MP.

Wist leaned around me. "Which healer confessed?"

Tempus seemed to agree with me that the answer was obvious. He sounded puzzled. "The one Ficus hurt. The one I marked as a person of interest. She talks like this." For that last part he switched to a falsetto whisper. A poor imitation.

51

"Ginko," Wist said.

"Ginko?" I parroted, stupefied. Then, just in case: "A little on the taller side. Skin and bones. Dark hair. No glasses. The one I gave a bond examination."

"Who'd you think I meant?" Tempus said irritably.

"She claims she murdered Miyu and Ficus?"

"It's obviously a false confession." He rubbed his forehead. "We aren't morons, Asa. She's clearly very troubled. Remember, I had both her and Ficus marked before the Extinguishers came. She never went anywhere near him."

"Does she still carry your mark?"

"I removed it."

"Very helpful."

"Can't slap those on an unlimited number of people. We need them for other cases. Whatever she says, she's innocent." He lowered his hand with a faint air of defeat. "Although she may have had reason enough to wish both of them dead."

"She won't recant?" I asked.

"She's very insistent. Too mentally unbalanced to serve anyone as a reliable healer, at this point. She's cloistered now, but the Shien cloisters aren't a charity home. Few clans would keep on a healer who can't be trusted to pull her weight."

"So—what, will they fire her? Throw her out in the street?"

He gave me a puzzled look. "Of course not. That would be irresponsible. I expect they'll have her committed."

I wondered if Danver knew—or if this were all happening in the Shien cloister, far from Follyhope.

Did she write Ginko letters? Would she swallow the loss of their friendship? Perhaps she'd interpret it as the price that needed to be paid for killing Miyu. Perhaps she'd accept that a peaceful life in the cloisters was the best sort of life that Ginko could hope for.

By persistently confessing to improbable murders, Ginko had eliminated the possibility of any other Shien ever trying to claim her as their bondmate. No one would want a crazy healer.

Which meant that it might have been a calculated move on her part. In the process, however, she'd ruined her future prospects. For her own sake, they'd put her in an asylum—and if she ever got out, what then?

Let me guess: no family to help her, no work history other than healing, no relevant education, no experience living outside the clan, no credit history, no savings.

How can I leave here? Ginko had asked me.

Get arrested, I'd told her, flippant as ever.

Tempus's underlings took the headless body away that same day—but that wasn't the end of it. Later in the week, more MPs and associates came by to case my room for evidence.

Eventually I got cleared to live normally in my own flat. By then, I'd already gone with Wist to view several other apartments. She was serious about helping me move out. The sooner, the better.

I liked having a place of my own in the city. But when I compared the cost of rent to how much time I would actually spend there, realistically speaking, my pride and independent spirit buckled. Frugality won out.

"Call the search off," I told Wist. "Let's just move the rest of my stuff to the tower. I'll terminate my lease."

"That's what you want?"

"That's what my bank account wants." I met her unblinking gaze, then relented. "Ninety percent of the time when I'm at home, I'm in the tower. If I need a city address for business purposes, I'll rent a mailbox."

Anyway, we didn't have time to run around inspecting other vacant apartments.

I'd finally used Nerium's business card. I'd made us an appointment at Follyhope. Not with Aunt Riegel—unlike most of our other recent visits—but with Nerium himself.

Once more we faced the iron gate. It was an unseasonably warm day. Overnight rain had melted any last traces of snow, and the ground felt spongy underfoot.

"Nothing good will come of tangling with the Shiens," Wist murmured.

"Don't rub it in."

Once more, Danver guided us to the manor. She wore her usual glasses in defiance of the drizzling gray air. A coating of magic on the lenses repelled all hints of moisture.

Nerium offered us tea in the Grand Salon. Wist drank only from a water bottle I'd brought in my bag. I ate jam-filled cakes. Always happy to feed myself at someone else's expense.

This space could've doubled as a ballroom. It dwarfed the three of us, but Nerium (and Wist, for that matter) appeared not to notice.

As if to compensate for the imbalance, someone had filled the salon with flowers. They rested in invisible vases. This made them look to be floating of their own accord in clear water that trembled when you breathed on it, but otherwise held its shape like ice. The stagnant clouds of flowery fragrance kept giving Wist sneezing fits.

"You've been apartment hunting, I believe?" Nerium said. "How's it going?"

"It's not going," I replied. "Also, we never told you that. Don't be creepy."

"I own real estate all over the city. I would have been glad to help, if only you asked."

Wist set her steel bottle down on the tabletop made of slick burled wood. She set it down hard enough to rattle our cups.

"Your guard dog is growling," Nerium said to me.

"Let's cut to the chase, then. Your brother's body."

"Yes—we're very grateful to have recovered the rest of him. We'd all but given up hope."

"It doesn't become you to play dumb." I waited a moment, and so did he. "Wasn't surprised when none of you acted all that broken up over Miyu," I said. "But you and Ficus were much closer. You seemed to like each other well enough. Which is more than I can say for most Shiens."

Perhaps Nerium and Ficus had gotten along because their interests overlapped in key areas—like brutally putting young Wist in her place—and diverged in others. Ficus would never try to found a company. Nor would he stand as a serious rival to become the next head of the family.

"Grief can be very private," Nerium said piously.

"Especially for high-class folk like your fine selves, eh?"

He was beyond provocation. He adjusted the rings on his age-thickened fingers and spoke in the tone of an educator. "The heart is always a private matter. But much of the work of grief has to be performed in public. Especially for Ficus. I can't count how many memorial events I've been called to speak at."

"That's rough," I said. "Hard labor."

"There's your answer, in any case. The rest of the country weeps for Ficus. He doesn't require my tears. Nor would he want them."

"That's all your brother gets from you? Lip service?"

The corners of Nerium's mouth deepened. "The truth is, I never thought he would live this long. None of us really expected him to make it past thirty."

"That's cold," I said. "Even for you lot."

"Not cold. Call it realistic. Ficus was always drawn to deadly forms of play. Little else drew his interest. He could barely even remember the names and locations of all his children. I knew that if he died, I would be the one who'd eventually end up going around to inform them. I rehearsed it many times in my head. He had a lot of close calls over the years."

So he was already dead to you, I thought. Dead to you many times over. Is that why you had so few qualms about taking out a hit on him yourself?

What I said instead: "Still. Seems a bit unnecessarily villainous to dump his beheaded corpse in my apartment. What'd I ever do to deserve that?"

"If only we could ask the Extinguishers."

"If only we could. Hey, I know—why not ask them yourself?"

He looked steadily at me from behind his fancy glasses, opaque with magic.

Next to me, Wist had wilted. She rested her chin on the table, eyes half-lidded in a way that suggested disgust, boredom, or just plain zoning out. We had to be careful not to unthinkingly nudge each other's ankles.

"Asa Clematis," Nerium said, "I swear to you that I had nothing to do with Ficus appearing in your apartment. I'm terribly sorry for your distress."

"Oh, for—I'm not *distressed*," I retorted. "You give me your word, then? Great. Your word means a hell of a lot."

"As it should." He disregarded my sarcasm. "I've stayed out of your path for just about two decades, haven't I? Ever since your first year at Guralta Academy."

I flicked a cake crumb off my plate. Wist caught it as if pouncing on a flying bug.

"This might surprise you," I told Nerium, "but I was always pretty careful with my address. Few people knew it, or had the means to find out. I rented that place ever since leaving prison, and the Extinguishers never came to my door."

"I'm sorry," he said again, all sincerity. "You've been made to feel unsafe in your own home. How awful."

"Hah. I just want to understand why. Placing that body there took a ton of effort. Creative thinking. Magical innovation. So what was the goal, if not to harm me—to impress me? I'm not impressed. I'm flat-out baffled!"

My voice rang out as if delivering the final lines of a poorly received play. Needless to say, no one applauded.

Nerium straightened in his seat and took hold of his cane. "Maybe that was the objective."

"What?"

"To get under your skin, by virtue of its very lack of an obvious purpose. To throw you off, or to reel you in. To linger in your mind. To sink deeper in you than any neat, sensible story with a proper beginning, middle, and end. To show you that nothing has ended yet."

In the next moment, his voice turned purely conversational. "Of course, you didn't just come here just to fruitlessly question me."

"I'll be the judge of what's fruitless," I said coolly. "Did you hear about Ginko?"

Nerium tilted his head.

"Miyu's bondmate," Wist said.

"Ah, yes. A sad story, isn't it? She seems utterly convinced that she killed them."

"Then you haven't heard," I told him. "We took her out of the cloister. With your grandmother's permission. Aunt Riegel helped put in a good word for us."

"Like rescuing a pet from a shelter," Nerium said affably. " A lovely act of charity."

"More like getting transferred from one corporation to another. Now she's on Wist's payroll, not the clan's."

"I see. Still getting paid by a Shien."

"Except that she won't have to bond anyone. She won't have to heal anyone. She won't get institutionalized for her so-called failures as a healer."

"And she'll receive a living wage for this?" He smiled at me as though indulging a child. "How is that not an act of charity?"

"We were badly in need of a cat sitter. She took good care of the cat living behind your boarding house. That's all the endorsement I needed." I pointed in a direction that was very likely not the actual direction of the staff boarding house, but I didn't care enough to let him correct me.

Right now Ginko was back at Wist's tower. Probably still getting shown around by Mori. Turtle had taken an immediate liking to her—scampering over and nuzzling her and smirking at me from between her ankles. I swear that cat has it out for me.

52

WIST SNEEZED into her elbow. I'd made sure she sat furthest from the flowers, but the scent was beginning to get to her.

I didn't recognize any of the cultivars in these freestanding arrangements. Some could've been from the same family as camellia or amaryllis. Or winter daphne, or forced tulips. All had more thickly layered petals than what you'd see in regular neighborhood gardens.

Servants streamed in to collect the remnants of our tea and clean the table. They were there and gone like a passing breeze.

When we got up to leave, I said to Nerium: "I'd like a favor."

He prodded the floor with his cane as though testing its solidity. "How surprising. Gratifying, but surprising."

"An extremely small favor," I warned. "If you've still got time now, take us to your doctor."

"Hazeldine?"

"That's the one."

He gazed at the curved glob of water clumped like clay around the base of a mass of flowers. The vessel that held the water in place had politely erased itself from our vision. Magic filled the air over the table like a soft scattering of sunlight.

Then, as if he'd come to a decision, he stopped playing with his cane. He looked at me frankly.

"I have time," he said, "but Hazeldine would gladly see you without another formal introduction. As long as you're with Wisteria."

"I know. We already came in to consult him a couple days ago. Before we took Ginko out of the cloister."

"Really. Then—"

"Is this his day off? Did he go on vacation?"

"No." Nerium wasn't smiling. "No, not that I know of."

"We were hoping to stop by today, too," I said. "Haven't been able to reach him."

Nerium started walking, cane in hand, a homely man parting a sea of flowers. I nearly made the mistake of grabbing Wist's arm to hurry her along after him.

Earlier this week, we'd spoken to Hazeldine at length. He kept his office in an unfamiliar wing of the manor, with windows that offered a distant view of water lilies.

It started off amicably enough.

He'd shown up dressed as sharply as ever, dapper from the cut of his jacket to the gleam of his monocle. He waxed on and on at the slightest prompting. About watching snow fall above the pool of water lilies (magic ensured that it never quite touched them). About the slender icicles that had hung from the eaves, now all melted to nothing. About the horror of what had happened to Ficus.

He gave us an elaborate pack of custom cuttings for Ginko. "For calm," he said, "and sound sleep. Let me know if she ever needs anything else." He lowered his voice. "This is so terribly good of you. Very charitable."

If Wist hadn't been hovering there like a disapproving grim reaper, he might have clapped me heartily on the back.

I changed the subject.

"I've met my share of originators"—a nod at Wist—"and the truth is, most of them struggle to invent new types of magic. The mere capacity for originating skills doesn't always translate to being any good at it. In fact, it usually doesn't. That makes you a rarity among rarities—you're very prolific."

There was a startled edge to his laughter. "Oh," he said, "oh—you flatter me! Don't compare me to the Kraken. I'm just a Class 2. I can create new skills, but I don't have much ability to retain them."

"You must keep very good records."

"I try, I try."

"So much paperwork," I mused. "A huge pain. You've got to submit every minute detail of every new skill you make to the National Archives and various other agencies. You do have all your skills on file with the government?"

His eyes were on Wist. He responded a beat too late. "Why, of course."

"The Kraken files all her skills, too," I lied, "but it's practically a full-time job. She's got an assistant who does almost nothing except make sure she sends everything in on time."

"Ah. The joys of bureaucracy," he said in a voice of strained modesty. "Must be far worse a burden for the Kraken than it could ever be for me."

Wist kept looking out the window at the water lily pond.

"You know," I said, favoring the doctor with a sunny smile, "anyone would think you're no older than Nerium. People really age differently when they understand the value of good health."

He preened. "The answer never changes—plentiful sleep, enthusiastic exercise, a varied diet, minimal stress."

"And knowing how to groom and dress yourself," I agreed. "Clothes can be so transformative. Your education must have helped, too—you were a med student when Nerium and Ficus went to Guralta Academy, I suppose? Or maybe you'd just gotten your degree?"

"Went through an accelerated program," he said genially. "Nothing special. But yes, I got my degree quite early."

Like I'd thought, he had to be around a decade older than Nerium. He'd already been working at Follyhope in some capacity when the clan first adopted Wist.

Before we came to see Hazeldine that day, I'd asked her what she remembered of him from childhood.

"He did his duty as a medical professional," Wist said. "When I got hurt, he took care of me. He gave me candy and small toys."

He'd offered kindly explanations for how all her injuries must be accidents. He'd repaired her when her own magic failed to rise to the occasion. He made her get better faster. And the faster her wounds vanished, the faster the next round would happen.

He was very skilled. She got burned all over her body once, and he treated her quickly enough to prevent scarring. He also implied that she must have entreated her siblings to build a dangerous bonfire. Maybe he'd even believed it.

I looked around his office. I cooed in admiration at his framed certificates and placards and commendations. I praised the taste evident in his choice of antique furniture, including a magnificent wooden apothecary cabinet.

Then, no longer smiling, I caught his eye. "We heard a lot of stories when we were innocent schoolgirls at Guralta."

"Stories?" he said. "Stories about—?"

"Stories of older students getting high off psychoactive cuttings."

"The same stuff was always popular with alumni, too," Wist said.

I nodded. "Not the sort of thing a student could cobble together. Cleverly designed magic—reliably effective. Replicable. And extremely expensive. Illegal, yes, but quite safe. An edgy little toy for rich kids. Not really any worse than alcohol, or high-octane coffee, or carefully cultivated mushrooms."

"I..." He wet his lips. "I graduated from Guralta long before either of you enrolled, I'm afraid. Can't say I know much about what's trending with younger generations."

"You have a daughter at the academy now, don't you?"

"Sometimes I think she's talking in code. Kids and their slang—I never have any idea what's going on." He pulled his mouth into half a smile. "I always embarrass her."

"I think you understand perfectly well," I said pleasantly. "You understand how to operate in gray areas. How to maximize your profit. I think your best work never gets filed with the government."

I stepped back, hands raised, forestalling his attempt to respond. "I'm not here to blackmail you. I'm not here to claim the moral high ground. You've built an impressive network of connections. Did you start by selling through Nerium? Or relatives of your former classmates?"

Somewhere in the middle of this, he stopped hearing me. His entire being—from his sumptuously oiled beard to his waxed wingtips—focused on Wist.

It was her opinion that mattered, not mine. If she stood in judgment of him, he would attempt to appease her.

"The lack of long-term side effects is impressive," she said woodenly.

Relief bloomed on his face.

I cut in again. "Yeah, about that—were Nerium and Ficus users, too? Always thought there were something off about both of them. In a different way from of Miyu. Were they bad seeds from birth? Did the crucible of the clan disfigure them? Or was it you and your magic?"

Doctor Hazeldine stared at me as if I were his teenage daughter, spouting off in the mysterious language of youth.

"Couldn't it have been some unknown side effect of your recreational cuttings that made them capable of, say, drowning a classmate in the Guralta caves? No, don't interrupt. They'll never be prosecuted, I know. It's ancient history. Students died in our time, too." I gestured at Wist. "What about everything they did to her, then? You know what happened years before anyone started calling her the Kraken."

I was making this argument in bad faith. I didn't care how many times Nerium or Ficus had taken Hazeldine's psychoactives in adolescence. They were unlikely to have been heavy users. Nerium would have focused more on the potential for distribution.

No, Hazeldine's magic wouldn't have altered their fundamental essence. But no one could prove that. Which mean it'd also be impossible for him to assert absolute innocence.

"Years later," I said, "Ginko came to you in terrible psychological pain."

"And I treated that pain of hers," he said stiffly. "Masterfully, if you don't mind me bragging."

"Yes. You treated her as if she were the one with the problem. As if she needed something excised. You never devoted even a second of thought to making her situation less—"

"Bonding is for life," he snapped. "That healer had a duty to Miyu. I did my part despite enormous difficulties. I ensured that she remained capable of carrying out her duty—unlike the healer before her. It's a shame that Miyu had to pass at such a young age, and I won't hear a word against her. There's nothing more despicable than slander of the dead."

I had nothing more to say. We left him bristling. He struggled to compose himself enough to say a curt farewell to Wist (and Wist alone).

I heard more when we brought Ginko out of the cloisters and found her a place at Wist's tower. I heard again how Miyu had been revolted by the barest hints of admiration from her bondmate. But she would also severely punish any shift in attitude that she perceived as a change in affection.

After the one and only time Miyu went berserk (courtesy of yours truly), Ginko got forced into counseling. A specialist in bondmate relationships informed her that the mage reflects the healer. Disturbances in Ginko's own psyche were, therefore, determined to be the sole cause of Miyu's instability. What a stunning coincidence that an expert hired by Shien mages would find themselves in agreement with Miyu's interpretation of every event.

It became Ginko's responsibility to fix the problems she'd planted in Miyu. Don't get caught up in your own self-centered distress, they told her. Don't be blinded by your guilt over failing her. Such wallowing would only further exacerbate Miyu's suffering.

They said to Ginko: you've become a source of poison to her, rather than a source of healing. If she's poisonous towards you, never forget where it comes from. A healer can't possibly understand the immense stress and pain of being a mage. Don't make it all about you. If she has anger problems and anxiety, if she loses control, if she lashes out, it's because of your inadequate support. You have to become a better healer in order to merit better treatment.

They said the same things many different times, and in many different ways.

They said: Miyu deserves a healer who can prioritize her needs, who can lie down beneath her feet to form an unshakable, rock-solid foundation. That's what's best not just for her, but for all of Osmanthian society. That's your sacred duty. No one else can support her like you can. You must shape yourself to become adequate to your greatest task.

They'd told Ginko this. And—directly or indirectly—they'd told Miyu, too, hadn't they? The mageocracy had taught her these principles ever since she was a small blond child. The impossible control that she craved must've always felt utterly right to her. It seemed like a supreme injustice when the world would not simply kneel before her and hand it over.

If I carried a magical axe … if I could stroll around Shien property and swing my axe as I pleased … well. Let's just say that Ficus wasn't the only one who would've ended up missing a head.

No—I wouldn't exact murderous vengeance for others without their consent. That's what stopped me, not my lack of a secret weapon. Wist would prefer for me not to use it, but I already had one. Functionally, what's the difference between an imaginary magical axe and the ravenous Void?

53

We'd parted with Doctor Hazeldine on bad terms. He'd ignored our attempts to make another appointment. But Wist was the Kraken—he wouldn't shut his door in her face.

I'd combed through the cuttings he'd given us for Ginko. Perhaps we could repurpose his talent for muting nearly every dimension of human pain.

One point of clarification: we didn't whisk Ginko away from the cloisters like kidnapping bandits. I explained to her that the Shien clan was about to have her committed. That she could take a job at Wist's tower, if she chose to come with us. She chose the tower.

I didn't describe the astounding magical prowess evident in its complete disregard of architectural norms, and indeed all the basic physical laws governing little things like mass and gravity and space. I didn't mention the subtle luxuries that Wist had copied from places like Follyhope.

Instead I mentioned the isolation, the view of the blue prairie, the uninterrupted sky, the innumerable empty rooms, the heavenly quiet, the immense freedom. I described how—if she wanted—she could go days, weeks, months, or quite possibly the rest of her life without setting eyes on me or Wist, much less any other human soul.

The only living creature we specifically requested that she interact with was Turtle the cat. And maybe, one day, Wist's assortment of nonmagical houseplants.

She left her healer robes behind. She walked out in a long wool skirt and a pale sweater with a few faded stains on it. She no longer wore gloves, and she no longer wore a bond thread.

Wist ported away the rest of her possessions in a single flick of magic.

As we showed Ginko to a room at the tower, I asked her why she'd falsely confessed to killing Miyu and Ficus.

Was she trying—as I'd suggested in jest—to escape the Shien clan by getting arrested? Or was it a misguided attempt to keep suspicion from landing on anyone else?

Wist and I knew the truth of what had happened with Miyu. But why bring Ficus into it? He'd been killed by a completely different group.

Turtle followed Ginko into her new room. The moment she sat down in a cozy club chair, Turtle bounded up to join her. An obnoxiously loud purring filled the space after I spoke.

"I think," Ginko said, looking down at the tortoiseshell bundle in her lap, "I think more people will die. I wanted to say that to someone. I didn't know who I should say it to. More people will die."

In the long term, there was no way for her to be wrong.

"At Follyhope?" I asked.

She lowered her chin in half a nod.

"Why?"

"Just a feeling."

"Who's going to die?"

"I don't know."

"Do you want us to save them?"

"............"

Fair enough. If I were her, I wouldn't have any tears to spare for the Shiens.

Murder aside, the next most likely people to die at Follyhope were Grandmother (already extremely old, although still intimidatingly sharp) and Aunt Riegel (who was also starting to get up there in years, and whose health seemed very delicate). Doctor Hazeldine would do his utmost for them. Not much Wist or I could add to that.

There was a reason someone in Hazeldine's position needed to be an originator. If a core family member developed difficult-to-treat cancer, he'd combat it with one-of-a-kind branch skills tailored to their case. No one had a better chance of living to a healthy old age than members of a moneyed mage clan.

Days later, Ginko's voice whispered at the back of my head as Nerium led us to Doctor Hazeldine's office.

More people will die.

We took a shortcut through a mirror. It wasn't that long of a trip. Even so, Nerium walked fast enough to visibly exert himself. His cane wasn't quite enough for him. He leaned on the wall when he knocked at Hazeldine's door.

No one answered.

Nerium knocked again, then let us in.

Before we saw the windows looking out on water lilies, and the grand apothecary cabinet, and the photos of Hazeldine and his wife and daughter posing by the most picturesque ruins on Guralta Isle—before we saw any of that, I knew what else we'd find.

Ginko had told me just this past week, hadn't she? *More people will die.* She had no real basis for believing that. She'd been cloistered away from Follyhope for over a month.

But she was right.

Nerium, still struggling to catch his breath, made a sound like he had a blockage in his throat.

Hazeldine sat slumped at his desk with his head down, one arm dangling. He didn't react to our entrance.

Wist's magic blinked through the room, there and gone in an instant. "He's dead," she said before anyone could reach out to take his pulse.

The room looked very bright and sharp to me. Hyper-real. There was a faint scent of old clothes, of something unwashed.

I moved closer to the doctor's body. His mouth gaped open like a pocket on ill-fitting pants. The desk beneath his face was spread with blank Shien letterhead. He'd drooled profusely, but the puddle was mostly dry now, the stationery dimpled and textured where it used to be wet.

Nerium snatched something off the other side of the desk.

Whatever he'd grabbed, he'd already pocketed it.

Wist, I said. *Did you see that?*

But there was no bond to carry my voice to her.

He swayed as if he were about to faint. Wist, impassive, caught his elbow. He thanked her weakly. Had he reacted like this to the news of Miyu dying, or even Ficus? Was it different when you were the first to come across the body?

If there were any shock in me, the Void had absorbed it without a trace.

Nerium spoke to Wist about telling Grandmother. I renewed my study of the tableau before us. Hazeldine's rich black beard had turned a chalky mottled gray. His monocle lay on the desk—either removed on purpose, or jarred off his face during his collapse. His clothing didn't look as nicely tailored as usual. Maybe nothing would fit well after the throes of death. Had he gone rigid, or was rigor mortis already receding? I wouldn't touch him to find out.

He'd knocked over a rosewood pen stand. A tin of slim honey sticks rested near his hand. The same type he'd given me in a bundle for Ginko. The same type I'd seen in Riegel's room. These were nothing but pure honey: no magic left in them.

The moment he died, all his cuttings would've evaporated, including those he'd offered Ginko and Riegel. Including those right here on his desk. Had the sparkle in his eye come from getting high on his own supply? Had he used a private stash of magic to keep his beard black, and his clothes fitting just right?

It'd be a lot of work for a two-branch mage to juggle so many different skills—for his role as a doctor, for illicit sale, and for vanity. Every time he ran low on a given cutting, he'd have to strip one of his branches, re-learn the skill in question, imprint it on his open branch, then painstakingly prune more cuttings till he'd built up his stock again.

This was a much slower process for most mages than it would've been for Wist. Whatever else you could say about him, Hazeldine must've had impeccable time management.

Wist and I obediently shuffled off to a drawing room while Nerium mastered himself and began to go through the morbid checklist of things to do after you find someone dead.

We ended up in the room where Lear and Ficus had played the knife game. The hanging fireplace still burned, but today it emanated no heat. The flames had turned a subdued lavender hue.

Danver and Lear passed by while we were waiting to be questioned. Both had wet hair. Danver was in a sweatsuit, her chin held high and her face flushed scarlet.

The estate had multiple baths and pools, both indoors and out—for sport, for leisure, for keeping exotic fish and plants. I could imagine Danver (thinking herself alone) walking in on Lear in some vast marble space, then being too stubborn to leave. Lear would appear unaffected. She'd keep chatting like normal whether they were both wearing bathing suits, or nothing at all. Danver would sink down in water up to her nose, stewing in humiliation.

Or maybe they had an ongoing competition to see who could swim faster laps. Or they'd gotten close enough to shower together on the regular. Who knows?

I caught Lear's eye. She shook her head at me—which could have signified anything from a warning to denial to solidarity.

The first words out of Tempus's mouth when he dragged himself in to see me and Wist: "We've been meeting altogether too often."

"You could say that about plenty of other people in this house," I countered. "No need to single us out."

"I need to face those *other people* with tact and courtesy."

"But you can be rude to the Kraken?"

He looked at us through his hands. "I've been rude to both of you since high school. Might as well not stop now."

"That's what I like to hear," I said happily. "I'll be glad to answer in kind."

"Don't overdo it."

He sounded awfully fatalistic. His mood had worsened as mine brightened—but then, that had always been the case, hadn't it?

We described everything we'd observed in Hazeldine's office.

"Was it his own magic that did him in?" I asked.

"I have no obligation whatsoever to—" Tempus stopped, abandoned his feint at pomposity, and continued in more ordinary tones. "I'm only saying this because the Kraken is a family member."

"Skip the disclaimers."

"If it was his own magic, all traces would have vanished after he passed. But he had no other injuries or signs of illness, physical or magical. We found an empty honey stick under his desk."

"Doesn't prove much."

"No," Tempus acknowledged. "Might be old trash from hours before he passed, fallen and forgotten."

"As a physician, he wouldn't deal exclusively in personalized cuttings, either. He'd have access to the clan's entire stock of generic medical magic."

"Could have been an accident," Wist said.

This wasn't just wishful thinking. Hazeldine must've been constantly inventing new magic skills—from legal to illegal, and everything in between. Whether intended for physical health, stimulation, sedation, or whatever else, his skills had powerful ramifications for the human mind and body.

If he were overconfident about his abilities, and if he'd gotten in the habit of testing his own wares on himself, one day he might inadvertently devise a skill with fatal side effects. A skill that could kill him before he realized his mistake.

It'd be a whole different type of problem if he'd accidentally done himself in with an off-the-shelf cutting—something that was supposed to be strictly regulated, proven safe.

"Doctor Hazeldine was being threatened," Tempus said.

I thought of the dark glee I'd felt when Wist and I cornered him in his office, when I dropped hints about his side business supplying Guralta students. And their hard-partying kin here in the city, too.

"Nerium," I said, remembering. "He took something off Hazeldine's desk."

"Oh, that."

"He showed it to you?"

"In confidence. It was a letter."

"A farewell note?"

"No, a letter to the doctor. From a would-be blackmailer. No name."

"So you'll treat this as a suicide." My eye kept going back to the low violet light in the fireplace. "Nerium pounced on the letter right in front of me, you know."

I turned to Wist. "Was it there from the start? Could he have been pretending to snatch it?"

"You want to accuse him of planting evidence?" Tempus frowned. "He didn't know you were planning to drop in on the doctor's office."

"Maybe he'd meant to discover the body on his own instead. What'd the letter say?"

"It didn't outright demand money from Hazeldine, or threaten to expose him."

"But the implication was there," I said.

"Yes. They were toying with him. Trying to make him wonder who they were. Trying to make him paranoid."

"Nerium seemed disturbed," Wist said.

I nodded forcefully. "Unusually disturbed. For him, anyway."

"He just lost another close relative—right after his brother and sister. Not everyone is as callous as you two," Tempus said tersely.

"Or you," I shot back.

"This is my job. What's your excuse?" He didn't wait for an answer. "It could have been a worse death. The doctor's heart slowed to nothing— it just forgot to beat. People react differently to an obvious case of suicide than to murder, or unfortunate accidents."

"Maybe Nerium's afraid it'll be him next," I said.

Tempus took this as a throwaway comment. Just more of the usual nonsense from Asa Clematis.

Indeed, it was wholly possible that Nerium hadn't been perturbed in the slightest. That he'd chosen to flex his acting skills, and Wist and I just so happened to be his audience.

That aside, there had been an unusual number of deaths in short order at Follyhope. If Hazeldine had killed himself, who could have driven him to it? If he'd been murdered, who'd wanted him gone?

Forensics specialists would try to determine whether Hazeldine's death had been magically induced. Sometimes hearts do choose to stop on their own. If it were magic that killed him, a specialist might also succeed in discerning whether that magic had been produced by anyone other than Hazeldine himself. According to Tempus, an in-depth analysis might take several more days.

Wist and I didn't appear to be suspects, at least. As soon as we finished hashing things out with Tempus, he gave us his blessing to leave.

Nothing connected the three deaths. Nothing except the fact that all three victims belonged to the Shien clan.

If you wanted to, I guess you could pluck out other common threads, too. They all had—whether through vicious aggression or negligence—contributed to Wist's childhood maltreatment. By the same logic, you could point fingers at Grandmother and Nerium and her adoptive parents and the rest of her siblings, all of whom remained mysteriously alive. For now.

Miyu and Ficus had, in varying ways, been potential liabilities to the clan. Hazeldine might fall in that category, too—but he seemed like he'd listen if Grandmother ordered him to tone it down. Had he gotten too used to living outside his means? Had he graduated from earning money under the table to outright embezzlement—or had he done too much secretive business with rival clans, splitting his loyalties?

Why did I care, anyway? Let the Shien clan consume itself from within. I had no interest in exacting justice for their dead.

If anything, it felt as though justice had already been meted out. You could argue that Miyu and Ficus had gotten the fate they each deserved. Hazeldine's hands hadn't been sparkling clean, either.

This sequence of deaths nagged at me because of how much it reminded me of myself. If I wanted to murder multiple people in the same household, how would I do it?

Rather: how would I do it without the Void?

I'd work meticulously to avoid carrying out the act myself. Metaphorically speaking, I'd set up a long, winding row of wooden blocks. I'd construct an elaborate chain-reaction contraption. I'd place myself as far away from the action as possible. I'd flick a tiny ball, knock over one little starting block, then watch the rest come tumbling down without any further interference or input.

That's also the approach Lear would take, if she were indeed attempting to sow as much havoc as she could in Osmanthus. But Lear wasn't quite that enthusiastic about exceeding her handlers' expectations. She seemed more like a reluctant low-level employee than a nationalist fanatic.

Maybe it was all an act—but then why settle for small fry? Why not attempt to take out the head of the family, if not the Kraken herself?

Was I looking at a picture of random chaos and attempting to perceive order where none existed? I could make up various motivations for Nerium and Grandmother. Not to mention Wist—and myself, for that matter. But Hazeldine's death really threw a wrench in my existing theories.

My theories weren't the only thing that had been lost with his death. Despite how hostile I'd been to him last time, I'd had every intention of taking Wist in for a serious consultation. He'd forgive everything in an instant if the great Kraken claimed to need him.

I'd hoped he could come up with a cutting that would make it bearable for us to touch again. To bond again. Or perhaps Wist could've studied his magic and then devised her own version. If we were capable of drawing close enough to hold hands and wade through hell together, maybe—on the other side of it—everything would be just like before. All we needed was a way to endure it. Like getting a numbing injection before surgery.

But Hazeldine was dead, his cuttings all gone. How much of his work had he recorded in a format easily accessible to us, in words we could understand? How much of it had been done under the table, or stored in his head? How much of it would be lost forever? And what other options did we have left now?

54

MY PATIENCE had begun wearing thin for a reason. I was terrified of my own growing hunger, a hunger to match the Void.

I had garbled lustful dreams of feeding on Wist. When I was in the thick of it, those dreams brought me nothing but pleasure, guiltless abandon. But I'd wake up cold with sweat, wishing I could go back to dreaming of my own death.

Memories of consuming her magic—of joining the Void in consuming her magic—intruded on my waking thoughts, too. Nothing smelled or tasted or felt as real as filling every last vulnerable space in her, becoming the Void between her branches.

I'd memorized the texture of all the veins lacing the back of Wist's detachable left hand. And thank god for that.

But it wasn't enough.

There was something increasingly wrong with me. I was afraid of what I might become. I was afraid that my deepest self, untethered, might be indistinguishable from the Void. Even if we fixed ourselves, even if we figured out a way to embrace again and bond again, there might still be no going back.

Life wasn't that kind, and we'd already spent more than our share of second chances.

The aftermath of Hazeldine's death was none of our business. Tempus dismissed us. But to leave for the tower would feel like admitting defeat. It would mean admitting we had no idea what to do next, no solution except some paper-flimsy hope that time might miraculously decide to cure us. Over the course of—what, decades?

I led Wist through the corridors to see Aunt Riegel.

Someone would be assigned to take over Hazeldine's immediate duties. Someone would eventually be deemed competent and trustworthy enough to tend to Riegel herself.

In the meantime, she'd suffer the most from Hazeldine's loss. Not more than his own family, but more than anyone else in Follyhope. Only Danver could tend to Aunt Riegel's magic, but only Hazeldine had years of experience with treating the physical effects of her condition. As well as assorted comorbidities. How many of the country's top medical professionals had ever seen a stunted mage in person?

We found Riegel sitting by the window overlooking the courtyard. A simple metal walker stood guard near her chair. I felt like an intruder the moment I noticed that she wasn't wearing her usual glasses.

She rested her hand on the vase of white chrysanthemums as though touching the back of an old and comfortable pet. Between Miyu and Ficus and Hazeldine, she'd never needed to change out her flowers.

Perhaps she'd kept them here since long before the first murder. The Shien clan was large enough to hear news of natural deaths on a fairly regular basis. Although most people dying in branch families would surely be relatives she'd never met.

The vase had a tinge of magic to it. These flowers might be the same ones I'd seen the first time I met her, preserved like sun cookies wrapped in paper. Or maybe Danver helped her replace them.

Wist and I gave our condolences. She already knew about Hazeldine. Even if no one came to inform her in person, Danver would've told her mind-to-mind.

I asked, uselessly, if there was anything we could do for her, anything we could get for her. Riegel blinked at us. Without the shield of those dense glasses, her eyes seemed small and wet and uncomfortably exposed.

"Always thought of him as a much younger man. Almost a child." Her voice quivered, then recovered its balance. "I suppose he wasn't that much younger than me, really. At least not compared to Ficus and Miyu."

She turned her face toward the window. The wisteria vine hadn't grown any leaves yet. "I keep wondering about his wife and his daughter. He talked about them so much that I felt like I knew them."

Would Grandmother tell them? Or Nerium? Or Tempus?

Riegel wiped her cheeks. Wist and I pulled up seats beside her. For a time, we all looked out at the sunlight in the secret courtyard. If companionable silence was what she needed most, well, we had plenty of it to go around.

That was the plan. Yet somehow I found myself babbling about my own fears again. Things I'd been trying not to voice in front of Wist.

While I had the presence of mind not to mention the Void, I rambled on about just about everything else. How we couldn't even touch anymore, much less make a serious attempt to bond again. How time had done absolutely nothing to soften or scar over our ever-raw broken edges.

Would it get better if we stayed further apart? How long would it take, then, and how would we know when it was safe to come together?

To truly heal, would I need not only to keep my distance but also to purge her completely from my mind and heart? Impossible, unless we consulted with a black-market memory butcher.

My voice poured out like a sickness being released. The only sign that Wist could hear me was a slight twitch of her fingers in her lap, a barely-there movement that could've been the first or last sign of life from a comatose patient.

When I'd spent myself, Riegel asked me to bring over her glasses. She fitted them onto her face. Before I could apologize for my ridiculous outburst, she took Wist's hand. She took my hand.

I jerked hard enough that she almost let go. I thought she'd convulse between us, felled by lightning. She'd inadvertently completed a deadly circuit. She'd become the path joining two people who could no longer be safely connected.

But no one cried out. She was just an ordinary older woman with dry gentle hands, and nothing horrific arced between me and Wist through the medium of her fragile flesh.

She looked first at Wist. "When you were a child," she said, "you saved yourself. You didn't know what you were doing. You devised magic to pack your wounds as if stuffing them with gauze. You learned to cushion yourself when they shoved you off the roof. No one taught you how to originate new skills, not back then. You discovered it for yourself, under the worst kinds of duress. But you did discover it."

Next she spoke to me. "Now that Hazeldine's gone, you find yourself wishing you'd asked him for help. His magic might have given you the ability to endure making contact. The ability to push through."

She squeezed our hands. Her grip was frail. "You're right—there are some things that time only makes worse. Time doesn't just cure; it corrodes. Pain doesn't always lessen with distance. When no answer exists, when the thing you want seems impossible, when no one knows how to help you—and it's so difficult to even ask—sometimes you just have to make your own way. Become your own teacher. What's impossible for other people might not be impossible for you."

"Like little Wist," I said. "But she was always the Kraken. Even before she knew it."

Riegel released our hands one by one. She patted our knuckles with a quiet air of satisfaction, as if to mark the covert completion of a restorative ritual.

"The truth is, few stunted mages live to forty," she said. "The oldest ever died just short of seventy. I'm not a record-holder myself, but I'm getting close. Very close."

Wist made a small inadvertent sound, one that fizzled out before becoming words.

Riegel wore a self-deprecating smile. "When you get to my age—well, this might have nothing to do with being stunted. I think a lot about how much time I have left. From day to day, I've got endless hours to ponder. But the years slip by in a blur.

"So—pompous though it sounds—I ponder my legacy. I never did give the nation a world-shaking mage like the Kraken. I didn't particularly want to, either. For a long while, it was more than enough to have these rooms for myself, and a budget for fabric, and to be left alone to decorate tiny hats. I love full-size hats too, you know, but I've been trying not to overflow my allotted space."

She brightened. "Did I ever tell you? Some of my hats sell on consignment. From boutiques in the city. It's all handled anonymously. I have fans, apparently. Collectors who buy all my latest works." She listed the names and locations of a couple shops.

"That could have been enough. But when I reached my forties—when I realized I'd already outlived most other stunted mages—I still wanted so badly to bear another child. I'd had no interest when I was young, and I'd had no choice in the matter anyway. My motivations weren't anything noble. I knew I could never offer a child as much as other mothers. I just had this growing desire in me—a selfish desire, mind you—to leave a living legacy."

"Other than your son," I said.

"Other than the boy I was forced to carry. Yes. The odds weren't looking terribly good. I was only getting older, and weaker, and all our efforts to date had miscarried. Hazeldine started to sound uncharacteristically pessimistic. Even if it succeeded, he said, pregnancy might kill me."

"But it did succeed." That was Wist.

"Goodness," Riegel said, suddenly flustered. "This isn't a very nice example of what I'm trying to tell you. What's gotten into me? I could have died. I know I was lucky. What I mean is that when I was a young woman, I couldn't ever have imagined deciding to have a baby just because I wanted to. It was the very definition of impossible."

She made a painful-sounding noise in her throat. Wist got up to fetch her a drink.

I asked if she needed medication. Hazeldine's magic had all gone defunct, but pharmaceuticals would still work fine—as would medicinal cuttings from other mages.

Wist rubbed her back until she'd recovered enough to speak again.

"Think back to before you became known as the Magebreaker," Riegel told me, hoarse but eager. "If you'd asked anyone about—what's the word for when you break a mage?"

"Hobbling."

"If you'd asked anyone about hobbling mages, wouldn't they have called it impossible? Bondbreaking, too. You see a path to it now. It was a path you made yourself, without any past precedent."

I grasped for words. "You mean—"

"You can survive this without pain relief from Hazeldine. Maybe magic itself isn't the answer to your problems at all."

"A bond is born from a magic branch," I said.

"And mages have never been able to work out the kinks in their own branches. To relieve their own magical pain."

"I'm not a mage, though."

"No. You're working with the mutilated aftermath of your own bond. Not with anything familiar like an ordinary core and branches. But you've always been good at forging ground in unfamiliar areas, haven't you? There was no one who could really advise you how to heal a mage like the Kraken. You figured it out for yourself. Branch skills and cuttings and mages might not hold the solution here. That doesn't mean no solution can ever exist."

She spoke like she'd been right there with us—at Guralta, and after Guralta. Admittedly, Wist and I would talk for hours whenever we came to visit. I couldn't remember with any confidence what we had and hadn't told her. Riegel had an incredible memory for other people's stories.

Her knobbly fingers clenched fitfully at the arms of her chair. She was trying so hard to make me see what she meant.

And I was finally starting to get it. Like lying down in a room with the lights off, and realizing half an hour later that I could see the gleam of Wist's eyes and the shape of her cheek and mouth. I could kiss her anywhere I liked without going wildly off-target—whereas just a little while before, my vision would've been a solid wall of black.

I started to tell Riegel that she was probably right. I'd been too consumed with everything I couldn't do. Couldn't touch Wist, couldn't whisper into her mind, couldn't feel where she was, couldn't heal her, couldn't neglect the Void, couldn't let our enemies know we'd been severed.

I started to tell Riegel that I understood now. But I was desperately afraid to hope.

I started to tell her, but no one heard me over the shouting in the doorway.

55

Danver burst into the room, yelling her head off. Lear followed a second later.

"Danny," said Riegel, sharp and unfamiliar. "Danny, are you hurt?"

"Am *I* hurt?" Danver cried. "You—"

Lear caught at her as if trying to stop a bar fight. "Danny, calm down."

Danver tore her arm away. "Nothing, *nothing* sets me off like you telling me to calm myself. You know that. You've encouraged it."

"Well, yes." Lear had the decency to look abashed. "But right now really would be a good time to take a deep breath."

"Not even a hello for us?" I asked. When I spot a fire, I get the urge to start pouring on oil.

Danver marched over. Her expression was thunderous. Lear and Wist tensed as though readying themselves to tackle her if she tried anything sketchy.

She pointed at herself, then at her mother.

"Break our bond," she said.

"Danny…" Now Riegel sounded teary.

I inhaled. I sighed. I motioned Danver over toward the sewing room. "Can we speak in private?"

"What?" she demanded. "You heard me. Break our bond."

"Ask more nicely. I'm not your servant."

I made for the sewing room without looking to see if she'd follow.

She did. After an extended pause, Lear and Riegel and Wist resumed speaking in muffled voices on the other side of the door.

Danver squared up in front of a pegboard mounted with scissors and rulers and a rainbow of thread. On my side I had a color-coded ribbon rack stocked so extensively that it could've been ported in straight from a craft store. The scent of incense lingered less heavily than in the adjacent bedroom.

"You changed your mind," I said. "Why?"

She stared. "What do you care?"

She was still in sweats, bare of makeup. Her mouth—always that odd bruised color—had gone thinner than ever with displeasure.

"Need to make sure you're not being coerced," I said plainly. "You were against it before. In fact, you specifically ordered me not to break your bond."

I waited.

"Hazeldine died," she said.

"I know. I found the body. So?"

I recalled, looking her over, that Hazeldine might've been her father. Her sperm donor, rather. Did she know? Had he ever acknowledged her? He'd seemed very proud of his legitimate daughter, the girl he'd sent off to Guralta. A full-fledged mage, presumably. Guralta didn't take subliminals, and he wouldn't mention his child in conversations with strangers if she were merely a healer.

"You got Ginko out of the cloisters," Danver said suddenly. "How are you treating her?"

"What's that got to do with breaking your bond?"

She glared. There was a wild tension in her that reminded me of the moments before Miyu's death.

More than anything, she bore an air of violent impatience, as if she saw some precious window of opportunity rapidly closing. As if she were the one running out of time. Not her aging mother—who, for all we knew, might currently be the oldest stunted mage anywhere on the continent.

"The doctor is dead," she said again. She pointed at the closed door. "My—Aunt Riegel needs the best healing, the best pain relief she can get. Now more than ever."

"I already know she's your mother."

"Just shut up and listen. You're the greatest healer alive."

"Uh, thanks." I wouldn't go out of my way to deny it. "Who gave you my credentials?"

"You've been the Kraken's chosen healer for years. That's proof enough."

I could've sent her argument off the rails by revealing that our bond had been violently shattered—and that, lately, I'd entrusted all Wist's healing to Mori.

"It has to be you." Her hands were in fists, as if she were about to turn around and start beating up spools of thread. "It has to be you. You need to heal her. I can't—I can't do a good enough job."

I was still confused. "Doctor Hazeldine had nothing to do with healing her magic. He treated different dimensions of pain. Can't you just wait for his replacement?"

"She's getting worse," Danver said in a rush. "She was getting worse long before today. He kept upping the strength of the stuff he gave her.

A different mage starting all over again, without any knowledge of her—they'd never produce the same results. It's a different dimension of pain, but it still piles up.

"You have no idea how much it hurts her, all the time—how well she hides it. I didn't want you to break our bond because I thought she … I thought she would...."

She choked, turned her back on me. Her hair remained damp enough to look yellowish-brown instead of warmthless platinum.

"She would never do it while we're bonded," Danver finished, still facing the wall. "She wouldn't want me to sense it happening. She wouldn't let me feel her leaving me. If she found a way to break our bond first—then she'd have no regrets."

"And now you think she won't … try anything?"

"I don't know!" Danver's voice cracked. "I don't know. She's already so much worse than just a month ago. Can't you tell? If I could heal her better, I could make up for the loss of what Hazeldine used to give her. If I could heal her better, I could at least make it so she isn't crushed by magical pain while her physical body gives out. But I can't. Even with the boost from bonding. I'm a good healer. I'm just not good enough for a stunted mage."

I rubbed my neck. Talk about pressure.

"I can break your bond," I said. "I can try healing her. No guarantees of the outcome, but I'll try. I can come back for touch-ups later, even, but I can't promise to always be available. This might just result in deferring her greatest magical misery to some later time. After the rest of her has become even weaker."

"I'll watch," Danver said fiercely. "I'll learn from you. I'll practice. I'll imitate you. Please. Just—please."

Her pride couldn't take this weight. She'd let it shatter like too-thin ice.

56

"Look," I said. We were back in the bedroom full of stained glass lamps and tiny hats. "There's no fancy ritual for this, okay? I'm making it up as I go."

"Thanks for the reassurance," Danver said, clipped.

She'd pulled her hair into a rough twist. Nothing as elaborate as her usual buns. She perched on the rim of a red chair by Riegel's bed—almost floating off the seat, prepared to box my ears for impertinence.

Lear leaned on the wall at the foot of the bed, unusually bereft of pearly jewelry and her signature eyeliner. She nevertheless looked completely in her element.

Ficus must have respected some rare quality he'd detected in her, something more than just her lack of fear or fawning. Her innate self-possession, perhaps.

"Didn't expect to be doing this in front of a voyeur," I said.

"Not a voyeur," Lear replied. "A potential future client."

Which I guess meant that everyone else in the room already knew she had a bondmate back in Jace.

She tilted her head at Wist. "Besides, I'm not the only one watching."

"Wist goes where I go," I said. "Unlike you, she's useful."

"Ouch."

"For one thing, she can guarantee that no one barges in on us."

Lear raised her hands in surrender. "We can't all be the Kraken."

Wist was poised by the door, although she could've served as a sentry from anywhere. Aunt Riegel had moved back to her bed. I assured her and Danver that I'd be gentle. That I'd make it a clean break. I promised myself (not out loud) that I'd pull back immediately if there were any danger of inflicting on them the same type of catastrophic magnetic repulsion that had taken hold of me and Wist.

I cautioned them that I didn't know if it would be possible for them to bond again afterward. Either with each other, or with anyone else.

"That might be for the best," Riegel said. Her voice only shook a little.

They'd originally bonded to prevent Miyu from claiming Danver. A drastic solution—but then, Wist and I had bonded under unusual circumstances, too.

Once Miyu got it in her head that she deserved a particular healer, it would've been extraordinarily difficult to make her back down. She might've sensed—nebulously, like an animal sniffing out weakness—that taking Danver would hurt Aunt Riegel. And that hurting Aunt Riegel might be a way to strike an unprecedented blow at Nerium.

Miyu was out of the way now, but that might not stop Grandmother from perceiving Danver as an underutilized resource. A healer who, if unbonded, could be better allocated elsewhere in the clan.

The end of their bond would not mean the end of their troubles.

"I want you to swear to secrecy," I told them (and Lear as well). "No one needs to know your bond is broken. Don't let them get suspicious.

They won't be able to prove it unless they bring in a notary. If it does get to that point—if you can't convince them you're still bonded—then tell them Wist did it. People will accept all kinds of crazy feats from the Kraken. Tell them—oh, I dunno—tell them she was so shocked to find a bonded mother-daughter pair that she split you as an act of charity."

Lear was the first to laugh. "Is that the Kraken's role in your relationship? To leap in front of you and take reputational bullets?"

"My reputation is beyond rehabilitation," I said huffily. "It's in both our interests to keep extra attention off me."

"I can be the Bondbreaker," Wist affirmed.

"See?"

"Just get on with it." That was Danver.

I rolled up my sleeves (for no particular reason—it wouldn't improve my odds of success). "It won't be flashy. Won't look like I'm doing anything special. But I'm not a fraud."

"Then prove it," Danver said witheringly.

"You don't have to sit still, like for a portrait," I told her and Riegel. "I'd prefer it if you didn't go dancing around the room—"

"That won't be a problem, I think," Riegel said drolly, eyes on her walker.

"Anyway, you can keep talking. Won't distract me."

"Mom, tell her if it hurts," Danver said. "You have to speak up."

Riegel nodded solemnly.

They did keep talking—softly, trying not to betray nervousness. Wist and Lear observed like a pair of dark-haired bodyguards.

Wist wore no identifiable expression. She absorbed the suspense of each creeping second with the empty intensity of a raptor on the hunt. Her mind could've been three worlds away.

Lear, even in stillness, had an arch half-smile. The look of someone always ready to riff on a joke, or to play the knife game at a moment's notice. But her wry liveliness betrayed no more of her inner self than Wist's absolute mask.

A new thought flitted through the margins of my brain. Lear had been born a stunted mage. Would she, too, face the looming shadow of a shortened lifespan? Or had the violent removal of her magic also removed any related threats to her health?

I sat cross-legged on the bed behind Riegel. It was soft enough to dip under my weight.

A bond might typically be compared to a length of thread. As with all things magical, though, no physical analogy or thought exercise could fully capture its essence.

I focused more on Riegel than on Danver. As a healer of magic, all my experience lay in working with mages. Severing the bond close to its root in one bondmate would be easier than severing it in the empty space between them. And it wouldn't dangle loose ends like a cut thread. Nothing would remain of the bond once I unwove it. It could only exist in the act of binding them: that was its nature. The instant I finished picking it apart, the instant it no longer bound them, it would vaporize, leaving behind only an invisible sense of absence.

Their phantom scarring—the emptiness where they used to have a bond—could harden into a stiff blinding shroud over their entire selves. Or it could heal as cleanly as thin fresh skin growing after a moderate scrape. A little shinier, a little more tender. The outcome would depend wholly on my skill.

Like I said, no bond really takes the shape of one neat coherent string. Still—even for me, that was the easiest way to conceive of it.

I pinched the bond down to a single stem near Riegel's back. She and Danver kept murmuring, their heads put together. They couldn't feel the pressure of my touch. That alone made it different from going through the ordinary steps of treating a mage's magic.

I could do this. Like how I could prod the end of a solitary magic branch and thus persuade all the rest of that mage's branches to tie themselves up in a tidy knot. I could tweak the bond in just the right way to make it twirl itself out of existence.

Before I performed my final manipulation on their bond, before I induced it to unmake itself, I already knew it would work.

It was a much simpler process than, say, healing a mage with double-digit branches. Easier, too, because breaking things is always easier: I can dash a porcelain cup to pieces on the floor, but I wouldn't know how to craft a new cup from scratch.

"Done," I said.

"That's it?"

Danver sounded ready to fight. But then she paled. Her upper body jerked against the back of her crimson chair as if I'd stood up and shot her point-blank.

She lurched from her seat. She veered over to the wall by the sewing room.

She stopped beneath a sumptuous floor lamp with a pattern of amber insects and grapes. Her shoulders were hunched, braced as if for a whipping. Her face stayed hidden.

I slipped off the bed. Riegel was not crying. She'd worn her glasses throughout. I couldn't read the light in her eyes.

"Come back, Danny," she said gently. The constrained throatiness of her voice was the only hint that anything had changed.

Danver shook her head.

Lear looked fixedly at Danver's misery as if savoring the priceless bitterness of a gourmet dish.

No surprise there. In an oblique sense, I could relate. But I could also judge her for making so little attempt to hide it. Right in front of Danver's own mother, no less.

I patted Riegel awkwardly on her soft shoulder. Surely one of the most inadequate gestures I've ever made in my life. I caught Wist's eye, and we headed for the door.

"Wait!"

Danver again, halting us with a shrill cry in the tone of *Stop—thief!* or *Run—fire!*

"You promised to heal her," Danver ground out as I peeked gingerly over my shoulder. Her face was a reddened mess.

"Indeed," I said. "And I will. You don't want to sit with your mother first? You know—reflect a bit? Have a moment?"

"Don't be lazy," she snapped.

"Hey. Get as emotional as you like, but don't take it out on me."

I heard a stifled snort from Lear's corner.

I turned back toward Riegel and Danver. "You both ... how do you feel?"

Neither had collapsed in convulsions. A good sign, hopefully, that I'd succeeded in undoing their bond without dealing out irreparable psychic or physiological damage.

"You were just as gentle as you said you'd be," Riegel assured me.

"I feel the way I look," Danver said tautly.

Wist hadn't moved from the doorway, but the shadow of her left hand kept flexing. Shadowy fingers—somehow more distinct than anyone else's—opened wide, then squeezed shut, fighting to master a nameless impulse.

She stopped when she caught me looking. Her shadow froze sheepishly, trying to pretend it had been still and docile all along.

Only then did I realize how queasy I was. The tension of bondbreaking had turned my skin clammy from my back to my ankles. I'd come too close to leaving Danver and Riegel utterly wretched. It could've gone so wrong.

Now that I let myself admit to the thinness of the tightrope I'd been walking, I could think of little else.

"Clem," Wist said. Her shadow stretched improbably across the floor to touch the back of my heel.

It was not a touch I could feel. She said nothing more than my name. But the sound of her voice was enough to right me.

I went over to Riegel again. I'd never healed a stunted mage before. Even so—compared to bondbreaking, this was much closer to my usual work. A retreat to more comfortable territory.

"Oh," Riegel said, when I was about halfway through healing her. She put a hand to her mouth, as though she hadn't meant to make a sound.

"Oh," she said again at the end. She swiveled her head as if looking for something missing.

The silence that followed lasted for a few idyllic seconds before Danver—eyes enormous and bloodshot—began interrogating me furiously about how I'd done it.

Riegel was still a stunted mage. Her branches still had a rigid, cramped look to them, all bent up and hardened like dead coral. Rather than fight their natural shape, I'd looked for hidden spots where I could ease the worst knots with the least intervention.

Danver ran to the sewing room and came back with a pad of paper. She scribbled down notes while I attempted to articulate principles that I'd never been very good at explaining to fellow healers.

"I feel so light." Riegel sounded awestruck. "As if you lifted out a growth the size of a melon."

I winced. "Nothing that dramatic."

I could already guess at how her branches would naturally shrink together over time, folding themselves at painful angles. I explained this to Danver, too.

Riegel waited till Danver's flood of questions receded, then beckoned me closer. She patted the stack of red embroidered pillows that propped her up, inviting me to sit beside her.

I dropped my voice. "Your daughter will be jealous. Besides, we should probably take off soon."

I figured she just wanted to thank me again. I could only take so much gratitude in one day.

"Don't forget what I said"—she twirled one hand in the air, an all-encompassing gesture—"before all this."

"About ... your hats on consignment?"

She laughed. "Oh, dear. You're being silly on purpose."

"Just a little bit."

"Not everything needs to be a contest of sheer forbearance," she said, now thoroughly serious. "Not every battle can be won through grit. Pain tolerance has no inherent correlation with nobility or worthiness."

True, I thought, but sometimes those things were hard to keep untangled.

She hadn't finished yet. "I don't think you would have needed Hazeldine's advice. Nor his magic. Nor anyone's magic. Not for your current dilemma. You're a healer, aren't you?"

What she meant: don't borrow magic to power through the agony of touching Wist. Don't try to solve your problems like a mage. Solve your problems like a healer—and not just any healer. Solve them in a way only you can. You, Asa Clematis, the healer who taught herself to hobble mages. The healer who discovered bondbreaking.

57

To DATE, I'd made no attempt to approach the site of my own wound like a healer.

I was, after all, a healer of mages. I had no reason to think I could heal myself.

Of course, I'd never had any reason to think I could hobble or hijack mages, either. Couldn't find those techniques in our textbooks.

Perhaps I should've immediately attempted to repurpose my abilities—to resurface the burning aftermath of what used to be our bond. I should've known that the pain that flared whenever I touched Wist was something I could learn to soothe on my own.

Being brilliant at fixing strangers doesn't necessarily make you any less dumb when it comes to fixing yourself.

And facing our bond scars hurt like hell. It hurt in a way that trampled every last fragile bud of rational thought. It hurt in a way that mocked hope, that sent memory sloshing and blurring as if my head were a fishbowl being shaken. The effects would linger like a concussion, further distorting my reasoning.

I shouldn't have needed Aunt Riegel to tell me to treat my own magical bond scars as if I were healing a mage. But it might have taken me an inconceivably long time to crawl to that conclusion without her.

I couldn't rush it. I couldn't hope for too much. The boulder I'd begun pushing uphill would roll back down to crush me. I might find healing myself to be truly impossible—a clever idea, a worthy attempt, but ultimately useless. Then what would we be left with?

I wouldn't try anything here at Follyhope. I wouldn't try anything before we went back to the tower.

But first we needed to pick up a few things for Ginko. (She'd also asked us to check up on her backyard cat, which had reportedly reappeared after the vorpal hole vanished.)

Tempus was still around; I found him and told him to walk with us to the boarding house.

"You may have business there, but I don't," he said curtly. "You can get there faster with a mirror."

"But the Kraken wants to chat."

"I'm excited to chat with you, Tempus," Wist said in funereal tones.

He shuddered. "Don't make it sound like a death sentence."

We ushered him outside. The air felt like lukewarm fog. I reminded him that Wist was a Shien, a vital member of the family, and she deserved all the latest updates about the progress of his investigation.

"How much do you think could have happened in the past few hours?"

"Tell us anyway," I said sweetly.

The umbrella pines in the distance were a dull hue today, closer to moldy black than green. Tempus kept trying to glower at me, but he'd chosen to walk on my right, close to my blind spot. It was easy to act oblivious.

"Magic killed him," Tempus said at last.

"His own magic?"

"No."

"You already confirmed it?" I asked, taken aback. "That was fast."

"There were traces on him. From another mage's cutting."

Hazeldine's own magic wouldn't have left any traces. The magic of the dead—like the hearts and minds of the dead—would vanish as if it had never existed.

"How long till you find out more?"

"A couple weeks," he said. "Give or take. We'll compare the traces to the national database. Might be able to narrow the cutting's creator down to a few possible candidates. Or we might hit a dead end."

"Think he took it willingly?"

Tempus flung his hands up. "Could be. Or maybe it got mixed in with his personal stash. Magic from a stranger, attached to the same type of honey stick."

I mulled over this. "Mixed in by accident, or by malice?"

"His magic perception was far below average," Wist said. "He wore the monocle to compensate."

I reached out as if groping at objects on a desk. "He could've been fumbling around on autopilot. He could've grabbed a cutting from his usual jar without peering too closely, without double-checking it."

"There've been cases like that before," Tempus said. "He may have failed to realize he wasn't taking his own magic. Particularly if the skill had been modeled after his work."

"Something similar," said Wist, "but strong enough to kill."

"Like an overdose in a single pill," I murmured. "That—or he knew precisely what it was, and he took it on purpose."

We skirted around the garden where there used to be a sprawling vorpal hole. It was tilled in stark rows now, interrupted here and there with large temporary greenhouses. As if Grandmother's staff had been ordered to transform the wreckage into something productive.

Hopefully they'd salvaged the butchered rosebushes. Roses could grow back from their roots, couldn't they? Some of the old thorny canes had been as thick as young trees.

"Any leads on Hazeldine's pen pal?" I asked.

Tempus leaned around me to address Wist. "How much do you know about the doctor?"

"Less than you seem to," she answered.

"I have a theory," I said, "that he helped propagate the market for psychoactive cuttings at Guralta. Even back in our day. You used one on me, remember?"

Tempus flinched. That particular encounter wouldn't be a shining memory of glory for him, either. Wist had made sure of that.

"Might be worth looking into," I added. "It's not defamation if he's dead."

"The psychoactives are a trivial matter."

"Huh. Well. Sorry for overstepping, Inspector." I was only a little bit miffed.

"He's propagated much more controversial cuttings." After saying this, Tempus stopped in the middle of the path. He mouthed something at Wist. Her magic enveloped us like a spreading mist.

"No one will hear us," she said, "or read our lips."

"Good." He didn't sound grateful. "You don't know about any of this, do you?"

She considered his words as if searching for a hidden message. "Any of what?"

Wist kept her involvement in high society as shallow as possible. Before the Follyhope vorpal hole, she could have counted on one hand the number of times she'd visited home as an adult.

"The privilege of the Kraken. You can afford to be aloof," he said, acid in his voice. "*I* only know because of my clan. An ordinary police inspector would never catch wind of it. If they did, they would know to ignore it. If they failed to ignore it, they'd be buried."

I spun my finger at him. "Very suspenseful. Hurry up and say it."

"Doctor Hazeldine was a prolific originator."

"So I gather."

"He invented cuttings to take during pregnancy."

"What, for morning sickness?"

"To increase the likelihood of the child being born a mage."

No one uttered a word. I closed both eyes for a moment, longer than I needed to, just to feel Wist's magic all around me like water.

"I assume there were drawbacks," I said.

"He also developed cuttings for young children. To stimulate the growth of more branches."

"I assume that had drawbacks, too."

"This is all hearsay," Tempus hedged.

"Yeah, yeah. Keep going."

"The cuttings for use in pregnancy—they did increase the likelihood of gestating a mage. They also dramatically increased the likelihood of having a miscarriage, or birthing a child with no head."

"And the cuttings for little mage kids?"

"Sometimes they did boost branch production. Kids who took that magic might end up a class or two higher. Half the time, they also developed incredibly rare and stubborn types of childhood cancer. Unbelievably difficult to treat, even with the best magic money can buy."

"I suppose he earned extra on the side by offering to cure it?" I guessed. "Custom cancer treatment was one of his strengths."

"How," Wist said, "how could he have needed so much money?"

Tempus stopped just short of rolling his eyes. "Not everyone can build the tower of their dreams out of nothing."

I tapped my lip. "He did appear to have expensive tastes."

In terms of positioning, he would've been closer to a high-ranking employee than a core member of the inner clan. He'd been adopted into a distant branch, one near the margins of the family registry. He and his nuclear family enjoyed plenty of lifestyle benefits, but his actual stipend might not have been all that generous.

"Guess the Shiens didn't accumulate wealth by overpaying their staff," I said under my breath.

"His cuttings built him connections, not just wealth." The cold polish of Tempus's voice instantly made me nostalgic for Guralta Academy. "The psychoactives are basically an open secret—"

"You would say that, wouldn't you?"

His face darkened. "A good number of people know about his magic for pregnancy and children, too. But that's a more flagrant violation of law and custom. Especially with the potential side effects. Parents who took a gamble and suffered for it wouldn't dare report him. Parents who won the same gamble would stop at nothing to protect him, and to protect their secret."

"So what you're saying is that he left a trail of dead children. Could be a whole bunch of regretful parents out there who've been living in hopes of getting him killed."

"Plenty of suspects," Tempus said grimly. "But I can't run around making enemies in other mage clans. Quite likely including my own. Quite likely including some Shien branch families, too."

"Your investigation will hit a wall, then." As it had with Miyu and Ficus.

This was bad enough for Grandmother to have wanted Hazeldine dead. He'd incurred enormous reputational risks—with all the benefits flowing to him alone. If even Tempus had heard rumors, there was no way she didn't know.

Maybe she'd gotten old enough to feel her time running out. What if all these deaths were the result of Grandmother Shien taking out her own trash? What if she'd started using her final years to put her house in order, to purge the unworthy?

Who would be next?

Riegel had spoken of pondering her own lifespan, her legacy. Grandmother might not be a stunted mage, but she was also decades older. She had just as much reason to wonder about what kind of clan she'd leave behind her. What kind of vermin she'd allowed to feast in the shadows of Shien glory.

Maybe she was old-fashioned enough to believe in the honor of the ruling class, and to believe that honor could be purchased with the deaths of the dishonorable.

Wist's magic dissolved from the air around us. The Void stretched luxuriously at the back of my new prosthetic eye.

"Decades ago," Tempus said, "criminals could buy under-the-table cuttings and stop the hearts of their enemies from hundreds of miles away. Do it cleverly enough, and no one would be the wiser."

"Were there ever such days?" I asked.

"Try reading up on murder cases from the last century."

"Of course," Wist said, "the cases you can read about are just the ones who got caught."

Tempus strode ahead as if he were the one who had things to do at our destination. The boarding house had just come in sight.

"Magic forensics have become much more powerful nowadays," he said.

"Not powerful enough to supersede social status," I countered.

"In some cases, yes. In some cases, no."

"The ambiguity would drive me crazy," I said.

He pulled vengefully at his mustache.

We exchanged a few terse words of parting at the door. We'd dragged him all the way across the Follyhope grounds, but he had no reason to step inside.

I was ready to forget about the three dead Shiens. Miyu, Ficus, Hazeldine: I wouldn't go so far as to invade the mausoleum and spit on their symbols. Likewise, I felt little compulsion to keep pursuing an elusive and thankless truth.

Even Tempus knew he wouldn't get any further. His investigations would only be permitted to interpret surface-level facts. No point in me wringing my hands over it.

I mentally closed the door on all three murders. Incidents, rather—Hazeldine's death seemed inconclusive. I decided to stop thinking about them, and the decision was easy. I needed to muster my mental stamina for the task of attempting to ... somehow attempting to reshape my own bond scars. Wist's scars, too.

We went up to Ginko's room in the boarding house. No one else had been assigned to it. The furnishings were the same as last time, right down to the hints of condensation rimming the lower edge of the window.

I swear to you, I wasn't dwelling on the Shien deaths. Why would I? They might've been victims, but none of them were innocent.

I have no idea what lit the tinder in my mind. Wist ducking her head to step through Ginko's door? The flap-flap noise of a passing bird? The cut flowers on the kitchen table downstairs? Unlike the grand display in the Grand Salon, these rested in a visible vase. Some were already brown, rapidly wilting.

I told myself: It's still none of your concern.

I told myself: No need to get involved.

I told myself: The whole damn thing is already over.

I told myself: No one has to know, anyway.

If I hid it well enough, even Wist wouldn't notice. No chance of me letting hints slip out through our nonexistent bond. Why disturb her with knowledge of things she couldn't control, couldn't change?

Frankly, if you ask me, I think it was all for the best. Good riddance to Shien Miyu, and Shien Ficus, and Hazeldine Shien. I wasn't the one who'd decided they needed to die. But I would never wish them peace. I would never wish them rest.

58

I BROUGHT Ginko the garden rocks we'd picked up off the chest of drawers in the boarding house.

These had not been included in her request. She'd mainly asked us to retrieve her private stash of cat toys (which the boarding house cat had never cared for) and treats. Plus other personal sundries she hadn't packed when she moved to the cloisters.

She peeked inside the bag of stones.

"If you don't want them," I said, "we can dispose of them."

I'd thought they might hold some sort of meaning. But they might also remind her of a time when Miyu's voice had constantly haunted her thoughts.

She began placing rocks on her windowsill, arranging them in order of size.

"You were right, by the way." I'd almost forgotten to tell her. "Hazeldine died. Seems like it'll get handled as a suicide."

She didn't stop moving.

"The doctor?" she asked. "He killed himself?"

"That's the official story, yes. The cuttings he gave you—they'll be useless now. Need us to look for alternatives?"

"Maybe," she said. "Maybe not."

"You don't want to go cold turkey."

"I've been tapering them."

"Already? Smart of you."

She was almost done placing rocks. I began telling her about the proud garden cat she used to care for in Follyhope. Danver had promised that it would want for nothing.

Later that evening, I turned my mind to the wounds left behind when the vorpal hole shredded my bond. I'd gained enough perspective to grasp that Riegel was right. Time would never mend this.

A bond had no self-healing mechanism. The searing we felt in our souls was not a sign of natural inflammation running its course.

I would have to pace it. I'd have to tinker with my own scars (and then Wist's) over the course of weeks or months. Spot-testing, never pushing too hard. My patience would be stretched to its limit.

This might actually work. But my concentration was shot. My thoughts kept darting back to the deaths at Follyhope.

I'd been so determined to let it all go. And I could have—honest to god. I'd have been totally content to keep the answer to myself.

The only problem was the body in the suitcase.

That body really had been Shien Ficus. Not a replica. Not the key to unlocking an elaborate new conspiracy spanning intelligence agencies, terrorist groups, and heaven knows what else.

He'd been a domestic spy, yes. He was also thoroughly dead, and he'd been dumped in my apartment. All of that was exactly as it appeared, and it was still the one element that made no goddamn sense.

I lasted two days before my self-control crumbled.

Wist and I went out onto one of the tower rooftops after a night of raging rain. Puddles collected on broad flagstones. Water filled gigantic leaves of ivy, too, making them sag like hammocks burdened with sleeping bodies.

"You're lucky it's still too cold for mosquitoes," I remarked.

"Would mosquitoes fly all the way up here to lay eggs?"

I shrugged. "Magic ones might."

"I don't think Osmanthus has magic mosquitoes," Wist said.

"Not yet. Just try not to breed them."

Her left hand (currently detached) had claimed a spot on my shoulder like a pirate's parrot. It warmed itself in the folds of my cashmere scarf.

"Wist," I said. "If I were the one who'd killed Miyu and Ficus and Hazeldine, would you turn me in?"

"It's difficult to give a real answer to hypothetical situations."

I pulled the other end of the smooth green scarf through my hands. The way a stage villain might stretch out a length of rope to intimidate hostages. Time to get tied up.

"We know what happened to Miyu. You know I didn't kill her in person. What if someone—what if I arranged for it to happen?"

The puddles were a perfect mirror of the sky above. Wist glanced up and down as if expecting something to have changed between reality and its reflection.

"You mean ... what if you ordered Danver to shove her in? Like what Ficus expected of Ginko."

"Nothing that direct. Nothing that certain," I said. "More like sparking a hundred tiny fires in hopes that one might eventually catch wind. Forget about the mechanics of it. What about intent? Would it make a difference if I'd gotten them all killed for noble reasons?"

"What's noble?" Wist asked.

She had me there. "Flip it around to the opposite of noble, then. What if I wanted them dead for money? Like so I could collect some special Shien inheritance. Pure personal profit."

"Did anyone make money off their deaths?"

"Just play along. How about this—what if I started murdering people as a fun intellectual exercise?"

"I'd stop you," Wist said.

"Even if they deserved it? Even if, realistically, they'd never have received any other punishment? You think the fact of me doing it for my own gratification would be a sin heavy enough to outweigh all their prior sins? Wait, no, don't answer that." This debate would take us to dangerous places.

"Want to go back to Follyhope?" Wist asked. She knew me all too well.

"No," I lied. "No—but now that I think about it, Ginko might like a chance to see Danver. And vice versa. We should ask them."

When I did go to ask Ginko, she fell silent for such a long time that I figured this in itself was her answer.

"We could arrange for you to meet her off the estate," I said. "At a cafe or whatnot."

"...Could Danny visit the tower?"

"Sure. Of course."

"It might be difficult."

"Why?"

"She'll need permission to leave the grounds."

"We'll work it out," I said, with unwarranted confidence. "Wist's a Shien. And she's the Kraken."

That was our excuse for our next trip to Follyhope.

Only once we were actually there did it dawn on me that, however warmly Danver felt toward Ginko, she might end up wanting nothing to do with the rest of us. After all, I hadn't come just to set up a loving reunion between friends. I'd come to scratch the incorrigible itch in my brain.

I hadn't said so to Wist, but she could tell something was up. The shadow of her left hand kept stirring even when the rest of her looked infuriatingly calm.

59

I MESSED UP three times in the corridors. Wist's left hand leapfrogged across the gap between us—I'd been speeding ahead—and urged me to slow my pace.

Wist took the lead for the rest of the game. Right now, at least, she did much better than me at spotting the difference.

At the end of the corridors, we let ourselves into Aunt Riegel's room.

She was resting near one of the bay windows again. Nondescript small birds chittered beyond the glass.

Wist's hand had reunited with her arm. She held her wrist as though she needed to physically screw it in place, make sure it didn't get loose and fall off at random moments. Her shadow took on a different shape: the silhouette of her hand touched her mouth, as if she were biting her nails.

Riegel insisted that we serve ourselves refreshments. I carried a tray over from the side room, but I had no appetite. I compromised with a small cup of hot spica. Wist picked at a crackly bag of yuca chips. Riegel drank from a mug of warm water scented with a fruit I couldn't name.

"Wist, seal the room," I said.

Her magic painted the walls and ceiling and floors and windows before I even finished speaking.

It didn't block our view of the viney pergola. No more so than the latent fragrance of incense would block our hearing. Magic perception and vision might often get conflated—I was as guilty of this as anyone—but they were still, in the end, two separate senses.

This space was now as secure as the innermost halls of the Palace of Magi. Riegel lifted her mug to her lips. The quilt around her shoulders had a pattern like a mountainous sunset. She betrayed zero surprise.

I pulled up a seat. Wist tucked herself into a window nook. The light from outside made it hard to see the look on her face.

"Do you have questions, dear?" Riegel asked.

It was the same grandmotherly tone she'd used when I first stumbled in here. When she'd encouraged me to introduce myself. My throat had felt painfully thick when I answered then, too. My voice had sounded strained to the point of snapping.

"I—"

I couldn't go any further.

"Take your time," she said. Again.

To my astonishment, I wanted to take it all back. To make Wist release the sealing magic. To tell Riegel I'd come just to check up on her.

Only a few days had lapsed since I'd severed her from Danver. Theirs was the first bond I'd broken by my own choice, with my own power. Surely I owed them some duty of care. That would've been a perfectly valid reason to visit. I wished I'd used it.

"Then again," Riegel said thoughtfully, "You might be able to answer your own questions."

"The body," I blurted.

She didn't ask: *which body?* She gave me space to find my voice—or rather, for my voice to find me. She gazed out at the withered seed pods dangling from the pergola. The wisteria vine looked gray and dead, the courtyard abandoned, but it would soon be frothy with new leaves.

"Ficus," I said. "The suitcase. My apartment. That was utterly pointless. Unless it was meant to frighten me off. You wouldn't misread me that badly, would you?"

Riegel sipped from her steaming mug of clear water.

My temples throbbed. "You wanted to stump me," I said slowly. "Dumping the body on me had no other objective—except to lure me back here. To force me to ask you. Of course I'd have questions."

However she'd gotten hold of it (through Nerium, possibly), she'd known my old address for a while now. She'd sent me an anonymous missive marked with the Shien clan emblem. She'd phrased it in a way meant to intrigue and provoke me.

Sending me Ficus's body was merely a grislier manifestation of the same tactic. He'd come packed in a suitcase embossed all over with the monoceros crest. Like how she'd penned her first message on Shien letterhead.

"That was one reason," Riegel agreed. "Not the only reason, however."

"You baited me."

"If his body stayed intact, if his body remained readily available, I'm sure Hosanna would have considered holding a grand public wake. The moment he died, his popularity would become more useful than threatening."

"You didn't want him put up on a platter for worship by the masses."

"People had to settle for eulogizing him in other ways," Riegel said. "No, I didn't much care for the idea of his corpse being showered in adoration. Is that petty of me?"

"I don't know. Was it personal?"

"Ficus wronged many people, in many ways. But I don't suppose he ever did anything to wrong me. When I saw him—which wasn't often—he always seemed to be on his best behavior. He could be very kind, you know."

"I don't, actually."

"His kindness was as unpredictable as his violence."

Well, that about summed him up.

I felt Wist searching my face. I'd told her shamefully little of what to expect in here—just that it would all come out once we talked to Riegel.

Inspector Minashiro Tempus might've felt differently, but I wasn't particularly concerned with the minutiae of how Riegel had influenced each killing. I assumed she'd worked through Danver and Nerium, and occasionally through Lear, Grandmother Shien, and trusted family servants. Rarely would any one person be asked to do anything overtly incriminating.

Consider the feud between Miyu and Ficus. It would've been easy to egg on Miyu's paranoia. Get Danver or some other servant to gossip loudly about strange tattoos on Ficus's forearms, about glimpsing him performing rituals by the rose garden. The murmurs that reached Miyu's ears—or the cryptic dropped notes left for her to find by accident—didn't have to be true. They just needed to point her in the right direction.

Riegel wouldn't have meticulously gamed out Miyu's reaction. She wouldn't have given Danver direct orders to wrestle her over the edge of a vorpal hole. That wasn't how Riegel worked. She'd make gentle suggestions and innocuous requests. She'd light small scraps of kindling. She'd move on without waiting to see whether her fires flickered out or grew large enough to ride the wind.

She could hardly expect to control every tiny detail. She was a sick woman permanently locked up at home by her own family. If she could avoid it, she'd try not to rely overmuch on her children. Although she wouldn't hesitate to ask for help when she needed it, either. She wouldn't ever get anything done without outside assistance.

In my estimation, she had a very good memory for all the disparate balls she'd set rolling. She had quite a knack for guessing at how their trajectories might intersect.

She was like a farmer sowing huge handfuls of seed, like a frog depositing thousands of springtime eggs. It would be fine if most came to nothing. In fact, you might expect the majority to die out in sudden frosts. Only a few would ever need to survive.

That was the joy of it, no? Waiting to see which seeds bore fruit.

Inconsequential actions could have outsize repercussions. Like delicately fanning the flames of Miyu's insecurity, her possessiveness towards Follyhope, her outrage over the vorpal hole, her long-simmering suspicions of Ficus.

Miyu would always assume the worst of him. She'd thought he'd flunked out of spy training. She'd think he'd fallen in with the Extinguishers just to be contrary. Wouldn't take much coaxing to set up a confrontation.

"You didn't explicitly tell the Extinguishers to saw Ficus's head off," I said.

"I never leave these rooms, after all." Riegel cupped her cheeks in a gesture of girlish embarrassment. "I don't have the power to demand that anyone do as I say. I don't suppose I've ever met an Extinguisher in my life. Well, unless we count Ficus."

"Someone must have hinted to the Extinguishers that they could mistreat his body, and expect to get away with it." Someone like Nerium. "Did they cook up nefarious plans for the rest of his flesh? You wouldn't know, would you?"

She responded with a helpless little smile.

"Whatever the reason, his headless corpse ended up being more of an inconvenience than a boon." My voice had finally warmed up. "Someone arranged for it to be dumped in just the right place to get under my skin."

That second someone might again have been Nerium. Or Lear. Or some other wild-card contact that Riegel had cultivated during her decades of quietly crafting mini hats at the heart of Follyhope.

I'd only found myself saddled with a suitcase holding Ficus's body because the Extinguishers no longer wanted it. If they hadn't chopped him up, if they hadn't spirited him away, then Riegel would've devised some other way to call my attention.

That irked me more than anything. Having the solution waved at me like a flag at a bull. I could've figured out the true mastermind without personally dealing with a naked male cadaver crammed into a mysterious teal suitcase.

I wanted to say that, but it didn't feel true.

I wouldn't put flowers out for any of the victims. Not from these murders. I would've forgotten them and moved on. Wist and I had bigger existential problems to grapple with. Without the strangeness of that body needling at the underside of my mind, I wouldn't have been invested enough to keep wondering.

You could see Riegel as a sad prisoner, condemned to live out the rest of her days under perpetual house arrest.

Or you could see her as a spider camouflaged deep in the safety of a woven den.

If you were going to suspect any elderly Shien lady of orchestrating coldblooded killings, it would only be natural to first suspect Grandmother Shien. If you were going to suspect anyone from the younger generations of knocking rivals out one by one, it would only be natural to point fingers at Nerium.

Riegel was a stunted mage: physically feeble, magically disabled, helpless in the jaws of chronic pain. She was *nice*, and her niceness came from the heart. I didn't think for a second that she'd ever been putting on an act. Wist and I liked her—we both still liked her. That wasn't something you could turn on and off like a switch.

I didn't even doubt the tears she'd shed for Doctor Hazeldine's wife and daughter. Despite the fact that she'd participated far more actively in his killing than she had in the deaths of Ficus or Miyu. She could weep for his surviving family, and mean it, but her tears hadn't been tears of regret.

"I'm curious," Riegel said, an incongruous brightness in her voice. She wasn't faking that, either. "You aren't puzzled by what became of the doctor?"

"His murder, you mean?" I asked baldly. "No. Not anymore."

She peeked playfully at me from above the rims of her bottle-bottom glasses.

She'd never openly discussed this with anyone, had she? Not ever. She kept her own counsel.

To some extent, Danver would've been able to glean Riegel's intentions by virtue of being her bondmate. Nerium was shrewd enough to figure it out for himself without any extra advantage. But Riegel would never invite her children to talk it over in unambiguous language. They wouldn't sip tea and reminisce about the building blocks of murder.

I made a gesture encompassing myself and Wist. "We have a close friend," I said. "Kuga Mori. Do you know him?"

"Oh!" Riegel covered her face, overcome by delight. "His research is just—it's fascinating. And he's still so young. Imagine what he'll have accomplished five, ten, twenty years from now."

I'd never met anyone outside academia who reacted to a mention of Mori as if he were a big-name celebrity.

"Ever send him fan mail?"

"A few letters here and there. Always anonymous."

"A few. Yeah. Sounds about right."

I watched Wist from the corner of my eye as I spoke. Would she understand where this was going?

"Mori told me that sometimes—very rarely—bonding converts certain mages into originators."

"He's brilliant," Riegel said earnestly.

"Lear told me that stunted mages can use magic."

"Yes. She would know, wouldn't she?"

"It's just—it's so horrible that it gets written off as impossible. Which it is, for all practical purposes."

Technically speaking, most anyone could pour oil over their head and then light a living fire. Most anyone could take a knife and flay their own skin—the parts within reach, anyhow. Anyone could do these things in theory, but for most of us, it might as well be deemed impossible. If not impossible, then too cruel to even think of. That's what it meant to be a stunted mage wielding magic.

"Dearest Magebreaker," said Riegel, "I'm so glad we met."

Her admiration was too much, too radiant. I couldn't take it. My throat made a swallowing motion, but there was nothing in my mouth to be swallowed down.

"Inspector Minashiro told me that the killing magic could've been modeled after Hazeldine's work. But it was someone else's cutting," I said harshly. "It was yours."

Riegel inclined her head like a queen acknowledging an envoy from faraway lands.

She had an arresting dignity to her. Even with her paunch, and the colorful quilt tucked around her back, and the streaky white powder applied to her quick-flushing cheeks.

She'd been a stunted mage all her life; she would never not be a stunted mage.

As a result, no one would've have bothered taking impressions of her magic for the national database. Tempus's analysts could pore over the traces left on Doctor Hazeldine to their heart's content. They could check every last citizen mage and registered foreigner—they would never find a match.

When she bonded her own daughter, Riegel had become an originator. A meaningless upgrade, cruel in its irony. No one would have known of it. No one would have asked.

She'd done what was commonly considered impossible. Just as she'd counseled me. She'd taught herself how to function as a branch-wielding mage and as an originator. She'd worked through intolerable pain. She'd crafted a poisonous imitation of one of Hazeldine's signature skills, and she'd welded it to one of his signature honey sticks.

She'd known Hazeldine for a very long time now. She'd learned which cuttings he took for his own solace and pleasure. Maybe she'd been mixing her own creations in his personal stash for months or years, with the innocent help of various staff or the not-so-innocent help of her daughter. Who—in a biological sense—might have been his daughter, too.

For that reason, perhaps she would've tried not to rely on Danver. Perhaps she'd summoned one of the few other maids permitted to access her suite. "The doctor forgot these," she'd say with a smile, handing over a bundle of the usual honey sticks. "Could you put them in the cup on his desk?"

Or perhaps this particular murder had demanded far more precision. Tempus hadn't located any unused honey sticks still loaded with suspicious skills. Given the intense effort it would've taken Riegel to prune even a single cutting, perhaps she'd only ever made one.

If she only had one, she could only have trusted it to Danver—who would do exactly as she said, and who wouldn't ask questions.

How much had Danver known of Hazeldine's dirtier dealings? Enough for her to have zero qualms about going to plant the deadly honey stick? Would she have found it easier or harder than her clumsy piecemeal assassination of Shien Miyu?

Unless Danver or an associate had placed it in Hazeldine's hands and made him take it, they wouldn't have been able to control the timing of when he picked the one deadly cutting out of the rest on his desk.

They could get a rough idea, however, based on the frequency of his indulgence and the size of his stock. Say he usually imbibed once daily—like drinking a glass of brandy after work—and there were seven sticks left in his tin of cuttings ... one might logically expect him to keel over within the week.

The fact that it had happened on the day we came to visit—that was the only true coincidence. Why had he been soothing himself with magic so early in the morning, anyhow? Had he been dead during our attempts at contact, or had he simply ignored us? Maybe the thought of facing us had driven him to gulp down all the magical relaxants he could get his hands on.

"You were entirely self-taught," I said to Riegel. "How'd you know your magic would work?"

"Why, that's simple." A teasing note entered her voice. "I tested it. Over and over."

I jabbed a thumb at the courtyard. "On insects? On animals?"

"Heavens, no! I could never."

"Sorry, sorry. No animal cruelty. Got it." Apparently humans were a different matter.

"I tested it on myself," she said.

"You still look alive to me," I muttered.

Wist sat up a little straighter. Her shadow stirred like windblown water.

"I made it very weak at first," Riegel explained. "The equivalent of a lower dose, one might say. Watered down. I upped the intensity notch by notch, until I began to get a feel for it. Until I grew confident that I could craft a version of the skill strong enough to do away with a grown man. A very vigorous and health-conscious grown man."

"You weren't afraid of it ... you know, working a little too well? On yourself, I mean."

"My condition is very closely monitored. Hazeldine called himself my guardian angel. He greatly pitied me, I suppose. He must have thought himself very gallant."

She placed a hand on her chest. "If I had a heart episode, he would've come swooping in to save me. No one would guess at it being magically induced. I'm a neverending fount of new health issues."

"Sounds like all the more reason not to give yourself watered-down heart attacks."

"Yet I'm still here," Riegel said simply. "And for all his exercise, and all his nutrition, and all his skin treatments, and all his stress management, and all his insufferable preaching—he's gone. The stunted invalid won out in the end."

She hated him.

I'd never gotten the impression that she truly hated Miyu or Ficus. Indeed, their deaths had happened at a distant remove from her.

With Hazeldine, it was personal.

"What'd he do to you?"

She looked at me as if to say: *Think for yourself, dear.*

I scraped together a thousand fragmented thoughts, scraps of recollection that had scattered like a lost fistful of sand.

He invented cuttings to take during pregnancy.

...Seven miscarriages along the way....

Riegel had tested her murderous magic on herself, and herself alone. Not even on birds or stinkbugs or squirrels or skinks.

How had Hazeldine tested the cuttings he'd developed in secret?

Of all the pregnant women he could access at Follyhope, who would be considered most expendable?

Low-ranking staff members. Subliminals. Healers. And a lonely stunted mage willing to spend years taking fertility treatments, trusting him to help her, longing to bear just one more child. Longing to bear a child on her own terms.

60

"You waited a long time to kill him," I said.

Riegel smiled wryly and looked down at her hands.

"I don't know how much longer I can keep making hats," she confided. "Every season, my rheumatism gets worse."

"Why now?" I said. "Why bring me into it?"

"Do you think Miyu was the first?" Riegel inquired.

"No. Not at all. It's ... in a way, it's like shaping and decorating your own tiny hats. A skill developed over long years of practice. You orchestrated the murders of other people, too, over the years. Infrequently enough that no one would ever suspect a connection."

"Why?" she said. "Why wouldn't I be content with my beribboned hats and my Danny and my little garden out there?"

"You tell me. Your victims—all of them, going decades back—must want to know *why* more than anyone. Why'd they have to die? Why them? Because you wanted revenge on the world? Because you got bored and decided to fill empty hours by making up your own grisly intellectual puzzles?"

She placed one hand over another in her lap. She regarded me and Wist with her head held erect. The round black mole on her cheek could've been a mark of shame or a mark of glory.

"I live here like our spare healers live in their cloisters. At first I saw myself as an inmate. Then I began to see myself as an observer. I learned so much more about the rest of the clan and the outside world than I'd ever thought possible.

"Then"—her voice softened as if in fond reminiscence—"I began to see myself as a judge. Isolated; existing at an impartial remove from the rest of society."

"You observed Miyu and Ficus," I said. "You watched them grow up. You observed Hazeldine, and others, too. You decided that they deserved punishment."

I didn't ask what crimes she'd judged them for. We'd already discussed Hazeldine. Miyu had driven her previous bondmate to suicide. Ficus had plucked his out of the Shien cloister for use in a fatal experiment.

Riegel worked like the best healers. Like me. The subtlest touch to the tip of a single magic branch, and I could make other branches dance seemingly all on their own, seaweed swaying in complex underwater currents.

I'd dabbled with being a vigilante, then discarded it. I'd gotten distracted by other things. International travel and such. Just like how all the revolutionary fervor bled out of me as soon as I got put on trial for treason.

A couple years back, I'd met a healer with abilities equal to mine, and—no need to mince words here—I'd killed her. For all practical purposes, this made me unrivaled. I could heal mages better than anyone. Which, ironically, was the one field I'd never aspired to excel at.

In other areas, I came up short. I was a flaky and heartbreaking daughter. My morals ran shallow: I'd met many truer rebels with nobler motives, deeper convictions, stronger principles.

Like Shien Riegel.

Forget about the rightness or wrongness of the murders she'd constructed as scrupulously as mini hats. Unlike me, drifting from one thing to the next, eager for the oblivion of a comfortable life, she'd committed herself to a single course for years. She patiently exacted judgment on those she deemed wanting, with no reward and no recognition. She was as inexorable as the karmic punishment that still awaited Wist and me after Manglesea.

"I won't get up on my high horse and spout off the sanctity of life," I said to her. "Someone should probably do that at some point. Don't think Wist feels quite up to it."

Wist shook her head with unusual vigor.

"Do you have criticism? I'd love to hear it." Riegel cast her eyes down shyly. "I never really had the opportunity to receive feedback."

"If you're so impartial, why'd you spare Nerium?" I demanded.

"Ah." She adjusted the quilt tucked around her back. Her hands were not steady. "You certainly do know how to go for the jugular."

I brushed this off like a fly. "That's why you like me, isn't? You must've heard about what he did at school. Would he get a pass for being a kid? Okay—he was eighteen when Wist came to Follyhope. He didn't stop hurting her once he came of age at twenty. You think he's fully reformed? You think he deserves more chances than anyone else?"

There was no merriment left in her face. Nothing but deep-worn lines of pain and age. "I can't excuse him."

"You sure can't."

"He's the one person I can't touch," she said.

"You need his aid. You'd have been a lot less effective without him."

"It's not just because losing him would introduce—logistical complications. I'm not qualified to judge him. If I had been able to love him, perhaps he'd be different. If I'd loved him like a mother—"

"Bullshit. Who was there to give Wist a mother's love, huh? You ever hear about Wist torturing small children? No?"

I couldn't rattle her.

"I can't judge him," Riegel said levelly, "but you can."

"Me? You want me to—"

"I won't stop you."

None of this was a surprise to her. She'd wanted me here. She'd wanted me to find her, to see her, to know what she'd done, to think I was smart enough to have discovered it all on my own.

Her past murders, killings of people I'd never met, may indeed have been (from her perspective) unbiased acts of judgment. Her latest three murders had unfolded at a much more accelerated pace. They'd taken place close enough together that Tempus had searched in vain for their hidden connection. These three murders had not just been a way for her to execute judgment and vengeance. They had been an invitation, a performance. And I was her intended audience.

"It's about legacy," I said. "You want to know that your legacy will continue. You want someone to carry on your work."

"Hosanna has struggled to choose an heir," Riegel replied. "But I won't."

"You have children. You have a daughter. I'm a stranger."

"Which means that you'll feel free to turn me down. Danny wouldn't. Danny would take it as an obligation. I've already narrowed the shape of her life far more than I'd ever intended. When she was little, I never imagined her staying in Follyhope as an adult, looking after me, never leaving my side. Please don't misunderstand—I'm so grateful. But that was never what I dreamed for her."

"Too bad you can't control her dreams," I said waspishly. "Why pick me? I'm nothing to you."

"Remember when Miyu went berserk?"

I furiously resisted the urge to exchange looks with Wist.

"Hard to forget," I said. "It was very dramatic."

"At the time, I was somewhat ignorant of what people meant when they called you the Magebreaker. When I heard about the circumstances—well, to be honest, I thought you'd done it."

I didn't trust myself to say a word in response.

"That's impossible, though, isn't it?" She didn't pause for me to react. "How could a healer—even a healer with your reputation—make a mage go berserk? That's the opposite of healing.

"But I heard the staff whisper that you'd been asking around about Miyu's previous healer. I couldn't help but think that you had something to do with how Miyu ruined herself. How it all happened on the very same day. She never really got over the shame of berserking."

"Good," I said

Riegel smiled. "I've been interested in the Magebreaker ever since."

"Years passed before you sent me a letter."

"At first I thought there was no need to rush." Her smile turned wistful. "Unfortunately, I'm not getting any younger, and my health isn't getting any better, and time just seems to slip by faster and faster. I'll never achieve everything I might wish to achieve."

"I won't achieve it for you."

"Who knows? You may not be interested now. At least the seed has been planted. Maybe, once you're my age, you'll find yourself pondering your own legacy." Riegel gave me a misty-eyed look. "Maybe you'll remember me. Or maybe you won't. I'm not capable of making demands."

"You're just planting seeds. Seeds that may or may not germinate."

"Yes." She brought her hands together as if closing a book. "This past fall, I began to feel a greater and greater sense of urgency. I looked for opportunities to quicken my plans."

"Who's next on your hit list?" I asked.

"Why, no one for now," she said, wide-eyed. "I actually have quite strict standards for judging people worthy of murder."

"Strict enough to rule out the mother who shunted you off to become an experimental brood mare for the government?"

Wist flinched. Riegel didn't.

"Ah," she uttered. "An excellent question. Here's an interesting little tidbit of trivia. Did you know? The greatest treasure belonging to any mage clan isn't their investments, or their real estate holdings, or their storehouses full of antiques, or their bloodline."

"They have to go out of their way to dilute the bloodline," I said. "As much as possible."

"To avoid making more dreadful accidents like me, yes." Riegel placed her right hand over her heart. "You tell her, Wisteria."

"...The greatest treasure belonging to any mage clan is their suite of proprietary skills," Wist said distantly.

"Proprietary? In what way?"

"Branch skills passed down exclusively within the family. Sometimes exclusively from one clan head to the next."

"It's all very secretive," Riegel said. "I don't know the details myself. Hosanna possesses at least a couple of skills not bestowed on any other Shien. Skills that even the Kraken might find utterly unfamiliar. My theory is that those skills have preserved her mind. Prolonged her life. Turned back every malicious attempt to wound her."

She held up her palm and pretended to stab it, mimed the arc of a blade veering aside at the last moment. "She survived multiple assassins in the years after she first ascended to become head of the family. She's made it through all kinds of deadly situations without getting a scratch. The Extinguishers who invaded the manor? They were never a threat."

I pictured the old woman: her pruney unamused face, her no-nonsense buzz cut. "You think she's invincible?" I asked.

"In some senses," said Riegel. "In any case, it would be unwise to make futile attempts on her life."

"You're here by her grace, after all."

"That, too."

I got up and stretched, stiff from sitting. What now? Time to shake her hand, congratulate her on a job well done, and get out of here?

"The only guaranteed way to hurt Hosanna would be to destroy something she loves," Riegel tacked on as an afterthought. "She doesn't love much."

"Sure seems that way," I said.

I'd obtained enough answers to quiet the itch in my head. Hadn't needed to pry them out of her, either. She'd laden us down with confession after confession like an overgenerous elderly relative handing out a bunch of needless gifts.

Funny how she'd picked the ideal successor for herself, I thought. Better than she could ever imagine.

I had the Void on my side. I could, in theory, commit the perfect crime. I could swallow up anyone who crossed me. I could swallow up every witness. Forensic magic had nothing on the Void. I could erase victims as effectively as a one-woman vorpal hole.

Only Wist would know.

I didn't think Riegel was crazy. I didn't think I was in any sort of position to earnestly critique her morals. I wasn't repelled by the notion of taking up her mantle—whether right now, or years in the future. I wasn't repelled by the image of myself as a killer by choice, an avenging judge.

I looked Wist in the face, and for an instant—just between heart-beats—it was as though the old lost bond still ran between us, stronger than ever.

There was no light in her eyes. She was afraid for me, afraid of me, afraid of the Void. But she couldn't show it, even if she wanted to. She couldn't tremble. Love held her back: she couldn't tell me what to do or how to be.

Meanwhile, the Void would keep adroitly muting my reaction to dead bodies, to violent murder. I had no magic to feed the Void, but it had nevertheless found something within me that it could eat away at. I couldn't prove what I'd lost—a piece of my conscience? My natural human sensitivity to the reek of the dead?—or that I'd even possessed it in the first place.

I couldn't inherit Riegel's legacy. I couldn't. I was the best person for it, and the absolute worst.

Over the course of two lifetimes, Wist had already grappled with the knowledge that she could—in her own way—erase anyone who displeased her. She'd adamantly chosen not to. Sometimes to the point of paralyzing herself, dreading the finality of any choice at all.

The world might lose some of is meaning, its weight, if it were solely of your own making. If you could sculpt it as you pleased, then maybe it was no better than a daydream.

Still, I knew myself. I wouldn't keep wrestling with it like Wist always had. I was too slippery: no manner of philosophical guilt could maintain its grip on me forever.

Only Wist could be the Kraken and still continue to qualify as a basically decent person. Only I could be myself, and I would have to be very, very careful about appointing myself as anyone's judge.

But Riegel hadn't demanded a firm commitment. Or any kind of commitment at all. Was it enough for her to know that I'd heard her?

I caught myself staring blankly at the white chrysanthemums stuffed into a black porcelain vase. They were practically overflowing.

"These flowers," I said. "Who are they for?"

Riegel made a sound just short of laughter. "Why, I thought you'd never ask."

61

"Seven flowers for each lost pregnancy," said Riegel. "And the rest ... would you like to count them?"

"Er, no thanks."

"One for Miyu. One for Ficus. One for Hazeldine. One each for all those who came before them."

"Hazeldine—already?"

"I like to plan ahead."

So the number of chrysanthemums really had increased since the first time I'd seen them.

"You don't have to linger just to humor me," she said suddenly. "I expect I've already given you plenty of food for thought."

"No kidding."

Wist got up from the bench near the window. Riegel, with only a modicum of assistance, clutched her walker and began shuffling determinedly back in the general direction of her bed.

A cloud must have passed over the sun: the entire room grew dimmer. A few lamps flicked on beneath jewel-tone shades. At Riegel's request, Wist went over to a shelf and lit a fresh stick of incense.

I helped Riegel get settled back in bed, enthroned among cushions.

"Normally, someone in your position would worry about getting turned in," I said.

"By you?" Riegel asked, astonished. "You and Wisteria? Oh, my. I never even thought of that."

It was my turn to be astonished. Surely she was pulling my leg.

"You must not have been very concerned, either," she continued, flipping it around on me. "If you were, you wouldn't have so readily accepted food and drinks from me."

I drained my cup of spica. "That's got nothing to do with it. Wist's always on the lookout for poison. What about Nerium? He seemed pretty disturbed to find Hazeldine dead."

She gave a firm shake of her head. "I'm not worried about Nerium, either. It's Danny who—oh, no, she would never report me. No matter what I do, Nerium will make his own way in the world, and Nerium will take what he wants. It's Danny who makes me lose sleep."

Did she understand who, specifically, had killed Shien Miyu? Would she have sensed the jolt of panicked adrenaline as Danver shoved her in the vorpal hole, shearing off her legs?

"Sorry," I said. "I can offer feedback on murderous machinations, but I can't give much useful advice about parenting."

She rolled the edge of her blanket, shaping it like dough. "If … if Danny ever wants to leave Follyhope, would you offer her a place?"

"Would she want a place with us?"

"It doesn't have to be forever," said Riegel. "I would be very grateful if you could give her an out. Like what you gave Ginko. It's up to her if she takes it."

"You're asking a whole lot today," I drawled. "First you want me to become a serial killer."

"A righteous serial killer."

"Oops—can't forget about that part. Now you want me to take in your adult daughter. I dunno, Auntie. Ginko is much pleasanter company."

She laced her fingers in prayer.

"We'll give it some thought," I said.

"That's all I can ever ask. If I were up to me," Riegel added confidingly, "she'd defect to Jace."

"With your favorite artist?"

"Who can say? But as long as I live, she'll never leave the country. Ah, well. I would miss her very much, and she knows it." She let out a lengthy sigh.

The strength in her voice had begun fading by the minute. It felt like time to leave. She'd played me like a fiddle, but I couldn't be too angry. Misguided or not, she'd been drawn to some cutthroat quality she perceived in me. She'd respected me and Wist enough to hand over her most dangerous truths. She hadn't required repayment.

"Stay a little longer," she said, just as Wist was about to undo the magic on the room.

I turned back toward the bed. "No offense, but it's probably time for a nap."

Riegel was looking at Wist. Her glasses bent the light, warped her eyes into uncertain shapes. "Wisteria."

Wist's shadow crept longingly toward the door.

"Wisteria, there's something I need to confess. To you in particular."

"Now?" I said.

Riegel disregarded me. She only had eyes for Wist. "Your parents," she began.

"Wait." Wist was all the way up against the door, as if she might melt right through to the other side of it. "Wait. I—"

"The parents who birthed you," Riegel said, quiet and clear.

"I don't want to—"

Riegel stopped her. "You already know in your heart. Have you ever seriously tried to search for them? Ever paid a PI to report on their lives after they lost you? Ever dug deep, deep into the memories that got mangled and repainted so you could be reborn at the age of six as a proper adopted Shien?"

She waited. It was a terrible pause, kindly and cruel all at once. I wanted to cover Wist's ears. But more than that—I'm sorry, Wist—I was dying to hear what came next.

"You've got a good instinct for what you can and can't bear," Riegel continued, soft-spoken as ever. "You didn't stay away from them out of some misguided sense of loyalty to the clan. You didn't stay away from them because you didn't care about where you'd come from. You didn't stay away from them to protect them, or because you never longed desperately for a loving family, or because you didn't need them, or because you didn't need anyone."

She was merciless. There were so many chrysanthemums stuffed together in that one black vase.

"You thought—below the level of conscious thought—that you wouldn't like what you'd find. You weren't wrong." She paused again. "It's not as bad as your worst fears. They were good to you for as long as they had you. They still deserved what they got."

"You..." Wist's voice creaked. "Aunt Riegel, you—"

"I judged them," Riegel said.

Wist remained deathly still. So did her magic.

I finally punched my curiosity back down where it belonged. "Wist, we can leave," I said rapidly. "You can port us to the city, the tower, anywhere on the continent, anywhere in the world. You don't have to listen."

"At first they were very reluctant to give you up, of course." Riegel didn't wear even a trace of a smile. "Then money came into play. They were not at all destitute, mind you. They didn't need extra funds to stay off the streets."

She explained in plain language—no room for misinterpretation—that the amount discussed had turned out to be a life-changing sum. Enough to change the lives of all their descendants for generations to come. To provide for their children—if they had others—and their children's children, and so on.

Their resistance weakened. In the end, they stopped fighting. They surrendered Wist to the Shien clan, knowing she would be compelled to largely forget them. Knowing they would never be permitted to see her. They surrendered her willingly. They took the money.

"They traded their first-born child for a bribe," I said tightly.

Riegel never took her eyes off Wist. "They stayed together. They managed their newfound wealth very smartly. Didn't lose their heads over it. And"—she stopped, sucked her lips in for a second—"they did raise more children. Oh, yes. You have quite a few fully blood-related siblings. Brothers and sisters.

"They're subliminals. All of them. No one ever told them about you. They formed a very large, rambunctious family. A sickeningly happy family. Yes, it sickened me.

"I did have some inkling, by then, of how the other Shien children were treating you. How your new parents turned a blind eye. How you had no memories left of being loved.

"Your birth parents sold you to the devil. Perhaps they'd assumed you'd be treated well. Perhaps they'd extracted various meaningless promises so they could feel better about abandoning you. Perhaps they'd been told that the Shiens would love you, adore you, shower you in praise.

"They had no way to know if we Shiens followed through. They never tried to know. They made their bargain and stuck with it. They never looked back.

"Nerium agreed with me, by the way," Riegel said. "Which might seem odd. But it's true. Even *he* found your birth parents repulsive."

Wist's left hand separated from her arm with the loud crack of a broken branch. I ducked hastily to catch it. Riegel paid us no heed, as if this sort of thing happened all the time in here.

At our feet, Wist's shadow swelled like a puddle of blood, swelled until it merged with mine. I cradled her lost hand like a wounded bird. It was the only part of her I could hold.

Riegel described how Wist's parents had died together in an industrial fire. An unquenchable magical fire. A dreadful accident. That's what people called it. An accident that, by some deeply perplexing miracle of probability, claimed no other victims.

"Your biological brothers and sisters aren't that much younger than you," Riegel said wearily. "They're all grown up now. Some with multiple kids of their own. Your bloodline certainly has an affinity for big families. If I had to mention a resemblance—hmm. Some of them are quite tall. Especially the women.

"They all live extremely comfortable lives. They've got enough wealth to pursue their passions. To spend their time on work for the love of it, rather than out of necessity. They donate a reasonable amount to charity.

"They know little of politics. They couldn't name more than four or five members of the Board of Magi. Controversies about mages and healers—and less well-off subliminals—go in one ear and out the other. They know about the Kraken, but they would never guess that they had any relation. By all appearances, they've bounced back remarkably well from the untimely loss of their parents.

"But do relax. Don't look at me like that. I wouldn't judge them," Riegel assured us. "Being apolitical isn't a sin in itself, at least not in my book. Why, if it were, far too many people would require judgment. Far more, Clematis, than you or I could ever get around to in our remaining years."

I'd left cruel marks on Wist's severed hand. I loosened stiff-clenched fingers.

"Wist's birth parents didn't make her great," I said. "Neither did you Shiens. Whatever she became, she became in spite of them. In spite of you. In spite of Nerium. In spite of everyone."

"I know," Riegel said. "Yes, I know."

She reached for her nightstand. Pill bottles and paper medicine packets clustered just beyond her fingertips.

"I'm sorry, dear. Could you help me get—"

"This one?"

"No. Right next to it."

I passed her a crumpled twist of paper. It looked as though someone had sat on it. She took the sachet gratefully and unfolded it, one seam at a time.

My heart still thumped as if we were in the middle of combat. Wist's shadow had spread across half the floor.

"I have to rely on pharmaceutical painkillers for the time being," Riegel murmured. Her throat must have been in a very delicate state. Her voice sounded like sandpaper. "They can only do so much, but I can't complain, can I? This is a situation of my own making."

She struggled with the paper packet. I almost leaned over and offered to help. But Wist's shadow flickered at the corner of my eye, and now Riegel was rambling.

"The longer I live, the faster time passes. Oh, did I say that already? You'd think it would crawl by slowly, always stuck here in these rooms. There's just so much to think about, so much to see and do. Rain running down the windows, new anthills in the courtyard, birds perched in my wisteria, the angle of the light changing with the seasons.... Every day, there's so much to take in. And the days whip by so quickly. It's dizzying."

This was the opposite of how Wist had described the ever-slowing experience of a dying world. A world that slowed so much, as it neared its last gasp, that it could fool you into thinking nothing would ever end at all.

At last Riegel managed to fumble the open packet to her lips. She came close to spilling powder all over her bosom. She hiccuped with laughter, then tipped the medicinal powder into her mouth. I glimpsed this on the very periphery of my one-eyed vision. The rest of me saw nothing but Wist.

Riegel swallowed her medicine down with water.

"Ah," she said with gratitude. "That's much better."

She closed one eye. Out of simple exhaustion, no doubt, but it looked like a wink.

"Thank you," she said hoarsely. "Thank you again. You're a miracle worker, Clematis. I'm so glad Danny can't feel this."

Her other eye closed.

Magic burst inside her, fast as a firecracker.

62

Did I do it on purpose? All I can say is that the thinking part of me didn't know what would happen.

You can blame me. I'll take it. I deserve it.

I was distracted, yes. At that particular moment, my attention span had room for little other than Wist. The empty look on her face. The roiling of her shadow. The ominous static sensation of ambient magic. The butterfly-wing shimmer that marked every surface of the room: her sealing skill to make sure no one heard us, and no one came in.

Under ideal conditions, my magic perception is equal to or better than Wist's. I could've noticed the cutting tucked inside Riegel's mouthful of medicinal powder. But I didn't.

Humor me for a moment. Imagine yourself grabbing a canned drink to pass to a friend. In the act of handing it over, would you read all the fine print on the back? Could you, if you had really good eyes? Perhaps. Would you?

I know, I know. Physical analogies don't work for magic. Never have. Never will. The point is—I missed it.

The point is—by the time I leaped forward, Riegel had no breath and no heartbeat. She felt unnaturally cold and hard.

I couldn't spot a single trace of magic anywhere on her body, inside or out. Of course not. She'd taken one of her own cuttings.

Her core and stunted branches and every last pruned snippet would've vanished in the same instant she did. Every last particle of her magic would've gone as dark as a drowned fire.

Her body floated off the bed. The room briefly went hot and humid as a jungle—the air thickening like water—as Wist flooded it with resuscitation magic.

The heat gave way to a refrigerated chill. Wist's magic thinned and scattered, dripping defeatedly down the walls. The body lowered itself onto the covers with a kind of awful dignity.

"Should we ... should we call for a doctor?" I sounded like a stranger, a child. "Medical magic isn't your specialty. But—would any mage know emergency skills stronger than yours?"

I could read the answer on her face.

Wist sank to her knees next to the bed. "It's been less than a minute."

"Lady Shien," I said. "The family treasure. Proprietary skills. Maybe she's got something that—"

"It's as if she's already been dead for hours. Dead for hours since the instant of her passing." Wist's voice shook. "Clem. What's the difference between resuscitation and resurrection?"

I couldn't answer. Neither of us could answer.

"I saw our old world again. On the other side of the vorpal hole."

"Wist—"

"I can't risk it. I can't cross that line, or let anyone else cross it. Even by accident."

"Wist, you don't have to convince me."

Her head was in her arms.

"You're right," I said. "You're right. She already feels like she's been on dry ice all day long. She didn't want to be resuscitated. She chose this."

When Wist rose from the floor, when I saw her face, it winded me like a blow to the chest. She looked as if she wanted to tear something out of herself—some deep-sunken shard of anger or grief or primal frustration—but she couldn't remember how. Now it was already too late.

Wist reattached her left hand. She unsealed the bedroom. The next steps were dully familiar. We needed to tell Riegel's children.

Danver came first.

She made an indescribable noise, a noise like—it made me think of someone holding her down and cutting her eyes out. No; it was more as if she'd grabbed the knife to cut her eyes out herself. The noise trailed in my ears long after she stopped making any sound at all.

Lear and Nerium were in the doorway. They watched with hardened faces as Danver climbed onto the soft bed and laid herself down next to Riegel's body. As if climbing into a grave.

Danver shook like she was the one dying. Each crunching sob made the bed shake with her, and Riegel moved just a little too, unresistant. She still wore glasses, because no one had taken them off her. Her eyes stayed closed, her face at ease, her lips not quite meeting.

Lear said something inaudible to Nerium. She passed her hand over her own eyes, as if she too were a corpse who needed to be laid to rest. She vanished into the hallway.

Nerium's mouth formed the shape of a word that might have been *Mom*, but it was a word without sound.

Wist and I, following Lear's lead, tried to softly excuse ourselves.

Danver's voice cut across the room.

"Who gave it to her?"

We looked back. Nerium observed from behind inscrutable glasses.

"Who gave her the medicine? Who gave her the magic?"

"Me," Wist said.

I managed not to react.

"She asked me to pass her one of the packets from the nightstand," Wist continued. "I'm sorry."

"The greatest mage alive," Danver breathed, "and you didn't notice anything wrong?"

"I'm sorry," Wist said again.

Danver rose from the bed. She drifted over to the window. She picked up the dark vase of chrysanthemums. Swiftly, she raised it as high as she could over her head, and then brought it down hard on the table below.

The vase smashed like an egg. Flowers scattered. So did splashes of a substance too gooey and pearlescent and pink to be regular water. Confused fragments of preservation magic clung to the shards of the vase on the floor.

The flowers started browning. It happened very quickly. They went from white to toasty brown to withered black like marshmallows thrust in a fire. Danver wheeled around, gaining momentum, and shoved over a floor lamp as though shoving a hated enemy in front of a train.

The lamp never quite hit ground. It was the one with a stained glass pattern of wisteria at peak bloom, pendulous flowers in hues of noble mourning. The base—textured like a long woody trunk—froze midair at a perilous angle.

It creaked. It slowly tilted back upright, guided into place by Wist's magic.

"Danny," Nerium said. "Control yourself."

"You killed her," she said to Wist, almost wonderingly. She'd badly damaged her voice: it was high and guttural all at once. "You took her from me. Why? Because she took your parents?"

"You knew?" I heard myself ask.

"I was her bondmate. I was her daughter. I knew more than she could ever guess."

Her breath came shallow and fast, too high in her chest. She might have said more, but Nerium motioned for us to leave.

The door closed behind us.

No one had left any sound-sealing magic on the bedroom. Something crashed. My shoulders jerked. Nerium spoke again, low and even. Danver howled, and kept howling.

63

"You DIDN'T have to cover for me," I told Wist.

"Better me than you."

"Why? Whichever of us gave her the packet, the result would've been the same."

"I'm a Shien. I'm the Kraken."

But Nerium interceded before we spoke with investigators. He pulled us aside and told us not to mention either the powder or the magic. He looked abruptly much older—as if he were in his late sixties, not his late forties—though he acted otherwise unaffected.

"Aunt Riegel was resting her eyes," he said. "You were getting ready to leave. Tiptoeing about the room. You noticed too late that she'd stopped breathing. It happened peacefully."

"Danver might disagree," I said.

"She won't. Trust me, Asa Clematis. She's smarter than she seems."

Later, when we spoke with investigators, I stuck to Nerium's story.

I almost came to believe it.

Why had Riegel asked me to give her the medicine? To make me culpable? To make me an accomplice? To make me suffer for my lack of enthusiasm, my reluctance to immediately take up the mantle of justice?

She'd been feigning weakness. She could have stretched a few inches farther and taken the packet for herself.

All I knew was that everything she'd done was intentional. She'd waited for the news of Hazeldine's death—for the results of her first and final human experiment. She'd tested the fatal form of her magic on one key living subject before using it again on herself. She'd confirmed that it would work as intended. In the very end, she'd left little to chance.

Neither Wist nor I would bear witness to Grandmother Shien's reaction. No need to wonder how she might take it: Riegel had already told us. She'd known of only one way to wound the nigh-invincible head of the family.

She doesn't love much.

Riegel's loss might hurt her mother more than anyone else could ever guess.

None of Shien Hosanna's other children had lived so close to her for so many years. They'd all dropped off the map one by one, inventing new ways to fall out of favor. The only daughter who couldn't disappoint her was the one from whom she'd expected nothing. Riegel's only job had been to stay alive, and to stay in Follyhope, and to remain unknown.

Riegel had never been a candidate to become the next head of the family. She had never been invited to participate in any important Shien enterprises, whether for business or for charity.

Turn this around, and you could argue that she alone had value by virtue of her mere existence. She was trapped, yes, caged like the toxic birds in Grandmother's office. She was also the one Shien scion who had been wholly excused from the constant exhausting scrum of competing for status.

Grandmother Shien had hidden Riegel away like something shameful, unsightly. Or like a greedily hoarded treasure. Or like a weakness she couldn't afford to show anyone, whether ally or enemy.

There had been outward signs of mourning over Ficus and Miyu, but little evidence of actual grief. How had their exiled parents reacted? Would it be any different for Hazeldine? And how ironic that the most grievous blow of all—at least to Grandmother—would be the death of a woman who, in the eyes of the public, had never even existed.

Afterward, in Wist's tower, I worked slowly at healing the edges of what used to be our bond. Mori, always reliable, came over to tend to Wist's magic whenever she needed it. He brought a bunch of small gifts, too. Sticky pastries from the city. Patterned handkerchiefs from museum gift shops. A set of wooden puzzles that clicked together to form a droopy-eyed bear. Books about local birds and plants and insects.

He always gave one to each of us: me, Wist, and Ginko. The gifts for Wist and me seemed rather unnecessary, but he wouldn't want to make Ginko feel singled out.

I sensed a tinge of survivor's guilt in the way he doted on her. He'd been protected by Wist the Kraken for a long time now. He'd never been forced to bond anyone. In a different life, he could have been Ginko—or Luka, Miyu's healer before her.

One cold, sunny day, Mori reported to me with great excitement that Ginko had all the makings of a born naturalist. She'd noticed different insects closer to the tower than further out in the prairie.

"Different how?" I said, skeptical.

"Some flicker in and out of sight. No, they're not jumping. They really go invisible. She showed me. Some chirp like crickets, or buzz like katydids."

I tried imitating cricket noises. "Like this?"

"You can only hear the sounds they make with magic perception. Not with your ears. Isn't that amazing?"

"I'm glad you kids are having fun," I said.

"The tower is a man-made—er, Kraken-made—magical object. One of unusual intensity and scope. It's been here for years now. Not at all surprising that it's exerted unpredictable effects on the local fauna."

"Just don't forget about your own research."

"Yes, Mom," he said blithely. What a comedian.

It was heartening, I'll admit, to see Ginko spend hours wading around intently in the swaying blue grass. I asked Wist to get her a couple bottles of sunscreen.

Wist and I went together to Osmanthus City: we visited the boutiques where Riegel's hats had been listed on consignment.

We didn't find any of her work. All remaining stocks had sold out as soon as the supply dried up. Each shop owner had been informed that the shy, mysterious artisan had decided to retire from millinery for the sake of her health.

We didn't let on that we'd known her, but everyone very much admired the mini hat pinned at a jaunty angle in Wist's hair.

Tempus hadn't even bothered saying *You again?* when he came to officially question us regarding the circumstances of Riegel's death.

To be fair, he didn't get much of a chance. I yelped as soon as he stalked in. "My friend," I said, "you don't look awful. You don't look awful at all."

"Who's your friend," he said prissily, "and why should I stand here and let you insult me?"

I traced my fingers over my lip as if smoothing a nonexistent mustache. "Back me up, Wist. He finally got rid of it. What do you think? Speak frankly. Tempus can take it."

Wist, who was seated, looked up into his face with dark bottomless eyes. Tempus fidgeted.

"You look more like yourself," she concluded, unhelpfully.

Tempus scowled. "I'm growing it back."

Later in February, Wist's birthday came and went. Even when we were completely alone, I couldn't do anything but kiss her left hand—divorced from the rest of her—and the air by her lips.

Worse still: the Void demanded feeding that very evening.

When she was well enough to speak, Wist enfolded me in her shadow. She told me again, as she'd told me before, that she'd never really thought about seeking out her biological parents. But that didn't mean she'd never thought of them at all.

There were times, as a child, when she'd wished death on them.

Once she grew older, she would imagine them recognizing her as the Kraken. Listening to news of her. Spotting her from a distance at public events.

They wouldn't brag. They would keep their end of whatever deal they'd made with the Shien clan—a deal that she told herself must've been forced on them with implied threats of extortion, ruination, fatal violence.

She never truly believed she would find them anywhere within reach. Part of her suspected that they'd been disposed of long ago. Why would the Shiens leave messy loose ends?

As long as she never went out of her way to find them, she could hold on to the possibility that perhaps they were somewhere out there, and they'd always been proud of her, and they'd spend the rest of their lives regretting her loss.

Somehow, she'd never imagined them with other children.

Hearing about her siblings had made her want to leave the country and never come back.

I made her look around her room—which, now littered with decor from my old apartment, had lost much of its minimalist flair. My scale figurine of her had embarked on a dazzling new career as a stand to hold earrings and other rarely-worn jewelry. My painting of kissing giraffes hung above the door, always watching us.

"How could you leave this?" I asked grandly.

"How indeed," she said, dry as bone.

It was May by the time I reached for a jar of sesame seeds and accidentally brushed Wist's hand.

Her right hand. Still attached to her body.

The pain of it had utterly changed. I wouldn't even call it pain anymore, not compared to before. It had been reduced to a bracing impact like being smacked with an open palm. It stung, but it was more than bearable. I welcomed it.

"Clem." She sounded stunned. "Clem?"

She didn't seem to know what to do next. Her entire shadow shrank beneath her—shrank into her like the Void hiding in my skull, like claws retracting, like something young and frightened retreating to safety.

I seized her in my arms and held her. A savage turbulence rocked us as if we'd gone tumbling together, over and over, down a steep pebble-strewn slope. It wasn't physical. It wasn't magical. It became almost too much at times. But I didn't let go.

64

I healed Wist's magic for the first time all year. At last we could liberate Mori to focus on his own work again.

That same weekend, Wist came home with a letter.

The air near ground level was rife with pollen blown over from anonymous trees in the distant forest. It made my throat itchier than ever before. I confined myself to the highest floors of the tower, prowling neverending terraces when I got tired of being indoors.

Warm rooftop wind billowed the ends of Wist's loose thigh-length shirt. It kept trying to snatch the letter out of her hands, too.

The letter had been penned on expensive paper marked with the monoceros crest. It was signed by Shien Nerium.

I skimmed past a series of elaborate greetings.

"Seems unlike him to put this in writing," I said. "Too incautious."

Then again, it would be far more incriminating for us than for him.

He wrote that the powder Aunt Riegel had swallowed was essentially a placebo masquerading as medicine. Its only purpose had been to serve as a medium to store her magic.

Danny knows that Aunt Riegel could have—would have—taken the cutting on her own. Danny knows it doesn't matter who physically placed the powder in her hands. Aunt Riegel would have been capable of plucking it off the table herself.

She was a stunted mage with the will and vision and talent to invent and use her own magic. No one else will ever believe that such a feat could be possible. But we know. She was in her right mind. More than that—she was indomitable. She laid her plans very carefully. In this, and in all matters.

She would rather have died alone than die in front of Danny. For different reasons, she would rather have died alone than die in front of me or Grandmother.

The two of you came to see her not long after Hazeldine's passing. Perhaps it was happenstance. But when you came by, she saw her chance.

Because of you—because you were there—Aunt Riegel chose not to die alone.

He mentioned Danver again lower down in the letter. *She's actually very shy,* he wrote. *Very sensitive.*

I snorted.

Left to her own devices, she might never again attempt to communicate with anyone outside Follyhope.

Aunt Riegel wouldn't have wanted her to be lonely. And I do believe she misses her friend.

"Ginko," I grumped. "Does he even remember her name? If he wants us to organize a playdate, why doesn't he just ask? We were going to do it anyway, before—before Riegel killed herself."

"Aunt Riegel's letter wasn't very straightforward, either," Wist said mildly.

"Think it runs in the family? She was *trying* to be intriguingly anonymous. That's different."

Wist pointed at a line toward the very end.

My special thanks to Asa Clematis for putting my card to good use. I'd be delighted to talk more.

"You spoke to Nerium?" She sounded too casual.

"Once," I said. "Months ago!"

I put a hand up under her long shirt, which kept flapping like a flag in the wind. She felt surprisingly chilly. Her stomach muscles jumped and tightened beneath my fingers.

A faint clanging shock still rang out whenever we touched. Which was often. I couldn't tell if that jolt came from our still-clashing bond scars, or if it was something I'd made up myself. A product of the overwrought sweetness of nerves and anticipation: expecting the prick of a medicinal needle, the stinging heat after an angry slap.

I had become a thousand times more attuned to her when I'd avoided bumping into her at all costs. My body stayed that way now, hyperaware of her, no longer inoculated against her presence.

"You won't distract me like that," Wist said coolly.

I'd mostly succeeded at distracting myself. "Right. What were we—?"

"Nerium."

The letter folded itself up with a crisp, censorious crackle of magic.

"Used his business card a couple months back," I said. "Just a quick chat—didn't seem worth mentioning, honestly. I asked him to let us know when it might be safe to pay one last visit to Follyhope. Without causing too much of a stir."

This letter, which Wist held between two fingers like a cigarette, was Nerium's answer.

We returned to Follyhope the following week, on a day when Wist could brush away other obligations. It felt as though it ought to be raining. The sky was streaked with stormy gray, and trees tossed in a humid wind.

I'd liked Aunt Riegel from the moment we met. I hadn't known her for long, though. The entire span of our acquaintance had already been surpassed by the months since her death. Maybe I didn't need to feel too bad about the fact that I thought of her more after her passing than I'd ever thought of her in life.

In certain segments of society, people murmured to each other that Lady Shien was on her way out. She was indeed the oldest living head of any mage clan. She'd long resisted retirement, but she'd started giving signals that it might finally be time to rest.

Perhaps it would take another year or two. Perhaps she would change her mind. For the first time in her entire career, though, she seemed open to naming an heir and stepping down.

Riegel had taken a deadly cutting because she was already deteriorating, slowly and surely. She'd taken the cutting because she'd found someone to offer her life's work. (By coming to confront her, had I sealed her fate?)

She'd taken the cutting to leave an invisible wound on Grandmother Shien. To strike at a woman protected by magic that allegedly made her all but unkillable.

She'd taken the cutting because she didn't want to keep tying her daughter to Follyhope. But she hadn't provided Danver with the means to go see the world, nor any reason to leave.

We met Danver and Lear in the entrance hallway with a water sculpture that never stopped moving. It floated high above us, much too high to touch, and sent sleek ripples of light and shadow playing incessantly over every surface below.

Danver was back in her designated dark robes, along with a lavender apron for mourning. Her old bond thread still encircled her neck. Lear wore culottes and a silk shell top printed with a brilliant mosaic pattern. The dancing, waving light made it look as if we'd all gathered underwater.

"You take them first," Danver ordered Lear.

She said it in Jacian. Maddeningly enough, her accent was close to perfect.

"Sure, but what about those?" Lear swept an arm toward Wist, who carried a substantial bundle of white chrysanthemums.

I switched to Jacian, too. "You've been practicing," I accused Danver.

She held her head high. "I'm naturally proficient at languages."

"When we first met you and Lear, you acted like you didn't know a word of Jacian."

"I'm also a proficient actress."

Lear smirked in a way that would've felled most blushing maidens. "Whatever you say, Danny."

Guess it wasn't just sheer inertia keeping Danver at Follyhope.

They were terribly mismatched, inappropriate for each other in every way. The wrong age, the wrong nationality, ill-fitting personalities.

Lear still had a bondmate leashing her to distant Jace. Could she ever let herself view Danver as anything more than a sort of sullen little sister?

My take on it: I used to be very good at fooling myself over how I felt about Wist. I could sympathize with those who preferred not to know themselves too closely.

No one else voiced the name *Danny* with quite the same intonation as Lear—not Ginko, not Nerium, not Aunt Riegel. There was always playfulness and mockery in the way she rolled those syllables around in her mouth, but also a peculiar note of respect, and the mockery seemed above all to be directed at Lear herself. Although I didn't think Danver could hear that.

But maybe there was hope.

Wist let them have their moment. After a generous pause, she let go of her flowers. Rather than falling, they swished out of sight as if darting behind a dressing room curtain.

"Well, that solves that," I said.

Danver stayed behind in the manor. We followed Lear to her atelier.

There were so many parts of the estate where I'd never set foot. Endless orchards of white peach trees, swathes of wilderness curated for recreational hunting, everything beyond the mausoleum.

Years might pass before the next time we took a stroll here.

"How much longer do you get to stay?" I asked Lear. (Not in Jacian. The sound of my own voice annoyed the heck out of me after hearing Danver's near-flawless intonation.)

"Till the end of summer."

"Then you go back home?"

"Not home. To Jace, yes, if that's what you mean. I'll be recalled to Central."

"Alone?" said Wist.

I gave her an approving look. See? I'm not the only nosy one.

"We won't know till I leave, will we?" Lear returned.

"Optimistic," I said. "You've already got her speaking Jacian. But I doubt you're trying as hard as you could. In fact, I bet you'll fade away in the night before she gets a chance to change her mind. Do you enjoy breaking hearts?"

"Who doesn't?" A throwaway response.

"For the record—if I do break your bond, you'll never be forced to take another bondmate."

"Because all my branches already got amputated?" Lear asked. "Convenient. Hopefully no one figures out a way to replant them."

It occurred to me, apropos of nothing, that her hair had always been mourning-ready. Look at those purple undertones.

Healers in Osmanthus often swapped tall tales of secret boats, of dashing smugglers who might resemble someone like Lear. For the right price, they could whisk you across the sea to Jace. In reality, no one seemed to know anyone who'd actually defected. The stories were usually about a cousin of a friend of a friend.

Lear unveiled the portrait I'd requested.

It was indeed a portrait of Wist.

"Hey!" I said.

Wist covered her mouth as if to hide a wayward smile. Lear had put me in the painting, too.

"You agreed to this," Lear said smugly. "Not my fault if you forgot."

"I had my mind on other things. There were murders happening all around us!"

"That's what you get for leaving it all up to my artistic vision. Come to think of it, I ought to charge extra. Two figures is more work than one."

"Breaking a bond in Jace will be a hell of a lot more work than breaking a bond in Osmanthus."

"Then I suppose you can chalk it up to my innate sense of fairness."

"I like it," said Wist. "I love it."

I tried to remember the last time I'd heard her make a positive comment about an image of herself.

Possibly never.

"I do know how to please my clients," Lear said modestly.

It wasn't that Wist had a complex about her looks. She truly didn't care. If we passed a bank of reflective windows while strolling around downtown, she wouldn't glance over to check her hair or the fall of her coat; she wouldn't even notice. But like it or not, the world was awash with countless depictions of the Kraken. By default, she usually attempted to dodge them.

The portrait was mostly from behind, although you could see part of our faces as we leaned together as if sharing secrets. I stood next to a seated Wist, one hand on the back of her chair. Her hair became a black twist that draped across me like the shadowy arm of a monster from the depths of the sea.

At the moment, her hair wasn't nearly that long in real life. It looked right, though. Even with the darker areas around my ankles and the legs of her chair blurring into an abstract and muddy confusion. Were we outdoors or indoors? Were those actually our legs, or were they old winter vines, the kind of vine that could grow powerfully enough to tear a house down?

"You did ask me not to paint in my usual style," Lear added. "So you'll have to forgive me if I'm not feeling terribly open to criticism. No revisions, by the way. Take it or leave it."

"Wist loves it," I said. "That means it's perfect."

"And you?"

"Sometimes I like being surprised, too."

Wist and Lear proceeded to have a lengthy discussion about frames. Afterward, Wist—who was being rather extravagant with her magic today—ported the portrait back to the tower without so much as a twitch of her little finger. Show-off.

Outside the atelier, I turned to Lear and said: "Perhaps one day we'll see you in Jace."

"It'll take a miracle of diplomacy for them to let in the Kraken."

"I got thrown in prison as a result of conspiring with Jacians."

"My condolences."

"My point is that it'll take just as much of a miracle for Osmanthus to allow me anywhere near your country, too."

"We'd better pray," Wist said under her breath. Lear gave us tickets to her upcoming solo exhibition, then waved us off with a laugh.

The white chrysanthemums rematerialized in Wist's arms as we went back inside the manor to meet Danver. She joined us beneath the stone arch with off-puttingly intestinal bulges and curves.

She led us briskly through corridor after corridor. She was an expert, all right. She scarcely looked from side to side, and yet she never missed a single discrepancy.

"You know," I said, "you're welcome at the tower anytime."

"The tower?"

"The Kraken's tower. Ginko would like to see you. Me and Wist, we can stay out of the way. Won't even know we're there."

"I'm not so rude as to demand that my hosts go hide in a corner," she said icily.

Wist stepped in to briefly discuss the logistics of arranging a visit.

Now that we had Danver alone, I found myself sorely tempted to needle her about Lear. Her exquisite Jacian pronunciation couldn't have sprung fully formed out of nowhere, after all. But I kept my thoughts to myself. Danver angered easily even when no one went out of their way to offend her. No need to make things any harder.

Apparently there had been no talk of commemorating Aunt Riegel in the family mausoleum. They kept her ashes in the same bedroom where she'd lived out the majority of her adult life. A hidden part of the manor that only a select few people knew how to access.

Danver opened the door and went in first. Her face was paler than I would've thought possible, her steps jerky. Even months later.

One of the paintings from Lear's loft now hung on the wall by the bed. A faithful rendition of Riegel's stunted magic.

For a while, no one said anything. Danver produced a large glass vase from a back room and thrust it at Wist. We filled the vase with our bundle of white chrysanthemums.

"Ginko helped pick them out," I said.

"They don't need water," Wist said. "They don't need anything. They'll last."

Danver pushed at the spindly frames of her glasses. "Is that your magic on them?"

"Yes."

Wist had told me about seeing chrysanthemums in Riegel's room when she came as a child. Just a few of them, at the time. She kept going over to look at them, though she hadn't known what white chrysanthemums meant.

"She could've hated the view from here," Danver said abruptly. "But she loved it. None of us wanted her to lose it."

Who was *us?* I wondered. Danver and Nerium? Grandmother? I didn't ask.

The wisteria vine on the pergola rioted with masses of new leaves and rebellious shoots. No hint of flowers: they must've already opened and fallen and vanished. No one had treated this courtyard garden with magic to stretch out each bloom as long as possible.

Danver pivoted toward the sewing room. She said to me, just as abruptly: "I have something for you."

"Oh, good. Thank you."

Wist shot me a wordless look.

"You'll see," I told her.

Danver emerged from the sewing room with a creamy handkerchief draped over her upturned hands. On top of the handkerchief coiled a slender cord of shocking blue thread.

I heard Wist's intake of breath.

"It's not the same," I said to Wist, "not in a literal sense, and it's not an exact replica—I was going by my memory of the color. The more I tried to remember, the harder it got. Maybe I should've asked you for input instead of doing it all on my own."

It was suddenly very difficult to meet her gaze. I barreled onward. "Riegel—Aunt Riegel ordered a bunch of samples from—see, I figured she'd know lots of ultra-specialist suppliers. For fabric and thread. Swatches of color. That kind of thing. I was right."

I stopped, indicating my willingness to take questions. None came.

"I first brought it up when she gave us her old sun cookies." I sounded as if I were making excuses for an appalling crime. "That's what I was asking when I stopped and whispered to her. I was afraid you'd be curious. But you had a lot on your mind.

"Afterward—when we visited later in the year—sometimes she'd ask me to go get her stuff from the sewing room, remember? That's when I'd look at samples. Felt like picking a criminal out of a lineup. Pretty terrifying that people can get convicted with nothing but eyewitness testimony, you know? I grew less and less sure of myself every time I compared one blue thread to ten others.

"I think this was the closest. Any color starts looking different after you've worn it for years."

And, before that, left it buried in a pot of lantana. And, before even that, carried it all the way from one world to another. I didn't say that part; Danver was listening.

"You don't have to take it," I told Wist.

"You do, actually," Danver said. "Take it and throw it away, for all I care. But it doesn't belong here."

I ignored her. "I know it can't replace—"

"Clem," Wist said thickly, and that was enough.

"Oh, for—get a room," Danver muttered.

"You're one to talk," I retorted.

"I beg your pardon?"

"You think you're very subtle. How about I list all the times I caught you looking at Lear's—"

Wist pulled me to her from behind. She clamped one hand over my mouth. Her other hand popped off her wrist and hopped neatly through the air to hook the blue bond thread.

Danver's jaw dropped.

"Her hand runs away from time to time," I said from behind my gag. "No big deal."

With Wist's intervention, we managed to have a mostly peaceful parting. We'd see Danver again soon enough, anyhow. We'd extracted a promise from her to visit the tower. Wist could take care of transportation.

But first it was time for us to retreat back to the tower on our own, just the two of us.

On our way out, we admired the wisteria in the courtyard. We made a few final adjustments to the clear vase of chrysanthemums. We appreciated all the shelves crammed full of tiny hats.

We turned together in the doorway and bowed to the bedroom where no one lived now, long and deep, as if bowing to royalty.

65

Back home, Wist said: "I'm glad she named me."

"It's a good name," I agreed.

"You weren't so enthused the first time you heard it."

"I was too young and callow to appreciate the sophistication of four full syllables."

I finished winding the blue thread around her left wrist. She'd begun saying things about using it to stabilize her wandering hand. And perhaps her testy shadow, to boot. I let her mumble to herself on and on, working out the intricacies of whatever magic she'd need to—well, never mind the details.

We were nestled together in the coffin she'd brought from Manglesea. The sky had cleared enough to splash a broken sort of light down through the glass of the sunroom. Most of her plants were doing unusually well right now. A verdant scent hummed in the air.

I asked her where she'd put Lear's painting.

"In the bedroom, for now," she said.

"How conventional."

"It's private."

"We aren't naked in it."

"I want it where I can see it every day," said Wist.

A little tendril of alarm budded in me. "This isn't going to be your new hobby, is it?"

"Mm?"

"Commissioning portraits of me."

Wist smiled. One of those blink-and-you'll-miss-it moments. Still very unnerving.

She was no longer smiling when she drew me closer and said: "Aunt Riegel's legacy."

"What about it?"

"Will you?"

"What, become a self-styled judge? Ask me again in a couple of decades."

Her arms tightened.

"You have to admit," I said, "I'd be just as effective a judge as her. More so, because I have so much more freedom of movement. Don't you think?"

The Void did a slow, pleasurable somersault against the back of my eye socket. I twisted in Wist's arms and pointed at my prosthetic. "Considering this"—I meant the hidden Void—"it's probably best for me to focus on *not* killing people. For the time being."

I leaned back again, relaxing against her. "Whatever we do, we've got to make sure we don't repeat the same thing all over again." I made a chopping motion. As if splitting a bond with a cleaver. "For vorpal holes ... would our bond stay intact if we passed through the hole together?"

"I don't have plans to leap into another vorpal hole again," Wist said. "Ever."

"C'mon. You never know. I never had plans to host an eldritch existence that could've destroyed the world, but here we are. I never planned on getting a life sentence—or on getting out early, either. I certainly didn't plan to—"

"You've made your point."

"Might be difficult to train the Void to tolerate vorpal holes," I said, undeterred. "But the new prosthesis seems to help. I've followed you to other countries. Why not other worlds?"

Wist touched the bond thread I'd put on her left wrist. She touched it as if she could hardly believe it was there.

"Are you ready?" she asked. She didn't look up.

My stomach leapt. "You mean—right now?"

"We both have our threads. What's a thread without a bond?"

"It might hurt," I said pathetically.

"Might not."

"Or it might not work at all."

Wist shifted against the side of the coffin. "Would you rather wait?"

I turned around and plunked myself down facing her. The coffin was very well padded. "This is extremely nerve-wracking," I said, irritated.

"More so than last time?"

"Last time, I was trying to make sure you didn't kill me. Or Fanren. That's a whole different type of nerves. I had a very noble reason for proposing to bond."

"And now," Wist said, "your only reason is wanting to be back inside each other. For the rest of our lives."

"Do you really have to put it like that?"

She studied me the same way she'd studied Lear's portrait of us. "You're embarrassed."

"Are you kidding?" This was my pride on the line here. "Nothing embarrasses me. I'm the goddamn Magebreaker. I'm beyond all shame. I swear—"

She touched the back of her wrist to my face. I felt the fresh texture of her new blue thread. I remembered Riegel, and how skillfully she'd translated my amateur attempts at characterizing a very particular color. No other shade of blue would do. I hadn't realized how many there would be to choose from.

I didn't yet have much experience with breaking other people's bonds. I'd proven I could do it neatly and painlessly. This came with trade-offs, however: from what I could tell, my method would make it virtually impossible for either partner to bond again in the future. That was the price of a clean and comfortable break. That was the price Danver had paid—in essence, I'd uprooted her ability to bond. With anyone.

It was different for me and Wist. Our bond couldn't have shattered more messily. If we succeeded in bonding again, it would be because of how inhumanely the vorpal hole had torn us apart. Our scars left us with the potential to come together once more.

If it worked—if it worked, this would be our third time bonding. Across two lifetimes. No one else would ever know. Not even someone as astute as Shien Nerium could guess the truth. Human lives weren't supposed to work like that. Bonds weren't supposed to work like that.

This time, she wasn't berserk. She didn't need saving. No one needed saving. This time, I had no real excuse.

"I offer my bond," she said, a whisper against my cheek, a closeness I couldn't have imagined during thousands of days in prison. Thousands of nights spent seething, curled up like a wounded animal around my inability to forget her.

That too had felt like a bond broken the wrong way, a shattered bone that would never be the same.

My fingers were in her hair. My hands quested across the nape of her neck, her beloved shoulders, her sides.

"I accept your bond," I said, for the second time in this one final life.

Wist hiked up my undershirt, exposing the small of my back. A hair-thin piece of magic would take root there to bind us.

This time, I didn't tell myself that I had no other morally sensible choice. This time, I didn't offer myself up like a flower waiting to be watered.

I wanted her bond more than anything. This time, I reached out and took it.

A Note from the Author

You've just finished reading Book 4 of the Clem & Wist series. But it's actually the fifth book if we count the prequel, *No One Else Could Heal Her*, which has key ties to this story in particular. Your support, your reviews, and your fondness for these characters have kept the series thriving all this time. Thank you from the bottom of my heart!

I love fantasy, I love romance, and I also really love classic whodunits. Suspects trapped together on a stormy island with no way in and no way out, eccentric detectives, impossible locked-room murders, dark family secrets, the suspense of wondering who will die next....

Three Murdered Mages, Two Broken Bonds isn't a mystery in the traditional sense. Even so, I hope it brought you a small taste of the joy I find when reading mysteries myself—which I do often, and ravenously.

If you haven't yet read *No One Else Could Heal Her* (the Clem & Wist series prequel), you may find that it offers a different perspective on several important characters also featured in *Three Murdered Mages, Two Broken Bonds*.

The next story I plan on publishing will be a standalone novel—but rest assured that there will also be more to come with Clem and Wist!

Follow my Author Page for future updates if you'd like to see more: https://amazon.com/author/hiyodori

Hope to see you again next time!

– Hiyodori